DOHANY STREET

Also by Adam LeBor

Non-Fiction

A Heart Turned East: Among the Muslims of Europe and America

Surviving Hitler: Choices, Corruption and Compromise in the Third Reich

Milosevic: A Biography

"Complicity with Evil": The United Nations in the Age of Modern Genocide

The Believers: How America Fell for Bernard Madoff's $65 Billion Investment Scam

Tower of Basel: The Shadowy History of the Secret Bank That Runs the World

City of Oranges: An Intimate History of Arabs & Jews in Jaffa

Hitler's Secret Bankers: How Switzerland Profited from Nazi Genocide

Fiction

The Budapest Protocol

The Yael Azoulay Trilogy

The Geneva Option

The Washington Stratagem

The Reykjavik Assignment

Danube Blues

District VIII

Kossuth Square

DOHANY STREET

ADAM LEBOR

First published in the UK in 2021 by Head of Zeus Ltd

9 7 5 3 1 2 4 6 8

A catalogue record for this book is available from
the British Library.

ISBN (HB): 9781786692764
ISBN (XTPB): 9781786693297
ISBN (E): 9781786692757

Typeset by Divaddict Publishing Solutions Ltd

Printed and bound in Great Britain by
CPI Group (UK) Ltd, Croydon CR0 4YY

Head of Zeus Ltd
First Floor East
5–8 Hardwick Street
London EC1R 4RG

WWW.HEADOFZEUS.COM

In loving memory
Brenda LeBor
1926–2020

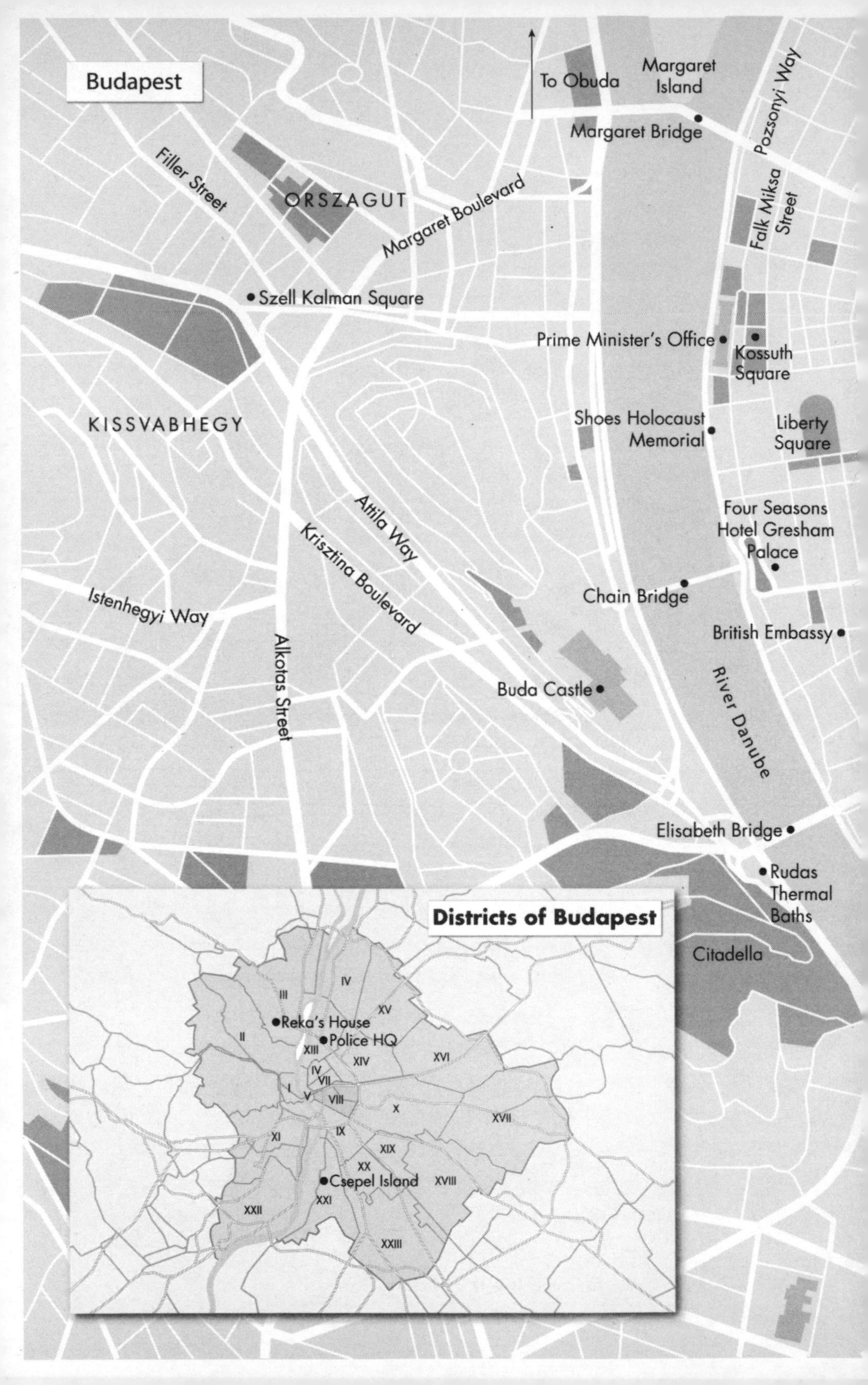
Budapest
To Obuda
Margaret Island
Pozsonyi Way
Margaret Bridge
Filler Street
ORSZAGUT
Margaret Boulevard
Falk Miksa Street
Szell Kalman Square
Prime Minister's Office
Kossuth Square
KISSVABHEGY
Shoes Holocaust Memorial
Liberty Square
Attila Way
Krisztina Boulevard
Four Seasons Hotel Gresham Palace
Chain Bridge
Istenhegyi Way
Alkotas Street
British Embassy
Buda Castle
River Danube
Elisabeth Bridge
Rudas Thermal Baths
Citadella
Districts of Budapest
IV
III
XV
Reka's House
II
Police HQ
XIII
XIV
XVI
IV
VII
I
V
VIII
X
XVII
XI
IX
XIX
XX
Csepel Island
XVIII
XXI
XXII
XXIII

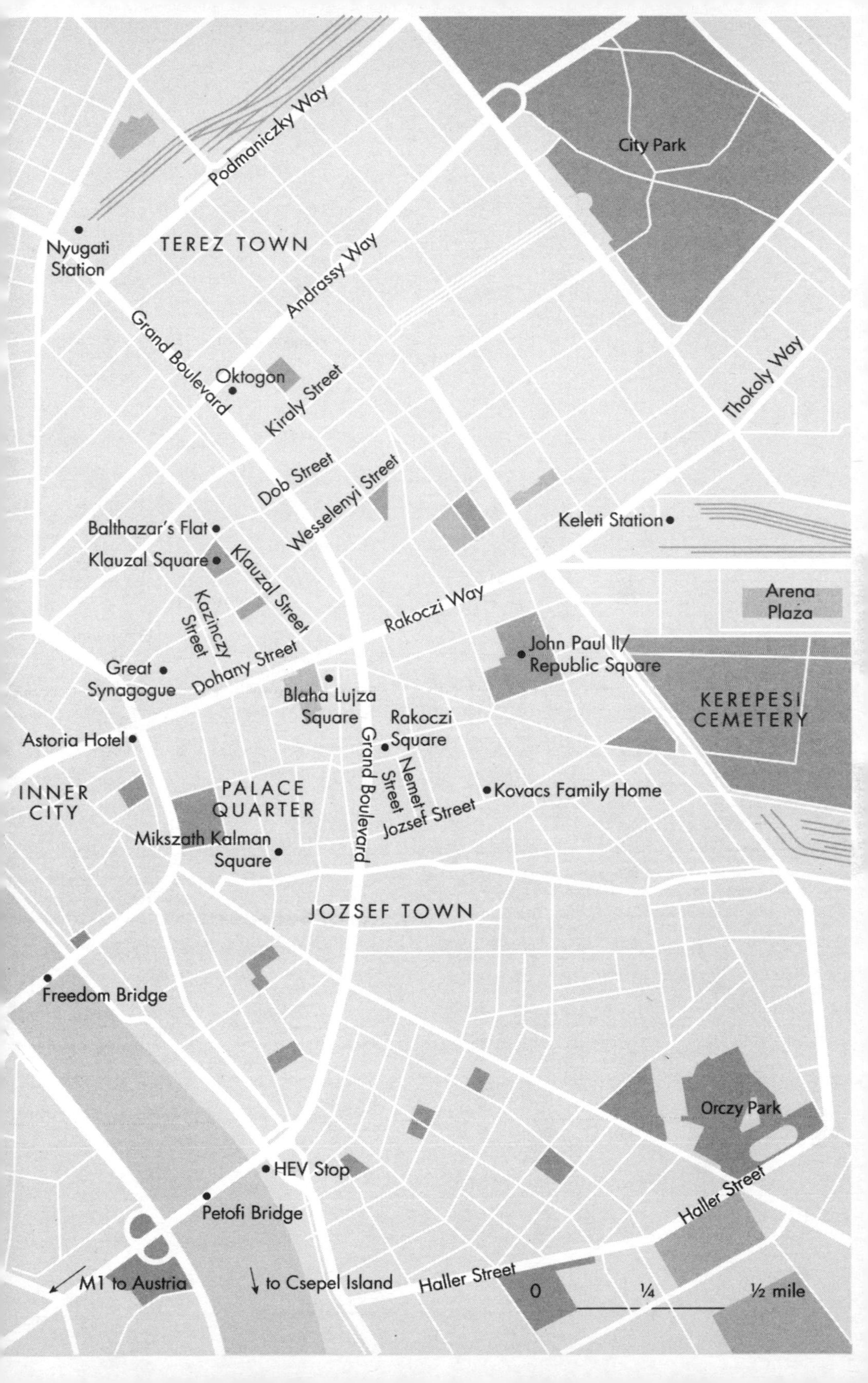

Podmaniczky Way
City Park
Nyugati Station
TEREZ TOWN
Andrassy Way
Grand Boulevard
Oktogon
Kiraly Street
Thokoly Way
Dob Street
Wesselenyi Street
Keleti Station
Balthazar's Flat
Klauzal Square
Klauzal Street
Kazinczy Street
Rakoczi Way
Arena Plaza
John Paul II/ Republic Square
Great Synagogue
Dohany Street
Blaha Lujza Square
KEREPESI CEMETERY
Rakoczi Square
Astoria Hotel
Nemet Street
Kovacs Family Home
INNER CITY
PALACE QUARTER
Grand Boulevard
Jozsef Street
Mikszath Kalman Square
JOZSEF TOWN
Freedom Bridge
Orczy Park
HEV Stop
Petofi Bridge
Haller Street
M1 to Austria
to Csepel Island
Haller Street
0
¼
½ mile

'The past is never dead. It's not even past.'

William Faulkner

PROLOGUE

Obuda hills, August 1987

She crouched down behind the rose bush, shut her eyes for a moment to help her concentrate, then pushed her fingers into the earth. It was damp and loose on top, packed thicker underneath, but still free enough that she could feel the dirt gather under her nails as she sought a cold, flat surface or sharp metal corner. The tip of her index finger hit something hard and she smiled as she traced its outline. But no – it was round and smooth. A pebble.

She frowned for a moment. Where was it? It had to be here. It was here last week. Nobody else knew about it. Perhaps she had the wrong rose bush.

She glanced across the garden at the house, checking that nobody was coming down the path. It was ten past six in the evening, almost time for dinner at six thirty, so she needed to be quick, but for a short while at least she knew she would be undisturbed. She stood up for a moment and counted the rose bushes that marked the end of the lawn, touching each of the seven with her right forefinger, checked she was behind the middle one. She nodded to herself. Three on one side, three on the other. This was the right place.

A Trabant sputtered past on the road behind the house, its underpowered engine straining against the hill, whirring like a hairdryer, gusting out clouds of exhaust. She wrinkled her nose as the acrid smell drifted through the hot summer air, crouched down again and began digging once more.

Her fingers pushed deeper through the earth, determined now, probing, scooping, until they brushed against a smooth metal surface. She pushed the soil away, sliding her hands down both sides of the box, loosening it until she could take it out and place it on the ground nearby.

It was a small, plain metal container. The blue paint had faded and the lid and its hinges were rusty. She could still remember how excited she'd been when she had found it a couple of years ago. The builders had been working on the pipes or foundations or something, and one day, when they went home, she looked into the big hole they had made and saw the corner of something blue and metallic poking out of the sandy mud. She had not said anything but that night she sneaked into the garden, pulled the box out and kept it hidden in the ground ever since. It was her treasure chest, and nobody else's. No one else in the family even knew she had it.

The box felt cold and heavy. She smiled as she carefully brushed the loose soil from the lid, sat down, rested it on her legs and opened it. She somehow knew, with complete certainty, that the moment she took her treasure chest inside the house, she would never see the box, or its contents, again.

She was only ten but she already knew about lots of adult stuff, like not telling other people that their home had eight rooms and two gardens, one in the front and one at the back, or that they had all these other people, like the maid, around to help all the time. She glanced across the garden to the far corner where the maid and her husband, the gardener, lived in a small cottage. It had a bright red roof and a thick wooden door, like something out of a fairy story. Sometimes they invited her in for lemonade and biscuits.

There were so many things she did not understand. They had learned at school that communism meant everybody was equal, but how could that be when they lived in such a big house and everyone else, or almost everyone, apart from her parents' friends, lived in flats? Her home was perched on a hill, overlooking Obuda. Alongside the wide road at the base of the hill, there were row upon row of *panel-lakasok*, panel flats made from giant slabs of pre-formed concrete, sometimes ten or twelve storeys high, whole families crammed together in small apartments. That didn't seem very equal.

She would think about that later. She looked down at the box and smiled. For now, she had her treasure chest. And there was real treasure inside: a red velvet box with four rings; a long white silk scarf, or something like a scarf, more like a shawl, with blue stripes and extra bits of white string knotted along the bottom; a book, like one of her exercise books at school but written in a strange alphabet like little blocks of ink. There was a photograph as well, of a young girl with curly blond hair in a dark dress with a single row of buttons down the middle.

She had taken the shawl out once, stood up and draped it around her shoulders. The garment was enormous on her and its bottom spread out along the ground, the white strings trailing in the grass. The shawl felt light and delicate, smooth against the back of her neck, but it didn't feel right on her, made her shiver. She had folded it up and put it back in the box. She had not taken it out since. How had the exercise book got here? she wondered. And what did the writing say?

She lifted it and held it to her nose. The paper smelled damp and musty. The pages had turned yellow but the heavy, black script was clear.

She looked at her watch. It was almost twenty past six. Time to pack up. They would be shouting for her soon and she needed time to hide the treasure chest again and properly cover it with earth. She put the book and the white silk shawl back inside carefully. There was just enough time to quickly check her favourite things: the rings in the red velvet box, one that looked like a woman's ring, with quite a big diamond, and another with a black stone – that was a man's one, she thought – and two plain gold bands.

The gold ones were her favourites. She took them out and placed them both in the palm of her left hand. One was bigger and heavier than the other. She guessed they must be wedding rings and then she had an idea, one of those ideas that when it came to her made her think *Why on earth didn't I think of that before?* She held the big ring up to her eyes and looked at the inside. Inscribed in tiny letters was: Miklos, 10 August 1933, Budapest. There was a name inside the small ring as well: Rahel, and the same date.

Somehow the names gave her a funny feeling, the same as when she had put the shawl on. She quickly put the two rings in the red velvet case, put that back in the blue metal box, closed the lid, placed it back in the space by the tree roots, covered it all with the loose dirt and smoothed it over. She stepped back, looked at her handiwork and smiled. Now nobody would know that anything was there. She rubbed her hands against each other, trying to brush the soil away. It didn't really work, but it didn't matter. She was a kid, and was expected to get dirty in the garden.

She skipped back to the house, looking forward to dinner.

She was hungry now. For a moment she felt the weight of the wedding rings in her palm again, heard the sound of the two names in her head: Miklos and Rahel, wondered about their fate. Then her mother appeared, calling her with her arms wide open, telling her it was time for dinner. Her stomach rumbled, and she ran towards her.

ONE

Dob Street, Thursday, 14 January 2016, 7 a.m.

Balthazar Kovacs peered through the narrow glass spyhole in his front door, trying unsuccessfully to stifle a yawn. It was an old-fashioned aperture, mounted high, that only showed what was directly in front of the viewer. He saw pale yellow walls, the dark-wood entrances of his neighbours' flats, the curved metal handrail that snaked around the building's art deco staircase. A weak winter sunlight seeped through the large window at the end of the corridor, streaked with rain and city dirt. So far, so familiar. So too was the top of a head with silver hair, trimmed and styled in a permanent wave that had been the height of fashion during the late 1980s.

The knocking that had first woken him sounded once more, sharper. This time there was a voice, speaking in a loud whisper. A female voice, one that he knew, but sounding unusually stressed. 'Tazi, are you awake? It's me.'

There were two women in Balthazar's life he could not refuse. The first was his actual mother and the other was Eva *neni*, Auntie Eva, his neighbour and surrogate mother, whom he saw far more often. And if Eva *neni* was knocking on his door at 7 a.m. there had to be a reason. He opened the door, gestured for her to come inside, closed it behind them.

Eva *neni* stood by the kitchen entrance. Just five feet tall, she was dressed in her usual faded pink housecoat, brown polyester trousers, and slippers. But her face was creased in anxiety and her blue eyes, usually bright, were red-rimmed.

'*Mondd*, tell me,' said Balthazar. Something bad must have happened for her to be knocking on his door this early.

'He's gone.'

'Who?'

'Elad. The flat's empty and he's not answering his phone. I couldn't sleep all night, I went over there just now. I'm sorry to wake you. I didn't know what else to do. Did I wake you?'

He shook his head. 'No, it's fine. I wasn't sleeping.' He gently squeezed her small hand. 'Don't worry, Evike. We'll sort this out. Come in, sit down, I'll make us some coffee and you can tell me everything.'

They walked through to the narrow kitchen. It was a small space with no street-facing window, that overlooked the courtyard. The plain white functional cupboards, the linoleum floor and the worn enamel sink were decades old. A corkboard hung on the wall above the red Formica-topped table. There were several photos there of Balthazar with his family: one of him as a teenager, arm in arm with his brother Gaspar, another as a child with his mother and father, and one together with his son, Alex, in a park downtown by the Danube. Two clippings from *Paprika*, the country's main tabloid newspaper, pinned to the board, were slowly turning yellow.

Balthazar pulled out a chair for Eva *neni* and she sat down at the table. They were both coffee drinkers, and he filled the kettle and spooned grounds into an old-fashioned cafetière, while Eva *neni* looked at the photographs one by one. Now she was inside the flat, and could see Balthazar was there for her, she was calmer.

'I haven't seen these pictures before,' said Eva *neni*, turning to him with an affectionate smile. 'What a handsome boy you were, Tazi.' She tilted her head to one side and gave him an appraising look. 'You still are. But you need someone to look after you. What happened to that nice-looking girl, Kati, the one who worked in the prime minister's office? I thought she had almost moved in.'

Balthazar laughed, good humouredly. 'So did I. Then she moved out.'

Eva *neni* shook her head, sighed. 'Tazi, Tazi, it's not good for a man of your age to be alone. It's not good for anyone. I lost my husband a decade ago and I still miss him every day.'

He glanced at her as he waited for the kettle to boil. 'You're not alone.'

She gave him a wan smile. 'I know.'

Two minutes later he sat down with the cafetière and two cups. '*Mondd*, now tell me the whole story. When did you see Elad last?'

'On Wednesday morning, yesterday. He was due to come over and pay the rent in the evening, around six o'clock. I was going to make him dinner. I called him several times during the day to check, left voicemails and sent some text messages. I didn't hear anything back. At first I wasn't worried. I know how busy he is. But he didn't turn up for dinner, didn't call back or reply to my messages. He's never done that before.'

Balthazar processed this information for a few seconds. A day wasn't very long. 'He's a young man, single, in a new town. Maybe he met a girl. He'll probably come home later today.'

Eva *neni* ran her finger over a crack in the red tabletop. 'Maybe.' She pushed down harder on the crack, moved her finger back and forth. 'I don't think so. Something's wrong. I can feel it. The flat is empty, it's been cleared out.'

Balthazar drank some of his coffee. His mind switched a gear, went into detective mode. 'Completely? None of his clothes or books or papers are there?'

'No. Nothing. Not even a toothbrush.'

Balthazar nodded slowly, fully alert now, the caffeine already working. 'Was the lock broken or the door forced open?'

Eva *neni* shook her head. 'No. Everything looks fine. But why would he leave like that, without saying goodbye, or telling me? Something's not right.'

Balthazar remembered how excited Eva *neni* had been to meet Elad. Her daughter, Klara, had relocated to London several years ago, so Eva *neni* rarely saw her or her grandchildren. Eva *neni* and Elad were related via a cousin in Tel Aviv who had left Budapest in 1945 for Palestine. The cousin had contacted her a couple of months ago. She had immediately offered Elad her small flat. It sounded like Elad really had packed up and left. But why would he do that without telling Eva *neni* where he was going?

'Was there any sign of a disturbance? Damage, scratches on the door, a broken window? Anything?'

Eva *neni* sipped her coffee for a moment as she thought. 'No, nothing. It looks fine, like nobody has been there for a long time. But he was there on Tuesday… Where is he?' She sniffed for a moment. 'What if something bad has happened? It's awful. It's all my fault. What will I tell his parents?'

Balthazar rested his hand on hers. 'Evike, we don't know what has happened, and anyway, none of this is your fault. We're going to find him. Give me a minute to go to the bathroom and freshen up first.'

Eva *neni* nodded. Balthazar walked through the flat to the bathroom and ran the cold tap in the sink. He looked at himself in the mirror. His thick black hair was dishevelled and his brown eyes looked bleary. He wasn't a big drinker and his head felt heavy and fuzzy from the two beers he had drunk alone the previous evening. Eva *neni* was right. Living alone did not suit him. But finding someone to live with was proving much harder than he'd thought.

He turned his head from side to side and stretched his arms out as far as they would go, feeling his limbs stretch. He rubbed his jaw and opened his mouth as wide as he could. He dipped his hands into the cold water, splashed his face and then switched on the radio to listen to the news while he brushed his teeth.

The radio announcer was speaking about the upcoming visit of the Israeli prime minister, Alon Farkas. He was flying in on Monday morning, in four days' time, to attend the commemoration of the anniversary of the liberation of the Budapest ghetto in January 1945. He would leave late that evening, after signing agreements on investment, tourism and scientific cooperation.

The upcoming visit had been all over the news for a couple of weeks. This would be the first visit by an Israeli prime minister to Hungary. Farkas, as his name indicated, was himself descended from Hungarian Jews and his visit was generally viewed as a PR and diplomatic boost for the shaky Social Democrat government of Reka Bardossy, Hungary's prime minister. The newsreader moved on to the steady decline in the value of the forint, Hungary's national currency, the rise in unemployment and the opinion polls showing that support for her government was sliding rapidly, with an election a month away.

Balthazar towelled himself dry, put his T-shirt back on and walked back into the kitchen. Eva *neni* was reading the two press clippings on the pinboard. The headline on one announced: GYPSY COP HERO TAKES DOWN INTERNATIONAL TERRORIST AT KELETI STATION; on another, HE'S BACK: BRAVE GYPSY COP STOPS PLOT TO BLOW UP KOSSUTH SQUARE.

Eva *neni* turned to him. 'You're famous. You know how excited all the *neni*s in the market on Klauzal Square get when you go and do your shopping? They talk about you non-stop.'

Balthazar smiled. 'Do they?' He hated the limelight, being recognised in public, but had little choice. Clips of the two incidents were also all over the internet. The last person he had arrested had even asked him for a selfie before Balthazar put the handcuffs on. He had refused.

Balthazar sat back down, feeling fully alert now. The sounds of classical music and a radio talk show host drifted up from the courtyard. The building was waking up. He looked at Eva *neni*. She picked up her coffee cup, took a small sip, put it back down, seemed about to say something, then did not.

'What's the matter, Eva *neni*? Is there something else?'

She nodded. 'I probably should have said before. But I thought he was just nervous because he was in a new town. And I didn't want to bother you.' She looked down for a moment and sighed. 'I should have.'

Balthazar rested his hand on hers. 'It's OK. You can bother me. What is it? What did he tell you?'

'Elad thought he was being followed. There was a car parked outside the Jewish Museum where he was working in the archives. A big, blue Mercedes with tinted windows. He told me it was there every day for the past week, whenever he came out.'

Large Audis and Mercedes were very common in Budapest, the favoured vehicles of government officials and local criminals. 'That's not necessarily something to worry about. A big Mercedes is about as common as a taxi, especially downtown.'

'Yes, I told him that as well. But then he said that earlier this week, he saw the same car drive past through Klauzal Square.'

Balthazar considered this for a moment. 'That still doesn't mean it's something to worry about.' Klauzal Square and the streets around it were used as shortcuts to avoid the heavy traffic on the Grand Boulevard. 'Maybe it was just passing through. And how did he know it was the same vehicle?'

'It was the same vehicle. It had a cracked right-side headlight. He was – I mean is – very observant. All those hours in the archives gave him an eye for detail, he said. And you know Israelis; they have to go in the army. He was in military intelligence, he told me. He's a historian, he's good with details.'

Balthazar nodded. 'I don't suppose he took the number plate?'

Eva *neni* gave him a worried look. 'Number plates, Tazi.'

'Plates?'

'Yes. He checked. Same car. Two different number plates.'

'Are you sure he was talking about the same vehicle?'

'Yes. A blue Mercedes saloon, with a crack in the right-side headlight.'

Balthazar sipped his coffee for a moment, let his memories of his encounters with Elad play through his mind. They had met several times in the building, passing encounters in the lift and by the entrance, and once properly when Eva *neni* had him over for her famous *turos palacsintas*, sweet cheese pancakes with home-made vanilla sauce, so they could get to know each other a bit.

Elad was in his late twenties, shorter and slimmer than Balthazar, with short black hair, watchful, green eyes and a wiry build. He was quite shy at first, but friendly, and when Balthazar proposed that they go out one evening for a drink and something to eat, he had responded enthusiastically. Why wouldn't he? He was a young man, alone in a new city, in the depth of winter. A postgraduate student at Hebrew University in Jerusalem, Elad was descended from Hungarian Jews. He spoke and read the language well and was writing his dissertation on the lost wealth of Hungarian Jewry after the Holocaust, tracing the fate of the assets of the once great Jewish dynasties of pre-war Hungary, the industrialists, businessmen and nobility who had lost everything. Balthazar had once enrolled in a PhD himself, researching the Poraymus, the devouring, as the Gypsies called their Holocaust, and he and Elad had chatted about libraries and archives.

More than half a million Hungarian Jews had perished in the Holocaust after the Nazis invaded the country in March 1944, swiftly and efficiently speeded to their deaths by the Hungarian state. But while many of the owners of the villas, companies, factories, and apartment houses had vanished in the camps or the icy waters of the Danube, their assets and property had continued existing – still did, in many cases. Their current owners were not usually to keen to discuss how they, or their forebears, had acquired them.

Balthazar asked Eva *neni*, 'Did Elad talk to you about his research? How was it going?'

'Not very well. People don't want to talk about those times, Tazi. He was very interested in one company, but they would not let him look at their archives. In fact they refused to cooperate in any way, sent him a lawyer's letter to stop bothering their staff or they would take legal action against him. They even threatened to get the police involved.'

'Which firm?'

'Nationwide.'

Balthazar stood up, gestured to Eva *neni* to follow him. 'Come. Let's take a look at the flat.'

TWO

Prime Minister's Office, Hungarian Parliament, 7.30 a.m.

Reka Bardossy looked through her briefing note, only half focusing, as the Israeli diplomat across the table introduced the final schedule for Alon Farkas's visit. Her mind kept drifting to the upcoming election. Unemployment, inflation: up. Her ratings, support for her and her party: down. Right down. The economy was sluggish. The young and the educated were leaving en masse for Vienna, Berlin, London. Even Edinburgh was jammed with young Hungarian migrants. Anywhere but home. The forint was losing value day by day. What would it be worth when the country went to the polls? And on top of all this, her uncle Karoly had somehow muscled in on the first high-profile visit of an international politician during her administration. It was at times like this that she missed her father the most. *Stop*, Reka almost said out loud, forcing herself to concentrate on the matter at hand.

She watched Ilona Mizrachi as she ran through the itinerary. By now Reka had spent so many hours on negotiating and planning the detail of the visit that she anyway knew it by heart. The Israeli government jet would land in Budapest on Monday at 11 a.m. local time. Alon Farkas would be accompanied by his wife, the ministers of trade, science and industry, other politicians and Israeli journalists.

Once they landed, everything had been timed down to thirty-second intervals: the walk from the airport runway to the armour-plated limousine that would bring the delegation down a pre-cleared road into downtown Budapest, the discussion with Reka and several ministers in parliament, the lunch, the ceremony at the cemetery next to the Great Synagogue on Dohany Street where the commemoration of the liberation of the ghetto would take place, the short meet-and-greet there with Holocaust survivors and former ghetto inmates, the ten-minute journey from there back to parliament to sign the trade and cultural exchange agreements and the small half-hour VIP reception in parliament's most prestigious salon. Ilona glanced at Reka as she explained how pleased they were that Karoly Bardossy, chairman and CEO of Nationwide, one of the country's largest business and industrial conglomerates, would be among the select group of guests.

Reka nodded and gave Ilona a politician's smile that did not extend to her eyes. The last person she wanted to see at the VIP reception was Uncle Karoly, but there was no need to let Ilona know that. Reka had seen Ilona in action before, in her public persona as cultural affairs attaché, shepherding a bedazzled Israeli author around the Budapest Book Fair, charming everyone she encountered. Now she watched Ilona as she spoke, marvelling at her self-possession and the way she dominated the room by sheer force of her presence.

Reka had once been to the Knesset, the Israeli parliament building in Jerusalem. It looked like a fancier version of a local government headquarters in a medium-sized Hungarian city, she had thought at the time, a very workaday building. Most visitors to the Hungarian parliament were impressed, if not awed, by its grandeur: the spectacular entrance hall, the long, gilded corridors, the vaulted ceilings, wood-panelled rooms, the priceless works of art, the sense of history.

Just a few minutes earlier Reka had watched as Ilona had walked into Reka's office. She had stopped at the door, slowly looked around as though she was planning to redecorate the room, nodded approvingly before she sat down. Where did it come from, this supreme self-confidence? She wondered if Ilona ever doubted herself, had a bad hair day? Not in public, she guessed. Another part of her was slightly envious at the way Ilona carried her sky-blue trouser suit and the wave of long black curls that fell down her back.

Reka glanced up and down the table. There were four of them in the room: Reka and Akos Feher, her chief of staff, Ilona and Anastasia Ferenczy, from the Hungarian state security service. She glanced through the windows as Ilona continued talking. On a sunny day the windows gave panoramic views over the Danube and the Royal Castle on the Buda side. Today the river was wreathed in a thick mist, as grey as the sky overhead. She could barely make out the arch of the Chain Bridge, a few minutes' walk away, let alone see across into Buda. The weather had been like this for days, and each time she thought the sun might break through, it retreated again.

Ilona glanced at Reka as if reading her thoughts. She finished her briefing, brushed her hair back needlessly and fixed Reka with her luminous brown eyes. 'Any questions, Prime Minister?'

Reka knew she was attractive. A blue-eyed blond in her mid-thirties with a model's poise, she turned heads wherever she went. She was an experienced politician who had survived numerous crises, both personal and political. But she was still slightly in awe of Ilona's supreme self-confidence. *Yes,*

Reka wanted to say, *How and when did you take over my office?* Instead she smiled and shook her head. 'No, none at all. Everything is under control.'

Reka put the briefing note down and slowly stretched out her fingers along the table, as though confirming possession. The dark hardwood felt cool and solid under her hand, a welcome stability in febrile times. This was her workspace, her inner sanctum, a large corner office in the heart of the neo-Gothic extravaganza that was the Hungarian parliament. She glanced around the table. Ilona had put on quite a show, and as a woman in public life Reka could admire her confidence, but now she needed to take back control. She glanced at Ilona, who was now leaning back in her chair and looking indulgently at Reka, as if giving her permission to speak.

Reka forced herself to stop smiling in return. Instead she tried to sound as prime ministerial as possible as she thanked Ilona for her comprehensive briefing and her team's cooperation with the Hungarian authorities. Last autumn Reka had been the toast of the country, after she had worked with Balthazar Kovacs to prevent a terrorist plot by her predecessor and former lover, Pal Dezeffy, to release a cloud of poison gas across Kossuth Square, in front of the parliament. Dezeffy was dead now, drowned after he fell in the Danube. So too were Reka's plans for a massive funding programme from the Gulf to modernise Hungary's rickety infrastructure and creaking health system after the Qatari investors pulled out. Which was one reason why she desperately needed this visit to be a success.

Reka glanced at the bright, modern watercolour on the facing wall. It was a painting of the Chain Bridge arching over the Danube at dusk. She had recently cleared out all the heavy, old-fashioned furniture and gilt-framed paintings of bearded luminaries of Hungarian history – there were no women – and refurnished the room with modern artworks by young Hungarian painters and photographers and new furniture produced by local designers. Small sculptures now stood on the mantel of the room's marble fireplaces. The thick, brown, upholstered padding on the back of the door, protection against eavesdropping, however, was still in place.

Hungarians had once won more than a dozen Nobel prizes, and it was time to reclaim that inventiveness, she had told the country in a television broadcast the previous week. This was a new era in Hungarian history, when the country would no longer battle modernity, but instead welcome it. Like other small nations with clever, talented populations. Like Israel, for example.

She remembered the reports she had recently read from the Hungarian ambassador in Tel Aviv. Many Israeli politicians – as well as the prime minister – had Hungarian ancestry. Like their Hungarian counterparts they spent most of their time fighting each other and handing out non-jobs to friends and allies. But somehow the country still managed to flourish. Unlike hers at the moment. But that was about to change.

'Does anyone else have anything to raise with our Israeli colleague?' Reka asked.

Anastasia Ferenczy nodded. 'Just to backtrack for a moment. As some of you know, I was stationed undercover last autumn at Keleti Station during the migrant crisis. Mahmoud Hejazi, the international terrorist known as the Gardener, travelled through the station on false papers. He was arrested by Balthazar Kovacs.'

'I've seen that, Anastasia. The clip is on the internet. Impressive work by Officer Kovacs,' said Ilona. Balthazar had arrested Hejazi among a crowd of refugees as they trekked from Keleti Station through Budapest, before heading to the Austrian border. Hejazi had fought back viciously, even taken a woman hostage with a knife before Balthazar took him down to the ground. A moment after he had handcuffed Hejazi, the Syrian terrorist had been killed, shot from underneath Balthazar by a single sniper round, fired from a long distance.

Ilona asked, 'By the way, did you find the sniper yet? Or the weapon? We all know that a lone gunman offers the greatest threat. Downtown Budapest and the area around the synagogue are very densely built up. There are plenty of apartment windows overlooking the cemetery and the synagogue.'

Anastasia replied, 'We have everything covered, Miss Mizrachi. On the ground and in the air. The security plan has been agreed with your colleagues. We will be deploying snipers on key roofs in the downtown area as well as helicopters. As you know, we are experienced in hosting high-profile foreign leaders. The visits of the Russian and Chinese presidents passed without incident.' She glanced down at the schedule. 'The meet-and-greet at the cemetery. The elderly people Prime Minister Farkas will be meeting, you have also pre-vetted and checked them to your satisfaction?'

Ilona smiled. 'Yes, of course. We do not see any danger from Holocaust survivors.' She turned back to Anastasia. 'You were about to tell us about the sniper who shot Hejazi.'

Actually, that was the last thing on my mind, Anastasia wanted to reply, but did not. She shifted in her seat for a moment. She normally dressed in jeans and T-shirts, but today she was wearing a white blouse and black wool business skirt, so new it was still stiff and scratchy. The outfit would go straight back on a hanger once she returned to her office at the state security service headquarters, a short walk away on Falk Miksa Street.

Anastasia saw that Ilona was watching her carefully now as she waited for her answer. Did she know something? Quite possibly. Israeli intelligence had long arms and a vast, efficient network of contacts and assets. It almost certainly extended to her headquarters on nearby Falk Miksa Street. The truth was that the gunman had never gone missing, although Anastasia wasn't going to share that information at this table. Anastasia – and those who needed to know – were well aware of his location: a Balkan restaurant on the corner of Rakoczi Square in District VIII, a restaurant that had been extensively renovated and refurnished after the owner had recently received a substantial sum of cash – part for an assignment cleanly executed, and part in exchange for surrendering his Dragunov rifle.

'We are still looking for the gunman. But we do have the weapon,' Anastasia said, careful to hold Ilona's gaze as she answered. 'And we have rolled up Hejazi's network and contacts here. They are all either deported or in custody.'

Ilona nodded. 'Good.'

Descended from a long line of Transylvanian aristocrats, Anastasia was in her mid-thirties but looked younger, with dark-blond hair, a smooth unlined face and strong features. She had large, clear green eyes, a straight nose and a full mouth – not classically pretty but certainly striking. 'But we are in Budapest. We know central and eastern Europe. Our Arab community here has been here for decades, since before the change of system. They do not want any trouble, and they certainly do not want any disruption to their lives and businesses. In fact they were very helpful in taking down Hejazi's contacts. Your strength is in the Middle East. My question is, have your people picked up any chatter about Prime Minister Farkas and his visit here since we last met a couple of days ago?'

Ilona said, 'No, nothing. We are monitoring all the usual channels. We will let you know if we hear anything.'

Reka looked around the table. 'Then I think we are done for now. Thank you, Ilona.'

Ilona stood up and Reka and her chief of staff walked her to the door, where they shook hands again. Once Ilona had left, Reka turned and gestured to Anastasia and Akos to move across to the corner alcove where four armchairs were gathered around a coffee table.

Reka sat back, stretched her legs out, ran her hand through her hair and closed her eyes for a moment. 'Four days to go. Then we're done.' She glanced at Akos. 'Tell me, is it too early for palinka?'

Palinka, or fruit schnapps, preferably home-distilled, was the Hungarians' great cure-all. Akos considered the question before he answered. 'If we were in the countryside, campaigning for votes, then not. In fact it would be rude to refuse if offered.' He sat back for a moment, shook his head. 'But here, now, probably it is. In any case we need to talk about the election campaign this morning, Prime Minister,' said Akos Feher. 'The numbers are not looking great.'

Reka was the first woman prime minister of Hungary. Like its neighbours, Hungary had been frozen in time for the forty-odd years in which it had languished under communism until the change of system in 1990. The great social revolutions that had reshaped Europe: the rise of feminism, gay rights, the student upheavals of 1968, had passed the Soviet bloc by. Central and eastern Europe were still deeply conservative societies. Even now, there were few women in public life, apart from sports stars and television presenters and only a handful of women MPs. The upside was a strong family orientation with an everyday respect for elders and a formal politeness and courtesy. The downside was that women politicians were mocked, even in parliament, with sexist jibes that were unthinkable in the west. The internet was awash with memes caricaturing Reka. One showed her in a kitchen, surrounded by smoking pans and a cooker on fire. Others were far cruder.

Reka said, 'There is still everything to play for. We have almost a month. Farkas's visit will help, assuming it all goes well.' Hungary was a small country with a strong sense of national identity and pride. It was important to be taken seriously on the international stage, for Budapest to host high-profile international visitors – all of which could translate into votes for the current prime minister.

Akos nodded. 'Of course, Prime Minister. And it will.'

Akos had just turned twenty-nine but looked younger. He was skinny, with spiky light-blond hair and a taste for tight navy suits. He had been working for Reka for about six months and his appointment had triggered furious envy among the older generation of apparatchiks who would normally expect to gain his position. His past with Reka had been short but intense. They were both the repository of each other's darkest secrets. But over the months their initial threats and attempts at blackmail had faded, evolving instead into a mutual trust and respect. Any destruction, they both understood, would be mutually assured.

Reka continued talking. 'Anyway, that's party politics, Akos, not government business.' The distinction, she knew, was a novel one in Hungary, and one she had blurred herself often enough when it suited her. But this time it was clear, and she did not want Anastasia to leave yet. 'And we don't want to make Anastasia feel uncomfortable. Let's have breakfast instead. And let Eniko in.'

Eniko Szalay was Reka's spokeswoman and press secretary. Farkas's visit was already garnering plenty of attention from the international press. Major international television networks were sending crews, the Budapest-based foreign press corps was demanding access, and there would also be a contingent of Israeli journalists travelling with him on the plane.

Just as Reka was about to call for Eniko, the double door to the room opened and she walked in. It was instantly clear that something was wrong. Eniko nodded briskly at everyone, but her face was rigid with tension and her mouth closed tight. At that exact moment Anastasia's phone rang. She stood up, excused herself, walked across to the corner of the office and took the call.

Eniko watched her go, then glanced at the others, sitting in their chairs, looking at her expectantly. 'We have bad news,' said Eniko.

'Which is?' asked Reka.

Anastasia walked back to the group, her telephone in her hand. 'An Israeli has gone missing.'

THREE

Dob Street, 8 a.m.

Balthazar walked briskly up to the front door of Eva *neni*'s second flat, as she followed behind him. The apartment was situated at the far end of the corridor. Its location meant that unfortunately the door was in easy view of the other flats.

A voice in his head told him that this course of action was a mistake. Neither he nor Eva *neni* knew what had happened to Elad, or what might have taken place in his flat. Balthazar was entering a potential crime scene, with no protection except a pair of latex gloves from the supply he kept at home. A neighbour might witness him entering the flat and if the police really descended on the building that would come out, potentially dropping him in a lot of trouble. Eva *neni* owned the flat so there would already be traces of her DNA. But he had never been inside the place before. He could easily contaminate it with DNA, or accidentally leave fingerprints, which could even make him a suspect.

If he really thought Elad had gone missing, he should call in the local cops from the District VII station. Each of Budapest's twenty-three districts had its own force. There were special city-wide squads at the Budapest police headquarters for serious crimes like murder, armed robbery and fraud. Balthazar was a detective in the Budapest police murder squad. There was no evidence of a murder, and, he hoped, there would not be. The District VII cops would send a team over and then open a missing-person case. That would involve calling in a forensics team and an investigator. They would seal the flat and launch a manhunt. That would be the correct procedure, the voice in his head said.

He ignored it.

There was movement at the other end of the corridor, a brief opening of a door, a glimpse of a head before the door closed. He sighed inside. Feri *bacsi*, Uncle Feri.

When Balthazar had first moved into the building many of the neighbours had been, at best, wary. Gypsies were often not very popular in Hungary and neither were cops. His being both had initially garnered a very cool response. Eva *neni* had been the only one to welcome him. But over the years, as Balthazar became a fixture in the place, and had used his connections to smooth out potential problems for a couple of neighbouring families with wayward teenage children – Klauzal Square was a popular place for teenagers to gather in the summer, drink beer and smoke dope – he had become accepted. Even more so, now that he was something of a celebrity. Accepted by everyone, except Feri *bacsi*.

Feri *bacsi*'s full name was Ferenc Balogh. A former full-time official in the Communist Party, he had lost his job in 1990 at the change of system and never found another. He did not bother to disguise his distaste for Balthazar and could frequently be heard muttering about how the building had been turned into a '*Cigany-haz*', a Gypsy-house, which was an insult. Nor was he a great fan of Eva *neni*, but he knew enough not to make that plain. Unfortunately Feri *bacsi* lived at the other end of the corridor and his front door gave him a clear view along the passageway.

The plan was that Balthazar and Eva *neni* would both go inside the flat, but Balthazar would just stand with his back to the closed front door. He needed to see the place for himself, and get a sense of it, but she would move around inside, searching for any clues or hints as to what might have happened.

Eva *neni* took out her key but just as she was about to put it into the lock, she dropped it. The key was on a ring with numerous others, including several large ones for the cellar and courtyard. She was nervous, Balthazar saw. The keys hit the floor with a loud crash. Balthazar saw movement at the far end of the corridor, a door open quickly, then close. Feri *bacsi,* again. There was nothing to be done about it.

Balthazar nodded encouragingly at Eva *neni* and she picked up her key again and opened the door. She turned to Balthazar, about to mouth an apology, but he put an index finger over his mouth. She nodded, and silently went inside. Balthazar quickly followed her inside and closed the door behind him.

The first thing he noticed was how tidy the place was. It was a small one-room flat, with a combined bedroom and lounge, a galley kitchen and shower room leading off the main room. An old-fashioned sofa bed took up part of the main wall. Opposite, on the other side of the room, stood a plain wooden chest of drawers and a narrow wardrobe, while a small table and chair stood in the far corner. The walls were pale yellow and the narrow parquet slats, the same size and pattern as those in his flat, were faded and worn. The windows, like those in his flat, were the originals, in ancient wooden frames that let the cold seep in.

Balthazar watched as Eva *neni* walked around, peering under the table, checking the bed and looking in the corners.

There were no signs of struggle here, none at all.

The aftermath of a crime, or malfeasance, left a kind of energy. That silent witness sometimes spoke to him. It was one of Balthazar's gifts, to sense something of what had happened in a place. His mother, Marta, had the same ability. Marginalised, expelled, hated by many for centuries, the Gypsies had developed survival instincts that were rooted in ancient ways, which could not be explained by science. The *gadjes*, the non-Gypsies, did not understand it at all. In the early days of his career he had tried to explain his sixth sense to his colleagues. They had laughed, looked at him like he was a mad person, or a shaman.

Nowadays, after he had found and arrested several murderers who would otherwise have escaped, his fellow detectives listened with more attention, but he knew that behind his back they still mocked what they called his '*Cigany boszorkanysag*', or Gypsy witchcraft. Perhaps that was one reason why he had become so close to Eva *neni*. She too could read the signs, which was one reason why she was still alive.

The air was calm. The flat felt peaceful. There was a faint smell of masculine deodorant, but none of that disturbed feeling, the bad energy that he often sensed in a place where violence had taken place. His instinct told him that if Elad had been abducted, it wasn't from here. It felt more like someone had come in and very methodically swept and emptied the room.

He watched Eva *neni* open the wardrobe. It was empty. So were each of the drawers in the cupboard facing the bed. She signalled that she would go into the kitchen and the bathroom. She entered one after the other and each time showed Balthazar her empty hands when she came out. So where were Elad's clothes, his notes, his laptop?

He thought back to his conversation with Eva *neni* in his kitchen.

Nationwide.

Nationwide was one of the wealthiest and most powerful companies in Hungary. Its main business was construction, but it also had interests and holdings in manufacturing, transport, property acquisition and had recently branched out into the media. There had long been rumours about how the company had been founded after the end of the Second World War. Questions too, about how both the firm, and its owners, the Bardossy family, had not only survived under communism, but had thrived. But Nationwide had powerful lawyers who soon descended on anyone asking uncomfortable questions or writing articles that displeased its boss, Karoly Bardossy. And now that his niece was prime minister, even fewer investigators were probing the company and its past – except for Elad Harrari, who doubtless would not care about Hungarian lawyers.

But had Nationwide really branched out into the abduction business as well? Kidnapping was a very complicated crime to organise and execute, which was why most kidnappings went wrong. It demanded a snatch team, a holding place, a supply of food and drink, a negotiator who knew what they were doing and for everyone involved to keep their mouths shut. Every crime demanded two questions at the outset of the investigation: who had the motivation? And who had the opportunity? Nationwide, or Karoly Bardossy, would have both, and the resources to abduct Elad. But he would be a very obvious suspect. Abducting a foreign citizen, especially an Israeli, was a serious matter. Still, it certainly sounded like someone was watching Elad and he had been followed. The first step would be to get more information about the blue Mercedes with the cracked right-hand lamp.

If Elad really had gone missing then there was no question: Balthazar would need to call in the forensics team to examine the flat. But the more he thought it through, the more he realised that the case would probably not be left to the District VII cops. They dealt with local crimes. This would be a very sensitive one. Elad was a foreigner, a citizen of a country whose relationship with Hungary was complicated, even fraught. The bosses would want the A-team on this. Which meant that Balthazar could ask to take it over.

They were about to leave when Eva *neni* stood still for a moment. She frowned for several seconds then stared into the distance. 'Wait, Tazi. I have an idea. I gave Elad a spare key to my flat, in case he needed to get in.'

'Where is it?'

'Hidden, of course. In a place where nobody would think to look.' She smiled at Balthazar as though he was a small child. 'We all need hiding places. Wait here.'

He stepped inside and watched as she walked across the room and opened a narrow door that led into the tiny bathroom. There was nowhere to sit down, only a shower cubicle and a small sink. Eva *neni* bent down, reached for the middle tile in the bottom row and pushed in the lower edge. The tile came loose in her hand. She put it down and reached inside the space, her fingers probing, until they found something.

She stood up and walked out, back to Balthazar, her palm outstretched. 'Look at this. I didn't leave it there.'

A small silver-coloured stick lay in her hand. Balthazar picked up the silver object. It was light in his hand, almost weightless, with a clear plastic cap over a narrow metal prong at one end.

'It's a memory thing, Tazi,' said Eva *neni*. 'For a computer.'

FOUR

Newsroom, 555.hu, Liberty Square, 8.10 a.m.

Zsuzsa Barcsy sat at her desk, watching the contents of her editor's hard drive scroll across her laptop screen. The rows of folders looked very tempting: story schedules, future projects, legal and personnel files. The correspondence with 555.hu's new owners was especially appealing. It might explain why an irreverent news site staffed by smartarse bohemians and hipsters had suddenly moved from a dilapidated apartment overlooking not-very-glamorous Blaha Lujza Square to a state-of-the-art office building in the heart of downtown – and why those who had survived the purge had received such substantial pay rises.

But she had one task to complete and very little time in which to do it. Zsuzsa's investigation into Nationwide had been held over for two weeks now. Each time she asked the editor Roland Horvath when it would run, he fobbed her off with increasingly feeble excuses about libel and lawyers. Zsuzsa was certain of all her facts and had double-checked everything – she had even sent the few sources prepared to speak on the record their quotes for authorisation. She had unravelled a web of front companies that reached from small villages in eastern Hungary and across the border in Ukraine to the Cayman Islands and Minsk, the capital of Belarus.

Zsuzsa had proved that Nationwide was gaming the system to produce immense off-the-books profits for its owners and directors – chief among them Karoly Bardossy, its majority shareholder. The mayor of one small village in the Ukraine had been astonished to learn that he was, on paper, a euro millionaire – but when he started asking questions he had been warned off in no uncertain terms.

And there was something else going on, Zsuzsa and several of her colleagues believed. Roland Horvath had never been the most collegial of leaders, preferring to issue edicts from his glass-walled bunker, but lately he had been positively secretive, lowering the electric blinds for hours for meetings with 555.hu's news editor, Kriszta Matyas. Roland himself just brushed away all queries, saying they were working on a project on a need-to-know basis and Kriszta was equally unhelpful. In fact neither of the two had let slip anything at all about what they were working on, which the rest of the newsroom had dubbed WTFATUT – *What The Fuck Are They Up To?* Was WTFATUT connected to the non-publication of her Nationwide article?

Zsuzsa looked around the newsroom, suddenly nostalgic for 555.hu's former offices, and a simpler life when her stories were published. That large ramshackle flat, on the corner of Rakoczi Way and the Grand Boulevard, had no air-conditioning or proper heating system. But its rattly wooden parquet floors, giant marble fireplace, high ceilings and toilets that pre-dated the change of system in 1990 gave it plenty of atmosphere. She especially missed people-watching from the balcony overlooking Blaha Lujza Square. Very little had survived 555.hu's move from its old offices. H. L. Mencken, the American journalist and guiding light to generations of reporters, still stared out from a tattered poster, a speech bubble recording his supposed epithet that 'The relationship of a journalist to a politician should be that of a dog to a lamp post'. A pile of boxes of files and reporters' research material had come with the poster, and were still stacked up in a corner of the room, but that was about it.

Zsuzsa's story, she was determined, would appear somewhere. OK, it was edgy, but that was her job. Her investigation, she was sure, was being held because of pressure from on high, but from where? Nationwide was the obvious suspect. Budapest was a small city and its political, business and media elites were closely entwined – to an unhealthy degree. In any case, if Roland continued to refuse to run the story, she would resign and take it elsewhere. Several of her former colleagues, sacked in the move, were now crowdfunding the launch of a new website called newsline.hu. It was a shareholders' collective, owned by the journalists, structured so that it could never be bought or sold. Survivor's guilt had already prompted her – and much of the remaining 555.hu newsroom – to donate to the fighting fund. If she did jump ship, the Nationwide story would make a great launch for newsline.hu. But first of all, she had to find out why it was being held over. Roland was a slow, methodical worker and she was sure that he would have kept the lawyers' notes and any other comments. There was also a chance that there were genuine legal issues – in which case she needed to know what they were.

She glanced nervously across the newsroom at the door again, then down at the printout of her instructions how to get into the computer system using Roland's login and password. The door was still closed; she was connected not to her work computer, but to her personal laptop, as she had been instructed. So far, so good.

This was the first day Zsuzsa had arrived in the office before Roland but he could still turn up at any moment as she prowled around his folders and files, now accessible on her laptop screen. A paunchy divorcee in his forties, Roland had little life outside the office and was known to appear at all hours of the day. His main topic of conversation, other than work, was his teenage daughter, Wanda, whom he saw once a week. Zsuzsa had once seen them in a popular hamburger restaurant, where Wanda seemed more interested in her telephone than her food, or her father.

Zsuzsa's desk was at the other end of the newsroom to Roland's office in the far corner. That would give her a few seconds to shut down her probe before he arrived at his desk, but no more. Part of her felt sorry for him, another slightly guilty for what she was doing. A few days ago Roland had asked her out to dinner, ostensibly to discuss his plans for the website, but his loneliness was almost palpable. But in the end she was a journalist and it was her job to dig out information – especially when her biggest story yet was being stonewalled.

Zsuzsa glanced again at her screen. She needed a folder called Misc. There, she had been told, everything she wanted could be found. The knot of tension in her stomach grew as the list of folders on Roland's desk expanded until eventually Misc appeared.

She took a deep breath. There was nothing remarkable about the newest icon on her screen – it looked the same as all the others. But this was the point of no return. Until now, she could, just about, concoct a story of a system malfunction that had somehow led her to Roland Horvath's computer instead of her own. She had not downloaded anything.

But once she started copying files onto her laptop, there would be some sort of data trail. That trail would not automatically lead to her computer – or so she had been assured – but it might be noticed and could trigger an investigation – in which Zsuzsa would be one of the most likely and obvious suspects. Who else would hack into a folder on the editor's computer where their story was stored?

This was the moment of decision. She looked around the room once more. It was empty and silent, the only sound the soft clicks of her keyboard.

A Bloomberg terminal stood in one corner for the newly recruited business reporters, next to a fancy chrome coffee machine with an impressive array of levers and switches, and bowls of fruit, cookies and muffins, all freshly delivered every morning at 8 a.m., in case of any early bird arrivals. She tapped her desk with her fingers for a few seconds. All of the journalists had a new wide, grey wooden desk, with a new Apple Mac desktop and silver keyboard, as well as a Mac laptop computer and a new iPhone 6, all paid for by the website's new owners. Once again she wondered why they were spending so much money. But that story would have to wait.

Zsuzsa watched her cursor hover over Misc. She dropped her thumb, let it press down on her touchpad until a faint noise sounded. It was done. She was downloading.

Misc opened to reveal two more folders: one titled ZB and the second, RB. ZB was obviously her initials. She opened the folder, her eyes widening as she saw copies of her article in various drafts as she had sent them to Roland. But there was much more material, which she had not and would never have sent to him: her source notes, transcripts of all her interviews, telephone log, contacts, research files, documents from international databases and web pages that she had saved.

Zsuzsa dug her thumbnail into her index finger as she tried to control her rising anger. She had been sitting here feeling guilty – while the whole time Roland and his bosses and lawyers had been inside her computer, pulling in everything to do with her work. *Feeling guilty* – for a moment she almost laughed.

A separate folder within Misc was marked Correspondence. She opened that to see various emails back and forth from the lawyers to Roland. That was expected and it was normal practice for lawyers to check contentious articles for libel. Then she opened one of the lawyers' emails. Her eyes widened as she scanned its contents, her anger turning to incredulity as she read through to the summary:

In short ZB's investigation has more than served its purpose. Her diligent and insistent probing has revealed numerous weaknesses in the structure of Nationwide Ltd., both in Hungary and its network of satellite organisations abroad, and the network of connections and financial channels between them, which leaves the organisation vulnerable to charges of money laundering and corruption in multiple jurisdictions – as suggest by ZB in her article. Ukraine is an especially weak node in the network and needs immediate attention.

Now that these vulnerabilities have been identified we can chart a clear path to eradicate them and so strengthen our position, both legally and in the many markets in which we operate.

She sat back, closed her eyes for a moment and exhaled. She had been duped. More than duped, she had been played. And how.

Part of her – a small part – was almost admiring. Whose idea had this been? In a way it was quite brilliant – use an investigative journalist to investigate what information could be discovered and so needed to be shut down. Probably not Roland. He was incapable of standing up for himself, or his reporters, but this level of betrayal, she thought, was beyond him. She glanced at her watch. It was after 8.20 a.m. She needed to speed this up. She copied the whole of Misc onto her computer, watching the download bar as it slowly crept forward.

Zsuzsa checked she had everything then closed the ZB folder on Roland's hard drive. Her task was completed. But the RB folder still showed, unopened. Then she realised what the letters probably stood for: the initials of the prime minister, Reka Bardossy.

She glanced at the newsroom door once again. It was still closed. The RB folder must hold something quite incendiary to be stored alongside her material. Furious now at the violation of her privacy, her workplace, and the confidentiality of her sources, who had trusted her at some risk to their jobs and careers, she clicked on the RB folder and opened it. There were two files inside, a Word document and a video of several hundred megabytes. Just as she started to download them both, the office door opened and Roland walked in. He looked across the newsroom, saw Zsuzsa and waved at her. She waved back, told herself to stay calm.

She glanced again at her desktop. The video file's download bar was showing just a few per cent. She looked back at Roland, who had started to walk over to his room.

Take control.

She stood up and walked quickly toward to the coffee machine. It stood in the centre of the newsroom, equidistant between their workplaces. As she arrived, Roland was almost at his door.

Zsuzsa called his name and he turned. 'Could you help me here, Roland,' she asked, gesturing at the array of handles and shiny tubes. 'I'm dying for a coffee but I still don't know how to work this thing.' She gave him her brightest smile. 'I think it's men's work.' Playing the ditzy girl worked without fail in Hungary, she had learned over the years – especially with anything mechanical.

Roland turned slightly pink, clearly pleased and flattered to be asked to help. He started walking over to Zsuzsa. 'Sure,' he said. 'What can I make you?'

'A cappuccino, if that's not too much trouble?' A cappuccino, she knew, would be the most trouble, what with all the steam and milk-frothing business, and so take up the most time.

Roland smiled, his saggy face creasing to reveal yellowing teeth. 'Coming right up. I'll make us both one. We can take them back to your desk, if you like. I can spare a few minutes to catch up; you can tell me how you are settling in.'

Zsuzsa nodded, hoping her extreme alarm at that idea did not show. The printout of her hacking instructions was still next to her keyboard. Even Roland would notice it. And what a screaming hypocrite he was. *How could you use me like that, you coward?* she wanted to yell at him.

Instead she smiled, stepped a little closer. 'Sure, I'd like that, but first could you talk me through how this works, so I can work it for myself next time?'

Roland nodded, and went through a long and detailed explanation about steam, pressure, milk froth, types of grind and beans. Zsuzsa pretended she was paying attention, but was actually watching the clock on the facing wall. Four minutes had now passed. That was plenty of time for the video file to download. Roland handed Zsuzsa her coffee. She thanked him. Now she had to get rid of him.

She looked at the clock again, tutted, shook her head and said, 'I'm really sorry, I completely forgot. I have to dash, a contact told me to call them before 8.45 a.m. and it's someone I have been trying to get for ages.'

Roland nodded, the disappointment clear on his face, and began to walk to his office. Zsuzsa quickly crossed the newsroom and sat down at her desk. The RB files had downloaded. She closed the folder, made sure Misc and all the other files were also closed.

She looked at Roland's office. He was hanging up his coat. Roland walked over to his desk. Zsuzsa cut the connection.

After ten minutes going through more of the material she had downloaded, her suspicions were confirmed. The website's new owner was a fully owned subsidiary of Nationwide Ltd. She was working for Karoly Bardossy.

FIVE

Dob Street, 9 a.m.

Javitas, next door to the entrance to Balthazar's apartment house, was the newest addition to the gentrification of District VII, much of which was focused on the streets around its epicentre, Klauzal Square. Javitas meant repairs in Hungarian. Until recently Javitas actually had been a repair shop for everything from typewriters to washing machines, run by Samu *bacsi*, an elderly Jewish man. Balthazar often dropped by for a chat and one of Samu's powerful coffees. The two men talked about how the neighbourhood was changing, as it evolved into the *buli-negyed*, or party quarter, the old shops and cafés slowly turning into trendy bars and eateries that were crowded with tourists every night, leaving the locals with fewer and fewer places to go. Even worse, in the spring and summer the pavements, especially in the morning, were often spattered with vomit or pools of urine.

Several months ago Samu had surprised Balthazar with the news that he was selling up. Balthazar was shocked: Samu *bacsi* was an institution. He kept erratic hours and charged almost nothing for his repairs, but everyone in District VII knew him. But soon he would be seventy-five, Samu told Balthazar, so it was time to retire properly. Somewhat to

Samu's amazement, the value of his premises was enough for him to retire and buy a new apartment for himself and his wife in one of the fancy riverside blocks in District XIII with a concierge, a balcony and view over the Danube. Even better, the purchaser was his grandson, Mishi.

It was Mishi who greeted Balthazar as he walked into Javitas. The old fading paintwork had been stripped away, the cracked parquet slats and the creaking wooden window frames had all been replaced. Javitas had a new floor of wide grey planks, white plaster walls, and a jumble of used furniture dating back to the 1970s and 1960s. Charlie Parker drifted from a Bose sound system, and the air was rich with the smell of brewing coffee.

Behind the counter was a blackboard with the day's specials: a new coffee from Ecuador, vegan stir-fry noodles with tofu, a gluten- and sugar-free banana cake. Javitas was a pleasant and welcoming place, the kind of café loved by hipsters from Budapest to Berlin and Brooklyn. But what lifted it from the legion of trendy eateries now colonising the city were the framed photographs of Samu *bacsi* at work. Some showed him as a young man, others just before he retired. The walls were also bedecked with souvenirs from across the decades: framed newspaper clippings, faded family photographs, posters for films and gigs by long-forgotten Hungarian rock bands. Perched on shelves and in various alcoves were some of the items Samu *bacsi* had worked on: an ancient black typewriter, an anglepoise-style lamp, a wooden radio. It was a loving homage.

Mishi put down the coffee cup he was polishing as Balthazar walked up to the long, zinc counter. Mishi was short and podgy with black hair tinged with grey, a goatee beard, soft features and shrewd brown eyes. Mishi had recently returned to Budapest after several years living in London, where he had opened several coffee bars in Hoxton, the area of central London known as 'Silicon Roundabout' for the number of tech firms that had opened up there.

He smiled when he saw Balthazar. 'Drink? Eat?' he asked. 'We have a fabulous limited-edition new roast from Ecuador. Notes of caramel and burned orange, a long finish.'

Balthazar laughed as shook his head. They both knew that he had no interest in the fine gradations of coffees from different countries. 'A Samu, please.'

A Samu meant coffee like Mishi's grandfather used to make: a thick, tepid sludge, brewed from a vacuum-packed supermarket blend of cheap robusta beans.

Mishi pretended to looked pained. 'OK. If you insist.' He looked at Balthazar, sensing there was a reason for today's visit. 'Something else I can help with?'

Balthazar looked around before he spoke. The only other customer, a teenage girl with green-streaked hair, was sitting in a far corner, deeply involved with her mobile telephone. He leaned on the counter, then asked, 'Is Vivi in?'

'So you're not here for the vegan stir-fry?'

Balthazar laughed. 'One day. Promise.'

'She's in the back. I'll bring your coffee through.'

'Thanks,' said Balthazar, as he started to walk around the bar to the door at the back.

'Wait,' said Mishi. He scribbled something down on the back of a business card. 'You'll need this. It's the door code.'

There were three back rooms behind the public café space. One had been converted into a kitchen, the second an office. Balthazar glanced inside the kitchen, watching the cook chop, fry and stir by the long cooker range. In the neighbouring space Noemi, Mishi's younger sister, sat by a computer, taking care of the café's paperwork. Balthazar stopped in front of the third room, where a large, grey steel door was firmly closed in a metal frame. He looked up to see a small CCTV camera pointing at him, waved and smiled at the lens. A entry pad was mounted by the side of the entrance. He tapped in 05101940 – Samu's birthday – and gently pushed the door open.

Inside the room a tall, pale, very skinny woman in her late twenties with a silver nose ring and buzz-cut black hair sat in front of a large desk. She turned when the door opened and greeted Balthazar with a raised hand. She was speaking on her mobile, he could see.

Balthazar waited a moment, but she gestured for him to come inside. As he walked into the room he caught the tail end of her conversation.

'Good, good. I told you it would work. Now put it all on the stick, then wipe all the files from your laptop with that program I gave you…' Vivi listened for a moment. 'No, don't worry. They might suspect something but they won't be able to actually prove anything, make sure you wipe everything from your laptop… OK, come over later.'

A 1980s fake leather armchair stood in the corner by a small wooden table. He sat down in the armchair, his nose prickling at the smell of burned rope that hung in the air. A large blue ceramic ashtray stood on the table. A bent stub lay in the centre, too thick to be a cigarette.

'No trace… wipe your laptop. That all sounds intriguing, Vivi,' Balthazar said.

Vivi put her mobile down and turned to Balthazar. The handset, he noticed, was an old-fashioned Nokia candy-bar model. She smiled. 'Doesn't it, Detective? Now how can I help?'

Balthazar picked up the remainder of the joint and sniffed it. Hungary had very harsh drugs laws. Mere possession of a joint was enough to earn a hefty fine or even a jail sentence. 'Firstly, don't do this in the square, at least for the next few days.' Klauzal Square was a popular haunt of the local dope smokers. 'The city will be crawling with cops, because of the Israeli prime minister's visit.'

'Thanks. I won't. But you didn't come here to tell me that.'

Balthazar put the stub back down in the ashtray. 'No, I did not.'

Vivi Szentkiralyi was a computer genius and had, until recently, worked as the systems manager of 555.hu. She had rescued the laptops of countless journalists after they dropped them or spilled coffee over the keyboard. She had saved 555.hu from a sustained DDOS attack, a distributed denial-of-service attack, when swarms of computers around the world had been hijacked and ordered to visit the news site and overwhelm its systems. She even knew how to navigate safely through the Dark Web, the secret internet where weapons, drugs, and many more illegal goods were traded, making it a rich source of stories. The new owners, however, had decided that Vivi's services were no longer required. She was one of many staff members who did not make the move to the website's new offices overlooking Liberty Square.

Balthazar had once seen Vivi's workspace at 555.hu: two massive desks, overflowing with hard drives, keyboards, tangles of cables, half-finished mugs of coffee, sandwich wrappers, pizza boxes and who knew what else. Her new workplace was the complete opposite: three sleek brushed-steel monitors and a single keyboard. A large steel cube hard drive with a blinking blue light stood at the edge of the desk, emitting a faint hum. The walls were painted white and the floor was the same wide, grey wooden flooring as the café's. It looked like there had once been a window on the other side but it had been bricked up and painted over. At the other end of the desk was a heavy, black old-fashioned IBM ThinkPad, which even Balthazar knew was very out of date. Vivi's outfit, however, had not changed and she wore her usual black long-sleeved T-shirt and ripped black jeans that showed the skin of her knees.

Balthazar looked at the three monitors and her orderly desk. 'It's a bit different to 555.'

Vivi smiled wryly. 'It has to be. I'm a grown-up now.'

She handed Balthazar a business card. He looked down. 'Information technology and security consultant. Sounds impressive. How is the hacking going?'

Vivi shrugged. 'Fine, I suppose. Mishi rents me the room. I bought the equipment with my redundancy. They gave us all a decent pay-off so we would go quickly and quietly. Companies pay me to break into their systems. Then I tell them their vulnerabilities. Then they give me quite a lot of money.' She looked wistful for a moment. 'But it was much more fun at 555.hu. I don't get a lot of visitors. In fact I don't get any. You are the first. That's it. So here I am. All legal and above board. Sorry I don't have anything to offer you.'

'That's fine, I ordered us both a coffee. Mishi will bring them in.'

'Great. So, what can I do for you?'

Balthazar leaned forward. 'I need your help, Vivi. With two things.'

'You have computer experts at police headquarters. I don't mean to be difficult, but why don't you ask them?'

'Firstly, because they are not as good as you.' He paused, let the compliment – which they both knew was true – sink in. 'And secondly, I need these done off the books.'

'Hmmm, sounds intriguing.'

'I think so,' said Balthazar as he reached into his pocket and took out the memory stick that Eva *neni* had found hidden in Elad's flat. He walked over to Vivi and showed it to her, lying in the palm of his hand. 'This is encrypted. I already tried to open it on my laptop at home. I couldn't get in.'

Vivi eyed the stick suspiciously then sat back for a moment. 'I don't mind doing things in a grey area, Detective, but it has to be for a good cause.' She hesitated for a moment. 'I know you are a decent guy and you used to be Eniko's boyfriend and you are the hero of Kossuth Square and everything, and Eniko is a good person, so you must be as well, but you are a cop.' She fixed him with a steady gaze as she spoke. 'So how do I know I am not going to get someone into trouble?'

Balthazar thought for a moment before he replied. It was a fair point and underlying it – which did not need to be said – was the fact that not all of his colleagues were decent. 'The memory stick belongs to someone who has disappeared, probably been kidnapped. I think it has some clues about what happened to him. None of that is public and the police have not even opened a case yet, so I am trusting you with that.'

Vivi frowned. 'Why the secrecy? If someone's been kidnapped it will come out sooner or later.'

Balthazar still stood with his hand outstretched. 'It will, you're right. But I need to get a head start. And it's connected to someone close to me. But if you feel you can't get involved, I quite understand...'

Vivi hesitated for a moment, then reached forward and took the stick. 'OK. I believe you. I'll help.' She looked down at the memory stick. 'I'll put it in the sandbox.'

Balthazar looked around, confused for a moment. There was no sand in the room as far as he could see. 'The what?'

Vivi reached across for the IBM ThinkPad, placed it by her keyboard and powered it up. 'This is the sandbox. It's never been connected to the internet and never will be. It's so obsolete it needs a card to connect to a Wi-Fi network. I filled the slot with epoxy glue just to make sure. I also glued up the cable connections so it can never be connected to a server.' She patted the lid approvingly, suddenly more animated than he had ever seen her. 'It's as safe as a computer can be. The hard drive is partitioned and runs on Linux, which is the safest operating system. Nobody writes viruses for Linux. Even if there is a virus on your memory stick it will only infect one part of the hard drive. The rest is safe. They call it a sandbox because you can play around there, with dangerous toys.'

Balthazar nodded slowly, as though he understood, although he was mystified by much of what Vivi was saying. *Linux?* His knowledge of computers was minimal at best. He could use a keyboard and a browser, run a basic Google search. He kept missing WhatsApp messages from his son, Alex, even though Alex had shown him how to set the notifications. 'Sure, sounds great.'

Balthazar watched the screen light up and Vivi pressed numerous buttons. A window appeared on the screen, with a flashing cursor at the top-left corner, and a line of code started spilling rightwards. It looked like nothing he had ever seen. Vivi inserted the USB drive. At that moment the door opened and Mishi walked in, carrying two cups of coffee, and handed one to each. 'A Samu for you, Detective, and today's special for you, Vivi.'

They both thanked Mishi and he left quickly. Balthazar sat back and drank his coffee while Vivi worked. He looked at Vivi as her long fingers, each tipped with glossy black nail varnish, moved across her keyboard. What did he know about her? Could he trust her? He didn't really have a choice. He didn't know anyone else in this world and he certainly could not take the memory stick to the police headquarters. Balthazar remembered Eniko telling him once that Vivi was a mystery, and never socialised with the reporters, even though they several times invited her for drinks after work. Nobody knew if she had a boyfriend or a girlfriend. She was very smart, that was clear. Perhaps she was just shy and even a bit lonely. He looked around the room. It wasn't much of a life, sitting here on your own all day without a window, even if the money was good.

Vivi's pale face was set in concentration as her fingers danced across the keyboard. Lines of code flowed back and forth, symbols appeared and disappeared. The coffee was perfect: thick, lukewarm and slightly bitter. He missed Samu and their conversations, he realised. The area around the square was changing more rapidly than ever, as though forty years of stasis and decrepitude under communism had suddenly erupted into an insatiable hunger for everything new and western and shiny. Mishi at least had made a great effort to keep the spirit of his grandfather's shop and incorporate its heritage. Which was why Javitas was Balthazar's go-to coffee bar – and also because it was underneath his flat.

The taste of the coffee was the taste of his childhood and teenage years. For a moment he was back at the kitchen table in the family flat on Jozsef Street, on the other side of the Grand Boulevard, in the heart of District VIII, explaining to his father, Laci, why he wanted to be a policeman, seeing the expression on his face, watching his incredulity turn to anger. Laci had expected him to leave school at sixteen. As the eldest son he would eventually succeed him in running the family business, running several topless bars and brothels. Laci, like many of his generation, had left school at fourteen. What was good enough for him was good enough for his sons, he exclaimed repeatedly.

But Marta, Balthazar's mother, had been determined that at least one of her sons would go out into the world and make his fortune legitimately. A short stint without cooked meals or other marriage benefits had quickly persuaded Laci to let his wife have her way. Balthazar was the first – and still the only – person in his family to go to university. Laci had even agreed that Balthazar could take a postgraduate degree at CEU. And when Balthazar had married Sarah Weiss, a Jewish student from New York, he and the whole family had attended the wedding, even though she was a *gadje*, a non-Gypsy.

But a policeman? In the family? His first-born son?

No. *Never.*

Balthazar's childhood home was just a fifteen-minute walk away, on the other side of the Grand Boulevard.

But it was out of reach. Laci had ostracised him, and forbidden any member of the family to have contact with Balthazar. That had not lasted very long. Balthazar was in touch with his siblings, his brothers Gaspar and Melchior, his sister, Flora, and his mother, Marta. Gaspar, the second son, now ran the family businesses, while Melchior was a musician, and spent much time travelling on the international festival circuit. Flora ran a small art gallery on Brody Sandor Street, on the fancy end of District VIII. But the unspoken accommodation was that while Balthazar could meet his relatives away from home, as long as they did not talk about it, he would not return to the family home. Jozsef Street was very near, but very far.

After a few minutes Vivi turned back to Balthazar, interrupting his reverie. 'It's encrypted, like you said, to a high level. I should be able to break it but it will take a while.'

Balthazar nodded. 'OK. How long do you think?'

'Maybe an hour, maybe a day. I can leave some programs running. What was the second thing?'

'Can you get into the Budapest city CCTV system?'

She smiled. 'That's not grey, Detective, that's illegal.'

'I know. I didn't ask you to do it – just if you *could*.'

Vivi laughed. 'Sure, but we both know what's coming down the line. To answer your question, yes, I could. The security is rubbish. Why?'

'Let's see what's on the memory stick. Then we'll know what to do next.'

SIX

Offices of 555.hu, 9.30 a.m.

Zsuzsa sat back in her ergonomically designed leather chair and pressed two buttons on the arm. A cushion gently pressed against her back as she slowly reclined. The sensation was enjoyable but tinged with a frisson of regret as she began to realise that she would not be sitting in this chair for much longer.

She had several options as far as she could see. Option one: she could ignore what she had discovered and carry on as normal, enjoying her salary and the comfortable office, the coffee machine and muffins, and let her investigation drift off into the holding file. That was not going to happen. Option two: she could confront Roland about what she had discovered. Which would get her sacked, immediately. That could also possibly involve the police down the line.

She took a bite of the chocolate muffin. It was rich and dense, thick with chunks of high-grade chocolate and definitely one of the best she had ever tasted. But in a way, Karoly Bardossy, Roland and the lawyers had done her a major favour. Nowhere in their correspondence did they say she had made a mistake, or misunderstood anything. Her investigation, she now knew, was accurate and correct. The smart move was option three: she would leave, and take her story with her. Nobody knew that she had downloaded the files – at least not yet and so far there was no reason for anyone to suspect anything.

And, neither Roland nor anybody else knew that she also had a copy of the video file of Reka. That footage, assuming it was genuine, was explosive, even by Hungarian standards – like something from a Jason Bourne film. Zsuzsa had never seen anything like it. The Word document that Zsuzsa had also download detailed Roland and Kriszta's plans: the video footage was to be kept confidential until 4.30 p.m. that afternoon when it would be uploaded onto the 555.hu website. Roland himself would write the accompanying article, calling for Reka's immediate resignation and a police investigation – both of which would probably follow quite quickly.

Part of Zsuzsa thought that she should let 555.hu run the clip. The material should clearly be in the public domain. But several doubts nagged at her. Firstly, it was clear that 555.hu had now been captured by a political interest group. Any important editorial decision – her Nationwide investigation, the footage of Reka Bardossy – was being taken not to serve the interest of the public but to further those of the owners. Zsuzsa wanted no part of that. She was a journalist, not a political operative. Secondly, she wanted revenge for being played, but one taken cold, not in the heat of her anger. She looked at her watch. It wasn't even 10 a.m. yet – she had some time to decide.

Zsuzsa idly checked her email, scrolled through the news coverage about the election and the forthcoming visit of Alon Farkas. That reminded her. Two days earlier she had met a young Israel historian at Retro-kert, the best known of Budapest's ruin pubs on Kazinczy Street, in the heart of the old Jewish district. What was his name? Eli, Alan something with an L. Alon? She shook her head, that was the prime minister. Elad, that was it. Elad H-something. He was a good-looking guy.

They had talked about his work at the Jewish Museum, where he was researching the history of several companies that had once had Jewish owners and how the companies were blocking him and refusing to give him access to their archives. This was a story, she knew. Then Elad had told her that of all the big firms he was investigating, Nationwide was proving the most obstructive. Not only would they not allow him access to their archives, they would not meet him or even reply to his emails. They had even threatened him with legal action, just for asking questions. All of which pointed, Zsuzsa and Elad agreed, to a cover-up.

Zsuzsa had told Elad a little about her investigation into Nationwide but nothing of substance. His interest was in the events of 1944 and 1945 and the fate of the companies, and their assets, that had eventually been absorbed into Nationwide, not its current activities, but still there was some overlap. They had exchanged numbers and agreed that Zsuzsa would contact him to arrange a proper interview. Once the work conversation was out of the way she realised that she was enjoying his company. They talked about their childhoods and schooldays, hers in her home village in the east of Hungary, his in an upmarket suburb north of Tel Aviv called Ramat Hasharon. He had even taught her a little Hebrew. Shalom, of course, she knew. But she could also remember *boker tov*, good morning, and *erev tov*, good evening. By the end of the evening she realised that she would like to see him again.

Zsuzsa picked up her private mobile and called Elad. The number was unobtainable, a recorded voice told her.

That was strange. She had called Elad immediately after exchanging numbers to make sure she had the right one. She did. She looked up the number of his workplace and called the switchboard.

'Good morning, this is the Jewish Museum. How can I help you?' said a friendly female voice.

Zsuzsa said, 'Good morning. Can I speak to Elad Harrari please?'

The female voice changed tone immediately. 'One moment, please.'

A few seconds later a male voice with a noticeable accent sounded. 'Who is this?' He spoke in English, his voice sharp and interrogatory. The word *who*, Zsuzsa noted, was pronounced '*ooh?*', without a W. *This* came out as '*zis*'. It was the same accent that Elad had.

'My name is Zsuzsa Barcsy. I am a reporter with 555.hu.'

For several seconds there was no reply, only muffled sounds. The mysterious man had put his hand over the mouthpiece, Zsuzsa guessed.

'Why do you want to talk to Elad?' the man eventually asked, his voice wary.

She decided to push back a bit. 'Why do you want to know? Who are you?'

'Dr Harrari is unavailable at the moment. I am dealing with his affairs. What is your business with him?'

Zsuzsa frowned. Something wasn't right here. 'We had agreed to arrange an interview about his work. When will Dr Harrari be available? And I did not catch your name.'

'He will call you back.'

Zsuzsa asked once more to whom she was speaking, but the line went dead. She put her handset down and pulled another piece off the muffin. This was very strange. Where was he, and what was the big mystery? She called Elad's number again: the same message that the number was unavailable.

Now what? She needed to think this through. Zsuzsa picked up one of her business cards, flexing it between her fingers as she pondered her next move. The material was thick, the letters raised and glossy. This was her first job but she had enjoyed a meteoric rise. Her ascent had several causes and she was self-aware enough to know why.

Yes, she was a talented reporter, a tenacious digger, with an innate, natural news sense but she had also hit a lucky streak, and every reporter needed luck as well as talent and tenacity. Her friend and former colleague, Eniko Szalay, now the prime minister's spokeswoman, had mentored her and shown her the ropes. Eniko had also given her a game-changing leaving present: the biggest story Hungary had seen for years, the refugee crisis of the previous summer and autumn, including her notes, half-finished stories and contacts. Several of Zsuzsa's stories had been picked up by the international media. She had been interviewed on the BBC and CNN, helped out the *Economist* correspondent with some research and interviews. Perhaps one of them could give her a job – it was becoming clear that she could not stay much longer at 555.hu.

Zsuzsa was a pretty young woman, with pale skin, large blue eyes, auburn hair and an engaging smile. It was easy, she realised, to get people to talk to her, which was half the job of a journalist and a skill that was not taught on her course. Women seemed to naturally trust her. Most men she spoke to had another agenda, she knew, which made them much easier to manipulate. She was surprised at how quickly she was learning to use her looks to get the information she wanted – especially since she had changed her style from the loose, baggy clothes she had worn as a student to more form-fitting, smarter outfits. But her people skills were no use if her stories were not being printed – and they had not stopped her being played by Karoly Bardossy.

A gust of strong perfume wafted up her nose and she sensed movement by her desk. 'Zsuzsi, I know the new chairs are wonderfully comfortable, but you aren't napping on the job, are you?' asked Kriszta Matyas.

Zsuzsi was the diminutive of Zsuzsa. It was used by her family and friends but was irritating and patronising in a work context. Still, Zsuzsa thought, it could be worse. At least she is not calling me Zsuzsika, dear little Zsuzsi, any more.

'No, Kriszta. I am wide awake. I was just thinking about' – she quickly changed track, slipping into the role of the frustrated reporter that Kriszta would expect – 'my Nationwide investigation. When will it run? There's a lot more to write about. We could do a three-parter. I think it would get picked up by the foreign press as well. Everyone is interested in Karoly Bardossy.'

The two women did not get on. An unmarried, thin brunette in her forties, Kriszta had formerly worked at the state news agency. She wore formal business clothes, elaborate make-up and heavy scent, and looked completely out of place among the hipsters and bohemians that made up the rest of the staff. 'It's with the lawyers, as you know. They still are going through your source notes and fact checks.'

Zsuzsa told herself to focus. Kriszta obviously had no idea that Zsuzsa now knew the real reason why her story was being held over. She needed to act like she was still ignorant of what was actually happening. Zsuzsa's voice was indignant. 'Still? I already gave them all that. They have had the material for days. How long do they need? Everything is correct and accurate. This is getting ridiculous.'

Kriszta raised a heavily mascaraed eyebrow. Her voice was terse. 'Lawyers go at their own pace. *I* will tell *you* what the next stage is.'

'The next stage is to publish the story,' said Zsuzsa.

Kriszta looked down at Zsuzsa. 'I'll be the judge of that.'

Before Kriszta's arrival, Zsuzsa had been tasked by her colleagues with finding out more about her. She had compiled a list of several articles Kriszta had written for the state news agency. They were mostly anodyne reports about the arrival of visiting dignitaries, usually from repressive former Soviet states, or new trade agreements signed with them. The worst, or best, was a hagiography of the president of Turkmenistan, who had renamed the days of the week according to his fancy.

Zsuzsa had also compiled Kriszta's top ten most obsequious lines, which had been greatly enjoyed by the staff. The document had been printed out in several copies and circulated by hand, so as not to leave a data trail, but at moments like this Zsuzsa sensed that Kriszta somehow knew it was her handiwork. Maybe the top ten had not been such a smart idea.

Kriszta continued talking. 'Meanwhile, I have some *very* exciting news for you. It's straight from Roland.'

'Do tell,' said Zsuzsa, trying not to roll her eyes. She had already learned that Roland's idea of exciting was quite different to hers.

Kriszta leaned forward, the light of triumph in her eyes. 'You are being seconded to the business desk for a while. They are working on a new directory of the top hundred companies in Hungary. It's a huge project. The new owners are very keen.'

Zsuzsa's face fell. A business directory. Checking names and addresses. This was work for interns. 'Why me? I am not a business reporter.'

Kriszta smiled. 'But you are, Zsuzsa. You did so well with your Nationwide story.'

'If I did so well with it, why aren't you running it?'

'We will, Zsuzsika. When we and your story are ready. Meanwhile, think of the new plan as part of your career development.'

Zsuzsa glared at Kriszta. 'I'll try. When do I have to start?'

'Now would be a good time.' Kriszta glanced at the remains of the chocolate muffin. 'But you can finish your snack first.'

Zsuzsa watched Kriszta walk across the office to Roland's room. *Thank you, Kriszta*, she almost felt like saying. *Now I know what to do.*

SEVEN

Margaret Island, 12.30 p.m.

Sandor Takacs shook his head. 'No. It's not your beat, Tazi. You are a detective in the murder squad. There is no dead body. No one's been murdered.'

'We don't know that, boss. He's disappeared. I think he has been kidnapped. I called the Jewish Museum. He has not been in since Tuesday. There is no sign of him at all, anywhere. They are really worried. There's no record of him flying out of the airport. Isn't that enough?'

The commander of the Budapest murder squad was wrapped in a winter police-issue jacket, with a Soviet-style padded hat jammed on his head. He pulled down the ear flaps before he spoke, tied them together under his chin. 'Enough for a criminal case, yes. Which will be passed to the missing-persons team. Maybe he took a train to Vienna or Bucharest, who knows where.'

He watched a barge slowly progress towards the island, laden with coal. 'Or a boat. Speaking of cases, you still have several remaining unsolved. How are you doing with Imi *bacsi*?'

Imi *bacsi*, owner of several nightclubs, had been found floating face-down in the Danube with his hands tied behind his back, a large hole where his nose used to be and most of the back of his head missing. His body had washed into an inlet in the far south of the city, near an abandoned factory.

Imi *bacsi* had been a well-known figure in the world of Budapest organised crime, with plenty of enemies. He had recently been seen entertaining several Russian businessmen in a private room at one of the city's most expensive restaurants. CCTV footage had just appeared, showing a top-of-the-range Mercedes parked nearby at a jetty in the early hours, not far from where the body was found a couple of hours later.

'I've traced the car,' said Balthazar. 'It was hired at Budapest Airport that afternoon.'

'Good. Who was driving?'

'A Chechen, apparently, travelling on a Russian passport. He flew out of Budapest the next morning on the dawn plane to Moscow.'

'A Chechen hitman. Poor Imi *bacsi*. You checked the passport?'

'Of course. It's genuine – government issue, but issued to a fake name.'

'How do you know?'

'I asked the airport for some screen grabs of him at passport control and sent them to Interpol. His first name is Aslan, his surnames change all the time. He's wanted by six countries.'

'Make that seven. Meanwhile, *do svidaniya*, Aslan.'

'And goodbye to our case too,' said Balthazar. They both knew there was very little that could be done now. The information would be reported to Interpol, and to the police's liaison in the Moscow force. Even if he was located somewhere in Moscow or Russia, Aslan many-names was highly unlikely to be arrested.

'I'll pass it upstairs. Meanwhile, there's the paperwork, Tazi. I'll need to see your report.'

'Sure. And once that is done, I can focus on Elad Harrari.'

The two men were sitting on a bench at the very end of Margaret Island, a few yards from the spot where the two sides of the riverbank narrowed and met in a point. In front, a wide expanse of water rushed towards them, before splitting down the sides of the island, south toward Serbia and the deep Balkans. Behind them stretched the Arpad Bridge, a brutalist concrete ribbon, by far the unloveliest of the constructions spanning the river.

The wind gusted hard, bringing a light sleet, and Balthazar shivered inside his coat. 'Can't we meet in your office, boss? I'm freezing here.'

Margaret Island was just over two kilometres long. Encircled by a running track, the green space was home to extensive parkland, the remains of a medieval nunnery, two thermal hotels (one of which had once been home for a while to Carlos the Jackal), a children's zoo, and a water tower. In the spring, summer and autumn the island was one of Budapest's prime attractions, jammed with locals and tourists alike, enjoying the verdant scenery and the pleasant breeze. In the winter it was almost deserted, unprotected against the freezing weather. A few determined joggers still ran around the track, their breath pluming white in the winter air. But even the hardiest, most inquisitive visitor did not venture to the spot that Sandor had chosen to meet with Balthazar.

'We can, usually. But you wanted to talk about this Israeli business.'

Balthazar frowned. 'And?'

Sandor raised his right index finger and spiralled it upwards. The gesture meant that someone was listening.

'How do you know?'

Sandor patted Balthazar's leg. 'I just do, Tazi.'

Balthazar nodded. The news that Sandor's office was bugged wasn't entirely a surprise. Rumours were swirling around the police headquarters that his boss would soon be retiring, to make room for his much younger deputy, Bela Szilagyi. Bela was adding more and more tiles to his roof – slang for protection – including several senior officials in the Ministry of the Interior. Bela's portfolio, Balthazar had heard, would soon be expanded to include liaison with the state security service. That would mark the beginning of the end of Sandor's career.

Short and tubby, with shrewd brown eyes and thinning grey hair, Sandor was a devoted family man, still married to his childhood sweetheart. Sunday lunches were an institution in Hungary, and Sandor never missed one, surrounded by his children and grandchildren. 'Don't worry about me. Everyone needs to know when their time is up. I've had a good run, Tazi. I'll get a decent pension. Very decent, actually. Several security companies have already been in touch to talk about consultancies. I'll be sixty soon. I want to enjoy the rest of my time, and my family.'

He reached inside his shoulder bag and took out a small metal thermos flask. He slid the white plastic cup off the top, unscrewed the cap, poured a pink liquid into the cup, steam rising from the surface, and handed it to Balthazar.

'That will warm you up,' said Sandor as he reached inside the bag for another cup and poured himself a drink. 'Winter fruit tea, *Takacs-modra*.'

Balthazar smiled as he accepted the 'Takacs-style' drink. He knew what that probably meant. The first sip confirmed it – a rich mix of peach-and-apricot tea overlaid with alcoholic fumes. Sandor was justly proud of his home-distilled palinka, Hungary's powerful fruit brandy. 'Is it your palinka?'

Sandor looked sideways at Balthazar in mock indignation. 'What a question, Tazi. Of course. Apricot, from our trees.'

The drink was warming and full of flavour. '*Nagyon finom*,' said Balthazar, and it was really as delicious as he said. But there was still the matter of Elad Harrari's disappearance. 'So here we are, boss. Let's talk.'

Sandor's voice softened. 'Look, Tazi, I asked about the case for you.'

'And?'

'This is no longer a police matter. Budapest and Jerusalem both want a news blackout on this. It's been passed upstairs. Leave it alone, I was told.'

Upstairs meant state security. Balthazar asked, 'By who?'

Sandor turned to Balthazar. He laughed. 'What do you want? A name? Someone.'

Sandor had been a policeman for forty years. He had not only outlasted almost all of his superiors, but prospered. Born into a family of smugglers in a small village in southern Hungary near the Serbian border, he might easily have slipped into a life of low-level criminality, like his siblings and cousins. But the communist regime wanted to promote young people from underprivileged backgrounds. Sandor did very well at school, so much so that a sharp-eyed party official spotted his potential and brought him to Budapest, where he joined the police.

The country boy thrived in the capital, the archetypal Hungarian who could navigate any system and the period of transition between them. The walls in his office were bedecked with photographs of Sandor with every prime minister since the change of system in 1990, although lately Balthazar had noticed that Pal Dezeffy had disappeared. Sandor had been Balthazar's patron, spotting his talent and intellect when he was a cadet at the police academy, and subsequently an officer on the beat in the rougher parts of Budapest, before recruiting him to the murder squad. And when, despite the force's supposed commitment to equal opportunities, Balthazar's progress had been stalled because he was a Gypsy, Sandor had stepped in to clear the obstacles. Sandor was close to Reka Bardossy and had helped her out over the years with useful information. But few believed Reka would survive the coming election and as her power faded, so did his.

Balthazar looked out over the Danube. The river was flowing hard now, the grey-green water spinning and eddying, shards of ice floating on the surface. Should he mention the USB stick? Probably. He did not like to play games with his patron. And Sandor would find out eventually anyway. He seemed to find out most things. 'There's more, boss,' he said.

Sandor sat back and finished off his tea. '*Mondd*, tell me.'

Balthazar told him about his and Eva's search of Elad's flat. Sandor tutted and shook his head. 'Tazi, that wasn't very smart. You do know how many police regulations and actual laws you broke doing that?'

Balthazar nodded. 'Yes. But we, she, found something. A memory stick, hidden in the bathroom, behind a loose tile. Eva knew where to look. The local cops would never have seen it.'

'Where is it?'

Balthazar explained how he had left the memory stick with Vivi, who was trying to break the encryption.

'Who else knows about the memory stick?'

'Just the four of us. You, me, Vivi and Eva *neni*.'

'Who is this Vivi anyway?'

Balthazar gave Sandor a quick précis of her career. 'Boss, do you think that Nationwide has kidnapped Elad?'

'That's a big move, if they did. But I do know what Karoly Bardossy is capable of.'

'Which is?'

Sandor took a long draught of his tea. 'If he feels threatened, anything.'

EIGHT

Liberty Square, 1 p.m.

Zsuzsa knelt for a moment and looked at the photograph of the young man and woman before she read the text on the sheet of paper inside the thin plastic folder. Miklos Berger had been forty-one and his wife Rahel thirty-three when they had been killed. Their story was one of many tied, pinned or pegged to a thin rope that ran across one side of Liberty Square. They had both been deported to Auschwitz in March 1944, where they were gassed on arrival.

The accounts were placed there by relatives or simply those who wanted to record the life of someone murdered in the camps or shot to death in the Danube. Underneath the pinned stories were mementoes as well: pieces of luggage, stones and rocks marked with names and dates, more photographs, a glasses case, a cigarette holder. All of the testimonies had been placed in plastic covers to protect them, but many were faded and several were nearly illegible. The Bergers' story, however, was notably crisp, their pictures clear, printed on thick, glossy, photographic paper – it looked like the account of their fate had been placed there very recently.

Zsuzsa knew that the story of Miklos and Rahel was unusual – the mass deportations began in May and June, and started with the Jews of the countryside and provincial towns.

Most of the Jews of Budapest, the last sizeable community in Nazi-occupied Europe, largely escaped deportation until after October 1944 when the murderous Arrow Cross, the Hungarian Nazis, deposed Admiral Horthy with the help of the SS. Then the transports, and the killings, resumed.

Rahel had been a primary school teacher, Miklos a businessman and industrialist. The photograph was a formal portrait, sepia-toned, and had been taken at a studio in 1935. Rahel wore a long, heavy skirt, a plain white blouse and matching jacket. She had medium-length hair, and dark, intelligent eyes, full of wonder and excitement at the life before her. Miklos stood handsome and erect. He wore a black suit and tie, his pride at his beautiful young wife beaming from his eyes.

Zsuzsa was steadily making her way down the line of family stories. Every few days she read another account, then sat on a nearby bench for a few moments, trying to process the enormity of what she had read. Rahel had been twenty-four when the photograph was taken, the same age as Zsuzsa was now. As she came to the end of Rahel's tale, she stared again at the photograph of the young woman. The wind gusted, flapping the sheet of paper back and forth, so hard it almost pulled it from Zsuzsa's hand, then stopped as suddenly as it had started.

A few weeks ago, before the weather turned too cold, Zsuzsa had gone on a historical walking tour of downtown and District VII, wanting to know more about the history of Hungarian and Budapest Jewry. Zsuzsa had grown up in the countryside in a small village in the far east of Hungary, not far from the Ukrainian border. She had never met anyone Jewish before she moved to Budapest to study English and Media at the city's Eotvos Lorand University.

She knew that there had once been a thriving Jewish community in her home town, but there was nothing left of it except an overgrown cemetery and a dilapidated synagogue that was scheduled for demolition. No Jews lived there, or in any of the neighbouring villages any more. Zsuzsa had once asked her grandmother about the Second World War and what she remembered about her Jewish neighbours. At first she started describing her school friend Vera and how they used to play together and share their sweets. Vera's father was a carpenter, and her mother ran a small grocery store. When Zsuzsa asked what happened to Vera, her grandmother started crying and could not speak. She got up and stood by the window, staring out over the fields. Zsuzsa's father had then become angry and yelled at her for upsetting her grandmother. Zsuzsa did not ask again.

A few yards in front of the makeshift memorial on Liberty Square was another, far more elaborate construction. In the middle of a row of jagged, broken pillars, stood a mawkish statue of the Archangel Gabriel. Above him an eagle swooped menacingly. The memorial had been put up by a previous government to commemorate the victims of the Holocaust. The Archangel Gabriel was supposed to represent Hungary, pure and innocent, until the evil German eagle had swooped down on a virtuous land to take away its Jews. The reality, Zsuzsa knew, was very different. It was true that for much of the war Admiral Horthy had refused to hand over Hungary's Jews to the Nazis, which was one reason why the Germans invaded in March 1944. But after that Hungary had turned on its Jews with a vengeance. The Hungarian state had proved so efficient at organising the ghettos and deportations that even the SS was impressed. More than 420,000 people had been deported to Auschwitz in less than two months – a record, even for the Nazis. Most had been murdered on arrival.

Zsuzsa stood back up and walked over to a nearby bench on the edge of a deserted playground. The trees around the edge of the square were stripped bare, and the café in the middle was closed. A few years ago the area had been pedestrianised, and the footpath was now slick with slush and ice. She glanced at the other end of the square, at the Soviet war memorial to the Red Army soldiers who had died fighting the Nazis and the Arrow Cross in the winter of 1944 and 1945: a plain, pale stone obelisk with a golden wreath in the middle, standing on top of a stepped, raised platform. Next to the memorial was the grandiose building that housed the American embassy, fenced off from its surrounds. During the war Carl Lutz, a Swiss diplomat, had operated out of here, issuing Swiss protection papers to desperate Jews to save them from the Arrow Cross and the Nazis. For a moment Zsuzsa was back at the makeshift memorial, kneeling down as the wind pulled the plastic envelope with the story of Miklos and Rahel back and forth in her hand. There were ghosts here, she knew.

Zsuzsa pulled her coat tighter but the wind was gusting hard now, the freezing air sliding down the back of her neck like icy fingers, and she shivered as she sat down. She closed her eyes for a moment, ignoring the cold, thinking of Rahel and Vera, her grandmother's childhood friend. Which was worse? To be Rahel, knowing that you would not live your life, never have a family, that you and your husband were being taken to your deaths; or to be a child and not understand what was happening while your parents tried to shield you from the coming horror? There was no answer to that question.

Zsuzsa opened her eyes. There were two benches in the park and a man in his thirties was now sitting on the other one. Something about him made her uneasy. He was holding a copy of *Magyar Vilag*, Hungarian World, the pro-government newspaper, but she could sense him glancing at her.

This was the fourth or fifth time she had felt that someone was watching her since she had filed her Nationwide article. There was nothing definite, but several times recently she had felt the hairs rise on the back of her neck. She had no idea how to tell if she was being followed, other than common sense, but today, of all days, she had no patience for this. She had to call Eniko Szalay, immediately. But not while this guy was around. Then an idea struck her.

She took out her mobile phone and let it fall from her lap onto the ground. Shaking her head at her supposed clumsiness, she bent down to pick it up, using the movement to glance sideways at the man on the bench and sneak a photograph of him. It worked and she looked at the snap on her screen, making sure not to look back at him after she did. He looked short, perhaps five feet six, wore jeans, a black parka, expensive-looking light-brown boots and a grey woollen hat pulled down over his head. His nose was slightly crooked and had a noticeable bump in the middle, the kind that comes from having it broken.

Now she had a photograph of him for her records but she needed to find out if he was watching her.

She turned on the bench and held her camera in front of her, as though she was taking a selfie. The man was visible in the background. She watched on her mobile's screen as he stood up and briskly walked away.

She smiled to herself, unnerved, yes, but also feeling that for once, she was in control of the situation. Now she could make her call.

NINE

Margaret Island, 1 p.m.

Sandor proffered the flask to Balthazar, who nodded. He filled Balthazar's cup and the two men sat in silence for a several moments, sipping their palinka-infused fruit tea, watching as a seagull hovered over the water, then banked and soared away.

'You know what day it is next Saturday?' asked Sandor.

'Of course. It's her birthday. She would have been thirty-six.' Balthazar swallowed for a moment, wiped his eyes, told himself it was the sleet.

'I think about her every day. She'd be married now. A mother with kids.'

Balthazar laughed. 'A grandmother, probably. You know how we are.'

There was another reason why Sandor had protected Balthazar and nurtured his career behind the scenes, beyond his natural talent for police work. The two men's lives were deeply entwined, bound together by far more than a shared profession. Balthazar had once had a cousin called Virag, or someone he thought was his cousin. The two were very close. A beautiful young woman with a singing voice to match, Virag, then sixteen, had been hired to perform at a fancy party at a grand villa in the Buda hills in 1995. The party's hosts were Pal Dezeffy, the former prime minister – at that time a rising young apparatchik – and his then girlfriend, Reka Bardossy. Something very bad had happened and Virag, who could not swim, was found drowned in the swimming pool.

The Kovacs family was devastated. Some of the hotheads wanted to take revenge, to make Dezeffy and his family pay. Balthazar and his mother, Marta, shut down the wild talk. Virag was gone, would be mourned and never forgotten, but more bloodshed would not bring her back – and would only end with the Kovacs menfolk incarcerated for a very long time. As for suing, no court would take the side of a family of pimps from District VIII against the gilded son of one of the country's most powerful dynasties. The Dezeffys, like the Bardossys, had supplied a steady stream of ministers and officials before and during the communist regime and continued to do so after the change of system in 1990. Even in 1995 Pal Dezeffy had been marked out as a potential future prime minister. The Dezeffys offered Balthazar's family the villa as part of a compensation package in exchange for not making a fuss. In truth there was very little the Kovacs clan could do but accept. The swimming pool was filled in and the villa was now an upmarket brothel, run by Gaspar, Balthazar's brother.

One day in the previous autumn, Marta had brought Balthazar lunch, her *csirke paprikas*, chicken paprika, his favourite childhood dish. She looked at the large, framed photograph of Virag and started crying. The story had tumbled out. There was a reason Balthazar felt so close to Virag. She was not his cousin. She was his half-sister. And her father was Sandor Takacs.

Marta and Sandor had fallen in love when he was a cop on the beat in District VIII. They began seeing each other in secret. Marta was seventeen, Sandor twenty-two. She became pregnant. Normally the couple would marry and settle down. But Sandor was a *gadje*, a non-Gypsy. Marta gave birth and the baby was handed to some cousins who were having trouble conceiving. She saw her daughter often at family gatherings. The longing for her, to tell her the truth, never faded, but Marta learned to manage it. Balthazar had blamed himself – still did – for not going with Virag to the party to protect her. He strongly suspected that Virag had been fleeing from Dezeffy's unwanted advances. Now Dezeffy too was dead, drowned in the Danube a couple of months ago, which was a kind of poetic justice.

Sandor looked out over the water for several long moments. The trees along the riverbanks were dark and bare, their long branches waving in the wind like spectral fingers. A police motorboat sped past, leaving a high white wake behind it. 'What's happening with the music school?'

A few days after Balthazar had foiled the terrorist attack on Kossuth Square the previous autumn, Reka Bardossy had called him into her office in parliament. It was clear that she wanted to talk about Virag. Balthazar had plenty of questions. Reka had told him that she knew nothing about Virag's death and had nothing do with it. She had been in another part of the house, busy with someone else, she had explained, blushing slightly. She was deeply, deeply sorry about the tragedy. Balthazar had believed her, more or less. Reka presented him with the plans for the new Virag Kovacs school of music, to be based in District VIII. The school would offer numerous scholarships and grants for 'underprivileged' – meaning Roma – children, if the family approved. They did and the school was due to open later in the year.

Balthazar shrugged. 'All going ahead as far as I know. They

have the premises, the construction is started. It should open later this September.'

'Who is doing the building work?' asked Sandor.

'Guess.'

Sandor laughed. 'The construction division of Nationwide.'

'Who else? As long as they do a good job.'

'They will, don't worry. Reka will make sure of it.' He turned to Balthazar, suddenly shy and uncertain. 'Do you think I could come to the opening?'

'Of course,' said Balthazar. 'She was your daughter. Everyone who knows what really happened will be glad to see you there. Nobody else will ask.'

'Thank you, Tazi.' Sandor sipped his tea. 'Back to business. What exactly was this Elad working on?'

'Investigating the lost wealth of Hungarian Jewry. Specifically whether several of our big companies are holding looted Holocaust assets and how they have responded to compensation claims from survivors or their descendants.'

'Which companies?'

Balthazar exhaled. 'All the important ones. But he was focusing on Nationwide.'

'That makes sense. There've long been rumours about how the Bardossys became so rich after the war, and then stayed rich under communism.'

'And how did they?'

'By meeting a need, I guess. Even a communist state needs some capitalists to deal with the outside world, to sell their products for proper money. This memory stick. How did Elad know where the hiding place was in the bathroom?'

Balthazar frowned. The same question had occurred to him, on the way to the island. 'Eva *neni* must have told him, I guess.'

Sandor nodded. 'Which begs the question, why would she show him where to hide things?'

'I asked her that. She said because everyone needs a hiding place.'

'She's right. Especially if you lived through what she did.'

'Maybe also because she knew that Elad's research might get him into trouble. He thought he was being followed. The same car kept appearing. A blue Mercedes, with tinted windows.'

'A blue Mercedes. That's a start, I suppose. Number plate?'

Balthazar shook his head. 'No, but it has a cracked right headlight.'

'That helps, till they fix it.' Sandor turned to Balthazar, shot him a quizzical glance. 'Why are you so keen on this one? The Israelis are furious, demanding that he is found before the prime minister arrives, or they will cancel the visit. Reka is frantic.'

Balthazar sat back for a moment, watching the river. The water was running hard and fast now, the sleet vanishing as soon as it hit the surface. 'You know that before I was a cop I was a postgraduate student at CEU. I was researching a doctorate into the Poraymus. Do you know what that is?'

Sandor nodded. 'The devouring in your language. The Gypsy Holocaust.'

Balthazar said, 'I spent a lot of time in the archives in Hungary, trying to find out more. It has not been written about that much.'

'And what did you find?'

'Death and misery. The family stories, whole generations just wiped out, including some of my family. The incredible sense of betrayal. Those old faded photos, the scraps of memoirs. It was the same as what happened to the Jews. Hungarian clerks drew up lists, Hungarian gendarmes rounded them up. Hungarian officials put them into ghettos. Hungarian trains took them to Auschwitz. Some of them came back – nobody wanted to know their stories. Nobody wanted to help. After a day in the archives I couldn't sleep. I was angry all the time. I kept fighting with Sarah. That's when it all started to go wrong. So I gave up and became a cop. I couldn't fix the past. But maybe I could help with the present.'

Sandor placed his hand on Balthazar's shoulder. 'That's true. You can and you have. You've never told me this before. Is that why Sarah left you?'

'Partly. And partly because she realised she was a lesbian,' said Balthazar, half laughing. 'So, in a way, I feel that Elad is carrying on the work I gave up. Someone has to call these people to account. Our skill sets are not so different. A detective is also a kind of historian, but working in a much more recent time frame.'

There was another reason, but he would keep that in reserve for now. He glanced at Sandor. 'Can I ask you something, boss?'

Sandor nodded. 'Sure.'

'What happened in your village, in the war?'

'We were smugglers. Mainly *szilva* palinka, plum brandy, or slivovitz, as they call it in Serbia. And tobacco, salami, cheese, whatever people wanted. I wasn't born then. But my dad and grandad before him, all smugglers for generations. They knew when the *razzias*, the round-ups of the Jews and the Gypsies, were planned. They kept the gendarmes supplied with the best booze. The gendarmes used to tip them off in advance. My family knew the paths across the border, where to hide in the woods or by the river.'

He poured himself some more tea, and refilled Balthazar's

cup. 'So my dad and grandad smuggled. People: Gypsies, Jews, Polish POWs, even two British airmen once. We got them to Yugoslavia. What happened to them after that I don't know.' His voice hardened. 'Sometimes they stayed in our house, for a night, for a week. Once we hid a Jewish family for a month. A couple from Budapest and their kid. They made it to Israel. We still get cards from their relatives sometimes.' Sandor was silent for a moment, then took a draught of the tea. 'But we did not hand anyone over to the Arrow Cross or the Nazis. Not a single one. Or stand by watching when they took the Jews away. Which is more than most people in this country could say.'

Sandor looked out over the water. Two seagulls soared, then dived. 'Looted Holocaust assets. The whole fucking country is built on looted Holocaust assets. Houses, shops, firms, factories, land. We took it all. From the Jews, from your people, Tazi. Hundreds of thousands of people we sent to be killed. Hundreds of thousands. Loyal Hungarian citizens. Businessmen, lawyers, doctors, teachers, craftsmen, some of the best we had. Families, their kids. In the summer of 1944, even after D-day. Everyone knew the war was over, the Allies were coming from the west, the Russians from the east, but still we carried on. And when the Nazis stopped the trains, even then we could not stop. We did it ourselves, shooting them into the Danube.'

He raised his hand, flicked his arm out and slid his thumb across his stubby fingers. 'That's five per cent of our population, *pffff*, up in smoke or floating in the river. For what? Why would any government do that to its own citizens?' He stopped talking, staring into the distance.

It was a question that Balthazar had asked himself many times. He still did not know the answer.

Sandor sat silently for several moments, slowly shaking his head, then shivered. He drank the last of the tea, carefully replaced the cup on the thermos and put it back inside his bag, looking slightly embarrassed at his outburst. 'We should go back, Tazi, it's getting very cold.'

Balthazar watched his boss with affection. He had never heard these stories about Sandor's family during the war, never seen him so animated about that era. One part of him wanted to probe deeper, but another sensed that now was not the time. The family stories would come out eventually. In his experience, they always did. In any case, he had a more immediate agenda. 'Elad?' he asked, his voice hopeful.

Sandor smiled, his anger dissipated. 'You don't give up, do you?'

'Would you?'

'Probably not.' Sandor's telephone buzzed. He took the call, listened for less than a minute then hung up. He looked at Balthazar, the skin around his eyes crinkling as he narrowed them. 'Good news, maybe. The Duchess has the case. So, Detective. Give me another reason why I should agree to this?'

Balthazar finished his tea, handed his cup back to Sandor. This was indeed good news. The Duchess was Sandor's nickname for Anastasia Ferenczy. She and Balthazar had worked together last autumn, first tracking down Mahmoud Hejazi, then derailing the attempt by Pal Dezeffy to release poison gas across Kossuth Square through the misting system used on summer days to cool the area down.

One day Anastasia had delivered a burner phone to Balthazar, via Eva *neni*. He smiled for a moment, remembering his neighbour's verdict on his new colleague: '*Nice teeth, spoke very well. No slang. Quite classy, I would say. You could do a lot worse.'*

Maybe Eva *neni* was right. Trusting his own judgement had not worked out very well so far. And he did have another reason to give Sandor. 'Because Elad Harrari is Eva *neni*'s cousin.'

Sandor had met Balthazar's neighbour several months ago, when he came round to check up on him after all the excitement of the previous autumn. Eva *neni* had immediately invited Sandor for some of her famous *turos palacsintas* with vanilla sauce, which he pronounced the best he had ever eaten – on the strict condition that nobody told his wife.

Sandor said, 'Her cousin. Hmmmm.' He crossed his arms, and extended his legs, amusement playing on his face. 'I'll need two things.'

Balthazar smiled. 'Sure. She'll send you a regular supply.'

'It will have to be to the office. With the vanilla sauce, and the sour cherries? And not a word to my wife.'

'With the sauce and the sour cherries. And not a word to your wife. Not one. The second thing?'

'The Duchess. If she agrees, you can work together,' said Sandor, his warm breath turning to steam in the freezing air.

Balthazar smiled. They both knew that was a racing certainty.

TEN

State security headquarters, Falk Miksa Street, 2 p.m.

The headquarters of the state security service took up half a block, flanked by Marko Street on one side, merging into the Ministry of Defence complex on the other. Amid the architectural elegance of its surrounds, the site struck a jarring, even shocking note. But the discord was intentional. It was one of the ugliest buildings in the city, a homage to communist-era brutalism: six floors of raw, grey concrete with rows of slit-like windows of reflecting glass. The message was clear: we are watching you – and this is where the power lies. More than twenty years after the change of system, much of it still did.

Anastasia Ferenczy's office was a cramped, narrow space on the corner of the fifth floor. It had grey walls, a filing cabinet, and a metal government-issue desk, on which sat a monitor and a keyboard. A small secure cupboard, where she stored her pistol, was attached to the wall. Two faded Picasso and Mondrian posters did little to brighten up the room. A pot plant sagged in a corner, the edges of its leaves turning brown.

Anastasia sat at her desk, sorting some papers for a few moments while Balthazar stood by the window, looking down Marko Street. She glanced up at him. 'I'll just be a minute.'

'That's fine,' said Balthazar. 'More time to enjoy the view.'

The two sides of the street made a perfect frame and he could see straight down the middle, over the river to the pale facades of the buildings on the Buda side and the hills in the distance. The grand Habsburg-era apartment house facing him had pristine cream and light-brown paintwork. Elegant curved terraces wrapped around the corner of each floor, their patterned ironwork black and gleaming in the pale winter sun.

'The view is the best thing about this place. And the exit,' said Anastasia.

Falk Miksa Street and its surrounds were the heart of District V, the most upmarket area of Pest, evoking an era when Budapest was the second jewel in the crown of the Austro-Hungarian empire, always competing with its big brother, Vienna. The street was lined with trees, the shops on the ground floors of the apartment houses home to antique dealers, art galleries and artisan jewellers. Some of the buildings were constructed in the art nouveau style, their doors covered with metal flower patterns, their facades home to frolicking nymphs and cherubs. Others, built in the 1920s and 1930s, were sparser, with the clean, rounded lines of the art deco era. Kossuth Square, the site of parliament, was just a short walk away.

Growing up in a crumbling block in District VIII, Balthazar and his siblings had been forbidden to even step on the tenement's rickety balconies. He could still remember stone chips flailing his legs when a large chunk of brickwork broke free from one after a heavy rainstorm, smashing onto the pavement a few yards away from where he and Gaspar played in the street.

Balthazar turned around, his eye falling on a framed certificate on the wall behind Anastasia's desk. He walked over, read the wording above the stamp and signature of the director of the service. 'Award for valour beyond the call of duty. Colonel Anastasia Georgina Ferenczy. 1 October 2015.' He turned to look at her. 'Congratulations. When did you get promoted?'

'The same day,' said Anastasia, blushing slightly. She looked down and energetically busied herself with her paperwork. 'A better room would be nice. I'm almost done then we can go.'

'Don't knock it. All I can see from my desk is the Arpad Bridge and the number-one tram.'

Balthazar returned to the window and looked back down over Falk Miksa Street. Two well-dressed tourists, German or Italian, he thought, stared into the window of the antique shop across the street. A guide holding a small blue flag on a stick shepherded a group of Japanese tourists down the street towards parliament. A block downriver, on Balassi Balint Street, was a super-modern playground with climbing frames shaped like ships and a soft bouncy floor, to cushion children's tumbles. Balthazar had often taken his son, Alex, there, although now he had just turned thirteen he was developing other interests. Which reminded Balthazar, this weekend was his turn to have Alex at home. He was due to pick him up on Saturday morning – and he needed to think of something to do with the boy. Assuming his mother, Sarah, did not cancel at the last moment.

As if on cue his telephone buzzed with a text from his son. Anastasia glanced up at Balthazar. 'It's Alex,' he said, reading the message. She nodded and returned to her work.

Dad what r we doing this wkend?

What do you fancy?

Burger, film – am I staying over?

Yup. Can't wait

Me 2 xxx

C u soon xxx

Balthazar put his mobile back in his pocket, smiling in anticipation, and looked down at the car park in the front of the building. It was surrounded by a mesh fence, painted turquoise. He watched as an elderly lady rummaged in a carrier bag, before scattering small pieces of food through the fence. Several cats instantly appeared and gobbled up the morsels, before scampering off.

'You may have a security breach,' said Balthazar.

Anastasia walked over to the window, stood next to Balthazar and looked down. 'You mean Agi *neni*? I don't think she is much of a threat.' She smoothed her hair back and deftly fixed it into a ponytail. 'I was in London once, at the headquarters of the Secret Intelligence Service for a liaison meeting.'

'Do they have an Agi *neni* as well?'

Anastasia laughed. 'I doubt it. The SIS headquarters is like a military fortress. Thick walls all around it, cameras everywhere. I've never seen so much security and so many armed policemen. We had to go through this sealed capsule, like a revolving door that closed on all sides, before they let us in. Whereas we have a turquoise fence and...'

'Agi *neni*. And the cats. Where do they live?'

'Under the cars, mostly. They especially like the director's.

I wouldn't mess with them. They get quite hissy if they aren't fed.' She turned to Balthazar. 'How old is your boy?'

'Thirteen.'

'It must be tough, only seeing him sometimes.'

'It is. His mother cancels on me quite often. She was better about visits last year but now she is back to making life difficult for me. Her girlfriend doesn't help.'

Anastasia raised her eyebrows. 'Girlfriend?'

'Amanda. That's why we got divorced. Well, that and other reasons. A graduate student at Central European University. She's German. Very earnest. First she persuaded Sarah that the police are part of the capitalist patriarchy, oppressing the working class and minorities. It was all I heard about.' He smiled wryly. 'And then Amanda persuaded her about some other things.'

'But you are a...'

'Minority,' said Balthazar. 'Exactly. But the wrong kind, apparently.'

He looked down again. Agi *neni* had gone, but the cats were still gambolling in the car park. 'Maybe Alex is better off with Sarah. At least he has some kind of stability. He's much nearer the American school, which is miles away, out in Nagykovacsi. I couldn't get him there on time every morning. And if he was living with me he would be on his own a lot.'

Balthazar knew that time was pressing. He was here to find Elad, not talk about his tangled personal life. But for a moment he just enjoyed the conversation. It was quite a while since he'd had any kind of relaxed exchange with a woman. Kati had left on 1 January. She had wanted to go to a riotous New Year's Eve party with her twenty-something friends.

He'd wanted to do almost anything except that. In the end he had surrendered and spent a miserable evening in a fancy converted loft with views over parliament and the river, not far from where he was standing. Kati's friends had gawped at him, made stupid jokes about being arrested for rolling a joint and then mostly ignored him.

Several kept disappearing to the toilet before emerging in a hyperactive state and wiping their noses. He had explained to Kati that he really could not hang out at a party where half the guests were snorting cocaine, but had agreed to wait until midnight. By the time they came home, shortly after, it was clear that they were on very different paths. She had gone home, then reappeared a couple of days later to pick up her clothes and cosmetics. They had not spoken since.

The parting had been a while in the making. Before she left, Kati had also helpfully listed his faults. The main one, it seemed, was his inability to commit, not just to their relationship, but to turn up on time when they had agreed to meet, especially when there were other people involved. He had been over an hour late, twice, and once had not turned up at all for planned evenings out with her friends.

The truth was, he did not want to meet them. The party disaster had proved him right. He had no desire to hang out with a new crowd, one several years younger than he was, drawn from the hoitiest sector of the *ujgazdagok*, scions of the nouveau riche who had gamed the system for immense personal profit. He did not want to settle down with anyone. He had been married once and it didn't work. After Sarah he had fallen in love with Eniko Szalay – and she had moved to London. He had liked Kati, a lot, but he wasn't ready for her to move in or start planning a future together. So it was probably for the best that she had left.

For a few seconds Anastasia was silent as she stood next to him. Neither spoke. A radiator hissed and gurgled in the background. Anastasia wore a close-fitting black polo neck and jeans. He could smell her shampoo and the faintest trace of perfume, something rich and musky that he had not noticed before.

He sensed that she glanced at him, perhaps with a hint of appraisal, before she spoke. 'So, Detective, let's get to work. Where are we with this case?'

Balthazar outlined the events of the morning, his visit to the flat with Eva *neni*, her connection to Elad, Elad's work on Nationwide, the encrypted memory stick that he had left with Vivi.

Anastasia gave him a quizzical look. 'Eva *neni*. She's wonderful. I'm a big fan. So this is personal for you, Detective?'

He nodded. 'Yes. Is that a problem?'

She shook her head. 'Not at all. But Karoly Bardossy will be.'

His mobile rang and he looked down. 'It's Vivi.'

He took the call, listened for several moments as she spoke. 'OK. No, don't tell me now. Not on the phone. We're on our way. We should be there in a few minutes.' He turned to Anastasia. 'She has something for us.'

Anastasia nodded, reached inside the secure cupboard and took out her pistol and holster.

Balthazar glanced at her weapon, a Makarov, an old-fashioned Soviet-era pistol. He patted his own, a Glock 17 in a holster on his belt. 'You don't want something a bit more modern?'

Anastasia shook her head. 'It's never let me down.'

He watched as she slipped on a shoulder holster and placed the weapon inside. Her movements were deft and fluid, and he watched her breasts rise and fall as she breathed in and out.

Her eyes caught his observing her and a flicker of a smile played on her lips.

'Come on, Detective, let's see what the story is.'

ELEVEN

Café Extra, Kossuth Square, 2.30 p.m.

Eniko Szalay sat back as the video clip ended, her mind working furiously.

This was a catastrophe in the making. It meant the end of Reka's government. The end of Reka's political career – and the end of Eniko's as well, certain to be one among many destroyed by the extensive collateral damage.

She sipped her coffee to buy herself a few moments. 'Is that it? Is there more?'

Zsuzsa shook her head as she closed the lid of her laptop. 'No. That's everything. I brought you a copy.' She handed Eniko a memory stick. 'It's on here.'

The two women were sitting in the far corner of the upstairs room of Café Extra. Located on the corner of Kossuth Square, with a view of parliament just a hundred yards away, it was a popular haunt of politicians and journalists. But the upstairs room, with its hard dark-red bench seats and utilitarian furniture, was usually deserted, as it was today.

Eniko took the stick, quickly put it into her jacket pocket. 'Thanks,' she said, her voice tight with tension. 'Are you writing this? Do you want a comment? Is that why we are meeting?'

Zsuzsa smiled, shook her head. 'No, no and no. I'm not writing it, Eni. I don't want a comment. And that's not why we are meeting. I'm here as your friend. Please believe me. Otherwise I wouldn't be here, giving you a copy of the video. I would be calling you from the office, coordinating with the website designer.'

Eniko nodded, even smiled at the irony. She had helped hone Zsuzsa into a dogged reporter. Now Zsuzsa had a video clip that could bring down the government, and take her with it.

Eniko brushed her bobbed hair away from her face. 'So why are we meeting? Why are you sharing this with me? You're a journalist. Your employer has an explosive video clip of the prime minister that will end her career, probably see her arrested soon after. Why are you telling the prime minister's press secretary what's coming… when exactly?'

Zsuzsa blinked. This was not quite the reaction she had expected. 'It's going live in just under two hours. You've helped me a lot, Eni. I thought I would return the favour.'

Eniko's demeanour softened a little. 'That's all?'

Zsuzsa nodded. 'Yes.' *More or less*, she was about to add, but stopped herself. There was no need for her to tell Eniko how she had been played by Karoly Bardossy's team.

Eniko smiled. 'Thank you, Zsuzsa. I really appreciate this, but be honest with me. What do you want in return?'

'In a few days, once we are through all of this and the Israeli prime minister is on his way home, I want an exclusive interview with Reka.' Then Zsuzsa would grill Reka about Nationwide, her uncle's company, but there was no need to tell Eniko that now. Zsuzsa's voice turned serious and direct. 'That means, Eniko, that Reka does not talk to anyone else for the next few days. No interviews with other media, print, web or broadcast. Only me, when we agree on a time.'

Eniko gave Zsuzsa an appraising look. That was exactly the right move. Zsuzsa had turned into quite an operator.

'That's all?'

'That's all.'

Eniko smiled. 'Sure. It's a deal.' She hesitated for a moment, then decided. 'Speaking of Israelis… there's something else you could look into.'

'I'm listening,' said Zsuzsa. She waited for Eniko to speak, the familiar tightening in her chest signalling that a tip-off was coming.

Eniko gave her a sharp look. 'Whatever you find out, you share with me. A full day before you go live on the website. Agreed?'

'I'll give you four hours.'

Eniko laughed. 'Then I won't give you anything. Twelve.'

'Eight. But not overnight.'

'Done,' said Eniko. The two women shook hands. 'Elad Harrari. Do you know who he is?'

Zsuzsa said, 'Yes. He's an Israeli historian. We met at Retro-kert. Why?'

'You did not hear this from me.'

'Of course not.'

'He's gone missing. I think he has been kidnapped. The Israelis are going nuts. They are threatening to cancel the prime minister's visit if we don't find him.'

Zsuzsa stared at Eniko, the questions – and answers – tumbling through her mind. That explained why Elad's number was unobtainable, why he wasn't at work, and the mysterious rude man she had spoken to.

Eniko could see that Zsuzsa was about to start demanding more information and quickly cut her off. 'That's it, Zsuzsa. Really. Thanks again for the video. I need to go back to work now.'

Eniko glanced at her watch, took out her phone and called a number. 'Kati, tell Akos and Reka that I need to see them both. Yes, I know it's their daily briefing time. I will be there in five minutes. Yes, of course it's important. It's a national emergency.'

TWELVE

Grand Boulevard, 2.30 p.m.

Five minutes after they left the headquarters of the state security service, Balthazar and Anastasia were stuck on the corner of Bajcsy-Zsilinszky Way, waiting to turn right onto the Grand Boulevard. The traffic jam was solid and stationary.

Just over fifty yards away, on the other side of the tramlines and the boulevard, Nyugati Station stood in front of them. Built by Eiffel's studio, its facade was an elegant construction of glass and blue-painted steel. Several of the panes of glass had been shattered by rocks in a recent protest and were still not repaired, Balthazar could see. Two long yellow trams on both sides of the 4/6 line stood at the stop in front of the station, neither of them moving. In normal times the drive from Falk Miksa Street to Dob Street should take less than fifteen minutes – a straight run once they hit the boulevard until they turned right – but these times were not quite normal.

The mood was febrile and had been worsening for several weeks. The refugee crisis the previous autumn, the collapse of Europe's borders, the botched attempt by Pal Dezeffy to organise a terrorist attack on Kossuth Square, the failure of the Qatari investment package; all of these had sapped support for Reka's ruling Social Democrats. The party stood at just twenty-three per cent in the polls.

Balthazar had seen the most recent police statistics: petty crime was rising and so were violent attacks in a normally safe and peaceful city. Domestic violence was growing. There was an epidemic of shoplifting as more people lost their jobs and stole food to feed their families. Support was steadily growing for a new neo-communist grouping, the Workers' Alliance, while the far-right National Renewal Movement was moving into double figures. Wildcat demonstrations were springing up across the city, apparently spontaneous but to Balthazar it seemed clear that someone was organising the mobs. The growing sense of lawlessness was eating away at the government's authority.

'Should we park and jump on a tram?' asked Anastasia, one hand on the steering wheel, as she peered ahead. 'This is not moving at all.'

'Those trams aren't moving either,' said Balthazar.

This corner of downtown was usually a busy interchange. He glanced rightwards. A crowd was gathering on Nyugati Square, some people emerging from the pedestrian underpass that led to the station, others from nearby side streets. Many held Hungarian flags with the centre cut out, a symbol of the 1956 uprising when revolutionaries had removed the hammer and sickle emblem. A middle-aged lady in a padded coat waved the Arpad flag of red and white stripes, an ancient Hungarian banner.

Many of the demonstrators held up posters and placards with Reka's face on them, superimposed with a red circle with a line through and the words *Eleg volt a komcsikbol,* We've had enough of the commies. A clutch of burly men in their twenties, each with a beer bottle in hand, stepped out into the traffic jam, banging on the roofs of the stationary vehicles, slapping the vehicles' windows, while they shouted *'Eleg volt a komcsikbol, eleg volt a komcsikbol.'*

Balthazar turned to Anastasia, shot her a questioning glance. 'Now what?'

'Pass me the blue light, please. It's on the back seat,' she said, still looking ahead and scanning.

Balthazar reached behind him and did as she asked. She opened the window and placed the light on the roof of the car. She turned to Balthazar. 'It's going to get noisy.' A second later the siren was howling, the racket filling the inside of the car as the blue light spun around.

The other drivers looked to see what was happening and started to inch sideways. As soon as a space opened up, no matter how small, Anastasia edged the car forward, sometimes veering rightwards, at other times to the left, pushing hard on the horn as well for good measure.

After a couple of minutes she had managed to clear a path through most of the jam. Only one car was blocking their escape onto the boulevard, a white Subaru SUV with tinted windows. It needed to jump onto the kerb at the tram stop. The edge was lined with concrete half-globes to prevent cars doing precisely that, but it would be an easy move for a large-wheeled SUV. Anastasia hooted repeatedly, the siren howled, but the car did not budge.

Balthazar picked up his phone and called the police headquarters. 'I need the name and address of the registered owner of this car,' he said, reading out the number plate. Half a minute later, he thanked the voice, hung up and stepped out of the car, his police identity badge in his hand.

One of the drunken protestors lurched forward at him, muttering about Gypsies, then took a wild swing at him.

Balthazar easily blocked the punch with his left hand, stepped sideways, gave him a hard shove to the chest with the heel of his right hand. The man went flying backwards, crashing into the door of a nearby car. He dropped his beer and stumbled off, banging into several vehicles along the way.

Balthazar approached the driver's side window of the white SUV and knocked. Nothing happened. He knocked again on the window. This time it opened.

A skinny woman in her mid-thirties with a tanning salon sheen and oversized lips was speaking on the phone. She glared at Balthazar, taking in his appearance. Her fingernails were long and painted white. 'What is it?' she demanded, then turned away to carry on her conversation. 'Someone's annoying me... He made me open the car window... I don't know who he is... I don't know if he is dangerous. Maybe you should get here or send someone.' She looked back at Balthazar. 'He looks like a...'

At that moment Balthazar showed her his police badge. Her manner changed instantly. She ended the call. 'Yes, Officer. How can I help?'

Balthazar pointed at Anastasia's Opel Corsa, the blue light still flashing, and the siren wailing. 'We need to get past. It's urgent. You can move out of the way, onto the pavement there.'

She peered forward at the row of concrete globes, frowning. 'But that will bump my new tyres. It might damage them. This is a brand new car. I'm fine here, till the traffic clears.'

Balthazar's tone of voice became harder. 'You are obstructing a police officer in his line of duty.' He quickly glanced again at the Opel, momentarily distracted. He knew very little about cars, except how to drive one, but weren't its wheels wider and larger than usual? And why were there were two exhaust pipes?

There was movement inside the SUV and Balthazar turned back to the driver. She was scrabbling inside her handbag and took out several 10,000-forint notes, smiling brightly as she held out the money. 'Is there a penalty? Or a spot fine?'

Balthazar shook his head. 'Put it away,' he snapped. 'Here's how it's going to work, Emese Bathory.' She started at the mention of her name. Balthazar pointed again at the expanse of pavement next to the tramline, and continued talking. 'You are going to park your vehicle there so we can get past. Or, I can bring you in for obstructing a police officer in the course of his duty' – he paused – 'and attempted bribery. That's prison. I don't think you would like being inside much. No tanning salons.' He glanced at her nails. 'Or manicurists. Although they might like you.'

Emese's eyes opened wide. She nodded quickly, dropped the banknotes on the passenger seat and started the engine. Balthazar stepped back and watched as she drove the car up over the bumps onto the edge of the pavement and waited there.

The other cars immediately started to move forward to fill the gap but he stood in the space, holding out his police badge. A few seconds later Anastasia's Opel Corsa pulled up. He opened the door and jumped in.

Anastasia said, 'Nice work, Detective.'

'Thanks. Threatening someone with arrest usually makes people cooperate.'

She gave him a cool glance. 'Not just her.'

'All in a day's work, Colonel,' he said, half smiling, then looked ahead. There was plenty of traffic on the boulevard, but enough space for Anastasia to clear a path. She put the siren back on and the cars quickly started to edge sideways to make room for her vehicle.

Instead she bumped up onto the pavement, drove around the SUV and down the tramlines, cutting two red lights. Balthazar watched the shops and cafés fly by as they headed towards Oktogon, where the boulevard crossed with Andrassy Way, the grandest of the city's avenues.

The trees were bare, their branches poking upwards like withered brown fingers. A light sleet began to fall on the windscreen as the engine growled. A tram appeared in front of them, its horn sounding loudly. Anastasia cut around it. He glanced at her, her face set in concentration, as the car sped down the tram path, dust clouding up in their wake.

At Oktogon, the lights were red. Anastasia pulled up on the tramlines next to a bus stop while the traffic flowed in front of them, the blue light still flashing, the siren quieter now.

Balthazar glanced at the bus stop. The three glass panels by the seats were methodically covered with much larger versions of the same poster that the demonstrators had been carrying at Nyugati Square a few minutes earlier: Reka Bardossy's face, the red line and the circle. Now they were still for a minute or two, Balthazar had a chance to take a longer, closer look at the image. The photograph had been altered, quite subtly, to make Reka's features look sharper, her eyes dark, glazed and fixed in a stare, her mouth slightly open. Underneath her face on one of the posters someone had written *Voros boszorkany*, Red witch.

Balthazar saw that Anastasia too was looking at the poster. She said, 'The image of Reka has been photoshopped, digitally manipulated. We checked. Someone's paying for these posters and those placards we saw at Nyugati Station. Probably those guys' beers as well. Those new parties, the Workers' Alliance and the National Renewal Movement, they are also getting plenty of money.'

'From who?'

'We're not sure yet. We are working on it. There are lots of front companies involved, going via the Cayman Islands, Ukraine and Minsk, for some reason. I'll keep you posted.'

The lights changed to green. The tramline ahead was clear and Anastasia accelerated away at speed. The force pushed Balthazar back in his seat.

'This is an Opel Corsa?' he asked. 'Standard-issue government vehicle?'

'Unless you merit a big black Audi or a Merc, yes. But yes, it was.' She turned to him for a second. 'They asked me if I wanted anything else when I got promoted. I had some suggestions for my car.'

'Which were?'

'Turbo-charged 2.5-litre engine, sports wheels, hard suspension. I like driving. And we are bulletproof.'

'All that for an Opel Corsa? Why didn't you just get a new car?'

'Camouflage. And sometimes it's just fun to surprise people,' she said, before turning to Balthazar. 'Don't you think, Detective?'

'I think that's a tram right in front of us, Colonel.'

The back end of a tram suddenly appeared in front of them as it trundled along the lines. The Opel slowed right down, hugging its rear.

'I do believe it is,' said Anastasia as she peered around the tram, spun the wheel and roared down the other side of the tracks. Balthazar could see a yellow shape in the distance as another tram started speeding towards them, getting larger by the second. Anastasia cut in front of the tram she had just overtaken with a few metres to spare as the tram on the other side rumbled past. Above the wail of the siren, Balthazar could hear both sets of bells ringing loudly and indignantly.

'Nicely done,' said Balthazar.

'You sound surprised,'

He smiled. 'I'm not, not at all. I was just remembering the last time we were in a car together.'

Last September Anastasia had been driving them at speed through a narrow maze of back streets in District VII and VIII, trying to avoid being arrested by the gendarmes, the national paramilitary police force, on their way to see Gaspar.

The Gendarmerie had been working for Pal Dezeffy, trying to destabilise Reka's government by taking control of Kossuth Square and the area around parliament. Despite Anastasia's skill behind the wheel, she and Balthazar had been captured by a Gendarmerie unit after they threw a spiked chain across the road, instantly shredding her car's tyres.

The unit's commander was Attila Ungar, Balthazar's former partner. When Attila had given Anastasia the option of arrest or joining the gendarmes she had called him a *kocsog*. The literal meaning of the word was jug, but it was slang for 'prison bitch'. Hungarian offered a rich and baroque vocabulary of insults, but *kocsog* was generally agreed to be the worst of the worst. Attila's men had tasered her immediately.

Anastasia laughed. 'I can't promise you that much excitement this time.'

Balthazar had then attacked Attila, even managed to grab his gun and try to escape, before he too was tasered. Dezeffy's planned terrorist attack was supposed to be the coup de grâce to Reka's wobbly government. In the end, thanks to Balthazar – and Anastasia – Dezeffy had failed, just. The gendarmes had since been disbanded.

'No tasers?' said Balthazar.

Anastasia smiled. 'I hope not.'

At Oktogon she turned right down Kiraly Street. Before the war, Kiraly Street had been the bustling heart of the city's downtown Jewish quarter, Budapest's version of London's East End or New York's Lower East Side, filled with kosher butchers, grocery and general goods shops. After the Nazis invaded in March 1944, it marked the edge of the Jewish ghetto. Now it was hipster central.

They drove past a run-down two-storey apartment house, the once-proud Habsburg yellow of its facade turned brown from decades of dirt and exhaust fumes. The ground floor was now an organic wine bar, with a blackboard outside detailing its special of the day – a red from Moldova. Next door two young women stood hand in hand pointing at the window display of a vintage clothes shop that took up the ground floor of an elegant art nouveau block of flats.

Anastasia turned left from Kiraly Street onto Csanyi Street. Here gentrification had not yet spilled over and the road narrowed and darkened. The buildings were lower, their grimy facades crumbling and dilapidated. Csanyi Street ended at the corner of Klauzal Square, where she would turn left onto Dob Street and park in front of Javitas.

'Almost home,' said Anastasia as she turned the blue light and the siren off.

She slowed down when she saw that there were four cars backed up at the end of the street. A policeman stood on the corner of Klauzal Square, checking each vehicle, then directing it to drive through the square and not turn left onto Dob Street.

Balthazar frowned. What was this about? There wasn't usually a traffic control here. And why couldn't the cars turn left onto Dob Street? Something had happened, he guessed, and nothing good. He could call in to ask, but he and Anastasia would see for themselves in a few seconds.

Anastasia glanced at Balthazar. 'I don't know either, but we'll find out very soon.'

The policeman waved the last of the cars in front of them through, glanced at the blue light on the Opel and walked over. Anastasia stopped the vehicle on the corner of Dob Street. Balthazar wound down the window, holding his police identity card in his hand. The policeman was young, he saw, hardly out of his teens. He glanced at the card, then looked at Balthazar. 'How can I help?'

'What happened?' asked Balthazar. 'Is anyone hurt?'

'Someone attacked the trendy café. But no injuries.'

'Thanks. That's where we are going,' said Balthazar.

The policeman nodded and stepped aside. Anastasia turned left and pulled up in front of Javitas. An ambulance and a fire engine were parked outside the café. Thick grey smoke poured from the inside. She and Balthazar looked at each other, jumped out of the car, and ran over to the entrance.

Vivi sat on a chair by a table outside, her pale face streaked with dirt and smoke.

THIRTEEN

Reka Bardossy's office, Parliament, 2.45 p.m.

Eniko sat back, watching Reka as she viewed the video clip until the end, then pressed the stop button on Eniko's laptop. She gave Eniko a wan smile, then glanced at Akos Feher. 'Well, it took a while, but we knew it would surface eventually.'

Eniko looked at Akos, then at Reka. 'So you both *know* about this?'

Reka looked embarrassed. 'I've got a copy. I've had one for ages, ever since the footage was taken.'

'How? Who gave it to you?'

'The Librarian.'

Eniko's mouth twisted in distaste.

The Librarian was the name of a former high-ranking communist official, the keeper of the elite's secrets. Eniko had heard rumours that he even used to have his own office in parliament, where he would collate the recordings he made from the bugs in ministerial offices – including that of the prime minister. She had seen him once in parliament, a shambling figure from another era, dressed in an ill-fitting brown suit, a shower of dandruff on his shoulders, his skin flaking from psoriasis. He had stared at her intently, looking her up and down, assessing her, his brown eyes like lasers behind his thick glasses, before walking off. There was nothing sexual in his gaze, but something far more chilling.

'Why did he do that?' asked Eniko.

Reka laughed. 'Do I really have to answer that, Eniko? Information is power. Information was his currency. He wanted me to know that he had it, and could release it at any time.'

Eniko said, 'But he's dead.'

Reka said, 'I know. I'm going to his memorial service tomorrow. And no, you don't have to come. But let's focus on today. When is this going live?'

Eniko glanced at her watch, 'At 4.30 p.m. But firstly, I have some questions.'

She turned to Akos. 'Have you got a copy, or did you just see an early preview?'

Akos shrugged. 'I was there.'

'Where?'

'On Castle Hill last year. I saw the whole thing.'

Eniko's eyes widened. This story was more and more incredible. 'Was anyone else there?'

Reka leaned forward, put her hand on Eniko's knee. Her voice was steady and she looked her press secretary in the eyes. 'Not at that stage, Eniko, no. Just Akos. But we need to deal with this. Now. We can worry about the backstory later.'

Eniko nodded. Her boss was right. 'So this is real? It's not a deepfake or concocted somehow?'

Reka nodded. 'Yes, Eniko, it's real.'

'Give me a moment here. I'm still processing this. A man tried to strangle you to death. You killed him instead.'

'I did, yes.'

'Where's the body?'

Reka shrugged. 'Disposed of. Does it matter?'

Eniko thought quickly. 'Yes, actually. Killing someone in self-defence is not a crime. We might be able to get away with that. Everyone likes a fighter and a winner. The problem is your cover-up afterwards. Illegally disposing of a body, tampering with evidence, that's two crimes already – carried out with clear intent.'

Reka glanced at Akos. He half-scowled, then nodded. 'Eniko is right.'

Eniko said, 'I know. What was it, by the way, that thing you stuck in his neck?'

'The heel of my Louboutin shoe. The hundred-millimetre version.'

Eniko closed her eyes, cataloguing the emotions running through her: incredulity, dread, but most of all, anger. How could she, as the prime minister's press secretary, not know about this?

Akos leaned forward, his tight shirt straining at his chest. His narrow face was creased with anxiety and his hair, already spiky, seemed to point in even more directions than usual. He asked, 'Are you sure that 555.hu are going to run this? How do you know?'

Eniko nodded. 'Sure I'm sure. I was tipped off.'

'By who?' asked Reka.

'It doesn't matter who. Someone I trust. Someone I used to work with. This is happening. And the clock is ticking.'

Akos asked, 'Why? Why did this person tell you?'

'To give us time to prepare a statement. This person owes me,' said Eniko, correcting herself before she gave away her source's gender. 'They will get into a lot of trouble if that comes out.'

Reka ran her hand through her hair. 'Not as much as we are going to be in. It would be much nicer if they just deleted it. Any chance of that?'

Eniko shook her head. 'No, Prime Minister. None at all. It's an amazing story. And you can be sure it will be picked up by all the international media. Anyway, it's out now. If they don't run it, someone else will.'

Her voice grew tighter. 'But before we talk about what to do about it, I have some questions.' She paused. 'As you might expect.'

Reka nodded, said nothing.

The three of them were sitting in the corner of Reka's office, on the new leather armchairs. A small table, designed by a young Hungarian artisan carpenter, stood in front. A basket of *pogacsas*, the small savoury scones that were an essential accompaniment to every Hungarian business meeting, stood on the table, next to baskets of fruit, bottles of mineral water and a coffee jug.

Eniko glared first at Reka, then Akos. Her nostrils flared as she controlled her breathing and beat back her growing anger. Eniko knew she had their attention, could feel the power in the room flowing to her. It would not last, she knew, and she must not lose her temper, but she would make the most of this moment. She reached for a *pogacsa* and bit into the salty pastry, chewed and swallowed.

Reka said, 'Go ahead.'

Eniko drew out the moment for a few seconds more, then started talking. 'Firstly, Prime Minister, how long have you had this?'

Reka thought for a moment. She had been given the clip by the man known as the Librarian in the middle of the refugee crisis last September. She counted off the months. 'About four months.'

'Where is the footage from?'

'From the cameras around the government offices in the Castle District. I was at a government reception. I stepped outside. Someone was waiting for me.'

'Who was he? The assassin?'

'A gendarme. Sent by Pal Dezeffy.'

Eniko shook her head. This story was getting worse and worse. First the killing itself, then the cover-up and now it turned out that Reka's predecessor as prime minister, her former lover and member of the same political party, had tried to have her killed. If all this came out, the government would collapse. Reka's own party would immediately disown her. There would be a vote of no-confidence in parliament. The opposition would win a landslide in the coming election. 'My next question is why didn't I – your press secretary – know about a video clip circulating of you fighting for your life in the Buda Castle before killing your assailant by sticking something into the side of his neck?'

Reka leaned forward, her voice conciliatory. '*Kedves* Eniko, dear Eniko, I understand, of course I do, that you are annoyed...'

'Annoyed is one word. Try amazed, appalled, flabbergasted,' said Eniko. She took another *pogacsa*, pulled it into pieces then poured herself a glass of water instead.

Reka leaned forward, her voice conciliatory. 'We did not tell you, Eniko, about the footage because it would put you in a legally difficult position. You would know about a crime and be obliged to report it. If you did report it, that would be the end of my premiership and your job, obviously. And if you didn't, and it came out that you knew about it, you could get into a lot of trouble. And that would also be the end of your job.' She smiled. 'So you see, I had your best interests at heart. And now, it's in all of our interests to deal with this. It's almost a relief in a way. I knew it would emerge sooner or later. So let's work out a plan.'

Eniko almost smiled. When Reka was good, she was very, very good. But she would not concede so easily. In any case, there was only one option open to her, Eniko knew, and they needed to move fast. There was a risk that Zsuzsa would be collateral damage, but something told her that Zsuzsa wasn't planning to stay at 555.hu.

Eniko also had to admit that she was quite impressed with what she had seen in the video. Reka kept herself in shape, with regular gym sessions, but she had put up a ferocious struggle – a physical fight against someone trying to kill her. That demanded a whole new level of tenacity and determination – and a willingness to take it to the end. If Reka fought that hard politically, maybe they could get through the next twenty-four hours with the government intact.

Eniko asked, 'Last question, how did you know how to fight someone sitting on you, trying to strangle you? Most people would just freeze.'

Reka smiled. 'My Krav Maga instructor. It's part of the syllabus. Defence against attack from the side, against attack from above with attacker at arm's length, attack from above with attacker close up and personal in your face. Defence against this, defence against that.'

'And which one did you use?'

'All of them. None of them. It turned into a giant blur. Real life is very different to practising in the gym. But I knew this man wanted to kill me. I just tried to control my terror and not flail around too much. He was much stronger. He would have got me in the end. But he didn't.'

Reka shivered at the memory, once again feeling the abject terror as his hands tightened around her throat, the resistance of his skin as she tried again and again to stab him with the heel of her shoe, the way his skin suddenly collapsed as the heel sank into his neck, piercing an artery, the blood fountaining skywards.

'Where is it?' asked Eniko. 'The heel, I mean?'

Reka glanced at Akos before she spoke, Eniko noticed. There was a longer backstory here, she sensed, but that could wait for now.

Reka shook her head, as if to rid herself of the memories, stood up, walked over to the window. She stared out over the Danube. The river was wreathed in mist and a fine drizzle ran down the windows. 'Destroyed. What matters now is, how do we stop this?'

She turned back to Akos and Eniko. 'OK. How about we buy a series of adverts at 555.hu, send them all our recruitment campaigns, all that boring public information stuff. Find out how much they need to stay afloat for another year. They must be struggling; all these hipster outfits are. Add another twenty per cent. It can't be that much.'

Akos nodded. 'Good idea, Prime Minister.'

Eniko shook her head. 'They won't agree. They don't need the money any more. They have a new owner; they have just moved to their fancy new offices on Freedom Square. This will drive an incredible amount of traffic to the website.'

Reka was silent for a few moments, leaned back against the window as she thought. 'OK. I've got it. A new law guaranteeing press freedom, the strongest safeguards in the world. Everything the journalists' union has been asking for.'

Eniko said, 'In exchange for killing a story? I don't think that works, Prime Minister.'

Reka exhaled. 'No, you're right. It doesn't.'

Akos said, 'A technical emergency. We shut down the internet till we work out what to do.'

Eniko shook her head. 'That won't work either. They will just give the video to an opposition television station. Prime Minister, we can't stop this. We need a strategy for dealing with it. Another question – Akos, you said you were there as well?'

'Yes. I had an iron bar to hit the guy.'

Eniko laughed. This was turning surreal. 'An iron bar. Why didn't you use it?'

'I was going to, but Reka beat me to it.'

'What were you doing there, anyway?' Eniko asked.

Akos said, 'I was… erm…'

Eniko could see him struggling to answer. 'It doesn't really matter, Akos. One last question, Prime Minister. How did you get rid of the dead body?'

Reka looked at Akos, back at Eniko, said, 'Antal.'

Antal Kondor was Reka's bodyguard and general Mr Fixit. He had worked for her since her earlier role as Minister of Justice. Eniko nodded. 'Naturally. Is there footage of that as well somewhere?'

Reka nodded. 'Yes. There is a longer version.'

Akos said, 'The director's cut.'

'Ha, ha,' said Eniko, her face unsmiling.

So there was more material out there. But if her plan worked it would not matter. She took a long gulp of her water.

'Eniko,' Reka said, her voice almost meek, 'we need to get on with this.'

'Sure, but before that, Prime Minister, my very last question. Are there are any more unexploded bombs that I should know about. Any skeletons in the cupboard? Perhaps literally? Because if there are, I really need to know.'

'Nothing. Now, Eniko, we can argue about this for the rest of the afternoon or we can deal with it,' Reka said, her tone sharp. 'Decide, please. Are you in or out?'

Eniko knew that her moment of glory was passing. She had taken the job of press secretary knowing that crises were certain to erupt down the line. Now she was in the epicentre of one, a crisis which if mishandled would bring Reka's career crashing down, and hers too in its wake. But if her plan worked, she could name her own terms. Eniko was wearing her favourite business outfit today, a black trouser suit that had been hand-made for her by a tailor in District VII, a grey satin blouse and black ankle boots. Somehow the clothes gave her energy. She knew she looked sharp, competent, professional – because she was all of those things. She felt Reka's and Akos's eyes on her, waiting for her reply. *OK, guys*, she thought, smiling inside, *just a little bit longer*. Eniko glanced down at her ankle boot, enjoying the soft feel of the leather and the sharp cut of the Cuban heel for a moment, then back up at Reka and Akos. They were both staring at her now, their anxiety clearly turning to annoyance.

Reka glared at Eniko, tapped her watch.

Eniko smiled. 'OK. I'm in. There is only one way to deal with this. We need to *own* this story. Then we can control it.'

Reka said, 'Great. How?'

Eniko leaned forward as she spoke. 'This is what we are going to do.'

FOURTEEN

555.hu newsroom, 3.45 p.m.

Zsuzsa was sitting at her desk, idly reading the latest opinion poll that showed the government's support sliding even further, wondering when to hand in her resignation and what Eniko planned to do with the video footage of Reka, when her phone buzzed to indicate an incoming text message.

Just as she picked up her handset, she saw that half the newsroom was also scrabbling for their mobiles. Anxiety knotted her stomach. Had the publishers, or perhaps Roland himself, discovered that someone had been inside his computer, and sent out a message to everyone? Maybe the building was going to be locked down while they searched for the hacker. She glanced at the door, half expecting to see security guards stomp into the newsroom, heading for her desk. But when she looked down at her screen, she felt relief. The message wasn't from Roland, or the publishers, or anyone she knew.

The sender was the National Emergency Messaging Centre. What was this about? The NEMC was supposed to deal with disasters like floods or earthquakes. It had the ability to message every mobile telephone in the country at once. Maybe an enormous blizzard was expected. Then Zsuzsa read the message:

Kedves honfitarsak, dear compatriots. I regret to inform you that our Hungarian republic is under attack from hostile forces. In response I have declared a state of national emergency. But we stand firm and we will never surrender. I will be speaking in a national broadcast at 4 p.m. on all television channels and on the internet at kormany.hu.

Eljen Magyarorszag, long live Hungary!

Vedjuk meg a mi koztarsasagunkat, defend our republic!

Reka Bardossy, prime minister.

Zsuzsa glanced at her watch. Four o'clock was in two minutes' time – and, she realised, thirty minutes before 555.hu was due to go live with the video of Reka killing her assailant on Castle Hill. This 'attack from hostile forces' was obviously connected to 555.hu's plan to release the footage.

She sat back for a moment, processing what she had just read. Reka was about to launch some kind of pre-emptive strike, which was, when Zsuzsa thought about it, the only smart play here. Eniko had, in effect, solved Zsuzsa's dilemma about when to resign. Her career at the website was over, that much was clear. Whatever was coming down the line would trigger an immediate internal investigation at 555.hu to find out how the prime minister knew about the video clip. It would take a while, but the data trail would inevitably lead to Zsuzsa. Only Roland's computer had the video, Zsuzsa was sure.

There would be a record of Roland's log-on on his office computer, twenty minutes before he arrived in the office. So if Roland had not been present when someone was logged in as him, who was in the office? Roland would remember that Zsuzsa was the only other journalist in the newsroom and that he had made them both a cappuccino. Maybe the little scene by the coffee machine had not been such a smart idea, after all. If she had stuck to finding out what had happened to her Nationwide investigation and not downloaded Reka's video file, she could probably have got away with it.

But hey, she was a journalist. It was her job to be nosy. In any case, it did not matter now. What was done, was done. The question was, what was she going to do about it? For now, she needed to gather her stuff and get out. Zsuzsa opened her web browser to kormany.hu and started gathering her phones, her most recent notebooks, her most useful contacts' business cards and slowly placed them inside her leather backpack.

The flat-screen television on the other side of the newsroom went dark for a moment, losing its feeds from the international news organisations, then only one channel showed: Hungarian state television. Someone turned the volume up so the sound carried across the room.

Zsuzsa looked across at Roland's office, tension rising in her stomach. The blinds were up. He and Kriszta Matyas were staring at the television in his room. The whole newsroom had fallen silent, the first time she had ever seen it so quiet.

Reka appeared on the television screen, right on time. She was soberly dressed in a light-blue blouse and navy jacket with a small Hungarian flag badge pinned to her left lapel. Her eyes were clear and her voice steady and well modulated as she began to speak. She thanked everyone for tuning in, and interrupting their work day or their personal business, but this was indeed a moment of national emergency, with the Hungarian republic under attack from a hostile force. She paused, stretching out the moment just long enough while every viewer mentally begged for more information, then carried on speaking:

> Many of you won't have heard of the term 'deepfake'. Why would you have? We Hungarians are an honest people. But not everyone is honest or interested in the truth. Nowadays computer technology and software is so sophisticated that it can conjure up video footage of a person and use their face and voice and so make it appear that a real person has said things they have never said, or done things they have never done. A deepfake is a piece of video that looks completely authentic, but it is not. It is computer-generated. It is completely artificial. It is a lie.

She paused after the word 'lie', looking straight at the camera, before saying again, 'A lie', then continuing.

> I regret to inform you, *kedves honfitarsak*, dear compatriots, that such a piece of artificial, computer-generated footage is in the possession of one of our best-known news organisations.

Zsuzsa watched her colleagues turn and stare at each other, realisation slowly dawning. Was this it? Was this What The Fuck Are They Up To? The secret project? Several of the journalists turned to look at Roland's office, where he stood completely still, his arms now crossed against his chest. Reka continued speaking:

> This news organisation – which I will not name, to save it from the righteous anger of our fellow Hungarians – plans to release this fake footage of me apparently carrying out a violent, illegal act, at 4.30 p.m. It is possible that the editors of this organisation believe the footage that they have to be genuine, that they have a genuine news story.

In this case, why have they not contacted me or my press office for a comment?

This is standard practice, even for this news organisation, which is well known for its unorthodox approach to journalism. They have not, because they know that this so-called footage is not genuine. It supposedly shows me committing an act which I have never committed, in a place that I have never been to.

It is a highly sophisticated example of a deepfake. In other words, it is a lie. Their plan, by releasing this footage, is to bring down my government. They are not journalists. They are activists. And yes, my government may yet fall – not now, but later this month, when you, the Hungarian people and voters, decide. Not because of a news organisation peddling falsehoods. Thank you.

Zsuzsa watched in wonder, her eyes wide. It was a smart move, the smartest she had ever seen from a government. In fact it was brilliant, a checkmate of stellar proportions. Roland and Kriszta had been totally outmanoeuvred. They could not release the footage now and anyway there was no point.

Reka – and Eniko – had completely taken control of the story. The clip would inevitably leak – perhaps even from the government press office – to show that it existed. The footage, she knew, was genuine. The prime minister of Hungary really had killed someone trying to murder her by sticking the broken heel of her stiletto shoe in the side of his neck. But the story had been framed as a lie and that is how most of the population would remember it. Initial perceptions counted more than anything. Roland, she knew, would be furious. He would call in the tech guys to see who had accessed the video file.

Zsuzsa scanned the newsroom as she prepared to make her exit. There was no sight of Kriszta, but the atmosphere in the newsroom was electric as the reporters swapped opinions about the footage.

This story was about to explode, and 555.hu's newsroom would be ground zero. It was a smart move by Reka not to name 555.hu – especially as her press secretary used to work there. But Zsuzsa was sure that Eniko would carefully leak the name of her old employer.

The media pile-on, Zsuzsa knew, would start immediately, and it would get nasty, possibly even personal. Zsuzsa had already seen during the refugee crisis how Roland and Kriszta were under pressure: they melted like a bar of chocolate in the heat. They would be furious, scared and then they would lash out, especially when they realised that Zsuzsa was somehow connected to the leak of their greatest scoop.

Zsuzsa needed to leave, ASAP, with her stuff, but without drawing attention to herself. But what journalist walked out of a newsroom when it was clear that a massive story was breaking? She looked around the office.

The main door was on the other side of the newsroom, past the reporters' desks and Kriszta's workstation from where she watched her underlings. That was too many desks and too many people. But behind Zsuzsa's workplace, just a few yards away, was the fire exit. The door was alarmed and opening it would set off a loud siren. But maybe that might help. She nervously took another bite of the remains of the chocolate muffin by her keyboard, checked her desk, then swept the newsroom once more from one side to another. Everyone was either reading Reka's message, showing it to each other or chattering on their phones.

Gyorgy, Kriszta's deputy, walked over to Zsuzsa's desk and sat on the edge. Gyorgy was a serious reporter, a refugee from the country's main independent centrist newspaper which had recently been closed down. He just about managed to conceal his disdain for his boss. Somewhat overweight, in his late twenties, Gyorgy had recently cultivated a goatee beard, but it remained a straggly effort. He had twice asked Zsuzsa out, but while she enjoyed his company, she did not find him physically attractive. The beard did not help.

'Big story,' he said, as he swung his legs back and forth.

'Very,' said Zsuzsa, hoping that her eagerness to get out did not show. 'Is it us? Do we have the footage?'

Gyorgy gestured at Roland's office, where the blinds were now down. 'Maybe. Something's up. Even if it's not, we need to report this. Why aren't Roland and Kriszta out here directing our coverage?'

'Good question,' said Zsuzsa. She looked down at her Instagram feed. Twitter had not really taken off in Hungary but the new social media platform had been an instant hit. Several of the most popular pop stars and models in Hungary were linking to Reka's broadcast, with a blizzard of hashtags #saynotodeepfakes, #dontbelievethehype #istandwithReka #istandwithhungary and more in a similar vein.

'Here's a story,' said Zsuzsa, showing the mobile screen to Gyorgy and passing him the handset. Eniko was really good at her job, she thought. 'Reka's already got all the influencers on her side.'

Gyorgy scanned through the feeds. 'Fast work. Impressive. They are taking control of the whole conversation.' He handed the phone back to Zsuzsa. 'Can you write this up for us?'

Zsuzsa shook her head. 'Sorry, I'm on something else. I have to go out now.'

Gyorgy frowned. 'What else? And now? In the middle of a national political crisis?'

'Yes. I'm seeing a contact who might know more about Reka's game plan. And I'm trying to persuade Eniko to meet.'

Gyorgy nodded. 'Ah, I forgot about Eniko. That's a really good idea. See what you can get from her. Even off the record. In fact off the record might be better. She can give us the inside story.'

I could do that, Zsuzsa felt like saying. *I am the inside story*. Instead she nodded. 'I'm on it.'

As Gyorgy walked off, Zsuzsa looked over again at Roland's office. The blinds were still up. The door opened and Roland and Kriszta started walking across the newsroom, heading straight for Zsuzsa's desk. At the same time two burly security guards walked through the main door to the newsroom. She grabbed her bag and walked quickly to the fire exit.

FIFTEEN

Dob Street, 4 p.m.

Vivi coughed several times, then took a long drink from the glass of water in front of her. She looked at Anastasia, her grey eyes red-rimmed from the fumes, but still wide and assessing. 'To answer your question, a smoke bomb happened. Several, actually. But who's asking?'

The two women were sitting outside Javitas at one of its small round tables. The sun had broken through the grey winter sky and a light breeze was blowing but an acrid stink still hung in the air. A space heater mounted on a long pole glowed red above them and Vivi was wrapped in one of the grey blankets that were usually draped over the chairs. Inside the café a police officer from the District VII station was taking down Mishi's account of what had happened, while another was collecting and bagging up the three empty smoke bombs.

Before Anastasia could answer Vivi, Balthazar stepped out of the door, walked over and sat down at the table with three bottles of water. They watched as a third policeman crouched down in front of them. Head to one side, he looked under the bonnets of the line of cars parked perpendicular to the pavements, their bonnets facing the buildings.

Balthazar turned to Vivi. 'Sorry, no coffee for now. Are you OK?'

Vivi shrugged, unperturbed. 'I'm fine. They didn't get to my room.' She leaned towards Anastasia. 'I was wondering about your friend. Is she a cop as well?'

Balthazar handed Vivi a bottle of water, passed one to Anastasia. She thanked him, took her wallet from the inside of her coat and showed her state security service identity card to Vivi. 'Not exactly.'

Vivi's eyes opened wider. 'Oh. That looks serious.' She turned to Balthazar. 'Am I in trouble now?'

Anastasia asked, 'Are you a threat or danger to the security of the state?'

Vivi shook her head. 'I hope not.'

Anastasia said, 'Good. Then you are not in trouble. Actually, I'm quite a fan of yours. It's impressive how you get past all the company firewalls and security.'

Vivi started with surprise. 'But how do you know...?' She paused for a few moments and smiled. 'Dumb question, huh?'

'Not at all. We could use your talents. We don't pay as well as big companies. But it's much more interesting. You could play with the most up-to-date technology and you would be serving your country.'

Vivi looked sceptical. 'Well, maybe. Let me think about it.'

Balthazar took a swig from his bottle of water before he spoke. 'Mishi says there is no serious damage. There were two of them on a red sports motorcycle, wearing silver helmets with tinted visors. The motorcyclist pulled up outside the door and waited. The passenger jumped off, threw three smoke bombs into the café, jumped back on the motorbike, then they escaped the wrong way down Dob Street, towards the Grand Boulevard. A couple of minutes later Mishi got three calls from an unknown number with nobody speaking. It's a warning.'

Anastasia said, 'For now. It doesn't mean they won't be back. Registration number on the motorcycle?'

'There wasn't one,' said Vivi. 'I already watched our CCTV.'

Balthazar coughed for a moment, the smoke still tickling his throat, then took a gulp of water. 'What could you get from the memory stick?'

Vivi reached inside her jeans pocket, and took out the memory stick that Balthazar had given her and another one of similar size. 'There were two folders. One with video footage and one with something that looked like scans of documents. I could open the video footage.'

'The documents?' asked Balthazar.

Vivi shook her head. 'Very little. A few words here or there. Bard-something. And bits of dates – 1944 was one. It's high-level encryption. It might be beyond my capabilities,' she said, looking at Anastasia.

'The video?' asked Balthazar.

'That's shaky but clear. I think it was filmed on a mobile phone. Footage of a blue Mercedes, mostly on Dohany Street by the synagogue and the Jewish Museum, some on Dob Street, outside here, in fact, and over at Klauzal Square.'

Balthazar put the memory sticks in his pocket. A blue Mercedes chimed in with what Eva *neni* had already told him about Elad's suspicion that he was being followed. Bard... must be Bardossy. What had the Israeli historian discovered about Nationwide? Was it really something explosive enough to get him kidnapped? 'I'm not sure yet. But this is really helpful. Thanks, Vivi.'

Balthazar scanned the area as he spoke. Dob Street was a one-way street that led onto the Grand Boulevard. There was no through traffic because of the temporary police checkpoint on the corner of Csanyi Street where it met Dob Street and Klauzal Square.

There were plenty of derelict or half-demolished buildings in the neighbourhood where it would be easy to temporarily hide a motorcycle. But for now everything seemed very quiet, unnaturally so. Dob Street and Klauzal Square were deserted. No tourists, no locals out shopping at the nearby market, no hipsters on their oversized skateboards. The green municipal bicycles were all stacked in their rack on the corner of Klauzal Square, unused for the moment. There was the usual line of empty two-shot bottles of industrial palinka along the window sill of the ABC grocery across the road, but even the drunks had disappeared.

Doubtless the recent excitement and the police checkpoint had also helped clear the streets. The wind blew hard and for a moment Balthazar shivered as the weak winter sun disappeared behind a thick bank of cloud. It would soon be dark. Something wasn't right here, he felt. There was a sense of heaviness in the air, something denser than the whiff of lingering smoke.

Balthazar stood up and turned to Anastasia. 'I'm going to have a look around.'

'Do that,' she said. 'Be careful.'

He walked back down Dob Street to the corner of Klauzal Square. The two policemen had rebased further down Csanyi Street, where it was easier to control the incoming cars. The centre of the square was a park, encircled by a metal fence. At first glance everything seemed normal as he stepped through the gate. The trees, their brown branches now bare, allowed him to see right across the open space.

The tables and stone benches where on warmer days locals played chess were deserted. The playground and the sandpit were empty. Even the dope-smoking teenagers that gathered in the far corner in all weathers had disappeared. Balthazar stepped inside and carefully looked around.

The only other person he could see was a man who looked to be in his thirties sitting smoking on the far side of the open space. He sat back at ease, his legs stretched out in front as he played with his mobile telephone. Balthazar started walking towards him. Perhaps the man had seen something, had witnessed the smoke bomb attacks. It was worth asking. He wasn't that tall, Balthazar saw, but he was well built with a pale face and a nose that had clearly once been broken. He wore jeans, a grey woollen hat, a black parka and an expensive pair of light-brown lace-up winter walking boots.

The two men's eyes met for a second. The man then looked away, apparently uninterested in Balthazar's presence.

Something about this guy.

But what? His look had been too unconcerned, Balthazar realised. Most people, when they saw a well-built man of obvious Gypsy extraction in a leather jacket walk towards them were not exactly fearful but were at least focused and alert. The man on the bench was neither. He did not move at all, just sat there looking super-relaxed. In fact he looked like he was almost smiling.

Balthazar stopped walking, kept looking at the man on the bench. Had they had met before? Why was this guy giving off such a strong 'fuck you' vibe? Then Balthazar realised. His heart speeded up. For a second he was back on Pap Janos Square, not far from Keleti Station, on a sweltering summer's day in early September 2015 at the height of the refugee crisis.

He had been standing by the half-demolished headquarters

of the Socialist Party, looking for the body of a murdered Syrian refugee when a black Gendarmerie van pulled up nearby. The six gendarmes had walked forward and positioned themselves around him: two squads of two on either side, and another standing behind him, all with their right hands hovering over their pepper spray and handcuffs. The commander had stood in front, his baton in his hand. Balthazar had not moved.

After a few moments the commander had slid his baton back into the holder on his belt and took off his sunglasses. 'Hallo, Tazi,' he said. The commander was Attila Ungar, Balthazar's former partner.

The man in the woollen hat sitting on the nearby bench was one of the six gendarmes who had surrounded him, Balthazar realised. He had a good memory for faces, especially when he thought he was about to be beaten up.

In the end he had not been hit, and had avoided arrest by calling in for assistance using a police emergency code. After Reka Bardossy had dissolved the gendarmes, some of their members, once vetted, had joined the riot squad of the Budapest police. Others had melted away into the underworld or, like Attila Ungar, had set up security companies.

So who was this guy working for? Was he connected to the attack on Javitas? Perhaps his presence was a coincidence. It wasn't a crime, after all, to sit at ease in Klauzal Square park on a freezing winter afternoon. But it was quite unusual. Somewhere in the distance an engine noise sounded, echoing down the now-empty streets.

Balthazar started to walk over to the man but then he saw that he had something in his hand. At first he thought it was a mobile telephone, but then he saw the aerial poking out of the top. It was a walkie-talkie. The man smiled at Balthazar and raised the walkie-talkie to his mouth. The engine noise grew louder. It was sharper and harsher than a car.

Balthazar's heart started pounding. He turned on his heel and sprinted back through the park, drawing his Glock as he ran. The engine noise now echoed across the square. The motorcyclist was now visible on the other side of the fence, rushing towards Vivi and Anastasia, getting larger by the second.

The motorbike was red, the rider and passenger both wearing silver helmets with tinted visors. The passenger was carrying an Uzi sub-machine gun.

Balthazar was halfway through the park, yelling 'Get down, get down', when he saw Anastasia launch herself onto Vivi. The two women crashed to the floor.

Anastasia crawled forward, pushing Vivi, showing her how to crouch down and shelter behind the bonnet of her car. She instantly understood and made herself as small as possible.

Balthazar sprinted towards Anastasia and Vivi, his Glock in his hand. He stood still for a moment and dropped into a shooting stance.

Time slowed down as he watched the motorcyclist approach Javitas.

There was movement, Balthazar saw, inside the café. At this range it was almost impossible to hit a moving target with a pistol. If he missed the gunman, the bullets would go through the glass front of the café and could hit the people inside.

He lowered his weapon, ran forward again.

The motorcyclist slowed as they reached the Opel.

The gunman aimed the stubby gun at the rear windscreen,

flicking quickly from left to right as he opened fire, the staccato sound of the bullets tearing through the air before they hit the glass.

After a couple of seconds the shooting stopped.

The motorcycle roared down Dob Street.

Balthazar reached the corner of Klauzal Square and Dob Street, aimed his Glock at the back of the motorcycle passenger as the motorcycle roared off towards the Grand Boulevard, distance growing rapidly by the second.

Now he had a clear line of fire.

Until two children ran out of a grocery store into the middle of the road to see what all the excitement was about. Balthazar turned around, his Glock still in his hand, to see if there were any more gunmen, or the threat was over. There were no more attackers.

Balthazar holstered his weapon, glanced at the Opel's rear windscreen. A line of holes was stitched across the glass. Large cracks reached from the top to the base, but it had not shattered. The bulletproof glass had held.

He looked at the pavement. It was covered in grey slush, streaked with dirt, dotted with cigarette ends. But there were no pools of red, or crimson streaks.

Balthazar shouted, 'Vivi, Anastasia, you can come out. He's gone.'

The two women slowly stood up. Both were unscathed. Balthazar exhaled hard with relief.

Anastasia said, 'We're fine. Did you hit them?'

Balthazar shook his head. 'I didn't open fire. There were people behind you in the café. By the time I got here they were halfway to the boulevard. Then some kids appeared.'

Anastasia walked around to the rear of the vehicle, pressed down on the windscreen. It gave way but did not break. She patted the bonnet, checked the two cars parked on either side. Neither was damaged.

Balthazar asked, 'Are you sure you're OK?'

She smiled. 'I'm fine. If they wanted to hit us they would have.'

Vivi said, 'Wasn't that exciting? I've never been shot at before.' She turned to Anastasia. 'Tell me more about this job.'

SIXTEEN

Dob Street, Friday, 9.30 a.m.

Zsuzsa slowly walked down Dob Street on the opposite side of the road to Javitas, observing her surrounds, without, she hoped, being noticed. Two policemen, one tall, the other short and tubby, stood nearby smoking, desultorily watching over the crime scene. The sky was the colour of gunmetal, the sun invisible, and the freezing wind cut through her coat, chilling her face and neck.

Two cars were parked in front of Javitas, but there was a space between them. They must have taken away the one that was shot up, she thought. The area in front of the café was sealed off by black-and-yellow crime scene tape stretching between small poles mounted on stands. The few pedestrians walking down Dob Street towards the Grand Boulevard had to navigate a path around the police tape by stepping into the road.

The shooting was a huge story, all over the television news and the internet.

The police had put out a statement that the attack had been gangland-related, insinuating that Mishi had failed to pay protection money. It was a warning, the police spokeswoman had said, as evinced by the fact that nobody had been hurt. Enquiries were underway and the police were confident that the motorcyclist and the gunman would soon be apprehended.

It was possible that the shooting was mafia-related, Zsuzsa supposed, but she doubted it. There were plenty of organised crime gangs in Budapest, but it was almost unheard of for rivals to engage in gun battles across residential streets. Back in the 1990s there had been a burst of bombings and shootings but nowadays the mafia wars were fought behind the scenes, not in public places. This was about politics, not crime, Zsuzsa was almost certain. The planned release of the video, Reka's pre-emptive media strike, the disappearance of Elad Harrari, this attack – all in the last couple of days – were were too big and too loud to be a coincidence or a mafia bust-up. Especially as she was pretty sure that this was the building where Elad lived.

Zsuzsa looked at the entrance to number 46/b, taking in the detail of the building, trying not to feel conspicuous. It was a typical 1930s Budapest art deco apartment house, flat-fronted, six storeys high, its glass-and-steel entrance door almost hidden between Javitas on one side and an organic greengrocer's on the other. Both were now shut.

The apartment house was in very good condition, painted a dark yellow. The middle of the facade extended further out, to make space for a balcony on either side. On each floor, between the double windows, was a finely sculpted relief showing stylised workers wielding tools or women holding babies. A faded wreath was attached to the wall by the door, underneath a small memorial plaque. The words were too far away for her to read but she already knew who it commemorated – the composer Rezso Seress. This was the right place, she was sure.

A few weeks earlier, before winter had really started biting,

Zsuzsa had been here on her walking tour of Budapest's Jewish history. The guide, a bright teenager called Sara, had taken them inside the Great Synagogue on Dohany Street, to tiny houses of worship tucked away in courtyards, to the city's last kosher butcher and cake shop. They had stood by the Great Synagogue where the gate to the wartime ghetto had been smashed aside by Russian soldiers in January 1945, seen the houses on Raoul Wallenberg Street in District XIII, whose wartime inhabitants had been placed under Swedish diplomatic protection.

They had gathered on Klauzal Square, a few yards away, to hear from an elderly Jewish man who had lived through the freezing, murderous winter of 1944 and 1945 when the square had served as an open mass grave. The tour had been a revelation to Zsuzsa, as the city's familiar streets suddenly revealed multiple layers of a dark, hidden history. The makeshift memorial on Liberty Square had told the stories of some of the Hungarian Jews killed in the Holocaust in far-off camps or shot into the Danube. Sara had shown Zsuzsa and her companions where and how those Jews had once lived and died in the same buildings that still stood today, on the pavements where Zsuzsa now walked. That walk had changed forever the way she saw the city.

The guide had also stopped outside number 46/b Dob Street, explaining how this was the former home of Rezso Seress, a Jewish Hungarian musician and lyricist. His best-known song, 'Gloomy Sunday', had been immortalised for an international audience by Billie Holiday. It inspired so many suicides – jumping off the Chain Bridge over the Danube was a favourite – that it was eventually banned by the Hungarian authorities. During the war Seress, like many Jewish men, was drafted into a forced labour battalion. He survived the Holocaust but his mother did not. Perhaps inevitably, Seress himself eventually jumped out of his apartment window. He lived but finally managed to kill himself in hospital.

The guide had wanted to take Zsuzsa's group inside the building, but there wasn't enough time. Zsuzsa remembered Elad telling her that there was a memorial to a 'famous singer' on the wall of the foyer in the apartment house where he lived. He also said that he had a nice view of Klauzal Square from his window. That wasn't exactly right – the memorial on the wall in the foyer also commemorated Rezso Seress – but this had to be the place.

The question was, where would Zsuzsa take her story about Elad, once she had it? 555.hu, obviously, was out of the question. Her escape plan yesterday had worked nicely. The alarm had gone off as she forced the fire door open. That had caused enough confusion in the newsroom to buy her a few seconds – and had also distracted the security guards as the central building hub had immediately started issuing instructions to the guards over their radios. By the time they had reached the fire exit by the newsroom, Zsuzsa was downstairs on the ground floor. There were two more fire doors in the back, by the commercial entrance. She had pushed one open and swiftly fled into the flow of afternoon commuters heading home. Roland and Kriszta had called her multiple times, but she did not answer.

Now the priority was to find out more about Elad Harrari. And her immediate task was to get into the building and find a neighbour to talk to.

That meant crossing the road, looking confident, and quickly finding a buzzer to try. The bored-looking policemen would notice her immediately.

A few seconds later Zsuzsa was standing in front of the entrance. She looked at the rows of names on the entry buzzers, glancing sideways out of the corner of her eye. One said KOVACS, BALTHAZAR. Was that the cop? Eniko's ex-boyfriend? Eniko had told Zsuzsa that he lived on Dob Street, near Klauzal Square. It must be him. Balthazar was not a common name. That was the last thing she needed, for him to appear now.

Meanwhile, the lanky cop nearby, she saw, was indeed watching her. He muttered something to his colleague and pointed at Zsuzsa.

She quickly scanned the names on the fourth and fifth floor. *Choose*, she told herself. She wasn't doing anything illegal, but the police were now on high alert.

She did not want to spend time explaining herself, producing her identity documents, waiting while they checked her out, nor leave a trail with the authorities about her presence here.

She pressed the button for BALOGH, FERENC. A grumpy voice said, 'Yes, what is it?'

Zsuzsa thought quickly. A man, elderly, cantankerous, probably lived here for decades, now on his own. She introduced herself then used the most formal of Hungarian's three registers as she continued speaking. '*Tiszteletem Balogh ur*, I am a journalist writing an article about how District VII is being spoiled by all the tourists and bars and noise and filth. It's not a *buli-negyed*, for local people, is it? The whole area is being ruined, don't you think, Balogh *ur*? I would really like to hear your views.'

She glanced sideways again. The policeman was walking towards her. The building intercom hissed with static. 'Balogh *ur*?' she said.

He really needed to press that button quickly. 'Balogh *ur,* I would really like to hear your opinion about all these awful changes,' she said, trying to keep the tension from her voice.

The policeman was just a few yards away. His radio crackled and he stopped for a moment to reply. The door to the building buzzed.

Zsuzsa exhaled in relief, pushed it open and stepped inside.

SEVENTEEN

Jewish Museum, Dohany Street, 9.30 a.m.

Balthazar stepped out of the lift and into a corridor so dazzlingly white he blinked.

He had last been inside Hungary's Jewish Museum on a school trip almost twenty years before. He thought it was a sad place, dimly lit and full of ghosts, with its Torah scrolls, Sabbath candlesticks and prayer shawls perched in old-fashioned wood-and-glass display cases with handwritten index cards.

Sad and not much of a memorial to what had once been one of Europe's largest and most flourishing Jewish communities. Still, he remembered thinking at the time, at least Hungary's Jews had a museum. There was no museum to commemorate or celebrate the country's Gypsies who had been killed by the Nazis in the Poraymus.

The director had made up for the gloomy atmosphere: a Holocaust survivor with a gravelly voice, bright blue eyes and a shock of silver hair. Erno Hartmann had brought the exhibition to life by telling the story of his family, who had moved to the capital during the war from Debrecen, a city in the east. After spring 1944 they had been incarcerated in the main ghetto, on Klauzal Square, right by Balthazar's flat. Erno, his parents and sister had lived in one room, sick and half starved. They had survived. So had six of his thirty-seven relatives who stayed behind in Debrecen and the surrounding villages.

Balthazar watched an elderly figure stride towards him. He looked familiar, if a little more stooped. The silver hair was now white, and thinner, the eyes a little rheumier, but the voice was still resonant. He wore a crisp white shirt and smartly pressed grey trousers.

'Detective Kovacs, welcome back,' said Erno Hartmann as he extended his palm. 'It's been a long time.'

Balthazar smiled as he took the old man's hand. His grip was firm, his skin dry. 'Thank you. You remember me?' he asked.

Erno nodded. 'Of course. You asked a lot of questions. You were curious. Unusually so. Balthazar is an unusual name. And you are a Gypsy. I wish more of your people would come to visit us. We have a lot in common.'

Balthazar said, 'We do. And one day, when we have a museum, I will welcome you.'

Erno smiled. 'I very much look forward to that, Detective. Let me know if I can ever help.'

'I will. Thank you,' said Balthazar. Erno Hartmann was as sincere, and as engaging as he remembered.

Erno said, 'I was reading about the shooting yesterday. A shooting with a sub-machine gun.' He shook his head slowly. 'It's unbelievable. This is usually a safe city. I read that you were there. You were not hurt?'

Balthazar shook his head. 'No. I was on the other side of Klauzal Square when it started.'

Erno fixed Balthazar with his gaze. 'Is it connected? Elad's disappearance? Gunfire outside his apartment building?'

'And mine. I live on the same floor as the flat he stayed in.'

'Ah, then you know his landlady, Eva *neni*, the *palacsinta* queen.'

Balthazar smiled. 'Yes, very well.'

'A wonderful lady. We went to school together. She must be worried sick.'

'She is.'

Erno, Balthazar could see, was watching him, not with hostility but a kind of curiosity. It was a common reaction when everyday Hungarians encountered a black-haired, brown-eyed detective who was obviously a Gypsy. But Balthazar sensed something more in Hartmann's appraising glance. The elderly man was assessing him, Balthazar knew. His instinct told him that Hartmann could be a valuable ally.

Balthazar decided to trust him. 'To answer your question, yes, I think all these things are connected.'

Erno gestured to Balthazar. 'Which is why you are here. And I am glad you are. Come, walk with me. You are not in a hurry, Detective?' It wasn't so much a question as a statement.

Balthazar glanced at his watch. Almost 9.45 a.m. There was a busy day ahead. He was due to meet Ilona Mizrachi, the Israeli cultural attaché, at a café on Klauzal Street, at eleven o'clock. After that he would meet Anastasia at her office on Falk Miksa Street, then join up with Sandor Takacs and head to the Kerepesi Way cemetery, for the memorial service for the Librarian in the afternoon. He was not going to mourn, but to observe. Karoly Bardossy, the CEO of Nationwide, would be there, and Karoly Bardossy, Balthazar sensed, was somehow key to all this. But for now Balthazar had some time. And Erno Hartmann, he sensed, would not be rushed.

'No, I am not in a hurry,' said Balthazar.

'Good, then we can take a few minutes,' said Hartmann. 'We are very proud of our museum. And no, in case you are wondering, I am no longer the director, I retired when the renovation started. The new director is thirty-five and a graduate from several universities. She has a master's degree in library and archival studies.' He shook his head in mild wonder. 'Who knew that such diplomas existed? But she is kind enough to keep me on as a consultant.'

Kind enough and smart enough, Balthazar thought as he looked around, increasingly impressed. He had been inside plenty of renovated properties in Budapest – the city was enjoying a building boom, but had never seen a transformation like this from shabby post-communist to London or New York gallery chic. The floor was lined by white-and-grey marble tiles, the walls were a pristine shade of white and massive skylights had been placed in the ceiling where the sunlight poured in. The exhibits were no longer jumbled together, but each was mounted on a cream board, and displayed in a pristine, floor-to-ceiling glass cabinet.

'It's beautiful. So light and modern,' said Balthazar.

'Thank you. We had some generous benefactors. The government, some private companies. One firm in particular has been very generous. But the most important thing is that our new prime minister has been very supportive. She has substantially increased our budget, enough to pay for all the renovations, these lovely galleries. And we are branching out, into – what's the word? – micro-history. We will soon have our first open-air exhibition outside the museum, in Klauzal Square, featuring local characters, past and present. Miss Bardossy was the guest of honour at our recent reception – you may have seen the media coverage.'

'I did. Not everyone was pleased.'

'What can we do, Detective? We have a very troubled history and some of our compatriots are still struggling with that,' said Erno, shrugging. 'It will take time. But some good things are happening as well. I'll take you through to Elad's office in a few minutes, but first, please indulge an elderly man.'

He led Balthazar to the first display case, pointing out a Torah scroll from the sixteenth century from Miskolc in eastern Hungary, a giant brass candelabra from the nineteenth century, and cloths to cover the bread on Friday night for Shabbat from Budapest. The adjacent display case held a medieval gravestone from a now-vanished Jewish cemetery in the Castle District, the Hebrew letters now just faded shadows.

They walked over to a long, curved ram's horn to be blown on the New Year, both ends wrapped in ornate silver plate embossed with Hebrew script. There was no one else around – the museum did not open till 10 a.m. so they had the place to themselves.

'A shofar,' said Balthazar.

Hartmann looked surprised. 'I'm impressed. Did you remember that from your visit?'

'Yes, but also because my ex-wife was Jewish. We came to Dohany Street synagogue for New Year and for the Day of Atonement.'

'Then you know something about our traditions. The shofar was supposed to be the grandest in the whole Habsburg empire. Grander than what they had in Vienna, that was the main thing. They blew it here, every year in the Great Synagogue, until the end of the First World War.'

For a moment he looked into the distance. 'My grandfather fought for the empire in that war. He was awarded a medal for charging a British machine gun nest. His brother was killed in action. When things got bad here, their military records helped, for a while. And then they didn't any more.' Hartmann blinked. 'Now come with me, Detective. You have not travelled all this way to listen to an old man's reminiscences.'

The two men stepped toward a door marked *Private: Staff Only*, and into the main administrative offices. These had also been renovated in the same bright, modern style as the museum's public space. Six pale-wood desks were spread around the room, each with a new monitor and keyboard and an Italian leather office chair in front.

Most of the desks were piled high with papers, files and books. Erno and Balthazar were the only ones present. One desk, in the far corner, was almost bare, with no computer or keyboard, although a modern-looking laser printer stood on a small table nearby. Three books were neatly arranged on one corner, next to a plain white mug. Balthazar walked over and looked more closely. He turned to Hartmann. 'Is this Elad's desk?'

Erno nodded. 'That's his, yes.'

'His computer?'

'He worked on a laptop. He did not leave it here overnight.' Erno gestured at the printer. 'That's his as well. A very fancy machine. Better than ours. It even scans and prints out photographs.'

Balthazar stood by the desk and put on a pair of blue latex gloves. The books were all works of Jewish history, about the war and the Holocaust. He picked them up, one by one, held them by their spines and flicked through the pages. Nothing fell out. He placed them back where they had been, then reached for the mug. He held it to his nose. It smelled of coffee. The desk had two drawers.

He pulled them open – both were empty. He ran his hands around the inside of the drawers, slid them back and forth, shook them from side to side, felt around the underside of the desk then checked the cushion and legs of Elad's chair. There was nothing there. Which made sense – Elad had hidden the important stuff on the memory stick, which Vivi was now going through.

Balthazar turned to Hartmann. 'Nobody should touch this desk. I will send over someone from the local station to put crime scene tape around it.'

Erno looked alarmed. 'You think something happened here?'

'It's possible, but on balance no, I don't think so. You have very high security here, CCTV everywhere, a direct link to the local police station and police headquarters. All the buildings' entrances and exits are covered. It would be very hard to get someone out of here without being noticed.'

Balthazar walked over to the window and looked out. The museum was part of the Great Synagogue complex on Dohany Street and was high on the government's list of protected buildings. Two uniformed police officers were standing by the synagogue entrance, and two more were patrolling nearby, all huddled in their padded winter jackets. Across the street, a police car was parked near the bus stop.

Leaning against the wall, by the entrance to an apartment building, a tall middle-aged man Balthazar recognised as part of the city's undercover squad stood smoking. Bela Siklosi, Balthazar knew, was much more alert than he appeared. The two men had worked together several times and sometimes met for a beer.

Another member of the undercover squad sat on a bench near the synagogue entrance, not reading the newspaper he was holding in front of him. Security, Balthazar was sure, had been boosted since Elad's disappearance.

But who was the young woman in her twenties wearing a black padded jacket and a blue hat, standing by the nearby bus stop, with a view of the entrance to the museum, looking at a map? She looked almost familiar – then he realised she had been twenty yards ahead of him for much of his walk from Dob Street to Dohany Street.

That was at least thirty minutes ago. At that moment she walked over to one of the policemen, gave him a big smile, pointed at the map and asked a question. Balthazar could see that she was nodding at the answer, but was also looking from side to side.

Balthazar turned to Erno. 'Would you excuse me for a moment? I need to make a call.'

'Of course. Is it private? Should I leave?'

Balthazar thought for a moment then shook his head. 'No, it's fine. Come here. You might enjoy this. Watch the girl with the map, talking to the policeman.'

The two men stood by the window. Balthazar picked up his mobile and scrolled through the numbers until he found Bela's then pressed dial. Balthazar spoke rapidly. Bela looked up at the window, nodded at Balthazar and Erno, then walked over to the young woman. He said something first to the uniformed policeman, showed his wallet. The uniformed cop stepped back.

There was a brief conversation between Bela and the young woman. She started to protest, then Bela said something that made her stop arguing and reach into her bag. She took out a wallet and showed Bela her identity documents. He took the card and looked down at it for several seconds then handed it back. The young woman jammed it into her pocket, folded up her map and immediately walked away, scowling.

Balthazar's mobile rang and he listened for less than a minute before thanking Bela and hanging up. He turned to Erno, who was watching the whole event with delighted fascination. 'Shoshanna Cohen, dentistry student at Semmelweis University,' said Balthazar. 'She's been living here for three years, two blocks up the road on Dohany Street, so I am not sure why she needs a map.'

'Someone is keeping an eye on you, Detective,' said Erno.

'It looks like it. When was Elad last here?' asked Balthazar.

'He came in Wednesday morning, stayed until lunchtime, packed up his at laptop and we have not seen him since.'

'Did he say anything about going somewhere, meeting someone?'

Hartmann shook his head. 'No. No meetings, no trips. It was not unusual. He wasn't a museum employee. He came and went as he pleased.'

Balthazar asked, 'What kind of person is he?'

'Diligent, polite, kept his desk in order. We had no complaints. What do you think has happened to him? Please tell me what you really think, Detective. I feel very responsible. He came to Budapest to work with us.'

'We don't know, and anything that may have happened is not your fault. But we think he has been kidnapped.'

'Yes, I think so too. Do you think he is still alive?'

Balthazar nodded. 'Yes, I do. I think whoever has him wants to scare him, stop him digging into something. I understand he was working on Nationwide. Maybe he found out something important, or threatening. Tell me more about what he was researching.'

Hartmann gave Balthazar another of his assessing glances,

then seemed to come to a decision. 'Let's go to my personal office, Detective. It's more comfortable there.'

He walked across the room with Balthazar to a door on the other side, stepped through and gestured at Balthazar to follow him. Erno's workspace had escaped the modernisation. The walls were a faded yellow, the floor a dull, worn parquet, its varnish long-since faded. He had a large, old-fashioned heavy wooden desk, that was piled high with papers, reports and books, and a dark-wood chair whose leatherette cushions were cracked and worn.

Several sepia and black-and-white photographs were carefully arranged on the surface of the desk, by an old-fashioned, thick-framed monitor and keyboard. Books were piled up on the windowsill, on the top of the filing cabinet, and on another, smaller, chair in the far corner. Erno lifted the books off the second chair, brought it over to his desk, sat down in his own chair, then patted the second.

Balthazar sat down and looked around. Hartmann's room even smelled different, slightly musty and dusty. It wasn't unpleasant. He took out his notebook and sat back as Hartmann started talking.

'They asked me if I wanted my space to be all new and fancy like it is outside. I said no, it was a bit late for me. I've been in this room for more than forty years and I don't want to change it now.' He rearranged some papers on his desk, to little or no effect. 'So, to answer your question, yes, Elad was researching Nationwide, focusing on its origins. As you may know, Nationwide was first formed after the war in the summer of 1945. It was a conglomerate, merging together several other firms with interests in property, industry and manufacturing.'

The previous evening, once he got home, Balthazar had

spent some time on the internet trying to find out more about Nationwide. The company website gave little away. There were plenty of articles about the firm in the Hungarian media, many alluding to its complex structure that seemed to lead to various tax havens and the growing prosperity of its owners and directors, first among them Karoly Bardossy. But none of the investigative journalists had looked at the formation of the company after the end of the war.

Balthazar asked, '*Merging* means what in this case?'

Hartmann exhaled sharply. 'Appropriating. Stealing, in plain language. Factories, villas, bank accounts, assets, foreign currency accounts abroad. Right down to the office furniture. All funnelled into the new structure. We half knew this, but Elad told me he was digging up new evidence.'

Balthazar took notes as Hartmann spoke. 'What kind of new evidence?'

'I don't know precisely. Elad did say he thought much of Nationwide's post-war wealth came from one company in particular, but he didn't say which one.' Erno smiled ruefully. 'I am sorry I don't have more details. Nationwide would not cooperate. No interviews, no access to the company records, no questions at all, then legal threats if Elad kept asking questions. A total stonewall, which surely tells us something. But he kept digging. We agreed that Elad would write a proper report once he had gathered as much evidence and verified as much documentation as he could. It all needed to be put in context as well and properly referenced. I did not want to know snippets of this and that. We needed solid evidence that we could evaluate.'

Balthazar nodded. 'What about restitution after the change of system? Has Nationwide returned anything to the heirs or the original owners?'

Erno laughed. 'Forgive me, Detective. No. Nothing. Their lawyers – they have some very fancy lawyers, not just here, but in London and New York – say that as Nationwide, as *now* constituted, was founded in 1948 and so did not exist in 1944 and 1945 when these properties and assets were *acquired* by a previous entity, as they put it' – his voice changed as though reciting very familiar lines – 'the company has no legal liability for the properties or holdings of any previous entities nor for any actions the previous entities may have or may not have carried out or any agreements entered into by previous entities. Even if the previous entity operated out of the same address, with the same staff and owned the same assets. It's a neat argument. Very popular in neighbouring countries as well.'

Erno sat back in his chair for a moment, picked up one of the sepia-tinted portraits, showing a distinguished-looking gentleman in his Sabbath best. 'This was my great uncle, Odon – the one who had charged the machine gun in 1916. He was a lawyer in Debrecen and the town notary. The keeper of Debrecen's secrets if you like. Which is probably why he was one of the first to be deported. He was a slave labourer at Auschwitz for IG Farben. He lasted six weeks.'

'I'm sorry,' said Balthazar.

Erno coughed gently, then wiped his eye. 'So am I. But I am sure you have more questions, Detective.'

Balthazar asked, 'Which company in particular was a generous benefactor?'

Erno smiled. 'I'll give you one guess.'

'Nationwide.'

'Yes. They paid for fifty per cent of the renovation, but they didn't want it made public. Karoly Bardossy asked for a private viewing, which I was happy to provide, of course.'

Balthazar wrote the name of the company in his notebook and scribbled a line about money for the museum. 'Why did they do that?'

'Who knows? If and when the whole story comes out, we are a useful alibi. Maybe Karoly Bardossy felt guilty. Maybe he wanted to see who we were and what we were doing. He did ask a lot of questions about our archives and what kind of documents we had. Maybe he was genuinely interested. He seemed to be when he was here. Probably it was mix of all of these.'

Erno shrugged, then continued speaking. 'People are complicated. They do all sorts of interesting things. Karoly Bardossy came a couple of months ago, before Elad started work. Elad was very interested in the Bardossy family. One branch of them were Arrow Cross, fanatical Hungarian Nazis. Some of them were executed after the war. The other branch, led by Karoly's father, Tamas, were communist sympathisers, before the communists even took power. They were secretly funding the party during the war, via Swiss bank accounts, even though they were rich capitalists. Tamas saw what was coming, I guess. He was minister of the interior, as you know, during the Stalinist times, and again after 1956. The most powerful position, even more than the prime minister. The interior ministers controlled the secret police. They knew where the bodies were buried. Literally, in some cases. It was a family business. Reka's father, Hunor, was also interior minister during the early 1990s, until he was killed in a skiing accident.'

'Is that how Nationwide stayed in business under communism?'

'Partly. But mainly because even communists need a window to the world, to trade and bring in foreign currency. Better to run that through Nationwide, then they could control it. The national archives had been wiped clean. We had very little documentation. Elad started contacting descendants of the families who had owned the appropriated companies. Some of them did not want to know. Who wants to go up against one of the most powerful businessmen in the country, whose niece is the prime minister? But one or two said they would help him, see what papers they had.'

Erno sat back and exhaled. 'We had tried ourselves, over the years, of course. But we get much of our funds from the public purse. At one stage, a few years ago, we actually took on a researcher to look at Nationwide.'

'And then?'

'And the stories started to appear in the newspapers about impending budget cuts to the cultural sector. Museums would be ranked according to the number of visitors they received.'

Erno smiled. 'In those days we did not receive that many. It was quite clever. We got the message. But when Elad arrived we thought we could try again. Our finances were finally in decent shape.'

Erno leaned forward, fixed Balthazar with his gaze. 'Look, Detective, I will trust you with this. But it is not to be made public in any way.' He glanced at Balthazar's notebook. 'Nothing in writing, by hand or by email. Agreed?'

Balthazar shut his notebook. 'Can I tell my colleagues? They are absolutely trustworthy.'

'I leave you to be the judge of that. Elad had a high-level source, he told me. Someone with direct knowledge of what happened, even evidence that they might share. He would not tell me who, or what, said it was too "sensitive". But Elad told me, if what he suspected was true, and he could confirm it, it would cause an earthquake.'

Erno paused. 'There's something else you might be interested in. I have a friend who works in Reka's office, in the foreign relations department. A big part of the agreement that Alon Farkas will sign on Monday is to do with scientific and technical cooperation. There is a confidential annex. Something to with an Israeli computer company and the technical research department of Nationwide. All high-tech stuff. I don't know the details. I didn't think anything of it when I heard, but now I'm starting to wonder. You might ask about that.'

Balthazar said, 'Thank you, Erno, all this is really useful. Is there anything else I should know or you would like to tell me?'

'Yes. Someone came to take a look at us,' said Erno as he started typing, his fingers surprisingly nimble as they skittered across his keyboard. The monitor switched on and a video file opened. 'This is some CCTV footage from Tuesday morning. This gentleman came to the attention of our security staff. Now, I doubt this is a coincidence. See what you think.'

The video file showed a man in a black parka wandering around the museum. He was shortish and well built with light-brown boots and a grey woollen hat pulled down over his head. He affected interest in the exhibits, but was clearly more interested in who was in the room. He kept looking around, sweeping the space until it was empty.

Once nobody else was around he walked across to the door marked *Private, for staff only*. He opened the door and peered inside, looking from side to side for several seconds, then staring straight ahead until a security guard quickly walked over. The man apologised and quickly left the museum.

A camera caught his round face and broken nose for a moment. It was the former gendarme that Balthazar had seen at Klauzal Square the previous afternoon.

EIGHTEEN

Boho Bar, Klauzal Street, 11 a.m.

Ilona Mizrachi sipped her café latte, her brown eyes assessing Balthazar. He could sense her calculating: *What does this guy know – and how am I going to get it out of him?* In the time-honoured fashion, it seemed. Ilona wore a close-fitting white blouse that was open to the top of her bust, where a silver pendant inset with a brown stone rested. Her olive skin and black curls seemed to almost glimmer in the bar's dim light.

She leaned forward, her voice warm and concerned as she spoke. 'How are you, Detective? You weren't hurt yesterday?' She tilted her head to one side, her hair rippling around her face, eyes holding his, not giving him a chance to answer. 'A shootout, in broad daylight, in Budapest. It's shocking. I'm so glad you are OK.'

Balthazar smiled inside. He had hoped for a less-obvious gambit. 'I'm fine, thanks. I was still in Klauzal Square when they opened fire. By the time I got there, it was all over and the motorcyclist was at the other end of Dob Street.'

They were sitting in the upstairs gallery of the Boho Bar where they were the only customers. The Boho Bar was a classic District VII establishment that would have sat happily in Brooklyn or Hoxton: bare-brick walls, second-hand furniture and recycled chairs salvaged from school classrooms. Soft jazz drifted through the space. Several pieces of toast smeared with a white paste rested on a plate in front of Balthazar.

Ilona asked, 'And your colleagues, Anastasia and the other girl, what was her name?'

'They are fine.' Balthazar did not reply to Ilona's question about Vivi, instead offered her the snacks. 'Would you like to try one?'

She looked down at the plate then at Balthazar, doubt written large on her face. 'What is it?'

'Vegan lard bread,' he replied as he picked up another piece of toast and bit in. *Zsiros kenyer,* bread and dripping, was the poor person's meal in Hungary: a thick smear of animal fat – goose, duck or pork – on bread or toast, sprinkled with paprika and topped with a slice of red onion. The Boho Bar's version was made out of tofu, laced with chilli, spread on sesame crackers. It tasted better than he expected, the chilli giving the tofu a nice bite. One of the house craft beers would wash it down nicely, but Balthazar was sticking to sparkling mineral water. He knew he needed all his wits about him for this encounter.

Ilona asked, 'Are you a vegan, Detective? You don't look like a vegan.'

Balthazar smiled. Why not play the game a little? 'What do vegans look like?'

Ilona's eyes opened slightly wider. 'Thin, pale, weedy.'

'No, I am not. Not even a vegetarian.' He offered the plate again. 'Try one.'

Ilona shook her head. 'No thank you.' She sat back, still looking at Balthazar, a slight frown on her face, clearly trying to work out who he was and how to deal with him. 'Tell me about yourself, Detective. Are you from Budapest? How long have you been a policeman? I've seen that footage of you on the internet, taking down the Gardener, stopping the attack on Kossuth Square. I'm having coffee with a celebrity. A celebrity detective.'

Balthazar obliged with a potted history of his life so far – growing up in District VIII, university, starting a PhD on the Poraymus, his work as a detective, but leaving out his marriage and divorce. Ilona listened and, as far as he could tell, was genuinely interested. The atmosphere began to ease, although he knew that this meeting was business rather than social. Still, she was a very pretty woman, and sometimes it was fine to just appreciate the attention, whatever motivation lurked in the background.

Ilona asked, 'And being a Gypsy and a cop, how is that?'

'Do you want the long version or the short one?'

Ilona smiled regretfully. 'I would like the longer one, but today I only have time for the short.'

'Overall, it's fine. My boss looks out for me. I am not always loved, but I believe I am respected.'

'Vitamin P, we call it. *Proteksia*. And when you have to arrest Gypsies?'

He gave her a wry smile. She was as smart as she was attractive, he realised. 'That's always interesting. Sometimes they yell at me, call me all sorts of things, question whether my parents were married, or suggest various farm animals I could connect with.'

Ilona laughed. 'May I?' she asked, gesturing at the plate of snacks. Balthazar nodded. She took one and bit into the cracker. 'You're right. Not bad.'

Balthazar continued talking. 'Or they just laugh and give me their hands for the cuffs. Prison sentences here are not usually very long. They know what's coming.' He paused for a moment. 'So, you've heard about me, now tell me something about you. Where is your family from, originally, before Israel?'

'The two Bs, Baghdad and Budapest. My father's family left Iraq in the 1940s, my grandmother escaped from here in late 1944, somehow made it to Romania, then Turkey and Palestine. She lived around the corner, on Wesselenyi Street, number 36.'

'So you are Hungarian?'

'One quarter, a very proud quarter.'

'Do you speak Hungarian?'

'A few words, not much more. I'd like to learn.' Ilona blinked for a second, sat up straight, as if realising she was opening up too much. Her tone changed, turned businesslike. 'Detective, I wanted to meet you today to find out more about the attack on Klauzal Square. We are obviously very concerned about this, a gunman on the loose a couple of days before our prime minister arrives, and the smoke bomb attack on a Jewish-owned café, followed by a gunman shooting up a car parked outside. At the same time, as you know, an Israeli citizen has gone missing. This changes the security situation. Do you think the gunman was after Anastasia and the other girl?'

'I think it was a warning. If he wanted to kill them, he would have, or at least tried to. He hit the windscreen then drove off. But still, this is very serious.'

Ilona considered this for a moment. 'Yes, it is, even if thankfully nobody was hurt. I'm curious, though, why was Anastasia there? Why this bar, Javitas, of all places?'

Because Vivi was decrypting a memory stick that Elad had hidden in Eva *neni*'s bathroom, Balthazar thought. Instead he answered, 'You must ask her that. She is not a police officer.'

'I will. The owner, this Mishi guy, he is Jewish, right? Was this an anti-Semitic attack?'

Balthazar shook his head. 'I don't think so.' The main dangers in District VII were being overcharged in a tourist restaurant, losing a wallet to a pickpocket or accidentally getting into a drunken brawl with a British stag party. Serious violent attacks in Budapest were rare outside mafia disputes, those against Jews even rarer, and gunfire almost unheard of. 'I hope not. It would be the first of its kind.'

Ilona's gaze sharpened. 'Still, all this is taking place right outside the building where Elad lives – and the day after he disappears. That's not by chance, is it?'

Balthazar took a sip of his water before he answered. She was right, of course. 'We don't know. We are working on that. But it may be a coincidence.'

Ilona sat back. 'A coincidence. I don't believe in coincidences. Not when an Israeli has gone missing. OK, Detective. Let's get down to business. What have you got for me?'

Balthazar had told Sandor Takacs that he was meeting Ilona. Sandor had warned him not to share anything important with her, at least until Balthazar and Anastasia had a much clearer idea of what was going on and how and why Elad had disappeared. Israel was a friendly country, and an ally of Hungary, but the interests of the Budapest police and the Jewish state were not necessarily the same. Balthazar had decided that he might trade a few snippets with Ilona, depending how the conversation went, but overall, he agreed with Sandor. In any case, as his grandfather had taught him, only family gets things for free.

Balthazar said, 'We have what you have – the CCTV footage of Elad in the city before he disappeared.'

Earlier that morning Vivi had managed to find several

recordings of Elad on Wednesday afternoon, video of the last time he had been seen, from the municipal network. Vivi had decided to try working with Anastasia for a few days' trial. If it worked out, she would join the state security service full-time. If not, she would go back to her room at Javitas, once the police allowed the bar to reopen.

The video showed Elad walking to Astoria, then down Rakoczi Way and over the Elisabeth Bridge to the Buda side. From there he vanished. Downtown was reasonably well covered by cameras – especially the area around the synagogue and the nearby headquarters of the Jewish community – but there was much less coverage in Buda, where the population was spread much thinner. Anastasia had sent the footage to the Israelis as soon as it was ready.

Ilona drummed her nails on the salvaged wooden table. 'I've seen it. It shows him taking a walk then disappearing. The footage was taken on Wednesday. Today is Friday. Where did he go next?'

Balthazar said, 'We don't know. We would like to, obviously. We are working on it, as fast as we can.'

'Try harder, please.'

Balthazar picked up another cracker and ate it in one go. Ilona looked at her watch.

Now his voice turned businesslike. 'Sure, we can do that, but what can you share with us? Your organisation has far more resources than the Budapest police. We could make more rapid progress if you would share the information you have on Elad. His background, his education, army service and so on. The more information we have, the more potential leads we can explore. We haven't received much from your side. In fact, we haven't received anything. Nobody has even replied to our request.'

Ilona said, 'The diplomatic service of the State of Israel is fully cooperating with our Hungarian partners. We are looking for the information you have requested.'

Balthazar took a drink from his glass of mineral water then looked around the room. Her bodyguards, two very fit-looking, shaven-headed Israelis in their twenties, stood nearby, one in the near corner, the other in the far corner. One of the bodyguards was watching Balthazar and Ilona, sensing the rising tension, while the second was scanning the room and the staircase that led to the upper bar. Diplomats in Budapest were usually protected by Hungarian police officers from a special squad. Clearly, the locals had been ditched.

He put his glass down slowly, and let the silence play out. Silence, he had learned from countless interrogations of suspects, was probably the most underrated technique in an investigator's armoury. Endless television cop series showed police officers yelling at suspects or threatening them to get information. But saying nothing often yielded far better dividends. People started to babble to fill the quiet, especially when they were concealing something.

Ilona blinked first. 'Have you been to the museum, to see Erno Hartmann? Does he know anything more about Elad?'

'This morning.' Balthazar paused. 'I met a friend of yours on the way.'

'Who?' she asked warily.

'Shoshanna Cohen. She had somehow managed to get lost, a few yards from her front door.'

Ilona's smile faded completely. 'I have no idea who that is or what you are talking about.'

Balthazar took another cracker and ate it in one go. 'If you say so.'

'I do. What did Hartmann tell you?'

The fencing continued. 'That Elad was investigating what happened to the wealth and the assets of Hungarian Jewry after the Holocaust.'

'We know that. He had dinner at the embassy a while ago, when he first arrived.' She leaned forward again, her eyes focusing on Balthazar. 'Did Hartmann mention any companies in particular that Elad was investigating?'

Yes, said a voice in Balthazar's head, Nationwide. The one that is somehow connected to your prime minister's visit next week. But something told him to hold back. 'No,' he replied, 'none in particular.'

'Any specific names or dates?'

Balthazar shrugged. 'No. It was just general stuff about what happened after the war.'

Ilona gave him a look that clearly said *I don't believe you*. She carried on talking. 'Look, Detective, this is all very badly timed. Our prime minister plans to announce a substantial investment programme, a new joint high-tech hub in Budapest and Haifa, and all the usual agreements on education and tourism.'

'I know. Believe me, we want to find him and wrap this up quickly as much as you do.'

'Good. Then we are on the same page.' She turned the charm back on, smiling and leaning forward once more. 'Balthazar, I wanted to tell you, our Ministry of Justice is launching a pilot scheme soon, liaising with friendly police forces. The plan is to bring promising young officers to Israel for two weeks. A one-week placement at a station in Tel Aviv, and one week touring the country. Flights, hotels, all expenses paid and a per diem as well of course. No need for receipts.'

She paused, then continued, 'The ministry has asked all our embassies to nominate potential candidates.'

Balthazar smiled inside. *Not bad.* Ilona was upping her game. 'That sounds very generous. I am sure that our international liaison department can give you a list of suitable candidates,' he replied, his voice deadpan.

Ilona's smile faded. 'Thank you for your time.'

Ilona looked around the room, caught the eye of both her bodyguards and held up the index finger of her right hand. Balthazar watched the bodyguards ready themselves as Ilona spoke. 'You should know, Detective, that earlier today we informed Reka Bardossy that Jerusalem is now considering if the prime minister's visit should still go ahead.'

'Why?' asked Balthazar. A cancellation would be a disaster for Reka – and could even hasten the collapse of her tottering administration. And if Reka's government collapsed, there would be chaos – and no Virag Kovacs Music School in memory of Balthazar's half-sister. All of Reka's personal projects would be ditched by her successor. Ilona had just thrown a grenade into the mix.

Ilona put her jacket on and readied herself to leave. Her manner turned icy. 'It is out of the question for the prime minister of the state of Israel to pay an official visit to and announce a partnership with a country where one of our citizens has just gone missing and where gunmen are opening fire on Jewish-owned businesses. This is on you, Detective – you and your partner, Miss Ferenczy. You have until Sunday midday, Detective, to find Elad Harrari.'

She stood up, gestured at her bodyguards. 'No Elad, no visit.'

***

Less than a minute later Ilona was sitting on the back seat of a Mercedes with diplomatic number plates, speeding down the 4/6 tramline towards the Margaret Bridge and the embassy in the Buda hills. She took a heavy black telephone from her bag, one much thicker and clunkier than a standard-sized mobile handset and pressed several buttons before she spoke. 'He knows something. Switch it on.'

NINETEEN

Dob Street, 11 a.m.

Zsuzsa Barcsy nodded politely as she sipped her fruit tea. The heating was blazing and the drink nicely warming. Feri *bacsi*, as he now insisted she call him, was coming to the end of his lengthy and slowly recounted life story. Once she persuaded him to open his door and let her in, his whole demeanour changed. He was obviously very lonely – a widower, with one son who had emigrated to Canada and who rarely visited and two grandchildren he had only met once.

They were sitting in the dark front room. The walls were covered in heavy green wallpaper, and the old-fashioned communist-era furniture was covered with a faint layer of dust. The tea, however, was served on blue-and-white, gold-trimmed Zsolnay porcelain, kept for special occasions, as he now described her visit. A copy of *Magyar Hang*, Hungarian Voice, lay open on the nearby sofa. SHOOTING TERROR IN DISTRICT VII proclaimed the front page. TRENDY BAR TARGETED BY GUNMAN. A plate of marzipan sweets from Szamos, one of the country's best-known confectioners, lay next to the newspaper.

Zsuzsa explained again about the article she was supposedly researching, on how much District VII had changed in the last couple of years.

'This shooting yesterday,' said Feri *bacsi*, shaking his head. He was a thin man of mid-height in his late-seventies, with a deeply lined face and badly cut grey hair. He wore a pair of shapeless grey trousers, a white shirt with a fraying collar and plastic beach sandals.

But his blue eyes were lively and his voice animated as he spoke. 'It's terrible. We never had anything like this. Budapest was a safe city. Now they are firing with sub-machine guns, right outside my front door. That Balthazar that lives along the corridor, on the same floor. He's a Gypsy and a policeman – if you can imagine such a thing. All the Gypsies I have ever met get arrested, they don't arrest people. He's famous now, I read about him in the newspaper. But what use is a famous policeman for a neighbour when they are shooting outside the front door?'

Zsuzsa noted the information about Balthazar living here, feeling slightly ashamed of herself. She knew she should engage with Feri *bacsi*'s prejudices but she was there for another reason and she needed him on her side. Instead she said, 'There's good and bad in in all types,' her voice emollient. 'At least he's trying to catch the criminals.'

She glanced down at the Zsolnay cup and saucer. 'Such beautiful porcelain.'

Feri *bacsi* smiled. 'Thank you. It belonged to my mother.'

He picked up the tray of marzipan candies and offered it to Zsuzsa. She looked down at the delicate sweets, each individually wrapped in foil, with a gold band around the outside. 'Please, take one,' he said.

Zsuzsa was about to refuse, but she could see the eagerness on the old man's face. She picked one from the tray, unwrapped it and ate it in one go. It was delicious, a rich concoction of almond paste and chocolate.

Zsuzsa drank some of her fruit tea and took out her notebook and a pen. 'Tell me more about the changes you have seen, Balogh *ur*. You have lived through so much.'

'Please, Zsuzsa, do call me Feri *bacsi*,' he said, before enthusiastically launching into a long and unexpectedly evocative description of the small family-run shops – like Javitas – that had been displaced by the gentrification of the area around Klauzal Square. The tailor where he once had a suit made, the butchers that made their own sausages, the cake shops, the small eateries that he used to go to, almost all had been displaced for hipster cafés and eateries serving tourists.

Zsuzsa scribbled as he talked, realising that she could actually write an article on this theme – working headline: 'The Lost World of District VII' – and her host's reminiscences would be a central part. That thought made her feel a little less guilty for deceiving the elderly man. But now was the time to finally steer the conversation to the real purpose of her visit. 'Thanks so much, Feri *bacsi*, your stories are really wonderful.'

His face broke into a smile. 'I'm pleased I could help. When will the article appear?'

'I am not sure, but I will definitely keep you informed. There was something else I wanted to ask you about, Feri *bacsi*,' she said, leaning forward and giving him the full-on wide-blue-eyes treatment.

Feri *bacsi* offered her the plate of marzipan once again. 'Please, ask.'

Zsuzsa smiled and took another one, ignoring her growing sense of guilt – was it really this easy to manipulate lonely old people? 'It's a long shot, but maybe you can help. I met someone a few days ago at a bar, his name is Elad and he is a historian. He's Israeli and I think he lives here. He said his flat was overlooking Klauzal Square and there was a memorial downstairs in the foyer, for Rezso Seress I suppose, so it must be here, I guess?'

Feri *bacsi* nodded. 'Yes, he was staying at the other end of the corridor, in Eva *neni*'s flat. I saw him quite a few times.' He shrugged. 'She was there yesterday, with the Gypsy cop. They went inside, came out about ten minutes later. I like to keep an eye on things, you know.'

Zsuzsa nodded. 'Very wise, especially nowadays.' She thought for a moment. 'Did you hear anything, noises, conversation?'

'No, nothing. This Elad, he's Israeli. The things you hear and read and...' Feri *bacsi*'s voice tailed off for a moment.

Zsuzsa flinched inside. Hungarian had a verb, *zsidozni*, meaning to go on about Jews, and not in a positive way. Was Feri *bacsi* about to indulge in some *zsidozas*? 'And what?'

'And he wasn't what I expected,' Feri *bacsi* said brightly. 'He was very polite and spoke quite good Hungarian. Seemed like a very nice young man. Maybe I'll invite him as well, next time you come for tea.' He paused for a moment, his voice hesitant. He looked down at his fruit tea then back at Zsuzsa. 'You will come again, won't you?'

Zsuzsa smiled, feeling even guiltier. She would, she decided. 'Yes, Feri *bacsi*, of course. That's good I found the right place. I lent him a book and I need it back. But he is not answering my calls or emails. Do you know anything about where he has gone, if he is coming back?'

Feri *bacsi* said, 'I don't know where he went, but wherever it was, it was in a very fancy car, that's for sure.'

Zsuzsa sat up, alert now. 'He left in a car? How do you know?'

'Because I was having a cigarette on the balcony. He came out downstairs carrying two bags, one on his shoulder and one that was a big hold-all. He got in a fancy silver Audi with tinted windows. Nice car, I remember thinking. There was a big guy there, broad-shouldered, shaven-headed. He looked like a hoodlum, but he was very polite, opening and closing the door for him.'

Zsuzsa tried not to let her surprise show, scribbled in her notebook. 'When was that?'

'Wednesday evening. I remember because my son called from Canada.'

'Did he get in the car willingly? He wasn't forced or anything?'

Feri *bacsi* looked puzzled and shook his head. 'Why would he be forced? They shook hands. Like I said, the big guy put Elad's bag in the boot, got into the car, and then they drove off.'

TWENTY

Falk Miksa Street, 12.10 p.m.

Anastasia pulled up Ilona Mizrachi's file onto her screen and opened it. 'OK, Detective, let's take a look at the Israeli cultural attaché in Budapest. What's she been up to lately?'

Balthazar sat down beside Anastasia. 'You have a file on her?'

'Of course we do.' She smiled. 'You think that's her real job?'

Anastasia opened a folder of images and video clips and began to scroll through the photographs. They showed Ilona at a variety of events, from the Budapest Book Fair the previous year when Israel had been the guest of honour, to Jewish cultural events in several of the city's synagogues, and at gatherings of the city's business and political elite. There were also several shots of Ilona out and about at glamorous parties and restaurants.

Wherever she went, she was always well dressed and immaculately made-up, zeroing in on the most important or influential person in the room. Anastasia played a video clip of Ilona at the congress of the ruling Social Democrats. There was no sound, but the film showed her moving with confident ease, working the room until she ended up at her destination: a chat with Reka Bardossy.

Anastasia glanced at Balthazar. 'She's very pretty, your new friend.'

'I've only met her once. She's not my friend.'

'Maybe she would like to be.' She lifted an eyebrow. 'I hope you weren't too dazzled by her.'

Balthazar smiled. Was Anastasia flirting with him? Yes, he decided, she was. 'Too glam for me. You know us *nyolcker* boys,' he said, using the slang term for District VIII. 'We prefer a more natural look.' He looked at Anastasia. 'Casual clothes, T-shirts, jeans, not too much make-up.'

Anastasia seemed about to say something. Instead she turned a faint shade of pink and busied herself at her screen. 'OK. What did Ilona tell you?'

'Directly, nothing new. Other than if we don't find Elad by midday Sunday, the prime minister's visit will be cancelled, which you already know. But indirectly, quite a lot.'

'Such as?'

Balthazar quickly summed up the exchange where Ilona pressed him about specific dates and the names of people or companies. 'I think she is worried about something. Something Elad has found out, or is on track to. There must be a reason why she cares what a historian might have discovered about a firm that was founded seventy years ago. And it must be connected to Alon Farkas's visit. There is some kind of connection. Otherwise they would not be threatening to cancel it.'

'I think you're right. For a small country, we make a lot of history,' said Anastasia.

'And we can never outrun it,' said Balthazar.

For a moment he was back at the Kovacs family home on Jozsef Street, one Christmas when he was fourteen. His great-aunt Zsoka was telling the story of how she and her parents were deported in the summer of 1944. She had been nine years old. The gendarmes took her parents first, forced them to join a long procession of Gypsies walking through the back streets of District VIII to Keleti Station, where the train awaited. She had come down the stairs with two more gendarmes, not really understanding what was happening. She reached for the hand of one of the gendarmes, as she had been told to do, to find an adult who could help in uncertain situations. He swore at her and slapped her around the face. His ring had gouged a deep line across her cheek. Decades later the scar was still visible.

He brought himself back to the present. 'Shall I talk you through what Hartmann told me?'

'Yes. But let's get Vivi in, see how that fits with what she has found.' She picked up the telephone on her desk and pressed a couple of buttons. 'Balthazar is here. Come through, please, and let's talk him through the material.'

The door opened a few seconds later and Vivi walked in, carrying a chair. She nodded at Balthazar, sat down at Anastasia's desk and made herself comfortable.

'You look right at home,' said Balthazar.

Vivi smiled. 'I like it here. I get to play with state-of-the-art technology. There's nobody throwing smoke bombs or opening fire on me with a sub-machine gun. My dream workplace.'

'Mine too,' said Anastasia. She turned to Balthazar. 'So what have you got, Detective?'

Balthazar took out his notebook and flipped through the pages until he came to what he needed. 'We know that Elad was investigating the origins of Nationwide. Some of the story of the company's foundation and early years is in the public domain, but only the bare outline. Nationwide Ltd. was formed in 1948 by Tamas Bardossy, grandfather of Reka and father of Karoly Bardossy, the current CEO and majority owner and Reka's uncle. Nationwide Ltd. was a conglomerate of several companies, including the original Bardossy family firm, which was already one of Hungary's biggest industrial conglomerates. Elad was especially interested in the Bardossy family's role, and the role of the family company in 1944 and 1945 before it was absorbed into the new holding company but most of the documentation in the state archives had vanished. Nationwide itself was not helpful, quite the opposite. They would not give him any access to their records, or allow him to interview any of their staff, or give him any contact details for former employees. They also threatened him with a criminal case if he continued asking questions.'

Anastasia said, 'So they have something to hide.'

Balthazar said, 'It looks like that. This kind of approach is unusual nowadays, Hartmann told me. Even the big German corporations who used slave labour for the Nazis have opened up their archives and let the historians in. They think it's better to let everything out in one go. There is a playbook: first the revelations, then the media furore, everyone gets outraged, the company boss apologises profusely, the company pays some compensation to whoever is still alive, they set up a historical foundation, fund a memorial, then the story fades away.'

Vivi asked, 'And does it?'

Balthazar nodded. 'Always. The war was a long time ago. The survivors are dying off. And if the story comes back, each time it makes a bit less noise. But Hartmann told me that Elad had a source, someone with what he called "direct knowledge" of how Nationwide was formed, who was feeding him detailed information about what really happened in 1944 and 1945. And that story would not go away. It would go off like a bomb.'

Anastasia asked, 'Did Hartmann have any idea who the source was?'

Balthazar shook his head. 'He said not. If he did, he was a very good liar. He said Elad would share everything with him once he could confirm and verify the information, and get the source's permission. Then he and Elad would evaluate and analyse everything. Which makes sense.'

Balthazar turned to Vivi. 'So what was on the USB stick?'

Vivi looked at Anastasia. 'May I?' she asked. Anastasia nodded and the two women switched places. Anastasia sat next to Balthazar, her leg briefly brushing against his as she sat down.

Vivi opened a series of windows. 'There were two batches of files. The first was a folder of video clips. That was quite easy to decrypt. Elad was definitely being followed. I guess he filmed them with his phone. Take a look.'

The footage showed a blue Mercedes, passing by the Jewish Museum on Dohany Street, parked nearby on Sip Street, then the same vehicle parked on Klauzal Square and driving slowly down Dob Street.

Vivi said, 'The Merc has three different number plates, but it's always the same vehicle. The right-hand headlamp is cracked. They are checking the number plates now.'

'Thanks, Vivi,' said Anastasia. 'And the second batch of files?'

Vivi looked slightly bashful. 'I'm sorry. Progress is still much slower, even with your technical capabilities. The decryption programs are still running. They are documents, but I don't have much more of their contents yet.'

Balthazar asked, 'What have you got?'

'Fragments,' said Vivi. 'A few words and phrases here and there.'

Balthazar nodded encouragingly. 'It's great you have anything. Tell us, please. Anything can be useful, even fragments of words.'

Vivi nodded, and opened her notebook. 'I thought you would say that, so I wrote down everything I could get. There will be more, I hope, but it might take a few hours, or even a day or two to get it. The document is encrypted to a very high level – military or government.'

She looked down at the notebook. 'Tam... ossy, several times. Could that be Tamas Bardossy? Then another name appears: Ber... something and Mik... something. Maybe Miki or Miklos? Then there is the word Swiss and then another word which I don't know and a number. That one I got: 500,000. Maybe 500,000 Swiss francs?' She turned the page of her notebook. 'Some full words: invalid, Picasso, Monet and Manet. The painters. I mean, that's me saying that, the painters.' She glanced down again. 'Oh, and I have a date for the second document: 20 March 1944. Is that significant?'

Anastasia nodded. 'Yes. It must be. The Nazis invaded on 19 March.' She paused and closed her eyes for a moment, thinking hard. 'So what do we have here? An Israeli historian asking unwelcome questions who goes missing, but who has a source feeding him super-sensitive, potentially explosive documents which seem to date from March 1944. The documents point to some kind of deal, I guess to do with payments and valuables.'

Anastasia's mobile rang. She looked at the number and took the call, listening for a few moments, thanked the caller and hung up. 'The car number plates have been checked. They are all fake – none of them exist.'

TWENTY-ONE

Kerepesi cemetery, 2 p.m.

A light drizzle began to fall as Balthazar watched Karoly Bardossy open his eulogy for the man known as the Librarian.

It was a chilly afternoon and the thin winter sun was already fading behind a heavy grey sky. Karoly wore an elegant black Italian suit, a white shirt and a black tie under a long black wool topcoat. His grey-silver hair was carefully barbered, swept back from his high forehead, and his blue eyes scanned the crowd as he spoke. 'Janos Toth was a patriot and a public servant. He devoted his life to safeguarding the security of our beloved homeland. He never enriched himself or surrounded himself with luxury even in the 1990s, and the terrible years of *vadkapitalizmus*.'

A wave of nodding passed through the mourners, as though he was dispensing great, unarguable wisdom. A tall man with short grey hair and a military bearing, also dressed in a black suit but with a less elegant topcoat, opened an oversized black umbrella and stood at Karoly's side, sheltering him from the rain as he continued speaking. 'While too many plundered the wealth and riches of our homeland, simply taking whatever they wanted in those dark times of chaos, Janos Toth lived a modest existence. No, there were no riches, no fancy cars or foreign holidays for him. Instead Janos stayed at his desk at the Ministry of the Interior, quietly and diligently working in the background, ensuring all of our safety.'

'Are you listening to this *loszar*, horseshit?' Balthazar whispered to Sandor Takacs, his voice incredulous. '"The terrible years of *vadkapitalizmus*". The years when Nationwide gobbled up half the country.'

The two men were standing a few yards away from the main gathering of mourners. Sandor looked at Balthazar, half amused, half impressed. 'I'm almost clapping. A fantastic performance by Karoly *bacsi*, especially here.'

Kerepesi cemetery was Hungary's most prestigious burial place, home to the graves of Hungary's national heroes. Not far from where Balthazar stood watching the funeral with Sandor Takacs lay the tomb where Count Lajos Batthyany, Hungary's first prime minister of a parliamentary government, executed by the Austrians after the failed 1848 revolution, was interred. Nearby was the even grander tomb of Lajos Kossuth, the leader of the 1848 revolution, whose multi-floor mausoleum was the grandest piece of funereal architecture in Hungary. Scattered all around were memorials for now-vanished noble families, adorned with marble columns, elaborate roofs and carved cornices, and statues of lachrymose mourners.

The Librarian's funeral was taking place at a section of the cemetery known as the Pantheon of the Workers' Movement. Built during the 1950s, its modernist architecture was a direct challenge to the grandees of the old bourgeois, monarchist order interred nearby. A plain path of granite tiles led the mourners between six giant standing stone blocks, three on either side, each adorned with reliefs of heroic workers and peasants.

Bardossy and his bodyguard stood at the far end, in front of a giant socialist realist statue of three rough-hewn figures: a male worker in the centre, holding hands with a woman next to him while also propping up another comrade. Behind them a slogan declared *A Kommunizmusert a Nepert Eltek* – They lived for Communism and the People. The Librarian had been cremated and his ashes placed in a small urn that stood on a nearby table.

Balthazar kept his voice low as he asked Sandor, 'Are you sure that Karoly *bacsi* is living for Communism and the People, boss?'

Sandor shot him a mock stern look. 'Shhh. If it wasn't for communism, I would still be living in a house with no heating and a toilet in the garden and running palinka across the border into Serbia.'

Balthazar looked around the small crowd of mourners. The numbers were not impressive, but much of Hungary's political and business elite were here, come to pay their respects – willing or not – to the man who knew so much about how they had risen up their respective ladders.

Balthazar spotted several MPs from the upper echelons of the ruling Social Democrats, the foreign and interior ministers, opposition politicians from the right and centre parties, the editor of *Magyar Vilag* and the two best-known newsreaders on state television. On the edge of the small crowd stood Reka Bardossy, her ministerial limousine parked not far away. Next to her stood Akos Feher, her chief of staff, while Antal Kondor, her bodyguard and fixer since her earliest days in politics, kept a watchful eye as he scanned the crowd and the surrounds.

Reka too was dressed in mourning clothes, in a well-tailored black wool coat and large black scarf. She saw Balthazar watching her and nodded at him and Sandor Takacs, shooting a quick smile as she rolled her eyes, while her uncle came to the end of his eulogy.

'Did you know Janos Toth?' asked Balthazar.

Sandor looked at Balthazar for a moment as if deciding how much to tell him. 'Yes, Tazi. I knew him very well. He was a couple of years older than me, another countryside boy, from Kecskemet, brought to the big city to make his fortune. We studied at the party academy together.' He paused for a moment. 'Actually it's true what Karoly said. He did live modestly. He had no interest in clothes or money or luxury. All he cared about was information. He had a lot of that. One of his brothers is buried here as well.'

'Where?'

Sandor gestured to the right. 'Over there, with the other '56ers.' The '56ers was the name given to the street fighters who had been executed by the communist regime after the failed 1956 uprising.

'If the communists executed his brother, why did he join them?'

'Janos Toth had three brothers. Gabor fought with the revolutionaries. He was wounded in the leg. They waited until he recovered, then they hanged him. Nandor, the youngest, joined the secret police when he was eighteen. He was at Republic Square when the crowd stormed the party headquarters. You know what happened next?'

'Yes,' said Balthazar. 'I've seen the pictures.'

A British journalist had started photographing as a furious mob gathered outside the building, convinced that the secret police were torturing people inside. Nandor and the other young recruits had come out with their hands up, clearly terrified. Some of the photographs captured the moment when the bullets impacted and the way the boys' faces contorted as they died in pain and terror. They were images that could not be unseen.

Sandor said, 'There were some dark times here, Tazi, not only in the war. Times when you had to pick a side. And sometimes you find yourself on the wrong side of history.' He nodded towards Karoly Bardossy. 'Or you switch early enough, survive and prosper.'

'And the third brother?'

Sandor smiled. 'Csongor was the sensible one. He moved to Szeged and became the director of agriculture for the whole county. He's retired now, spends his time in his vineyard and with his fruit trees.' He scrabbled in his pocket, took out a hip flask, and offered it to Balthazar. 'There's some of his in here now. Fancy a drop?'

Balthazar shook his head. 'No thanks, boss. What will happen to the Librarian's archives? There must be a lot of very worried people.'

Information was power, especially in country with such a murky past as Hungary's. The Librarian's archive was priceless, its secrets able to make or break not just careers and companies but whole dynasties.

Sandor nodded. 'That is the question everyone is asking. That's why they have come. Do you think any of these people are actually here to mourn? They all sighed with relief and raised a glass once he had gone. That's what they all want to know. Where are his files on me? And they don't want to ask on the phone.'

For a moment Sandor was back on the windswept bench at the end of Margaret Island where he had sat with Balthazar the previous day. That was the same place where he had last seen the Librarian alive, the previous October. They had both known that the Librarian was slowly dying.

'And Balthazar, and his boy?' Sandor had asked. 'They are safe? I have your word?'

The Librarian turned towards Sandor, his rheumy eyes locked on his. 'Don't worry, Sandor elvtars, *comrade Sandor. I give you my word. Nothing will happen to them.'*

Balthazar asked, 'And what will happen to the archive?'

'How would I know?' asked Sandor, a smile playing on his face.

'A little bird told me you might. Almost certainly would, in fact.'

Sandor took another slug from his hip flask. 'Wait a few minutes. You may hear something interesting.'

Karoly Bardossy stepped back and another mourner took his place, a tall, silver-haired elderly lady in a fur coat that had seen better days, lavishing praise on the dead man in a similar vein. She was followed by Reka Bardossy.

Balthazar watched Reka as she nodded briskly at her uncle, then began to speak. He had spent quite some time with the prime minister over the past few months, dealing with the aftermath of the arrest and shooting of Mahmoud Hejazi, the terrorist known as the Gardener, and Pal Dezeffy's failed attempt to pump poison gas through the sprinkler system on Kossuth Square. They had talked at length about her dreams of modernising Hungary, of fixing the health system, overhauling education, creating a transparent business environment. Balthazar believed her, but all that was much easier said than done, especially in a country as haunted by its past as Hungary – and where her plans threatened so many powerful vested interests. Reka, he thought, could barely manage to contain her distaste for the dead man, but still managed to mouth some platitudes about Janos Toth's record of service to his country, before continuing.

'As many of you know, Janos Toth left his archive in the charge of his lawyer, Andras Zsigmund.' Reka nodded towards a portly, grey-haired man in a brown raincoat, standing among the mourners. 'In his will, Janos ordered that this archive be destroyed. Zsigmund *ur* was of course ready to carry out his client's wishes.'

Reka paused as a wave of almost physical relief washed through the mourners. Several turned to each other, smiling, as Reka continued speaking. 'But before executing his plan, he contacted me.'

The mourners stopped smiling. Several glanced at each other.

Reka waited, enjoying the moment before she spoke. 'I thought long and hard when I was informed of this provision. After consulting with my advisors, and several historians, I have decided that the overwhelming historical importance of the materials means Janos Toth's archive must be preserved for current and future generations. We Hungarians, more than most peoples, know how important a nation's history is to its wellbeing and sense of itself.'

By now Balthazar, like all the mourners, was completely focused on what Reka was saying. Her gaze moved around the mourners and seemed to settle on her uncle.

'It is inconceivable,' she said, 'that such a rich source of information about our country, reaching back to the end days of the Second World War, should be destroyed. Therefore, I have issued an executive order to preserve all the materials in Janos Toth's archive, including his notes, correspondence and recordings. Mr Zsigmund has agreed, of course, to comply with the order and his colleagues have proved very helpful in compiling the material in question.'

Reka paused for a moment, letting her words sink in. A loud murmur carried through the air.

Preserve all the materials in Janos Toth's archive.

Balthazar had to stop himself grinning as he watched the mourners looking urgently at each other, back and forth, hissing and whispering, near-panic written on their faces.

Reka resumed speaking. 'Janos Toth's archive is being moved to the state national archives as we speak. I speak for the nation when I say how grateful we are that a man of such unflinching, clear-eyed vision kept such a detailed, contemporaneous record of how so many important decisions in our political, economic and diplomatic history were kept. A record that will be preserved for posterity.'

Reka waited for a moment, a half smile playing on her face. She caught Balthazar's eye and subtly inclined her head in recognition.

Sandor Takacs looked at Balthazar, nodding slowly, his eyes wide in recognition of Reka's gambit. '*Ugyes lany*, clever girl.'

Balthazar said, '*Nagyon*, very.'

It was indeed an impressive move. Reka was now untouchable – if she won the next election. Otherwise, she had just made an awful lot of powerful enemies. Balthazar looked at his watch. It was coming up to 2.30 p.m. He needed to be back at Liberty Square at 3.30 p.m. to meet Attila Ungar at the office of his security company. He did not think there was much more to learn here, but with much of Hungary's business and political elite gathered in one place, it was always worth looking around. He spoke quietly to Sandor. 'I'm going for a walk. I'll be back in a few minutes.'

Sandor nodded at him. 'Good idea.'

Balthazar walked away from the pantheon, into the main ground of the cemetery. The rain had stopped now and the air smelled damp and fresh. It was a peaceful place, well looked after, with trim paths and verdant greenery. Balthazar stopped for a moment to look at the grave of Norbert Szilard, 1859–1934. *Father, brother, son, much missed* said the inscription on a plain black marble headstone, now dull and weathered with age. A statue of a hooded mourner stood by the slab, covered in ivy. One eye peeked out at him from behind the dense greenery.

A long line of vehicles was parked in the pathways – the usual array of expensive Audi and Mercedes saloons, with several Range Rovers, the newly favoured vehicle of the city's *uj gazdagok*, new rich. He walked down the pathway, idly checking out each car. One of the Mercedes, he saw, was dark blue, with tinted windows. It was a few years older than the cars parked next to it, grubbier and needed a clean.

He crouched down in front of the car and checked the left-side headlight. It wasn't cracked but looked dull and worn. He ran his finger down the plastic casing. It was smeared with dirt and grease and scored with tiny indentations and scratch marks from stones and gravel thrown up by other vehicles.

Balthazar checked the side headlight on the right-hand side. It too wasn't cracked. In fact the plastic covering was shiny and pristine – it was, he realised, brand new. He took a photograph of the number plate, then turned back and returned to Sandor Takacs.

TWENTY-TWO

Liberty Square, 3.30 p.m.

Attila Ungar held Balthazar's phone in front of him as he watched the footage Vivi had captured from one of the street cameras overlooking Klauzal Square. It showed Balthazar walking through the park, almost up to the man sitting on the bench, until he raised the walkie-talkie to his ear. At that point Balthazar turned and started sprinting back towards Dob Street.

Vivi had zoomed in on the man and added a few seconds of still footage of his face into the main clip. He was clearly visible and would be recognisable to anyone who knew him. The footage ended and Attila handed the phone back to Balthazar.

'Do you know him?' asked Balthazar.

'We'll get to that.'

That was a yes. 'Who is he?'

'I told you. We'll get to that. Be patient. But are you sure you want to pursue this one, Tazi?'

'Why wouldn't I?'

Attila wrinkled his nose, waved his hand back and forth in front of his face. 'Smells bad. Uzis, shootouts. Israelis. Historians poking around places best left undisturbed.'

'You know about that? The historian?' asked Balthazar.

Attila shrugged. 'I hear things. Thing is, Tazi. You've put me in a bit of a spot here. A couple of weeks ago we signed a substantial contract with Nationwide. I'm now their chief security officer. That means overseeing everything from the doorman at the headquarters to threat analysis.'

Balthazar thought for a moment. Attila was CSO for Nationwide. This was news. Maybe it had been a mistake to come here. The most elementary threat analysis would have Elad high on the matrix, and now Balthazar too, poking around with his questions. The footage of the man on the bench was clear enough – someone else among Balthazar's contacts would know who he was.

'And what kind of threats is Karoly Bardossy worried about?' asked Balthazar.

Attila smiled as if to say, *Let's stop fucking around here*. 'Look, Tazi, essentially we are on the same side. I want to know where Elad Harrari is and what he has found out, and so do you.'

Balthazar and Attila had once been partners, starting out as beat cops in the District VIII station, working the streets together. Attila had grown up in poverty in a *panel-lakas*, a small flat in a tower block in a remote part of the city, far from Liberty Square. His father had killed himself when he was young and his mother's subsequent boyfriends had been spongers, alcoholics, or both.

Attila leaned forward as he continued, 'So really, if you think about it, we would both be so much better off, Tazi, if you came to work for me.'

Attila had come a long way since their days in the back alleys of District VIII. Barely five foot six, he wore a crisp white shirt, one that looked tailored and showed off his impressively muscled physique, the result of years of weightlifting. He gestured around his modern office, with its pale walls dotted with framed prints of Hungarian classic paintings and stylish modern furniture. 'Look at this place. Beats our old station in District VIII or the police headquarters.'

As if on cue a knock on the door sounded. Attila shouted to come in. An attractive, miniskirted young woman in her twenties with a bob of brown hair walked in, carrying a tray laden with coffee cups, milk and Italian biscuits. She smiled at Attila and Balthazar, placed the tray on Attila's desk and walked out. 'Much nicer scenery, too,' said Attila as he watched her leave. 'Csilla is an intern. Very eager to please. You'll love it here.'

Attila had been an excellent cop, sharp-eyed, street-smart and able to see through any concocted alibi or story, no matter how plausible. But eventually the complaints from suspects that they had been knocked about, even beaten up, in the holding cells became too numerous to ignore. Attila had resigned and joined the Gendarmerie.

Last autumn, while working for Pal Dezeffy in his attempt to bring down Reka Bardossy, Attila had arrested Balthazar and detained him in the basement of an abandoned villa in Buda, once used by the communist-era secret police as a torture chamber. But when Attila found his father's initials scratched on the wall, together with the dates of his incarceration, he had changed sides and helped Balthazar escape. After Reka Bardossy had dissolved the Gendarmerie, Attila had founded his own security company. Its headquarters was in a neighbouring building to the 555.hu newsroom, also overlooking Liberty Square.

Balthazar looked around Attila's office. It was true, it was much more comfortable than his rickety desk and worn-out decor and fittings at the Budapest police headquarters. Attila had once offered Balthazar a position in the Gendarmerie. He had immediately declined.

'Again?' Balthhazar asked. 'So many job offers.'

Attila had grown some hair and looked almost respectable, less a thug and more the kind of businessman that would be useful in tough negotiations with questionable partners. But his shirt could not quite disguise the tattoo of talons on the side of his neck.

'This is not the Gendarmerie. No rough stuff. That's all over,' Attila said, emphatically shaking his head. 'I am a respectable businessman now. Apart from Nationwide we have some nice fancy clients – American CEOs living the expat high life, Chinese businessmen, German bankers. I have to focus on Nationwide now, but the others need looking after. I'll at least triple your salary, Tazi. You can have a modern office, a hot secretary, expenses, a car – whatever you want.'

He looked down at his desk for several moments, exhaled, then looked back up at Balthazar. 'Look, Tazi. I owe you one. I was going down the wrong path.'

Balthazar thought before he answered. On one level, Attila's offer was tempting. A tripling of his salary – even a fifty per cent increase – would be welcome. Much of it already went on maintenance payments to Sarah and lately she had been asking for more to cover Alex's fees at the American school, even though she was paid far more than him in her job at Central European University.

There was a chance, he guessed, that at least part of Attila's company was clean and legitimate, probably the part dealing with the expatriates. But if he ever left the police force, it would be to work for his people in some way, not for an overpaid job in a private security company. His conversation with Erno Hartmann still echoed in his mind, about a museum commemorating the Poraymus and the Gypsy contribution to Hungarian culture.

Balthazar said, 'Thanks, Attila, really. I appreciate the offer. But no thanks, at least for now.' He leaned forward. 'So, the guy in Klauzal Square? Because I remember the face,' he said, raising his eyebrows. 'But not the name.'

Attila had the grace to look almost embarrassed at the reference to their encounter last September on Republic Square, when Balthazar had been surrounded and threatened by Attila and his fellow gendarmes. 'OK, Tazi, this one I will give you. Geza. His name is Geza. I offered him a job when we set up the company, but he said no, said he had some freelance offers.'

'Geza what?'

'Geza Kovacs.' He smiled. 'Maybe he's a relative of yours.'

Kovacs was Hungarian for Smith. And Geza Kovacs, whoever he was, was clearly not a Gypsy. 'Very funny. He's not.'

Attila looked thoughtful for a moment. 'OK. Let's be serious. So what's this Kovacs doing sitting around in Klauzal Square with a walkie-talkie in his hand, being stalked by the country's best-known cop a few seconds before a gunman on a motorcycle shoots up a car and nearly kills our favourite state security officer?'

Attila had not lost his ability to sum up the situation in two or three sharply focused sentences. Balthazar smiled. 'I was hoping you could help me with that, Attila.'

'Like I said, Geza's gone freelance.'

'For who?'

'*Nem tom*, dunno,' said Attila, sliding into street slang. 'Really. Otherwise I would tell you.'

'Where does he live?'

'That I do know.' Attila took out a pen, wrote down an address on a slip of paper and handed it to Balthazar. 'Tazi,' he said, his voice serious, 'be careful.'

TWENTY-THREE

Liberty Square, 4 p.m.

He would be careful, but before going anywhere, Balthazar decided, he would head home and grab something to eat. He stepped out of Attila's office building onto a small piazza that led onto Liberty Square. From there to Dob Street was just a ten-minute taxi ride, but he would walk at least some of the way, he decided.

The walk would help clear his head, and give him to think through where he was with this case. On the way he would call Anastasia and send her the address Attila had given him, so she could send someone over there to meet him. Or maybe she could come herself. He smiled at that prospect, realised that would be his preferred option.

A memory flashed through his mind. One day last September, before things had turned violent with Attila and his henchmen, Balthazar and Anastasia had been sitting in her car when he had threatened them.

'The Duchess and the Gypsy. A real Hungarian scene. Someone should paint you both,' Attila had said, with a smirk on his face.

Still, it was quite a sharp line. The Duchess and the Gypsy. One descended from a line of noble aristocrats and the other from a dynasty of pimps. Could that ever work? Was she even interested? Perhaps, he thought. He remembered how she had blushed when they were joking about Ilona Mizrachi, the times when their eyes had met, the way her leg had brushed against his in her office. Or maybe Anastasia was just being polite and friendly, overcompensating a bit like many liberal-minded Hungarians, to show she wasn't prejudiced? Sooner or later, he knew, he would find out.

Meanwhile, he had something more pressing to deal with. He needed to speak to Alex. Text messages were generally fine – Alex's generation seemed to live by them – but he needed to hear his son's voice. Partly because that was more intimate than staring at characters on a mobile screen, but also because he could hear the timbre and tone of his voice, and sense Alex's emotions and mental state. Now that Sarah had started playing power games again with his access to his son, he made sure to speak to him every day.

Balthazar glanced at the makeshift Holocaust memorial as he walked through Liberty Square. A young woman with pale-blond hair and wire rimmed glasses was poring over the testimonies in the plastic folders that were pinned to the rope. He walked over for a moment and watched a tour guide point at the statue of the eagle swooping over the Archangel Gabriel, explaining how inaccurate the imagery was, that Hungary had been many things during the Nazi occupation, but an innocent angel was not one of them.

He was about to walk away when one of the testimonies caught his eye. The photograph and the testimony were very clear – the photograph especially so. He walked over to take a closer look. Miklos and Rahel Berger had been attractive couple, he thought, clearly devoted to each other. The names meant nothing to him but there was something about them that looked almost familiar – why was that?

He read through their brief biography until the last line – *Tragically, they were too trusting* – then his telephone rang, breaking his line of thought.

He took the call – it was Gyula, a contact of his in the municipal vehicle registration department, ringing with information about the number plate Balthazar had photographed at the Librarian's funeral. Balthazar had not made an official request to check the plate, as that would be logged and go through the system. Instead he had used every Hungarian's favourite entranceway: the *kiskapu,* the little gate where a contact would do an unofficial favour, one to be banked for future credit.

'That Merc's registration number you asked me about. I checked it,' said Gyula.

'And?'

'It's a company vehicle, registered to Nationwide. There's no more information, no name in particular, just the usual company details.'

'Thanks, Gyula. I owe you one,' said Balthazar and hung up.

Distracted by the call, he turned away from the memorial, and headed down Oktober 6 Street. The drizzle had stopped, the wind now just a breeze and the air pleasantly brisk before the chill of the night set in. The building on the corner was a former communist-era office building, now a bank, covered in pale marble. At first glance it looked yet another identikit homogenous structure. But Budapest could still surprise and delight. On its side the architects had preserved a giant fresco of two-metre-tall, sturdy, jolly peasants leading a horse as they brought in the harvest.

So what was his harvest with this case? It was now Friday afternoon. Elad had been missing since Wednesday evening.

Balthazar had checked with Eva *neni* earlier in the day. There was still no sign of him or any messages. She was frantic with worry.

At least he now knew that it was a Nationwide vehicle that had been following Elad. But would Karoly Bardossy really be that unconcerned about leaving a trail of images and evidence that led back to his company, then arrange to kidnap Elad? Especially when he was such an obvious suspect? Maybe Karoly thought his wealth and connections made him invincible. Perhaps he was, for the moment. But nothing lasted forever, especially in Hungary, and Karoly would know that. Why bring so much heat down on yourself?

And what was the connection with the gunfire on Klauzal Square? That was a warning, but from whom? Had Karoly Bardossy, or someone at Nationwide discovered what Vivi had found on the decrypted memory stick? And if they had, then how? Vivi had not told anyone about the contents of the memory stick, except him and Anastasia.

And all of this against the backdrop of the forthcoming visit of the Israeli prime minister in three days – and Ilona Mizrachi's not very subtle fishing expedition at the Boho Bar. Hopefully, Geza Kovacs would be able to help make sense of this – if he was ready to talk about whoever was paying him.

For a moment Balthazar felt a familiar, unwelcome pressure on the back of his neck as he walked down Oktober 6 Street. The kind of pressure that signalled someone was watching him, perhaps even following him. Then it faded and he was suddenly hit with a burst of nostalgia, displacing everything else.

This part of downtown, the heart of District V, was home to Central European University where Balthazar had for a while been a PhD student. He strolled past the spacious Israeli-owned falafel bar where he had spent so many lunchtimes experimenting with the menu of unfamiliar dishes, and Bestsellers, the English-language bookshop whose friendly owner, Tony, was always happy to recommend his latest choice – and which had always proved enjoyable.

A clutch of students exited one of the CEU buildings on the other side of the road, a 1970s communist-era horror of smoked glass and concrete in the middle of a row of elegant Habsburg apartment houses. Their laughter and happy chatter carried across the street as they discussed where to go for a drink. For a moment Balthazar envied them, not just their youth, but the world of possibilities that they would soon face, where decisions were still to be taken, of life paths that could still go in a myriad of directions.

And what of the decisions he had taken? He could have had that life, had he wanted, spending his days in the not very arduous world of academia, surrounded by the young, smart and quite often beautiful.

All the doors had been open. His supervisor in the history department, an amiable New Yorker of Hungarian background called Misha Fekete, had made it clear very quickly that a comfortable career was in easy reach if he finished his PhD. Misha was well connected in academia. There was talk of scholarships to Oxford or Harvard, tenure at CEU. The Holocaust was thoroughly documented, and still pored over by academics around the world. The Poraymus was neither.

Balthazar had been in prime position to contribute to the study, even build a new discipline – and who better to do that than a Gypsy historian? Yes, there was the suspicion that he would be a *disz-Cigany*, a decorative, token Gypsy, in place to highlight the liberal credentials of those around him, rather than on merit. But really, so what? Everyone needed a patron – at CEU it would have been Misha Fekete; at the Budapest police he had Sandor Takacs.

To himself at least he could be true. Balthazar would never tell Sandor, or indeed anyone, but one reason – perhaps the real one – he left academia was the prospect of seeing Sarah every day at the CEU building, in the café, the lifts and the libraries. Losing his wife – and to another woman – had been a hammer blow, even a humiliation. Perhaps he should have listened to his parents' warnings before the wedding – Gypsies and *gadjes*, their culture, their values were too far apart for a mixed marriage to ever work. Gypsy women did not leave their men.

His family had been stunned – even more so when he had eventually explained that Sarah had moved in with a woman. Every one of his relationships after Sarah had seemed to prove that true: Eniko had left him, for reasons he still did not fully understand, and now Kati too. Still, he had a son, handsome and smart, to whom he was growing closer as he grew, and that was something that made everything else worthwhile.

Balthazar turned the corner from Oktober 6 onto Zrinyi Street. The narrow pedestrian thoroughfare led onto St Istvan's Square and the Bazilika, which housed the right hand of St Istvan, Hungary's first king. He paused for a moment to take in the view of the church. Dusk was falling now and the Bazilika looked magisterial, its giant domed roof and two towers softly illuminated against the darkening sky, streaked with grey.

The wind picked up and the pressure on the back of his neck intensified.

This time he took notice. Was he being followed? He stopped for a moment, glanced at his watch, then looked up and down the street as if looking for someone. The pedestrians flowed around him: commuters hurrying home for the evening from their jobs in the nearby ministries, a few hardy tourists and the CEU students.

Nobody stopped, but that did not necessarily mean anything. A professional team might be following him in a box, with one tracker behind him, another to the side and the third in front.

He really needed to call Alex, and also message Anastasia the address that Attila had given him. But first he needed to see if he was being watched. Surveillance detection drills used all sorts of techniques to see if someone was following: taking the suspected watchers into a chokepoint, like an underground passage or a staircase, to see if they followed, getting on a bus or train then getting off at the very last moment, going into a department store and moving up and down between floors or simply stopping and checking as he was now.

Sometimes it was necessary to lose watchers without them knowing that they had been detected. At other times it was more useful to get up close and personal, to let the watchers know that they had been busted. This, he sensed, was one of those times.

There were six benches spread out along Zrinyi Street. Balthazar sat down on the one in the middle, which faced an art gallery on the other side of the street. He took out his phone and scrolled through the numbers, as though he was looking for someone's contact details, but was actually watching the street with a sharp, intense focus. Several tables stood outside a café on the other side of the street, a few metres further towards the Bazilika.

Nobody sat down next to him – that would be a very amateur move. But among the crowd two people stopped walking. One, a woman who looked to be in her late twenties, suddenly became very absorbed in the painting on display in the window of the facing art gallery.

She wore a grey skiing jacket and had black hair under a black baseball cap and stood with her back to Balthazar. A few yards further up the street, a man of similar age in a brown skiing jacket, stopped, turned and sat down at the café's outdoor table. Both had white wires trailing from their ears.

He watched them for a moment. Neither caught his eye. None of this was evidence that he was being tailed. Lots of twenty-somethings had Apple earpieces and wore skiing jackets in winter.

Balthazar looked again at the young woman and the man at the café table. Where were they from? There was something about them, their gait, the way they held themselves, their alert, hyper-confident manner, that made him think they were not Hungarian. Were they British or American? He didn't think so. In any case there was no reason for the British or the Americans to be following him. There was a reason for another country's operatives to be doing so.

A waitress appeared at the table and handed the man a menu. He held it high to his face. Balthazar dropped his head, apparently absorbed in his telephone. In reality he was looking across the street. The man glanced at him over the edge of the menu. The young woman was still staring inside the art gallery. The door opened and an assistant invited her inside. She declined and her head turned rightwards for a fraction of a second at the man sitting at the café table before returning to the gallery window.

Balthazar smiled to himself.

The man, or the woman? The woman, he decided.

He walked across the road and stood next to her. 'Nice paintings. I like the one in the corner,' he said, pointing at a colourful portrait of an elderly lady looking out of a window at the sea. 'She looks like she knows someone is watching her.'

The young woman took a half step to the side, glanced at Balthazar, not quite able to keep her irritation from showing. 'If you say so.'

'I do.' He tilted his head to the side, looked intently at her. She had brown eyes, full lips and a plump face. 'You know, you really look like a friend of mine.'

She stared at Balthazar, her eyes darting sideways for a moment. 'That's nice. But I'm waiting for someone, so thanks but no thanks.'

'I'm sure you know my friend,' said Balthazar.

'I doubt it. Please stop bothering me, or I will call the police.'

Balthazar took out his wallet and showed his identity card. 'I am the police.'

She stepped further away. 'I have no idea what you are talking about. Please leave me alone. Or I will shout for help. There are lots of people here.'

'I don't think you are going to do that. But I'll tell you my friend's name anyway; that might help. She is called Ilona Mizrachi.'

The young woman stiffened and a pink flush crept up the side of her face.

'Give Ilona my regards,' said Balthazar.

TWENTY-FOUR

Mariahegyi Way, Obuda hills, 4 p.m.

Karoly Bardossy stood on his terrace and sipped his single-malt whisky as he looked out over Budapest. Far in the distance, past fields and woodland, the city glimmered faintly, as dusk fell. His city.

Sometimes he felt intensely protective of the Hungarian capital. He had reshaped it, moulded the skyline, scraped forty years of dirt off grandiose Habsburg apartment houses, demolished communist-era concrete piles, put up new towers of glass and steel, dragged Budapest into the twenty-first century. Here and there he could make out the faint shapes of Nationwide' constructions – tall office blocks, residential parks, new museums, shopping centres, gated residential compounds. Whatever was coming – and he sensed that something was – nobody could take away his legacy.

The air here was fresh and clean, sharp with the coldness of winter. The ten-room villa stood high on the top of Mariahegyi – Mary's hill – and could only be reached by a winding, narrow track through the surrounding woods.

At the end of the track was a security cabin, manned twenty-four hours a day by armed guards. A CCTV network covered the track and the surrounding woodlands, as well as the entrance to the house, the terrace and every room inside, except of course his bedroom and bathroom.

A short tarmacked path led from the security cabin to the entrance of the villa, and the house itself was surrounded by a high wall. There were no neighbours here for several hundred metres in every direction, which is how he liked it. He had designed the villa himself and overseen the construction in conjunction with an Italian architect whose usual clients were Russian oligarchs. All the materials, from the imported marble tiles to the custom-made furniture, and the labour had been run through the construction division of Nationwide. The architect had accepted payment in 500-euro notes from the company's petty cash.

Karoly turned to look at the house, its angular modernist facade softly illuminated by light-sensitive LEDs. His home had not cost him personally a single forint, which only increased his pleasure.

He took another sip of his whisky when a soft cough sounded to his right. He turned to see Porter, his butler, standing expectantly. 'Will sir require the jacuzzi later tonight?'

The jacuzzi sat on a raised teak platform and took up most of the corner of the terrace. Thursday nights were his midweek break and time for female company, lately in the shape of two nineteen-year-old countryside girls who claimed to be sisters. He had no idea if that was true, but they certainly seemed very well acquainted.

He had first met them in the VIP suite of his favourite brothel, a villa in the Buda hills, on the recommendation of the madam. Karoly had been a customer there for many years, as was much of the city's business and political elite. After his wife died last year there was no need for him to spend two hours travelling there and back. Instead he had asked the madam to send the girls to him.

The owner, an overweight Gypsy, had agreed, but had asked for an extra fifty per cent. Money wasn't an issue and Karoly had paid. Usually, the three of them would bathe together, drink a substantial amount of vintage champagne, then retire to the master bedroom. It was Porter's job to have the drinks ready on ice as well as a supply of gourmet snacks.

Karoly shook his head. 'No thank you, Porter. Not tonight. Please call the agency and cancel the visit. I'll call you if I need something.'

Porter had served in the British army for twenty years before retraining as a butler. He had previously worked for a Kazakh oilman until his master was found slumped at the wheel of his Ferrari with a small hole in his forehead. Six feet tall, with laser-sharp hazel eyes and close-cropped steel-coloured hair, the Englishman was the very soul of discretion. Still, Karoly kept the cocaine in his bedroom, where he parcelled out the lines himself. It would not be fair to ask Porter to engage in illegality, and anyway, by that stage even the most discreet butler would doubtless prefer not to be a witness to what followed.

Porter nodded as he retreated into the house. 'Very good, sir.'

Karoly glanced at his watch, a vintage Patek Philippe that had cost him €50,000. He had bought the watch for his son Fulop as a thirtieth birthday gift, an attempt to repair their fractured relationship. But Fulop had moved out the day after his mother died and cut all communication with his father. He was now living in London, in a part of the city Karoly had never heard of, called Shoreditch, working for an internet start-up, or so the private detectives he had employed told him. The private detectives had found out details of Fulop's bank account in London. Karoly had transferred £5,000. Fulop had immediately sent it back.

Karoly tipped back his glass and finished off the whisky. The bottle, from a small distillery on the isle of Jura where he had bought a controlling interest, stood on a small table nearby, with a crystal bowl of ice and jug of water. He looked at the drink then shook his head.

He needed a clear mind for this evening. Instead he walked over and poured himself a glass of water. He took a long drink, sat down on one of the chairs on the terrace and picked up a cream-coloured cashmere blanket from a nearby pile and wrapped it around his shoulders. For now he had more immediate problems than a son who refused to communicate.

His relations with Reka had been cool for years, but had turned glacial after the death of his brother, her father, in a skiing accident more than twenty years ago. He had hoped that when Reka became prime minister he could repair things – Hungary was a small country, where the political and business elites were entwined and her predecessors had usually courted him. Instead she had cancelled a number of major state contracts with Nationwide, citing irregularities in the tendering process, and refused to meet either him or anyone from his company.

This was problematic, not just because of the immediate loss of income, but also because of the way he – and Nationwide – were now perceived. News of the government cancellations spread quickly. Nobody wanted to be tainted by association. Suppliers were putting their prices up, demanding faster payments. Other company tenders, from different divisions and for non-government work, were not chosen, even though their price was the lowest. Still, none of this would matter if he could make this deal with the Israelis work. Unimaginable riches would follow.

He drank some more of the water as he stared out into the night. Far overhead an airplane passed on its way to land at Budapest's Liszt Ferenc airport, its wing lights blinking in the night. Fulop, Reka, sliding turnover, cancelled contracts, all of these he could deal with. The first two were probably not fixable and the others would not last forever. The company had enough cash in the bank to tide over several lean years. But the real problem was the Israeli historian.

Karoly had used his contacts in the police and security service to track Elad Harrari's communications and internet research. But the Israeli was very security-conscious, almost as though he knew he was being watched. He used a network of VPNs and proxy servers to disguise his trail across cyberspace. One of Karoly's people had told him that he thought Elad was filming the car that was following him. Elad's emails were just brief notes to his family at home; he rarely spoke on the phone and much of his work was carried out in the archives of the Jewish Museum, none of which were online. Karoly had told the firm's communications people to stonewall every request, and then sent the lawyers in with threats of criminal prosecution. None of that had worked. They all knew that Elad was not breaking any laws. The smarter play, perhaps, would have been to welcome Elad with a smile and promises of cooperation then drip-feed him bits and pieces of information that led nowhere significant. But it was too late for that. Elad Harrari, Karoly sensed, was onto something. Which made him dangerous.

So where the hell was he?

Karoly had put out an alert at the borders and at the airport, but nobody going by that name, or answering his description, had left. Still, Hungary bordered seven countries and there were no checks on the road to Vienna. He could be anywhere by now, writing up his report.

And that was what worried Karoly the most. There were two dark secrets in his family and both were inextricably bound together. For a moment he was back at the funeral of the Librarian, watching his niece speak to the crowd, all of whom were asking a question she was about to answer:

After consulting with my advisors, and several historians, I have decided that the overwhelming historical importance of the materials means Toth's archive must be preserved for current and future generations.

This was a disaster waiting to happen.

The Librarian had known everything. Somewhere in that pile of musty papers, he would have made the connection between those two events. And if that came out it would be the end of everything: of Nationwide, his comfortable life in this house, of any chance of reconciliation with his son and the deal with the Israelis. Especially the deal with the Israelis. Instead he would be looking at shame, disgrace and a lengthy prison sentence. Anxiety twisted inside him.

He would have a little more whisky, he decided. He stood up and walked over to the table and poured himself a small measure, topped with a few drops of water. He sipped the mix, trying to focus on the complexity of the bouquet and the aftertaste. Honey, bitter oranges and notes of dark chocolate, the whisky master had promised him. But the alcohol was sour in his mouth. He could definitely taste bitter oranges, but not much else.

Still, at least the long-term project was coming to fruition. The money spent on funding the Workers' Alliance and the National Renewal Movement was really proving its worth. The hoodlums and thugs rampaging around on demonstrations were also earning their pay. Support for the ruling Social Democrats was leaking in all directions. It was commonplace now to hear that the government was losing control, that law and order were collapsing.

Karoly smiled at the memory of the first time he had seen the mock-up of the posters declaring *Eleg volt a komcsikbol*, We've had enough of the commies. And those pictures of Reka, sharpening her features, adding shadows, making her look devilish. What did they call it – photoshopping? It was a marvel. Technology made it so easy to manipulate people. There were no communists any more, had not been for decades. That system, the idiotic ideology of equality, had only ever been a front, a gloss to ensure that once the old, bourgeois elite had been disposed of, a new one could take its place. With the Bardossy family front and centre, and profiting handsomely – at least until Reka became prime minister. His greatest enemy was his own niece. For a moment he wondered what his brother Hunor would say, then quickly banished the thought.

Instead, he considered the events of the last couple of days. The smoke bomb at the bar and the shooting outside had not worked. The cop, the state security woman and her hacker sidekick were all still on the case. And the video file that he'd hoped would bring Reka down had fizzled into nothing. Part of him was admiring. His niece had played that gambit rather brilliantly. All of which meant he would now have to escalate. It was dangerous, but there was no option.

And if the Israeli had disappeared, the cop had not. He lived in the same building as where Elad had been staying. There was some connection to a neighbour, an old Jewish lady. The cop was key, Karoly knew. He was a Gypsy, could not sit still, roamed around the city day and night. How hard could it be to bring him in? This should have been a job for the new security company that he had hired – which he would never have done if he had known that Attila Ungar was the cop's former partner.

But that didn't matter in the end, because people a lot more efficient than the hoodlums and ex-gendarmes that Attila employed were on the cop's trail.

Karoly glanced at the house. Once he had him here, he would find out exactly what he – what they all – knew.

TWENTY-FIVE

St Istvan Square, 4.45 p.m.

Balthazar stepped away from the young woman, and carried on walking up Zrinyi Street into St Istvan Square. Once he was a few yards in, he turned back for a moment. The young woman was sitting with the guy in the brown jacket at the café table. They seemed to be arguing.

He smiled and walked down the side of the Bazilika. The church entrance was higher than street level and the building was surrounded by a low wall and several steps. He sat on the steps for a moment watching the flow of people around him and called Alex. Nothing happened. He looked at his iPhone, an old model that lately was frequently playing up. The screen had a hairline crack and volume control barely worked. The handset was definitely coming to the end of its useful life. It was time to change it, he knew. He tried again – this time the call went through. The phone rang and rang but eventually the boy picked up.

As soon as he spoke, his dull, resigned 'Hi, Dad' told Balthazar that something was wrong. He let Alex speak for a while, with his usual chatter about school and his friends, then asked, 'What's the matter?'

'It's not *fair*,' he exclaimed, his voice full of youthful indignation.

'What isn't?' asked Balthazar. He sighed inside, as he knew exactly what was coming. The only question was why – what would be the latest reason?

'Mum says I can't come now on Saturday. I have to be with her. I have to go to American *nagyi*'s birthday.'

American *nagyi* – grandma – was Sarah's mother Elsa Rosenbaum, a well-to-do New York socialite and widow who spent her time doing good works. Elsa had just made a substantial donation to a new library wing at CEU and was also close friends with the American ambassador, a person of considerable influence in Budapest, as Sarah often reminded Balthazar when they argued about his access to Alex.

Balthazar watched a tourist couple stare at the menu of the small restaurant across the road. 'How? American *nagyi* lives in New York.'

'She's flying in tonight. Mum says we are going to the Four Seasons for dinner to celebrate. She's seventy or something. She's OK, but it's going to be *soooo* boring. I don't want to go. I want to be with you, Dad.'

Balthazar felt a familiar anger start to rise up. The divorce agreement gave him one day with Alex every other weekend and two hours one evening a week. His erratic work hours meant he could not always arrange to see Alex for the two hours in the evening. Sarah sometimes let him trade that evening for an overnighter on the weekend and that had been their plan for Saturday.

'Let me speak to Mum,' said Balthazar. 'Give her your phone.'

'She's not here. She's gone to the airport with Amanda.'

At one stage a year or so ago, Balthazar had seen so little of his son that he had taken to borrowing an unmarked police car and parking across the road from the entrance to the

American school in the village of Nagykovacsi, just outside Budapest, simply to get a glimpse of Alex.

Sarah had complained to her mother, who had complained to the American embassy, which had eventually filtered through to Sandor Takacs. He had been sympathetic, of course, but had warned Balthazar off. For a while last year Sarah had been more cooperative, even easy-going. Sarah and Alex had been on Kossuth Square last autumn when Balthazar had stopped Pal Dezeffy's attempt to spray poison gas through the sprinkler system. Balthazar became the most famous cop in Hungary. After that Sarah had, he sensed, basked in his reflected glory. Certainly Alex had been immensely proud of his father. Sarah had even let Alex stay overnight several weekends in a row.

The problem wasn't Sarah, but Elsa. Elsa was always polite to Balthazar but could never quite hide her disapproval of her daughter's former choice of husband. Amanda, Sarah's girlfriend, was another matter. A daughter with a female partner gained substantial points in Elsa's social circle and Amanda was always lavished with gifts. Lately there had even been talk of Sarah and Amanda getting married. Maybe he could arrange to switch Saturday night to Sunday, and then take Monday off and spend the day with Alex.

'I'll sort it out, Alex. Don't worry. I'll take a day off on Monday. We'll spend the day together. Don't sulk with Elsa. Be nice with her. Use your Gypsy charm. Big smile, big eyes. She'll melt. We'll sort it out.'

He could sense Alex smiling down the line. 'OK, Dad, you got it.'

Balthazar ended the call and put his handset away. He shivered for a moment. The remaining daylight was fading rapidly now and sitting still had chilled him.

He would take a taxi home, he decided. There was a line of cars on the corner of the street. Several were private vehicles whose drivers looked like they were hoping for a naïve tourist that could be taken on a long, winding and lucrative route. Balthazar looked up and down at the cars until he saw one registered to a reputable company.

He walked over, opened the door and sat next to the driver, a dishevelled-looking man in his fifties with sparse grey hair. He glanced at Balthazar, asked, 'Where to, boss?'

'Klauzal Square.'

'Which way?'

'Take Dohany Street. Let's go via the synagogue.'

The driver nodded, and turned onto Bajcsy-Zsilinszky Way, a wide, eight-lane road that cut through the heart of downtown. Balthazar sat back, glad to sit still for a moment and watch the city slide by.

The driver, he saw, glanced at him in the mirror several times. This wasn't unusual. A tall Gypsy man in a black leather jacket wasn't welcomed everywhere. But the driver, he sensed, was curious rather than wary or hostile. Like every Budapest taxi driver he had a plastic card on display with his name and registration number: Zoltan Lukacs.

'Zoltan,' said Balthazar, 'have we met?'

The driver shook his head as he cut into the bus lane to avoid the traffic. 'No, boss, I don't think so. But you're that cop, aren't you?'

Balthazar smiled. 'Which cop?'

'The famous one with the fancy name. The one who took down that terrorist last autumn, then stopped that nutcase Pal Dezeffy from gassing everyone on Kossuth Square. I'm sure it's you.'

'It's me. You're right.'

The driver smiled at Balthazar with a row of crooked teeth. 'I knew it.' He turned the meter off. 'This one's on me, Detective. And there's something else you should know.'

'*Mondd*, tell me.'

'People are asking about you. The word's out. Anyone picks you up and takes you anywhere, there's 20,000 forints in cash for information.'

Balthazar sat up, alert now. Twenty thousand forints, around sixty euros, was a lot of money for a tip-off. Zoltan glanced at him again. 'I won't say anything, of course.'

The car turned left onto Deak Square. A large island divided the road, itself bisected by the 49 tramline. Balthazar watched a yellow-and-white tram pull away, heading towards the Freedom Bridge and Gellert Hill. Balthazar looked at the driver. Could he believe him? He had no choice, and Zoltan had given him some useful information, if it was true.

'Tell me more. Who's offering the money?'

Zoltan laughed. 'I don't know, boss. He didn't say his name. But he's been doing the rounds of all the taxi ranks downtown, handing out 5,000-forint notes like sweets. Told us to take this, and if we had anything for him, there would be another 15,000 in it for us.'

He glanced at Balthazar again in the mirror. 'Lots of the guys took it. I didn't.'

'That's OK. What did he look like?'

'Fancy clothes, but rough-looking bloke. Looked like he's been in a fight once and not done very well. His nose had been broken, set badly, it looked like. He gave out a telephone number to call.'

The road narrowed as Deak Square became Karoly Boulevard. The car moved into the left-hand lane, ready to turn into Dohany Street. Balthazar glanced at the Great Synagogue as they drove by. Built in the neo-Moorish style in the late nineteenth century, it was the largest synagogue in Europe, a statement of pride and belonging by a once great Jewish community.

He had first visited the building on a school trip. Like the neighbouring Jewish Museum, it had been a run-down place, its once ornate decor and fittings worn. The rows of wooden benches still had the nameplates of the families who had once sat there. But if the building was scruffy, it was deeply atmospheric and he had thought it a haunted place. Over the years it had been painstakingly renovated and restored to its former glory. He had been inside several times with Sarah, accompanying her to services on the major holidays. The interior was stunning. Now it glowed like a golden sentinel, its imposing facade and twin towers looming over the edge of the city's Jewish quarter.

Balthazar asked, 'Did he give his name, or any name?'

The driver shook his head. 'No. Said there was no need. Whoever answered the phone could help. They would send the rest of the money over.'

'Have you got that number, Zoltan?'

The driver nodded. 'Of course. I'll give it to you when we arrive.'

The car turned onto Sip Street, then weaved through the narrow back street of District VII until they arrived at Klauzal Square a few minutes later. The pavements were already crowded as the *buli-negyed*, the party quarter, slid into the weekend. Balthazar smiled as he watched a man in his twenties, wearing a pink tutu over his jeans, direct his friends, each with a beer bottle in hand, into a nearby bar. Even in January the stag parties still poured in. On the other side of the road, two ultra-orthodox Jews, dressed in their Sabbath best, walked briskly to synagogue.

The car arrived in Klauzal Square, and pulled over on the corner of Dob Street. The driver turned and handed Balthazar a slip of paper, with a mobile number on it. 'That's the number.' He shook hands with Balthazar. 'Pleasure to meet you, Detective. I hope it all works out for you.'

Balthazar thanked him and stood for a moment, watching the car drive off, when he noticed a young woman watching him.

She was leaning against the fence around the park, smoking a cigarette, several yards away. She wore a puffa jacket, miniskirt and knee-high black leather boots and looked familiar. She looked up as he walked closer.

Balthazar was right, he realised, he did know her. Her name was Marika, and she came from a small Hungarian-speaking village in northern Romania, near the border. Marika was twenty and worked for his brother Gaspar.

She had been walking the streets for a few months, but was likely to get promoted soon to one of the brothels. Marika was a pretty girl, with soulful brown eyes, and long black hair. She was supporting a family of five brothers and sisters, most of whom were unemployed, an alcoholic father and a mother who sometimes found work as a cleaning lady.

Marika saw Balthazar looking at her and waved at him. 'Hallo, Tazi,' she said. Tazi came out as Tathi, as Marika had a lisp. 'Sure you don't need warming up, Detective?' she asked, laughing.

Balthazar smiled, shook his head. It wasn't a serious proposition. 'Thanks, Marika, but not tonight.' Not any night, not with any of his brother's girls, not ever, but there was no need to tell Marika that.

There were Gypsy girls like Marika across eastern Europe, he knew. Bright, entrepreneurial, street-smart but with little, if any, agency over their lives. Across the post-communist world, from the Baltic coast to the Balkans, Gypsy communities were stuck in the same cycle of deprivation and grinding poverty. Much of that was due to the endemic prejudice and discrimination that they faced, but their own community's mores and customs were also part of the problem.

Much of Roma society was not well prepared for modernity and did not know how to adapt to it. Women might rule at home, but Gypsy society was still deeply conservative and patriarchal. Teenage girls were still often quickly married off and encouraged to have as many children as possible as quickly as they could. The young mothers had little education and there were rarely books in the house.

The children came quickly but they were often classified as mentally handicapped by teachers and education authorities, even though most of them were not. They received a sub-standard education which gave them few or no life skills for the twenty-first century and so they too left school at sixteen, got married and began raising a family and thus the cycle of deprivation continued. Or, like Marika, they worked the streets. That said, a growing number of young Roma were entering education, becoming entrepeneurs and building careers, often in the creative fields. Balthazar's sister Flora ran a gallery that frequently showcased Roma artists and his youngest brother, Melchior, was a musician. Successive Hungarian governments had launched several initiatives to help break the cycle of poverty and unemployment but there was still a long way to go.

The sight of Marika made him sad, churned up all the complex, contradictory emotions he felt about his father and his brother. Yes, his father had ostracised him, but Balthazar knew that he had self-exiled as well. Balthazar had known full well what his father would do once he joined the police.

But once this case was over, and they had found Elad, he would continue the conversation with Gaspar that the two brothers had started recently. The Kovacs family business was under pressure – the refugee crisis and the collapse of Europe's borders had opened up a space for new gangs from the Balkans to muscle in and move up through central Europe to the west.

In the old days the heads of families from across the region had met together and carved up the region into spheres of influence like the diplomats at Versailles redrawing the post-war map of Europe. The newcomers, some from the former Soviet Union, others from Albania, cared nothing for those agreements, positively relished tearing them up, sometimes using extreme violence. The Kovacs family, like many of the city's veteran criminal dynasties, could not – would not – compete.

Balthazar's plan was to become legitimate. The brothel in the Buda hills would be turned into a proper hotel, the bars would no longer offer extra 'services' but would provide food instead. Tourists were pouring into the city, foreign investment was soaring. Even the eighth district now had its own fancy 'Palace Quarter', where it bordered District V downtown. There was plenty of money to be made, without exploiting anyone. Gaspar was open to the idea – like many businessmen operating on the edge of legality, he yearned for respectability. The problem would be persuading Laci, his father.

But that was in the future. The immediate question was what was Marika doing here? District VII was out of Gaspar's territory, controlled by another Gypsy family, the Lakatos clan – and they were under pressure from a new alliance of Serbs and Albanians. Sending Marika here was exposing her to danger.

Balthazar asked, 'Marika, why are you here? You're well out of your patch.'

She shrugged. 'Gaspar said to try my luck.'

Balthazar shook his head. 'Bad idea. It's not safe.'

Balthazar reached into his pocket, took out 10,000 forints and handed it to Marika. Her eyes widened. 'But I thought you said you didn't…'

He smiled. 'I don't. This is for you, keep it, don't tell Gaspar. Go home. Buy yourself a proper dinner. Tell Gaspar I told you to. Tell him I said he needs to stick to District VIII.'

She swiftly pocketed the money. 'Thanks, Tazi, but he'll be angry.'

Balthazar rested his hand on her arm. It felt thin under her puffa jacket. 'He won't. I'll tell him myself not to send any more girls here – that I gave you the evening off.'

Marika leaned forward and kissed Balthazar on the cheek. 'Thanks, Tazi.'

TWENTY-SIX

Andrassy Way, 7 p.m.

Ilona Mizrachi watched the three dots on the screen of her laptop, each pulsing steadily on top of a map of Budapest. Two, red in colour, were stationary at a fancy hotel on the Great Boulevard near Rakoczi Square, where the operatives were waiting in a café for their instructions.

The third, blue dot was moving up Dob Street towards the Grand Boulevard, where it turned right, in the direction of District VIII. Ilona knew immediately where the phone's owner was going. Her sense of unease, which had been growing exponentially over the last twenty-four hours, took another leap forward.

The main point of Alon Farkas's visit was buried in a small secret annex to the agreements he would sign on Monday. Everything else – education, trade, the reception for the Holocaust survivors – was theatre. Farkas knew what was contained in the secret annex, of course, but he had a notoriously short attention span – his main focus was keeping his fractious coalition together so he could stay in power. But most of those involved in his visit to Budapest had no idea of its hidden provisions. The secret annex was even being kept from the Israeli ambassador to Budapest – and from Reka Bardossy. But Ilona had a copy.

The annex was one page long. It outlined how Nationwide Ltd. would sign a licensing deal, the first of its kind, with its new Israeli partner. Hayam was a software firm set up by veterans of Israeli military intelligence and Mossad. Ilona had just discovered that Shlomo, the deputy ambassador and her head of station, sat on the board of Hayam.

Hayam had a sure-fire winner of a product, but it needed Karoly Bardossy's contacts and introductions to sell it. Few Muslim or Arab countries would buy from Israel, but a Hungarian label was a very different matter.

Everyone loved Hungary, handily situated in the centre of Europe. The country was a member of the European Union and NATO but was still the gateway to the west for the east, and vice versa. Hungary had excellent diplomatic relations across the developing world. Karoly Bardossy had a network that stretched back decades and still reached across the Middle East, the former communist states and Soviet Union. Not just of businessmen and women, but of former intelligence operatives who either still ran the domestic security services or used their contacts to enrich themselves. Bardossy's contacts were a potential goldmine. If all went well in Hungary, Nationwide – and Hayam's owners – would make millions. Shlomo would finally be able to buy himself one of the villas in Herzliya, an expensive beachside city, that he spent of much his day looking at online.

Ilona had signed up to her agency to serve her country, to guard against threats, whether physical, economic or political, to the state of Israel. On balance, she could just about rationalise the trade deal to herself. There were many ways to serve one's country and helping its exports was one. It was not for her to judge how ethically acceptable Israeli exports were. Russia, China, even the United States were all working on similar programmes. It was just a question of who got to market first.

But being part of some kind of off-the-books black operation that involved a gunman opening fire with an Uzi on two women and throwing smoke bombs into a café owned by the grandson of a Holocaust survivor wasn't what she had signed up for. She knew from personal experience that once the gunplay began, it was hard to stop – and nearly always triggered retaliation.

Perhaps it was because she was partly Hungarian, but either way, she was not about to let District VII, or any part of Budapest, get turned into a shooting gallery. Ilona had a very good sense for people, which was one reason she had been recruited by her service and given her current job. She had once met Karoly Bardossy. Underneath the faux charm, she had thought him utterly ruthless.

For a moment she was back in the Boho Bar, listening to Balthazar recount the short version of his life story. She really would like to hear the longer version, she realised – and perhaps take the time to tell him her story. It would certainly be better than another night sitting here on her own, watching television.

Ilona sat back and looked around her apartment. Andrassy Way was a glamorous address, home to some of the city's most spectacular apartment houses. Her flat had high ceilings, ornate plasterwork, marble fireplaces, glossy wooden floors. Budapest was her first foreign posting. Initially she had been thrilled to move here, loved the sense of space and history in her grandiose nineteenth-century apartment building, which was a listed monument. But lately it had palled. The flat was far too large for one person. The lounge alone was bigger than her place in Tel Aviv. It wasn't permitted for her to date anyone who was not Israeli. The medical and dental students were too young, the businessmen too old, and frequently too touchy. Anyone at the embassy was out of the question. She was lonely.

She looked at her watch: it was 7 p.m. The Sabbath had commenced. Her grandmother would be bustling around her flat in Bat Yam, just south of Tel Aviv, where the family gathered every Friday night, serving soup, passing the *cholla* bread.

After the meal was finished the stories would begin, of life in Budapest and Baghdad. Ilona never tired of her grandmother's stories, hearing about how she had escaped from the Budapest ghetto and the year-long odyssey before she arrived in Haifa. Without the help of Gypsy smugglers, Ilona's grandmother would never have made it to Palestine. They had helped her escape across the border into Romania, and passed her along a network of relatives that reached across the country to the border with Bulgaria and then through to neutral Turkey.

Ilona's phone rang and she took the call. She watched the blue dot move along the Grand Boulevard as she listened to the angry voice before replying. '*Slicha*, Shlomo, I'm sorry. Yes, we have the target address. No, I don't know where he is. The program is not working. It's new, it's still buggy.'

She held the handset away from her ear, the angry male voice audible around the room, and allowed herself to get annoyed. Sometimes it felt like all her life men had either been shouting at her or trying to get into bed with her, her boss included. 'Listen to me, Shlomo. Fix your shitty software. Is it my problem that you are out somewhere and don't have your computer with you? I don't know where he is. Yes, I'll call you as soon as I hear anything.'

She ended the call. Shlomo could fuck off. The tracking software was working perfectly. The lies came easily, but Ilona had been well trained. She spoke fluent Hungarian but was under orders not to let it be known – appearing ignorant of the language frequently brought a rich harvest of information as she eavesdropped.

The red dots were still stationary in the hotel café, waiting for her instructions. The blue dot was almost at Rakoczi Square. She had no intention, she realised, of calling Shlomo, or anyone else, to keep them updated.

The two operatives were freelancers brought up from Serbia. This wasn't a termination mission, but their instructions were to take Balthazar somewhere and rough him up enough so that he told them what he knew about Elad's research – and where he might be. That prospect, and the events so far, were enough to make up her mind about what to do next.

Ilona looked at her screen again. The blue dot, Balthazar, was inside the building.

She looked at her screen again. The red dots were moving now, toward the target address. It was just a couple of hundred yards on foot, but they were moving faster than walking pace – they must have jumped on a tram.

She took out a burner phone, tapped out a text message, sent it, then made a call.

'David,' she said, 'it's me. I need a courier. When? Now, of course.'

TWENTY-SEVEN

Rakoczi Square, 7 p.m.

Balthazar stood outside the entrance to the flat where Attila had said he would find Geza Kovacs and pushed the doorbell.

A shrill ringing sounded then faded away. He waited for a few seconds then pressed again. The bell rang again, then nothing. The door was narrow, its dark-brown paint streaked with grime, a match for the gloomy decor of the cramped, dimly lit corridor. A single light bulb hung from a cable halfway down the passageway. The air was stale and unmoving and the smell of frying drifted up the main staircase. A few feet away someone had painted a giant letter Z in black and silver on the wall.

After several seconds of silence Balthazar stepped forward and listened for the sounds of movement or voices inside. There were none. He checked the piece of paper that Attila Ungar had given him: Flat VI/VI, 14 Rakoczi Square. Flat number six on the sixth floor.

He was in the right place. This was number 14, and this was the sixth, top floor of the building. The dwellings here were smaller than those lower down, their ceilings lower and their rooms more cramped. Many had lacked indoor bathrooms until recently.

Balthazar had prepared for his visit. He had several plasticuffs in the pocket of his leather jacket and was also carrying his Glock 17. He had checked the floor plan on the land registry database before he had arrived. Flat VI/VI was a one-room studio, with a small kitchen and bathroom.

The flat was a couple of metres from the old tradesman's staircase at the rear of the building, which opened onto Nemet Street. The apartment looked out onto the inner courtyard. It was the kind of place he knew well, where many of his relatives had lived, with two, sometimes three, generations somehow eating, sleeping and living together in the same space. Some of them still did.

Balthazar stepped to the side and gently pushed the door with his forefinger.

It swung open.

He suddenly remembered that in all the excitement of losing the people following him, he had forgotten to tell Anastasia where he was going – but now it was too late.

His heartbeat speeded up and he drew his weapon. He stepped inside. The flat stank – a sour mix of stale cigarette smoke, sweat, rancid fat and more. 'Armed police! Is anyone here? Make yourself known,' he shouted. 'I repeat, this is the police,' he exclaimed, his voice fading as he saw what the room contained.

Geza Kovacs was sitting on a worn green-and-brown sofa bed, his legs splayed, what was left of his head resting against the wall behind him.

His T-shirt was splashed with red, as though someone had squirted him with paint. A grey-and-crimson smear crept up the wall. It did not look like he had tried to reach for a weapon or fight back.

There was no sign of forced entry. That meant two things:

Geza probably knew the gunman and had let him into the flat, where he had despatched Geza with chilling efficiency. This was a professional hit.

Balthazar's heart was pounding as he looked around the room, once, twice, rapidly scanning the space from side to side. The adrenalin dump turbo-charged his senses. The thick, stale air filled his nostrils, the sound of distant traffic hummed, pale fragments of bone peppered the mess on the wall. A large flat-screen television was switched on in the corner, a game of *Grand Theft Auto* frozen in mid-play. The screen showed a black SUV charging through the night, with several bodies in its wake.

Three pizza boxes were piled on the coffee table in front of the sofa, crusts curling inside. Cans of beer and Coca-Cola were strewn around the room.

Balthazar's breathing turned ragged and he tried to calm himself by slowly inhaling and exhaling through his nose. The stink of spilled beer and food almost made him gag.

The floor plan had shown two doors leading from the main room – a kitchen to the right and a bathroom to the left. He stood to the side of the kitchen door, then pushed it open, his gun in his hand as he stepped inside.

The walls were a faded shade of yellow, spattered with grease behind the ancient gas cooker. Two wooden chairs stood on either side of a creaky table, topped with worn blue Formica. An ancient fridge hummed in the corner. A white enamel boiler was fixed to the wall, its narrow hot-water pipe leading into a cracked sink.

He looked in the fridge – it was empty apart from a box of margarine and half a salami. A half-full bottle of cooking oil, turned dark with age, stood by the cooker.

Balthazar stepped back into the main room, walked across

to the bathroom. He pushed the door open, shouted again, stepped aside for a few moments, then moved inside, his gun at the ready. This room too was empty. The fittings were of similar vintage to the kitchen, another sink with its enamel cracked and scored, a bath with large dark stains. He walked over and looked at the stains. They were brown, dry and ancient, encrusted dirt, not blood.

The room smelled as stale as the kitchen with an extra layer of damp and mould. The flat had not been properly inhabited for a long time. There was nobody else here, he was sure.

He holstered his Glock, took out the scrap of paper the taxi driver had given him, blocked his outgoing number, and called the number written on it.

A few seconds later a mobile sounded in the flat. Balthazar listened for a moment and looked around.

The phone was ringing in the dead man's trouser pocket.

Just as he was about to call the District VIII police station to report the body and to send backup, his screen lit up with the notification of an incoming message. There was no number. He opened the message:

MR CELEBRITY DETECTIVE GET OUT NOW!

TWENTY-EIGHT

Remetehegyi Way, Obuda hills, 7 p.m.

Reka placed the single sheet of paper on the coffee table in front of her, sat back on the leather sofa and carefully placed her stockinged feet on the sheet of smoked glass as she processed what she had just read. The table was an original 1980s Philippe Starck and one of her favourite pieces. The glass top rested on four rubber balls perched on top of each leg and she felt a slight bounce as she settled back. A glass of sparkling water, slowly warming, stood in the centre.

She and her ex-husband Peter had bought the table in Milan on a shopping trip a decade ago, in what now felt like another life. They had loved its quirky style and the high price was no object. Nothing had been too expensive in those days, when money and power flowed towards them like the Danube at high tide.

Reka picked up the glass and took a sip of the water as she contemplated another evening alone. The wine fridge on the other side of the room was crowded with some of Hungary's finest vintages. But she never drank alone, especially since she became prime minister. Peter was gone now, shacked up with his twenty-seven-year-old executive assistant. The news had not been a surprise – their marriage had been one of form only for the last couple of years; and really, how unoriginal to run off with an awestruck twenty-something – but she had still valued his advice and his company, no matter how sporadic. Now she went home every night to an empty villa in the Obuda hills. There was nobody else to take his place, or even on the horizon. And for now at least it was inconceivable to let another man get close to her.

The envelope had arrived by courier, half an hour ago. The motorcyclist had pulled up outside Reka's villa, at which point the two police officers on permanent guard had approached him. He had thrust a slim package at them, then roared off. Neither had caught his number plate, which was anyway smeared with mud, doubtless intentionally. The police officers had handed the package to Antal Kondor, Reka's chief of security. After running it through several checks, he had brought it to Reka.

The envelope inside contained a 'memorandum of understanding' between Nationwide and Hayam, an Israeli tech company based in Tel Aviv. Hayam produced a software program called Shomer, Hebrew for guardian.

Reka already knew about Shomer.

Shomer was the world's most advanced covert surveillance system to be commercially available. It could be implanted on a person's mobile phone without them knowing. It would track their movements, all their internet and social media activity, their banking and shopping and of course would listen in to all their calls. Every phone had its own file in a giant database to where all the information, including sound files of conversations, was sent back.

All the phone's files, browsing, emails, texts, photographs and conversations, could be cross-referenced and analysed for patterns. Several intelligence agencies had this capacity, but there was always a question as to what to do with the deluge of information. Shomer had the answer. It analysed not just the content of individual phones but also used advanced pattern analysis to map networks of contacts: their frequency of interaction, their distance from each other, their shared interests and activities. Shomer's most important USP – unique selling point – was that it used artificial intelligence to predict future patterns of behaviour and network development.

Shomer was fantastic news for authoritarian regimes. But for dissidents, free-thinkers, anyone wanting to organise and challenge the established order, Shomer was a catastrophe. Especially as the software was virtually undetectable, except by the most sophisticated intelligence agencies. Anastasia Ferenczy had already circulated a note to all members of the government and civil service above the level of assistant state secretary, warning them that Israel had developed the world's most advanced spyware. Anyone involved with the forthcoming visit of Alon Farkas was to be extra vigilant when using their telephones and assume that all communications were being listened to. Meanwhile, the technical division of Hungary's state security service was working on a means of finding out if Shomer was present on a mobile phone.

What Reka had not known was that her uncle was secretly planning to go into business with Hayam and use Nationwide, and Hungary, as a cloak for a worldwide marketing drive. The memo explained how. So what was she going to do about this?

Cold water, she decided, that would help. She walked across the lounge to the adjacent bathroom and switched on the cold tap over one of the twin black marble sinks. The water system could be adjusted for freezing cold as well as hot. She turned the temperature dial down as far as it would go and put her hands inside the icy stream. Once her skin was thoroughly chilled, she bent over the marble sink and splashed her face several times, rubbing the water into her face.

Reka closed her eyes for a moment, relishing the icy sensation and hoping it might re-energise her, before staring at herself in the mirror. She saw a woman in her late mid-thirties, still attractive but definitely more care-worn than when she first took power the previous autumn.

The skin around her blue eyes was scored with deeper lines and the whites were marked with tiny veins. She tried smiling at herself, watched the thin lines as they shot out of either side of her mouth. She massaged the skin around her lips and smiled again. There was no change. She ran her hands through her dark-blond hair. It was, thankfully, as thick as ever, but its bounce was fading. Her tresses fell more easily through her fingers, and lay flat on her head when she moved them away. She peered up at the top of her head in the mirror. Her highlights needed some attention too, she saw.

Reka splashed herself again, then took a white hand towel from the small pile by the taps. She closed her eyes as she held the soft cloth to her face.

Did she still miss him? Sometimes, she admitted, yes, she did.

Peter was gone, and she was sad about that, but in truth her ex-husband had only been a means to fill the Pal Dezeffy-shaped space in her life. She had known Pal since they were children, the gilded youth of Hungary's ruling elite. They had been on-off lovers since their late teens, the ultimate power couple.

Marriages, flings, long- and short-term relationships, all these came and went but somehow they could never escape each other. Even at the end, when Pal went berserk, her hold over him had not diminished. Using the gendarmes to take control of Kossuth Square, trying to hijack the sprinkler system, gas the passers-by, all these, she thought, were also a last, desperate, attempt to get her attention.

Now, looking back, she realised that she could have guided Pal in a different direction, one that served the interests of Hungary instead of filling his – and her – families' Swiss bank accounts. Or even done both.

There had been plenty to go round back in the days of *vadkapitalizmus* – wild capitalism – in the early 1990s. Both the Bardossys and the Dezeffys had profited mightily as Hungary transitioned from a one-party state to a free market economy. In Romania the Communist Party had organised a violent uprising and executed its crazed leader Nicolae Ceausescu and his wife, Elena, to ensure that behind the scenes, the same apparatchiks remained in power. Czechoslovakia no longer existed and had split into two countries. Yugoslavia had plunged into years of war and murderous ethnic cleansing.

But Hungary had managed a smooth transition to democracy. There were no riots, no fighting, no mass arrests. The old one-party system had just faded away. The idealistic democrats and dissidents had, for a while, taken political power. But real power – control of the economy and national assets – had remained with the former communists, reborn and renamed as Social Democrats. When the state no longer existed, who owned its assets? Whoever grabbed them first, it turned out.

Reka, Pal, all the former comrades had gorged on the nation's wealth like greedy diners at a *svedasztal*, a buffet brunch at one of the five-star riverside hotels. And yes, she had been part of that, had never questioned the sense of entitlement that had paid for her walk-in wardrobe of designer clothes, this bathroom with its Italian fittings and wet room or the abstract modern art bought in auctions in London, Zurich and New York that hung on the walls of the lounge. But that was then. Enough was enough.

She dropped the face towel into the aluminium basket under the sink. That era, of plunder and corruption, was over.

She would bring Hungary into the twenty-first century, turn the country into a modern state, with a transparent administration and the rule of law for all, not just the privileged elite. That battle would be long and arduous, she knew. The old, dark forces had already begun their fightback to stop her and destroy her government – led, she knew, by her own uncle.

The release of the footage showing Reka killing her assailant had been their first attempt to bring her down. But Eniko's plan had worked brilliantly. The girl was a marvel. A snap telephone poll Reka had commissioned yesterday showed sixty-five per cent of voters believed Reka's line that the video was a sophisticated deepfake – with an even higher proportion of voters under thirty believing so.

The story had exploded across social media but was now fading away. Eniko's hashtag blitzkrieg, and promises to several influencers of a dinner with Reka soon, had also helped. Reka gave herself an ironic smile. Her drive for honesty had started with a gigantic lie. How was she any better than her opponents? Because she wanted to improve the lives of all Hungarians, she told herself.

Reka walked back through the lounge and through the French doors that opened onto a wide, curved balcony, picking up a black merino wool shawl on the way. For a moment she shivered as a cold wind gusted in her face and she pulled the shawl tighter around herself. The house looked over the river and the Pest side of the city. The Danube was a wide ribbon of black, and a single set of lights moved slowly downriver, a barge heading south into the Balkans. The headlights of the cars on the riverbank traced patterns like fireflies. A sea of apartment houses stretched into the distance, windows glowing where families gathered for their evening meal.

Once, it felt like a lifetime ago, she had company in this house – when she had a family, or at least parents. Her father, Hunor, had been killed in a skiing accident in the winter of 1991, soon after the change of system, when he was serving as minister of the interior in Hungary's first post-communist system. He was an excellent skier and the cause of the accident had never been fully explained. Reka's mother had never really recovered from his death and two years later had died of a heart attack.

A memory flashed through her mind: Reka was back in her office last autumn, speaking to the Librarian. One of her first acts was to remove the microphones that he used to bug the prime minister's office. He had walked in immediately:

It would be a mistake to think of me as a fool, Doshi. Your dear father could explain that to you, if he were still with us.

The threat was clear enough, but had the Librarian, or whoever he worked for, really had her father killed? And in whose interest would that be? Now she had taken control of his archive, she might finally find out the truth, or at least some clues.

Why had he gone off-piste and crashed at high speed into a very visible tree, without wearing a helmet, even though he was normally a cautious man? And what had happened to his ski helmet, the one that she had bought him for his fiftieth birthday? It had never been found, and would have saved his life if he had been wearing it.

Part of her was convinced that he had been murdered, but she could not understand why. Sure, her father, like his elder brother Karoly, had done well during the start of the *vadkapitalizmus* in the early 1990s. Like most of the country's ruling elite, they had realised by the 1980s that the old regime was no longer tenable and had started preparing for its collapse. Hunor was no saint. Once the Communist dictatorship started to fall apart he gamed the system to make sure that his family was comfortable and would remain so.

But once the family's wealth was secured, Hunor focused on politics. Unlike his brother Karoly, he did not want to build a massive business empire or compete with the new would-be Magyar oligarchs. Instead his motivation was to build a new democratic Hungary. They had talked about that so many times.

For a moment she wondered at her own motivation. One part, she knew, was her long-running feud with her uncle, who refused to repurpose Nationwide away from being a money-making machine for a handful of directors into something more socially useful. She had commissioned a confidential study from one of Hungary's leading economists to show how easy that would be and sent it to Karoly.

The economist had suggested breaking up the main holding company and redistributing its assets to a network of local firms, especially in the deprived east of the country. Karoly had never even acknowledged the document. Instead he had recruited the economist at double his previous salary, buried him in the firm's research department. Another part was Reka's anger at being manipulated and kept out of the loop over the Hayam deal. Her country would not be used as a front for dictators and corporations around the world to spy on those who threatened their interests.

But overshadowing all of this was the growing realisation that the strands of her life were being woven together into a dark thread – one that reached back through the decades, beyond her childhood, to the most terrible era in Hungarian history: 1944. She needed to make a decision. One which, if she followed her conscience, would have irreversible consequences.

Her relationship with her uncle would not survive. For a moment she felt a pang of regret. For a while, in her younger years, she and Karoly had been close. She had learned a lot from him about the world of business and its intersection with politics – until she had, perhaps, learned too much. The knowledge of how Nationwide Ltd. had been born, and at what cost, had been a burden on her for as long as she could remember, like a heavy weight dragging her down, souring her comfortable life.

Reka had never confronted Karoly with what she had discovered but each time she had tried to steer the conversation to the origins of the company he had made it very clear that this subject was off limits. Once he had walked out of the room.

She watched another light move down the Danube, this time much faster than the barge. It looked like some kind of speedboat. The pilot seemed to be enjoying himself as it weaved back and forth across the waters. Now, she realised, was the time. The weight was about to be lifted.

Reka walked back inside, suddenly feeling almost elated. Firstly, she called Eniko, asked her to come over immediately. Eniko agreed. Then Reka called Antal Kondor and outlined what she wanted him to do. Her request, he said, would take about half an hour to organise.

She sat back and waited, idly flicking through the channels before watching the state television evening news programme.

Her government ratings had stabilised, the newsreader, a handsome former water polo player in his late twenties, announced. There was still a long way to victory in the coming elections, she knew, but it was a good sign.

She looked closer at the newsreader. She had met him once or twice at various government receptions for sportsmen and women. He had made it clear he found her attractive. Perhaps for her looks, or perhaps for her power – most likely a combination of both. For a moment she considered inviting him round later.

She wasn't looking for intellectual conversations, but something more elemental. That would be one way, in her experience a very effective one, to release the stress and tension she felt. Perhaps in a few days, once she was through this crisis.

She checked her watch – twenty-eight minutes had passed since she had called Antal. At that moment, her doorbell rang.

She walked over to the video screen above the entry pad. Antal stood in front of the camera with a thumbs up then held four fingers up. Reka smiled, mouthed 'thank you' and walked back to the sofa. The four fingers meant that the number of the mobile telephone she was about to call ended in four. There were ten handsets in total, each with the same first ten digits in their numbers, which she had memorised. The video entry phone buzzed again – this time it was Eniko. Reka let her in, thanked her for coming over at short notice, took her coat and led her through the lounge.

There the two women sat down. Reka explained her plan and the backstory. It took several minutes.

Eniko listened carefully, asking a couple of questions along the way until Reka stopped speaking. She looked shocked at first, then thoughtful. 'Your grandfather Tamas really did that?'

Reka nodded.

'And how long have you known this?'

'Ever since I can remember. It's been a burden my whole life.'

Eniko exhaled sharply. 'Sorry, but you don't get the sympathy vote. At least your family survived.'

'I know, and I'm not asking for sympathy. Or understanding. But I need you to work with me on this, and to know that I can rely on you.'

'And do you have the paperwork to prove it? We will need evidence if you want to go public about your family's secrets.'

'Yes. I do.'

Eniko slowly shook her head. 'First the video of you on Castle Hill, now this. Is there anything else I should know about, Prime Minister?'

Reka looked her in the eyes. 'Actually, there is one more thing you need to know, and I promise you that you will, very soon. Meanwhile, if this is too much and you want to go, you are free to leave, of course. I trust you to keep what I have told you confidential. But please decide, Eniko, are you in or out?'

Eniko sat back for a few moments in silence. They both knew that she was not going anywhere. 'OK, I'm in. But meanwhile, why release this now? What's the rush?'

'Because it's time. Nothing stays secret forever.'

'Maybe, but there will be severe consequences. It will be the end of Nationwide – or at least of your uncle's business career. That will blow back on you. It's your family story, which means it's your story as well, especially if you knew about this all these years and did nothing. It may blow up the trade deal with the Israelis. You do know that?'

'Of course. But it will be out there. And on our terms. What did you say yesterday? – we have to own the story. That worked very well. So will this. We will own this story.'

Reka walked over to the wine fridge and took out a bottle of Siller, a rosé so dark it was almost a light red. 'Will you?' she asked.

Eniko nodded. 'Sure, but only a little, and only once you have made the call and she is on the way here.'

'Agreed,' said Reka as she walked across the room to a minimalist Scandinavian sideboard and extracted two wine glasses.

'Prime Minister, are you sure…' Eniko said, suddenly hesitant, 'that this is not some kind of elaborate revenge on your uncle? I hope I am not speaking out of turn. But I know you two have fallen out.'

Reka smiled. 'No, Eniko, of course I am not sure.' She paused for a moment, turned serious. 'Who knows? Maybe I am working out some childhood trauma. But that trauma is rooted in what my family did in 1944 and what my uncle covered up for decades. And that needs to be told. No more secrets.'

Eniko half-smiled. 'What a story. Then let's do it.'

Reka nodded then picked up her phone, entered a new number and pressed call. There was no answer at first.

Reka waited a few moments then called again.

This time she heard a female voice that said 'Hello, who is this?' in a very uncertain tone. That was understandable.

Reka started speaking, her voice calm and confident.

TWENTY-NINE

Rakoczi Square, 7.10 p.m.

Balthazar quickly read the text message as he stood in the bathroom, his palms wet with sweat, his heart still racing, then read it again.

MR CELEBRITY DETECTIVE...

Ilona.

Was this a genuine warning, or another of her mind games?

Decide.

The man he had come to see sat dead in the next room. His brains were splattered up the wall. He had been asking around about Balthazar, offering money to strangers for information.

The message was real. The only reason for Ilona to tell him to get out now was that more trouble really was on the way. How she knew that – and where he was – was something he would think about later.

The dead man on the other side of the wall had been killed within the last hour or two – there was no sign of rigor mortis. Whoever had shot him was probably a long way from Budapest by now, if not out of the country.

Rakoczi Square was very close to Ulloi Way and the road to the airport. For now, the first thing he needed to do was call the District VIII station for backup and the white suits, the forensics team who would seal the flat and look for prints and other evidence. Balthazar had already informed the local cops that he would be in the area and told them to possibly expect a call from him – but he did not want to give any more information about his mission in case it leaked.

He slipped his Glock back into his holster, took his phone from his pocket but his hands were sweaty and he fumbled. The handset fell to the ground, hitting the bathroom's tiled floor with a sharp snapping sound.

Balthazar swore to himself and picked it up to see the small crack on the screen had turned into a much larger one. He tried quickly to dial the police headquarters but no numbers came up, no matter how many times he jabbed at the digital keypad. The phone was dead.

He slipped it back into his trouser pocket and quickly walked through the main room and into the kitchen. He picked up the bottle of cooking oil and exited the flat, closing the front door quietly behind him as he stepped out into the gloomy, unlit sixth-floor corridor.

The building had no lift. He could hear voices and two sets of rapid, distant footsteps getting steadily louder as the men came up the main staircase.

Balthazar unscrewed the light bulb hanging in the corridor and placed it in the side pocket of his leather jacket, then moved down to the entrance to the rear staircase. He opened one of the double doors, stepped through and closed it behind him, stepping out onto the landing – a small flat area.

He was in luck – the double door had two round handles, one on each. He took out a plasticuff from his leather jacket, looped it around the two handles, slid the end through the ratchet and pulled it tight. A few hard kicks would soon snap the plasticuff, but it would buy him some time.

The rear staircase was narrow and unlit, unused by the residents. A Bakelite handle poked out of an ancient light switch on the wall by the door.

Balthazar flicked it up and down several times. Nothing happened. He instinctively reached for his telephone to use the built-in torch until he remembered that it was broken. The voices were much louder now, almost on the other side of the door. A few seconds later the door shook as the men tried to force it open.

Balthazar upended the cooking oil on the floor behind him, pouring from side to side to make sure all of the landing was covered, then dropped the empty bottle down the middle of the staircase. He stepped over the oil and took the stairs quickly, one hand on the rickety banister, almost slipping on the stairs' worn, rounded edges.

In a few seconds he was on the fourth floor. A loud bang suddenly cracked the silence, followed by two more. By now he was on the third floor, moving as fast as he could in the dark, the ground hardly visible from the light seeping in through a filthy window.

Another bang sounded from behind the door, then another, the clamour echoing across the staircase. Sooner or later one of the neighbours would call the police.

He passed the second floor, then the first and jumped the last three steps to the ground floor, almost slipping as he landed by the back double door that opened onto the street. There was a wide space in front of the door, and a bricked-up tradesman's lift shaft, long disused, protruded from the wall.

Balthazar pushed the double door to the street several times but it stayed in place. It was locked, he saw, although the wood was old and cracked. He stepped back and kicked the door edge by the lock as hard he could. That was the door's weakest point. The lock shook and a loud cracking sounded.

A sharp snapping noise echoed down the staircase. The plasticuff on the double door on the sixth floor had finally broken. Balthazar waited for a second, then heard a crashing noise as one of the men fell to the ground, then another in rapid succession, followed by a furious string of oaths in what sounded like Serbian.

He could hear the two men coming down the stairs, but much slower now, their steps irregular and their breathing loud and harsh.

He pushed the back door onto the street again, felt the lock strain in its holding. The men's voices were getting louder. They would reach the ground floor in a few seconds.

He kicked the door again. The wood cracked and splintered further. A final kick and it broke and flew open. The sound of the outside world flooded in – children playing in the distance, the buzz of traffic, a siren wailing somewhere far away.

He turned to see figures moving on the first-floor landing on top of the curved staircase. There were two of them, he saw, one tall and almost stooped, another shorter and stocky. Both were limping, their clothes torn and smeared with oil and dirt. The tall man had a gun in his hand; the other, he saw, was about to reach for his weapon.

Balthazar threw the light bulb at them. It exploded nearby with a sharp bang, triggering a further stream of swearing.

'*Jebacu ti mater*,' I will fuck your mother, one of the men yelled. '*Jebi ga*, fuck it,' the other man shouted.

He was right. They were swearing in Serbian, Balthazar realised. He did not speak the language properly, but had spent enough time in Belgrade on international investigations to recognise a Serbian accent and pick up some street slang and swear-words.

It took the men a few seconds to realise that they had not been injured, giving Balthazar time to take cover behind the disused lift shaft and unholster his Glock. He swerved out for a second and fired twice, above the men's heads. The sound of the gun boomed around the enclosed space. The bullets smashed into the underside of the staircase above the men, sending out small clouds of dust.

'Drop your weapons, place them on the ground, then kneel down with your hands behind your head,' Balthazar shouted. 'I am a police officer. You are surrounded. Drop your weapons.'

The siren was getting louder.

The two men looked at each other. The stocky man, Balthazar saw, did as he ordered, and lowered himself to his knees, sliding his pistol in front of him. But the tall man ducked back.

'Can you hear that? The police are coming. There is nowhere for you to escape,' Balthazar shouted, his Glock still trained on them. 'Do not shoot. Drop your weapons. Whatever they are paying you, it's not worth going to prison for the attempted murder of an police officer.'

A burst of furious Serbian echoed down the staircase. The two men were arguing.

A bullet smashed into the wall high above Balthazar's head. He ducked instinctively and fired back instantly, placing two shots a foot apart above the tall man's head. 'I told you. Do not shoot. Drop your weapon. The police are on their way. Next time I won't miss.'

Balthazar fired once more, placing the shot in the centre of the underside of the staircase above the men, sending more dust and chips raining down. 'Drop your weapons,' he yelled.

The tall man shouted, 'OK, OK.'

He dropped to his knees, next to his companion, and slid his weapon away, a foot from his companion's pistol. Balthazar walked over to the bottom of the staircase, his gun still trained on the two men.

His right hand still holding his Glock, he took two plasticuffs from his jacket pocket. 'Catch these,' he said as he threw them up at the two Serbs. 'Cuff each other, keep your hands in front of you, then get back down on your knees. Don't be smartarses. You have opened fire on a police officer, so no fast moves.'

A second siren sounded in the distance.

The two men did as Balthazar ordered, scrabbling and almost falling over. A few seconds later they knelt on the ground, their hands bound in front of them. The guns lay on the ground a few feet away.

Balthazar walked up the stairs and kicked their weapons over the edge of the stairwell, under the metal banister, all the while keeping his Glock pointed at them. Two sharp cracks sounded as both pistols hit the hard concrete surface.

'Stay there,' said Balthazar.

He walked backwards downstairs, still aiming at the two men, making for the two men's weapons. The guns, he saw, were Glock 34s, a more advanced version of his Glock 17, with a longer barrel and greater range and accuracy. Whoever was paying these guys had plenty of money. He kicked the guns further away, into the corner under the staircase.

The first siren sounded even louder now.

Balthazar turned to open the door and looked outside to see a black Toyota SUV with tinted windows coming down Nemet Street. It bumped up onto the kerb and parked on the pavement on the corner, by the back entrance of the apartment building. The vehicle had been repainted, but its contours were very familiar, right down to the metal grill over the windscreen and the windows. Balthazar looked hard at the side of the car. The outline of the word *Csendorseg*, Gendarmerie, was still just about visible under the new paint.

The door opened and Attila Ungar stepped out. He shook his head as he spoke. 'Tazi, Tazi, I told you to be careful.'

'What the hell are you doing here, Attila?' Balthazar asked, although he was already starting to understand the answer.

Attila smiled. 'Nothing that you need to worry about, Tazi. It's all under control.'

Attila walked into the back entrance of the apartment building, looked at both men on their knees at the top of the stairs on the first floor, and shook his head. He turned to Balthazar. 'Nice work, Tazi. Not a scratch on them and they both surrendered. Now don't worry; we'll take over from here.'

He looked at Balthazar's pistol, still in his hand. 'You can put that away. You're quite safe now.'

Balthazar stepped forward. 'These men need to be taken into custody. And not by you. You have no authority here.'

Attila smiled. 'Tazi, you're still a believer. It's quite touching, in a way.'

Balthazar raised his gun hand and pointed it at Attila, who immediately stopped smiling. Balthazar said, 'I told you. You have no authority here. These men will be taken into custody.'

Attila nodded. 'Yes, they will. Our custody.'

He gestured at the black SUV. Two men came out, both burly with buzzcuts. Both carried long-barrelled pistols in their right hands. The weapons, Balthazar saw, were also Glock 34s. The two men stood still, waiting for Attila to give them their orders.

'Your move, Tazi,' said Attila. 'Three of us, and one of you. I would consider de-escalation, if I were you. We don't want a shooting match, do we? And think of all the paperwork afterwards.'

Balthazar looked down Nemet Street.

A police car had parked nearby, its siren sounding and blue light flashing. He could see a driver in the front seat. The black SUV, the two armed men and the unfolding scene would all be clearly visible to him. The siren stopped, the blue light went out. Why weren't the police intervening?

Balthazar waited for several long moments.

There was no movement inside the police car. The driver switched the engine off, sat back and watched.

Attila smiled. 'They're not coming, Tazi.'

Balthazar holstered his weapon.

The two men in T-shirts walked up the stairs to the Serbs, helping them up.

Attila slapped his arm lightly. 'That's better. We don't want any accidents, do we? Don't worry, Tazi, they will be fine. And they will soon be out of your hair, en route to Belgrade.'

Balthazar damped down his anger. Why weren't the cops coming to help? Although he was already starting to understand the answer. 'And Geza Kovacs, dead upstairs?'

Attila looked surprised. 'Geza? Dead? That's nothing to do with us. Really. Nobody is supposed to be dead.'

'Well, he is.'

'That's a shame. He was a good guy. Meanwhile, I need to take care of these two jokers. They were supposed to bring you in for questioning, but I never thought that was very likely. Still, I thought I would drop by and check, just in case.' He smiled. 'Lucky I did, eh? See, Tazi, I still have your back.'

'Attila, what the fuck is going on?'

Attila walked nearer to Balthazar, and spoke quietly in his ear. 'Nationwide, Tazi, that's what's going on.' He looked at Balthazar as he stepped back. 'I told you to be careful. Where are their guns?'

Balthazar gestured under the curve of the staircase. Attila walked over and quickly located the two Glocks on the floor in the corner.

He picked them up and nodded at Balthazar as he walked straight to the SUV. 'And a disarm as well. Nice work, Tazi. Remember, my offer still stands.'

Balthazar watched as the men in T-shirts guided the two Serbs into the back of the black SUV, their hands still bound in front of them. He exhaled hard, ignored the anger he felt. There was nothing to be done. The tall man glared at Balthazar, his face smeared with dirt and oil, spitting insults in Serbian. Attila got in the front seat and the vehicle pulled away.

Half a minute or so later, once Attila's vehicle had disappeared from view, the police car started moving down Nemet Street. It stopped on the next corner, by Rakoczi Square. There were three people inside, he could see: two forensics officers dressed in white suits and the driver, an overweight man in his fifties, who was still talking on his radio.

The driver looked familiar as he levered himself out of the car. His name was Istvan Sandor, aka Pisti *bacsi*. Pisti was the custody sergeant at the District VIII station. It was many years since he had been seen on the streets, not least because his substantial pot belly made it difficult for him to run after or chase any a suspect. Back in his days as a beat cop Balthazar had sent so many local criminals to him that Pisti had asked him to slow down a bit as the system could not cope.

Pisti had worked at the local station for almost twenty-five years and nobody knew District VIII like he did. Pisti had been a helpful mentor to Balthazar and had several times slapped down other officers for off-colour remarks about Gypsies. This may have been because Pisti was friendly with Balthazar's brother Gaspar. The two men often dined together at one of Budapest's high-end restaurants, although Balthazar had been careful to never enquire precisely how that relationship worked.

So why, Balthazar wondered, was Pisti away from his cosy office on a freezing, filthy night like this? Unless Pisti had asked for a transfer to the street, which was unlikely, the answer, Balthazar realised as Pisti approached, was not likely to be good news. Pisti wheezed as he stood still for a moment, his winter jacket straining at the zip.

Balthazar said, 'You saw what happened. Two guys shot at me. Attila Ungar took them away. In plain sight. Where were you? Why didn't you do something?'

Pisti shrugged. 'We got here too late. Sorry.'

'No you didn't. You were parked at the end of the road, watching the show. Who's running law enforcement here? Us or Attila?'

Pisti took Balthazar's arm in his right hand as he spoke.

'*Nyugi,* Tazi, *nyugi*. Take it easy and listen to me for a moment.'

Balthazar stopped talking, feeling Pisti's hand on his bicep, staring at him with his red-rimmed eyes. Something bad was coming, Balthazar could sense it.

Pisti said, 'The bosses want you in at midday tomorrow. Someone will call you soon with a formal request.'

'Why?'

Pisti looked up at the top floor of the building, his hand still resting on Balthazar's arm, then back at Balthazar. 'There's a dead man in there, Tazi. They've got footage of you on Klauzal Square, walking towards Geza Kovacs. You were one of the last people to have any interaction with him. You called in earlier saying you were in the area and that you might be calling us in later. Now he turns up dead. How does that look?'

'Like I anticipated a crime might be committed and warned the local police station so it could deal with it?' Balthazar paused for a moment. He had not called the killing in – his phone was broken. 'How do you know that he's dead, anyway?'

Pisti blustered. 'It doesn't matter. We just know. Look, I believe you, Tazi. But there are other ways to look at this.'

'Do they think I killed them? Because I didn't.'

Pisti said, 'I have no idea what they think. But these are strange times, Tazi. I've got your back, as much as I can, that's why I am here, instead of sitting in my nice warm office. But not everyone is your friend. Bring a lawyer with you when you come in tomorrow.'

Balthazar started with surprise. 'A lawyer? What for? Do they want to charge me?'

'I don't know.'

'Am I in danger?'

'Two Serbian gunmen have already opened fire on you. What do you think? That was a warning.'

Pisti squeezed Balthazar's arm harder, spoke sotto voce. 'Drop this Israeli business and there will be no problem tomorrow. This missing historian will turn up sooner or later. The brass wanted you brought in at dawn with a raid and everything. I pulled in a favour to get you midday under your own steam. You can decide overnight. If you don't come in...' he said, his voice trailing away.

'If I don't, then what?'

'You will be arrested on suspicion of murder.' Pisti let go of Balthazar's arm, moved closer and to the side, his breath warm on Balthazar's ear as he spoke even more softly. 'This is me now, not the police, with some friendly advice. Don't come into the station tomorrow. Don't go to police headquarters, either.'

He stepped back, resumed his official voice. 'Are we clear now, Detective Kovacs?'

Balthazar nodded. 'Completely.'

THIRTY

Hollan Erno Street, 7.40 p.m.

Zsuzsa stared at the ancient Nokia handset lying in the centre of her coffee table.

It shook as it rang, skittering as though it were alive, but eventually the noise ended, without her picking it up. The handset had just arrived by motorcycle courier. The courier had come to her front door, asked Zsuzsa her name and when she said it, had thrust a small padded envelope into her hand, said, 'This is for you', wished her a pleasant evening and left.

The telephone had started ringing a few minutes after she unpacked it. She had been so taken aback by the delivery she had not thought to ask the courier to wait while she opened the envelope, and ask him any of the questions that were now buzzing around her mind.

Who had sent her this museum piece and why, and what was this about? Perhaps this was an elaborate threat. She might even be in danger, she thought, various half-formed scenarios flitting around her mind. She had been lurking at the scene of a shooting, had been observed by the police, asked questions of a suspicious neighbour. Who knew what was really going on in this country?

Zsuzsa picked up the handset and checked the call list.

There was one listed, from an unknown number. She looked at the contacts list: it was empty.

She put the Nokia back down on the table, feeling unsettled, and stared at the framed 1970s Hungarian Railways travel poster on the facing wall. It showed a tranquil, blue Lake Balaton under a yellow summer sun. Holidays, warm weather, perhaps some male company, all that seemed like another world at the moment.

The most immediate question was how she was going to pay her rent. Roland Horvath had called her an hour or so ago, and this time she picked up. He told her not to come back in and that she would be soon in receipt of a letter from the publishers' lawyers, with several detailed questions about her action and movements over the previous few days. She would receive the bare legal minimum of redundancy, which meant, in effect, nothing. All the former employees of 555.hu who had survived the purge had been re-employed by a new company, only formed a few weeks ago, so her previous record of service counted for nothing.

Still, she had made it to the capital, found a place to live and she was a working journalist. She was young, smart and good at her job. She would get through this. Zsuzsa looked around her small studio flat, liking what she saw. The main room served as both bedroom and lounge. One part had been converted to a galley kitchen and another walled off as a bathroom with a stand-up shower. This was the first place she had rented in her own name, where she could live and decorate as she liked.

The flat was sparsely furnished, with a sofa and bed from Ikea and an art deco-style coffee table she had found on the street in last year's *lomtalanitas*, or throwing-out day. The armchair she had bought at a nearby antique shop. The best part was the wide balcony that looked over the pedestrianised street.

She heard the sound of a mobile ringtone and looked down suddenly at the Nokia. The ringing was in a nearby flat, she realised.

She felt jittery, looked back down at the Nokia, unsure if she wanted it to ring again or not. Meanwhile, *rent*. She had enough in the bank to keep going for a couple of months, but that was all. Decent jobs in Hungary's shrinking media landscape were scarce, properly paid ones even rarer. She could, she supposed, take her Nationwide story to newsline.hu. But newsline.hu was running crowdfunding appeals to pay for its staff and premises, so that was no financial solution.

Lately she had been thinking about writing for one of the big western newspapers, like *The Times* or *The Guardian*. *The Times*' correspondent had recently moved to Berlin, so they needed someone in Budapest. But the first thing the editors would ask is what stories she had to offer. What she had on Nationwide would be huge news in Hungary, but was a bit local for the international press. Although the Bardossy family connection did give the story a decent lift. Or maybe she needed a different, bigger story. A decent interview with Reka would be very sellable, she knew. And Eniko had promised her one, once all this was over – whatever *this* was.

She glanced at her watch. She had no other plans for the evening other than watching the evening news and looking through the notes she had downloaded about her Nationwide story from her former editor's computer. Maybe there was something buried there, something she had not noticed yet that could boost the story.

Or maybe this strange phone could get a her a coveted stringer's position with one of the big foreign papers. For a moment she smiled to herself. A minute ago the Nokia was a potential threat. Now it might be the catalyst of a new career. Whatever the mobile represented, whoever had sent it needed to call again so she could find out.

A minute later the ringtone sounded.

Zsuzsa took the call.

A female voice said, 'I wish you a good evening, I am Reka Bardossy, the prime minister. I hope I am not bothering you. There is something I would like to talk to you about.'

Zsuzsa took the telephone away from her ear, held it in front of her and stared at the handset. What was this? The prime minister? Was this a prank? Or Roland's revenge? Or some kind of threat?

Zsuzsa said, 'Is this a joke? Who is this?'

'No, it is not a joke. Not at all. This is a matter of the utmost seriousness. This is the prime minister of Hungary. My name is Reka Bardossy.'

Maybe this really was the prime minister. It certainly sounded like her. Zsuzsa said, 'I know the name of the prime minister. But how do I know that you are really her?'

'Because I just sent you the dark-blue Nokia which we are now speaking on.' Zsuzsa took the phone from her ear and glanced at it. It was a Nokia and it was definitely dark blue.

Reka continued speaking. 'But still, I understand you want more proof. Let me hand you to Eniko.'

A familiar voice greeted Zsuzsa.

Zsuzsa asked, 'Eni, is that you? What's all this about?'

'Yes it's me. Really.' Eniko paused for a moment. 'Zsuzsi, we have a story for you. You've already done half the work.

We can give you the rest. It's massive. The missing part which goes right back to the war and the Holocaust. And you will be able to sell it to the western newspapers you wanted to write for. I can guarantee that.'

Eniko would not lie to her, Zsuzsa knew. Zsuzsa felt that quickening, a subtle excitement, an alertness of the senses, that every reporter lives for. 'I'm listening. Tell me more.'

'Not now. I'll hand you back to Reka.'

Reka said, 'I can't speak on the phone. Eniko has already said too much.'

'OK. I believe it's you. But what do you want from me?'

'Your time, your energy and your expertise. And your trust.'

Zsuzsa's heartbeat speeded up. This was real. And maybe it would be the start of a new opportunity for her. Her dad had always told her in times of disappointment that when one door closes, another one opens. Perhaps this was it. 'So what happens next?'

Reka said, 'This. You pack a bag with several days' worth of clothes and toiletries. Bring your laptop. Take the battery out of your phone. Bring the Nokia. My security chief will come and pick you up. You will be staying with me. It's not secure for you to work on this in your flat. But you will be safe here.'

Zsuzsa frowned for a moment. The prime minister wanted her to move in for a few days, because she was going to give her a story that would put her in danger. 'Can I think about it? This is quite a lot to process.'

'Sure. You have five minutes,' said Reka. 'That's four and a half more than you need. In or out. You decide. I will call you back.'

Zsuzsa hung up and put the Nokia back down on the table, staring at the handset as though she had never seen a mobile telephone before.

She stood up from her armchair and slowly paced back and forth across the flat. That familiar adrenalin rush began to course through her body. It was the same feeling as when she uncovered Nationwide's network of money laundering subsidiaries. This was obviously for real, and something very serious. The war, and the Holocaust, Eniko had said.

Eniko had told Zsuzsa a little about what happened to her family, how her grandparents had survived in an apartment building a block away on a street now named for Raoul Wallenberg, the Swedish diplomat who had saved thousands of Budapest Jews by placing them under Swedish protection, how her mother had changed her name to Terez after the war to disguise her Jewish origins.

Zsuzsa walked outside to the balcony, shivering for a moment in the cold night air as she peered down at the evening street scene, deciding what to do. In warmer weather she always enjoyed sitting here, looking down on the streetscape like a secret spy, staring at the passers-by, imagining where they were rushing to – a date, a secret liaison, a visit to a relative.

In the summer the bars and cafés put out tables and chairs and the street felt almost Mediterranean. But now there were only a handful of pedestrians hurrying home. Two homeless people were bundled up in blankets by the bakery on the corner of the Grand Boulevard. The falafel bar and hipster coffee shop were deserted. Even the patisserie was closing for the evening. This part of the city, in riverside District XIII, was one of the most pleasant downtown areas, with plenty of neighbourhood bars, cafés and bookshops. But Hollan Erno Street and its neighbours were haunted, she knew.

The streetlamps glowed orange over the layer of slush coating the pavement. Zsuzsa peered across the street. She could just make out the two small brass plaques embedded into the pavement on the building facing hers. The brass plaques commemorated Jews killed in the Holocaust who had lived in the adjacent buildings. There were many scattered around District XIII.

During winter of 1944, Hollan Erno Street and its surrounds were known as the International Ghetto, where tens of thousands of Jews were confined in houses nominally under foreign neutral diplomatic protection. But as the Russians advanced, the Arrow Cross became crazed with bloodlust, rounding up Jews from the protected houses, marching them to the nearby riverbank and shooting them into the freezing water.

A few days ago Zsuzsa had finally remembered to stop and read the wording on the plaques outside the building facing hers. She still remembered the terse phrasing: the names, dates of birth of David and Eva Kun and their fate. David was thirty-two, Eva twenty-nine. They were both shot into the Danube in January 1945.

She wondered how it must have been, that last walk to the river nearby, David and Eva knowing these were their last few steps, that they would never have a family, build the lives they had hoped for.

Were they holding hands as the Arrow Cross gunmen screamed at them? Had they shivered in the line-up on the riverbank, heard the sound of the rifles being readied, felt the icy cold of the embankment on their feet as they took off their shoes so the gunmen could sell them later, heard the crack of the bullets as they hammered into their victims? Perhaps they had prayed, or merely sobbed silently.

The Nokia rang again. Zsuzsa took the call. She did not bother with a greeting. 'Yes,' she said. 'I'm in.'

THIRTY-ONE

Tito Grill, Rakoczi Square, 8 p.m.

'So what are you going to do?' asked Goran Draganovic.

'First I am going to finish this. Then I will think about it.'

Balthazar jabbed the last *cevapcici* with his fork, dipped it into a smear of *ajvar*, a spicy pepper paste, and ate it with relish. He drained the last of his beer, put his knife and fork down, and sat back, replete. Despite his plan, he had only grabbed a banana when he arrived home before heading out again to Rakoczi Square. Once the adrenalin had worn off and the excitement of the evening faded away, he was ravenous. 'Thanks. That was very good. Best meal I have had for several days, in fact.'

'Then drop by more often, *brat*,' said Goran Draganovic, using the Serbian word for brother. 'Not just when you're in trouble.' He picked up an unlabelled wine bottle filled with a clear spirit and poured two generous measures into the two small glasses in front of them. 'Now some *sliva*, to aid the digestion.'

'OK,' said Balthazar. 'But just a little.'

As Balthazar ate he had explained part of the story to Goran: about Elad going missing, being followed by the Israelis, about Geza Kovacs and the two Serbs who had tried to abduct him. Goran had listened without saying much.

Unlike many of his Serbian compatriots, he was not voluble, which was one reason the two men got on well. Another was that Balthazar felt at home here.

Nobody stared at him, made remarks or otherwise bothered him. Balthazar rarely went out to eat in District VII, apart from a small old-fashioned eatery on Klauzal Square, run by a Jewish family. He did not feel comfortable in the hipster places. He had several times run into students or academics who he knew from his days at Central European University who looked at him with a kind of horror when he said he had left academia to become a policeman. He occasionally met someone for a drink in one of the less well-known ruin pubs, but even there he was often the only Gypsy male.

In the Tito Grill, however, he could relax. All were welcome, but it was well understood that this was a place where the diners valued discretion and privacy – at least until the slivovitz started flowing on a weekend night and the sound of the Boban Marković Orchestra or another Balkan Gypsy brass band started booming around the room and the dancing started.

It was also where deals were made and sealed, sometimes between 'businessmen' it would be best not to cross. There was no menu and only two dishes were available: *cevapcici*, small kebabs, and *pljeskavica*, a hamburger, both made from a mix of minced beef and pork. Both were served with *ajvar*, fat chips, raw onions and a slice of tomato on a lettuce leaf described as 'salad'. The *cevapcici* were served in either five or ten. Balthazar had opted for five, not sure of his appetite after the events of the evening.

After Pisti and the forensics officers had gone upstairs to the flat where the dead man was, Balthazar had sat for a while in Rakoczi Square, processing the events of the day. Until recently the square had been the centre of Budapest's red-light district, its meagre greenery lined each evening with prostitutes and their pimps. Balthazar's father, Laci, had started out as a pimp here, back in the 1970s, running streetwalkers who serviced their clients in the back streets and narrow alleys.

But the gentrification that had transformed District VII had inevitably spread to District VIII, especially this part immediately behind the Grand Boulevard. The park in the centre of the square had been kitted out with modern equipment, dozens of trees had been planted and new pathways laid. Even the metro station had a fancy new glass-and-steel entrance. The grand old apartment buildings were no longer home to prostitutes, but a new wave of young families looking for affordable flats near the centre. On Saturdays farmers from the nearby countryside gathered to sell their produce and vegetables. There were still a handful of dark, tiny grocery stores that survived by selling *parizsi*, the cheapest form of processed meat, and huge loaves of *fel-barna*, heavy half-brown bread, cheap cigarettes and beer, but they were falling one by one.

Balthazar's encounter with Pisti, and his warning, combined with the recurring image in his mind of Geza Kovacs with most of his head blown away, meant that part of him just wanted to go home – not to his empty flat on Dob Street, but to his proper home, that of his childhood, just a few blocks away on Jozsef Street, to eat his mother's *csirke paprikas* and go to sleep.

But that couldn't happen. After a while, he realised that he wasn't only cold but also ravenously hungry and he walked over to the Tito Grill. The first five *cevapcicis* had disappeared in a few minutes and another five had quickly appeared as if by magic.

The Tito Grill was still holding out against gentrification, a stubborn remnant of another era, not just of the old District VIII, but also as a homage to a country that no longer existed. Framed and mounted over the wooden bar was a red, blue and white Yugoslav flag with a red star in the middle, a prized antique from the partisan era. Ancient faded travel posters for JAT, Yugoslav Airlines, showed the tourist sights of London, Paris and Berlin.

Many of the customers hailed from the former Yugoslav states. During the wars of the 1990s, Hungary had given refuge to thousands of refugees and some, like Goran, had stayed. Still, Balthazar thought, as he looked around the room, there was something different about the place. It had kept its ramshackle charm, but had definitely been spruced up. The walls were now a proper shade of white, not a mucky light grey. The wooden bar was still pockmarked with cigarette burns but had been smoothed and polished, glowing warmly in the dim light. The partisan flag had been reframed. The refurbishment had been subtle, but was definitely noticeable. Balthazar looked down at the plastic table cloth – the familiar red and white checked pattern but the cloth itself was definitely new.

Balthazar said, 'You've redecorated.'

Goran nodded. 'You have a good eye. We are doing well. I thought it was time. But we still have same Balkan charm, yes? Not too shiny?'

Balthazar shook his head. 'No. It's perfect. It looks great. You got it right. You always do.'

Goran smiled. 'Thank you.'

The two men clinked glasses, both saying *ziveli*, Serbian for cheers. Goran knocked his shot back in one; Balthazar took a sip.

Goran's slivovitz was brewed by his grandfather in Subotica, just across the border, and smuggled across. It tasted fresh and clean with a long fruit finish, warming him inside as it slid down.

'Do you know this guy, Geza Kovacs?' asked Balthazar.

'Not in person. But I know his name,' said Goran.

'How?'

'He was asking around, after Reka Bardossy dissolved the gendarmes. Looking for work.'

Balthazar poured himself a glass of water from the jug on the table. 'He found some. He was sitting in the park in Klauzal Square with a walkie-talkie just before the gunman on the motorbike shot up the car.'

Goran shook his head. 'Bad for business. Nobody likes this gunplay.'

Balthazar's mobile rang. He looked at the number, then at Goran. 'I need to take this.'

Goran nodded. 'Should I go?'

Balthazar shook his head. 'No, it's a short call.' He pressed the accept button, listened for a few seconds, said thanks and hung up. 'It was my contact in forensics. They found the bullets in the wall. They were small, 0.25s.'

'Probably Beretta. Maybe the 950. Is very small pistol, short barrel, very easy to conceal.'

The two men spoke English together. Like many Slavs, Goran struggled with using definite and indefinite articles, which did not exist in most Slavic languages. Tall and well built, somewhere in his late forties, Goran had black hair tinged with grey, blue eyes and bushy eyebrows that met in the middle. Over the years he had built an extensive – and expensive – network of contacts across the police, border guards and customs agents.

Goran smuggled more than illicit alcohol. His family had been outwitting every kind of authority for centuries, from the Ottomans to the Austro-Hungarians, the Nazis during the war and the communists afterwards. Goran had never met Sandor Takacs, Balthazar's boss – the two men saw no benefit in being seen together – but his and Goran's families knew each other and had occasionally cooperated.

Goran was now a people smuggler, although not of girls lured to jobs as barmaids only to be forced into prostitution. Instead he ran a kind of travel agency. The JAT posters showed the destinations on offer. An enquiry would elicit the current price. Anyone turned back would receive a full refund or unlimited attempts until they made it through. Balthazar had heard that during the war Goran had served as a sniper with the Yugoslav army, but when he had once asked about those times Goran had changed the topic immediately.

'The question is,' said Balthazar, 'who was Geza working for?'

'Leave it with me. I will ask around.'

'What about the two Serbs who were shooting at me?'

'How do you know they were Serbs?' asked Goran. 'Maybe they were Russians, or Bulgarians. Or Croats.'

Balthazar smiled, looked up for a moment as he tried to remember the oaths sounding down the staircase and his visits to Belgrade. 'Let's see, we had *Jebacu ti mater*, *jebi ga*, lots more about mothers and all sort of suggestions about my future. And I thought Hungarians could swear.' His voice turned serious for a moment. 'Goran, I would like to know more about who these guys are.'

Goran nodded and stood up. 'Let me call someone. I have special phone in the office. I will be back.'

Balthazar watched Goran walk to his office, a small room behind the bar. His network reached across the Balkans but was especially strong in his home country of Serbia. If anyone could find out about the two toughs, Goran could.

A wave of tiredness suddenly washed over him. He closed his eyes for a moment but all he could see was Geza Kovacs. At the time his adrenalin was pumping so hard that the gruesome death, the blood and gore and splatter did not really register, then there had been the action on the staircase, and after that the encounter with Attila and Pisti.

But now the danger had passed and the adrenalin dump had faded. Balthazar shivered for a moment, took several deep breaths. Over the years he had seen plenty of corpses but it was a long time since he had witnessed the effects of several bullets at such close quarters.

He took another slug of the slivovitz. But even the slivovitz could not numb the question that increasingly had been nagging at him – where was his life going? Sometimes it seemed that he had intentionally exchanged the paper stories and accounts of murder in the Poraymus for real, actual dead bodies and that had been a mistake.

Goran returned, interrupting his reveries. 'I have some information. Bad guys are part of clan based in Novi Sad.' Novi Sad was the largest city in northern Serbia, an hour's drive from Belgrade.

'Did they kill Geza Kovacs?'

Goran shook his head. 'No, definitely not. Nobody knows anything about that. Sounds like professional job. These two do rough stuff, but they are not hitmen.'

'They had guns. Glock 34s. Expensive guns.'

Goran shrugged. 'Of course they have guns. They are Serb criminals. But the bullets in the flat were small calibre, you told me. Maybe Beretta, but not Glocks.'

'Maybe they had Berettas as well.'

Goran laughed, shook his head. 'Ladies' weapon. In any case, these are not hitmen. They are second division.'

Goran looked at Balthazar and raised his glass, an amused glint in his eyes. 'Lucky for you.' He peered closer at Balthazar. 'Are you OK? You look pale.'

Balthazar sat back and took a long drink of water, glad to see his hands were not shaking. 'I'm fine. It's been a long day. Who were they working for?'

'This is strange part of story, which I don't understand. I heard one Hungarian businessman, very important guy, wants to stop your investigation.'

'Karoly Bardossy?'

'Yes, that is name I heard. You are making powerful enemies.'

'Seems like it.'

'But my guys in Novi Sad say also maybe Israelis are involved.'

'They are. Tell me more, what exactly did you hear?'

Goran shrugged. 'Just that. One Hungarian businessman and one Israeli ready to pay a lot of money for two guys to find out what you know and give you a message to stop. Why are Israelis hiring Serbs to scare Hungarian cops?'

Before Balthazar could answer Goran, Biljana, the vivacious Serb bar manager, gestured to her boss from behind the bar. Goran stood up, telling Balthazar that he would be back in a few minutes.

Balthazar nodded, glad of some time on his own to think things through. Why were the Israelis trying to scare him off?

He was their best hope of finding Elad Harrari. There was a news blackout on the Israeli historian's disappearance – rumours were flowing around but editors had been told that delicate negotiations were underway for his freedom, which news coverage would endanger. It was a lie, but the editors, for now at least, believed it.

MR CELEBRITY DETECTIVE GET OUT NOW!

But if Israelis were trying to abduct him, why had Ilona warned him to leave? And what to do tomorrow? Pisti's warning had been very direct. If he went to the police station he would likely be arrested and charged with murder. If he did not go to the police, a warrant would be issued for his arrest. He blinked and rubbed his eyes for a moment. How did he end up here?

He yawned deeply. The day's events were now hitting him and the food and alcohol was making him sleepy.

Goran returned and sat back down. 'Our other waitress is leaving, getting married, Biljana says. We need a new one. Do you know anyone?'

Balthazar looked over at Biljana. She was in her early thirties, he guessed, with jet-black hair, high Slavic cheekbones and a deep throaty laugh. She waved at him, smiling widely. She was an attractive woman and good company the few times she had sat with Goran and Balthazar. He smiled and waved back.

'I can ask around,' said Balthazar.

'Thanks.' Goran shot Balthazar a look. 'She likes you.'

Balthazar smiled. 'Really?'

'I think Slav girl is better for you. Not so many games as Hungarians. Yes, we are together. No, we are not. Maybe you, maybe Csaba, maybe Zoltan. Serb girls make their mind up.'

'You are probably right,' said Balthazar, but now wasn't the time for that conversation. Now he needed sleep and to wake up with a reasonably clear head. 'How's the car?'

The car was a turbo-charged Lada Niva, a rugged four-wheel-drive vehicle that was far tougher than its fancy Japanese equivalents that cost at least double the price.

Goran smiled, and knocked back his glass of *sliva*. He held the bottle over Balthazar's glass, but Balthazar shook his head.

'Car is fine,' said Goran. 'Do you want a ride?'

Balthazar nodded. 'Yes, please.'

Goran laughed. 'Fun ride, like last time? Or normal ride?'

Balthazar had last sat in Goran's vehicle the previous September, during the refugee crisis. Goran had accompanied Balthazar to a cage fight between two migrants where the prize was a Hungarian passport. On the way home they had been stopped by two gendarmes pretending to be policemen.

Goran had burst through the fake checkpoint. When the gendarmes pursued them he led them through a wooded area, and managed to get several of the gendarmes' cars to bang into each other. Balthazar and Goran then threw several stun grenades, blinding and disorientating the drivers even more, causing a second set of crashes, before escaping.

Balthazar said, 'Normal ride please. Home.'

Goran looked across the room and nodded at a dark-haired, wiry man in a white T-shirt sitting at a corner table, nursing a coffee and reading a two day old copy of *Blic*, a Serbian tabloid newspaper. This was Memed, a Bosnian Muslim from Sarajevo and one of Goran's lieutenants. Memed never touched alcohol. Memed walked over, shook hands with Balthazar and said, '*Hajdemo*, let's go.'

The two men stepped outside and began to walk down Nemet Street, where Goran's Lada Niva was parked nearby.

THIRTY-TWO

Margaret Bridge, 8 p.m.

Zsuzsa sat in the back of the Audi, waiting for the traffic to clear so that the car could turn right from Jaszai Mari Square onto the Margaret Bridge.

The evening scene looked familiar, almost comforting. An orange tram trundled across the bridge onto the Grand Boulevard as it headed towards Nyugati Station. A gaggle of teenagers loafed around the McDonald's on the corner while a middle-aged lady in lycra with a determined expression on her face pedalled her mountain bike down the cycle path.

Zsuzsa felt nervous, excited, but also reassured by the company of the two men. Antal, who had picked her up, was sitting in front of her, while another man called Gyuri was driving. Both were tall, burly and shaven-headed, and looked like they could handle themselves. The two men wore small radio earpieces under which she could see a pale cable, tightly curled, stretching into their jacket pockets. They were tense, on alert, she sensed.

Antal turned round for a moment as the car slowly began to move forward. 'Everything OK?' he asked.

'Fine,' she replied, nodding. 'Where are we going?'

He glanced at his watch, a large Rolex, she saw. 'Obuda. Remetehegyi Way. We should be there in twelve minutes.' He paused for a moment, looking at Zsuzsa in an unusual way, as though assessing her – not whether or not she was attractive, but as though trying to make a judgement. 'Strapped in properly?'

Zsuzsa nodded. She was held in place by a four-point seatbelt that reached around her hips and over her shoulders, the kind usually worn by flight attendants sitting by the emergency exit on an airplane.

'Good. Keep your seatbelt on.'

She nodded. 'Sure. Why? Are we going to crash?'

Antal seemed to come a decision. 'Not with Gyuri driving. But there may be some… interference ahead. I'll let you know. You've been on an airplane?'

'Of course.'

'Think of this car like a plane, Zsuzsa. If I shout brace, lean back and push your head back into the cushion on the headrest. You'll be fine. The seat belt will hold you in place. Just make sure your head does not fly forward. Got that?'

Zsuzsa blinked. *Brace?*

What had she got herself into here?

Antal said, 'Show me, please.'

She did as he asked, resting the back of her head into the front of the head rest. 'Push harder, and tense yourself, squeeze your muscles, so you can't move,' said Antal.

Zsuzsa pushed harder, tensing her back and shoulders, forcing her head into the headrest.

Antal nodded. 'Better. Sit back now and enjoy the ride.'

She would try, she told herself, as the car turned properly onto Margaret Bridge and she looked leftwards to take in the night-time view. The city could still take her breath away with its luminous beauty. The Danube shone black, its waters sleek and glistening. The neo-Gothic extravaganza of the parliament building loomed over the river, its sharp spires and domed roof glowing golden, like some fantastic castle in a fairy story. Across the water the lights of Buda were spread out like a carpet of jewels reaching high into the hills, blinking and shimmering in the dark. Two flags flew from the lampposts spaced along the bridge – the red, white and green of Hungary and the blue-and-white ensign of Israel.

Margaret Bridge wasn't straight. It had a large kink in the middle from where a feeder road ran down onto the island. The few pedestrians around were bundled up against the cold, and by now the commuter traffic had finished and the roads were quite clear. A metal fence separated the edge of the road from the bicycle path that ran along the bridge. A teenager in a lime-green hoodie zipped past her in the opposite direction, on a scooter with tiny wheels.

Gyuri took the bend at speed, the G-force pushing her back in the leather seat. No need to brace yet, but it would be a relief when they finally arrived, and Eniko and Reka could tell her what all this was about. Still, she was enough of a reporter to take mental notes of the journey so far. She could already start to write the colour story to go with the main one, the story of how she got the story. A headline something like 'How I Was Smuggled Into the Prime Minister's Residence at Night' would work nicely, she thought.

A few metres before the tram stop at the end of the bridge, the Audi cut into the traffic without indicating, triggering several indignant bursts of hooting from nearby drivers. Gyuri moved across into the far-right lane and turned right.

A red light showed at a zebra crossing, but there was nobody in sight and the car went straight through at speed. Zsuzsa glanced at the apartment block at the side of the road. She could see a young couple through the window, sitting down to their evening meal. The man leaned forward across the small table to kiss the woman before they started eating.

For a moment she envied their cosy domesticity. It had been a long time since she had shared a meal with a guy. She had thought that city life would automatically bring an exciting social life, but it was much harder here than at home to make friends. And her choice in men was abysmal. The last guy she had dated, Adorjan, was now in prison. Somehow she had managed to get involved with a man who was working with Pal Dezeffy in his attempt to derail Reka Bardossy's Qatari investment plan.

Adorjan had supplied the fatal fake Viagra which had killed the key Qatari financier in the fancy brothel in the Buda hills – a brothel owned by the brother of the city's most famous detective. How did that relationship work? she wondered. That would make an amazing article – two brothers: one a cop, the other a pimp. Although somehow she knew neither would ever give her an interview.

The car turned right again at speed then took a sharp left, cutting in front of a slower-moving vehicle and sparking some outraged hooting. Well, she thought, she had always dreamed of an exciting life as an investigative reporter, and now she had one.

She had taken the battery out of her phone as Reka had instructed so could not use Google Maps but by now she knew the city well enough to guess their route. They would follow the path of the river for a kilometre or so until they turned left at Szepvolgyi Way and climbed up into the Buda hills and the district of Obuda.

She was right and a few moments later the Audi was

speeding along the wide three-lane road that ran parallel with the river, parallel with Margaret Island. So far so good, but there was still a way to go.

'Where might there be interference?' she asked.

As if on cue Antal's earpiece hissed and crackled. He held up a hand to both acknowledge her question and ask her to wait. 'There is a police check on the corner of Szepvolgyi Way. We need to take another route.'

Zsuzsa frowned. 'Why are we worried about the police? It's not illegal to go to the prime minister's house.'

Antal said, 'No, it's not. But it seems you are making some powerful enemies, who don't want you to get there, Zsuzsa. I just heard that there is a warrant out for your arrest,' he said, his voice amused. 'What have you done?'

Zsuzsa's doubts turned to anxiety. 'Arrest? On what charges?'

'Theft, unlawfully accessing a computer, possession of stolen goods, stolen data, unlawful acquisition and retention of private data. You've been busy.' He turned to the driver. 'Gyuri, be careful, we are transporting a criminal. She might be dangerous.'

Gyuri laughed and sped through another red light.

Antal looked intrigued, tilted his head sideways as he spoke, as though assessing her again. 'Zsuzsa Barcsy, I think you are not as innocent as you look.'

Zsuzsa smiled, in spite of her nerves. Was Antal flirting with her? Yes, she decided he was. 'I hope so. So what happens next? Are you going to hand me over?'

'What do you think?'

'I think not.'

'Smart girl. But when I say brace, you...'

'I know.' She paused for a moment. 'Will there be shooting?'

'Possibly. But I doubt it. In any case you don't need to worry about that.' Antal lightly slapped the windows. 'This car is bulletproof. Even the tyres. Relax. Enjoy the ride.'

Antal's earpiece crackled again. He looked straight ahead and his voice turned serious. 'They've got a drone up. There are police on every route, looking for us. Take the next left.'

The Audi moved across into the left-hand lane as the car approached the turn-off at Zsigmond Square. It sped past a line of green municipal bicycles each parked neatly in its stand, then turned right onto Uromi Street, a much narrower residential road that also led north towards Obuda.

Every now and again Zsuzsa found herself in a street that reminded her of her home village. The Buda side especially was composed of suburbs that had once been small settlements. They drove past a house, a single-storey building with a yellow facade that looked like just her grandmother's.

For a moment she felt a pang of homesickness, then looked straight ahead. The police checkpoint was positioned towards the end where the road bent leftwards. There were two cars parked horizontally across the street at an angle, their front bumpers a metre or so apart. One cop was standing on either side of the road, a torch in hand while another sat in the driver's seat of each car.

The Audi slowed right down as it moved towards the police cars. There was a single vehicle in front, a white Toyota saloon.

The police officer on the right-hand side of the road waved his torch.

The Toyota stopped and one of the police officers peered inside. He gave the driver a cursory glance and waved it forward. The drivers inside the two police cars reversed for a couple of metres to let the Toyota pass.

'Speed through now, boss?' asked Gyuri. 'There's a space.'

Antal shook his head. 'Only for a few more seconds. They will drive back into position. And this is a residential street. All we need is for Erzsi *neni* to appear with her dog when we are doing seventy kilometres an hour.'

Zsuzsa tried to damp down her growing sense of alarm. Antal sensed her unease and turned back around to speak to her. 'Don't worry. Gyuri knows what to do. He's an expert. Aren't you, Gyuri?'

Zsuzsa looked in the driver's mirror to see Gyuri grinning at her. '*Nyugi*, miss, relax. It's going to be fine.'

Zsuzsa nodded uncertainly and braced herself.

She expected the car to rev up and smash its way through the police vehicles at top speed, sending them spinning out of the way like a scene from a Jason Bourne film.

Instead the Audi carried on creeping forward.

She glanced at the speedometer: they were going at ten kilometres an hour. One of the policemen waved his torch at the Audi, frantically gesturing for the car to stop.

Gyuri kept driving, calmly holding the wheel, keeping a low but steady speed, until the Audi was just a few yards from the two police cars.

'Brace now, Zsuzsa,' said Antal.

The Audi suddenly lurched forward as Gyuri floored the accelerator. She pushed herself back into her seat, leaning back as hard as she could and pushing against the headrest.

The Audi hit both vehicles with a crunch, smashing the police cars' headlights and crumpling their bonnets.

The impact pushed her back into her seat but both police cars spun outwards, one to left, the other to the right, absorbing much of the energy of the impact. Both police officers jumped out of the way, just in time.

A fraction of a second later the Audi was roaring up Uromi Street.

Zsuzsa glanced leftwards as the Audi came onto Szepvolgyi Way, where one of Budapest's best-known cake and ice-cream shops stood on the corner. It was a wide road, with two lanes in each direction, the main artery in and out of Obuda.

Last summer she had sat on the low wall overlooking the road with her then fiancé, eating lemon sorbet as he had explained to her that he hated Budapest and wanted to go back home to their village, and he would like Zsuzsa to come with him and to get married as soon as possible.

She had gently explained that would not be possible and it would be best to go their separate ways. He had packed up his clothes and moved out of their tiny flat that evening. The episode now seemed like a scene from another life.

The Audi was speeding up now, hitting eighty kilometres an hour as it raced up Szepvolgyi Way towards Obuda, running several sets of red lights, then turning onto Folyondar Street, a residential road that led onto Remetehegyi Way.

Now they were coming into a fancier part of the city, Zsuzsa could see. For a moment they were stuck behind a taxi, then Gyuri overtook, moving into the opposite lane then switching back just in time to avoid the oncoming traffic.

Zsuzsa flexed her shoulders, turned her head from side to side. Everything moved smoothly. She relaxed a bit, now writing the paragraph in her head about how the Audi smashed its way through the police roadblock. She asked, 'Are we expecting any more interference, Antal?'

He turned and smiled at her. 'I don't think so. The drone will have seen what happened. They tried but this is a big beast. It's going to take a nice chunk out of the police budget if we have to keep smashing our way through their cars.'

Gyuri kept a steady pace as the car whizzed through the quiet, tree-lined streets. A few minutes later the car drove onto Remetehegyi Way and parked outside Reka's villa. Two policemen walked over immediately, but raised their hands in greeting when they saw the car and Antal exit the vehicle.

He opened the boot and took out Zsuzsa's bag, then opened her car door. She stepped outside, looking around curiously. She had never been to Obuda before.

The air smelled different, she realised, sharper and fresher than downtown. Reka's villa looked very grand, set back from the road behind a high fence, with a carefully manicured garden in front. The view of the city from here was spectacular.

Antal handed Zsuzsa her bag. 'I wish you a lovely and pleasant rest of the evening,' he declared, lapsing into a formal register, an amused glint in his eye.

'Thank you. It's been very interesting so far,' she said.

'Let me know when you want a ride back into town.'

'I will,' she said, watching Antal as he turned and walked away.

The front door opened and Reka stepped out. She walked down the path to the gate, which opened silently. She stepped through and greeted Zsuzsa. 'Thank you for coming, Zsuzsa. I'm very glad to have you with us. I hope your journey wasn't too difficult.'

Zsuzsa tried to recover some of her composure. This was actually happening. She was really coming to stay with the prime minister. 'It was more exciting than I expected.'

'So I heard.'

Reka patted the Audi, walked around to the front. The headlights were cracked and white paint was smeared down each wing, but there seemed to be no structural damage.

Antal saw Reka looking at the car. 'I'll get it checked tomorrow morning, Prime Minister.'

Reka said, 'Thank you, Antal. And thanks to you and Gyuri for getting Zsuzsa here safely.'

She turned to Zsuzsa. 'Come with me and I will show you to your quarters. You can freshen up then come into the main house. Eniko is waiting for you.'

Zsuzsa followed Reka through the gate and down a path at the side of the house. The garden was enormous, big enough for a small cottage in the far corner with a wooden door and a red roof. Reka led her to the door and opened it.

There were three rooms inside, Zsuzsa saw, a kitchen at the back, a lounge in the front and a bedroom to the side. The lounge had cream walls and was comfortably furnished, with a sofa, a large coffee table and two armchairs. A man was sitting on the sofa and stood up as she entered. He was good-looking, in his late twenties.

Zsuzsa blinked for a moment, wondering if she was perhaps hallucinating after the excitement of the journey across then city. She was not.

'*Erev tov*, Zsuzsa,' he said.

THIRTY-THREE

Rakoczi Square, 8.30 p.m.

Balthazar and Memed walked down Nemet Street to Goran's car. It was parked nearby in Nemet Alley, a narrow cul-de-sac that cut across the road a couple of blocks further down.

Nemet Street and its surrounds were a typical inner-city mix of dilapidation and regeneration. Most of the apartment blocks were grimy and run-down, their windows thick with dirt, their cracked facades marked with colourful graffiti tags. Here and there a restored building stood out, its front a splash of dark yellow, or a sharp-angled new office block of gleaming brick, glass and steel. Between them were empty lots, waiting for construction to start.

Balthazar glanced at a young woman walking slowly on the other side of the road as he and Memed walked towards the corner of Nemet Alley. The night had turned cold and he shivered for a moment in his leather jacket. She stopped for a moment, leaning against a wall surrounding a construction site, looking in their direction. A giant sign announced that the Nationwide property division had started building a business centre there.

He thought the girl looked familiar, but the street lighting here was dim and it was hard to be sure.

The two men turned left and walked several metres into Nemet Alley. The narrow passage was reasonably well lit – two blocks on either side had recently been converted into *garzonlakasok*, modern studio apartments – which was why Goran liked to park there. Halfway down the alley were modern steel park benches on either side of the pavement. Nearby, a row of new saplings grew in narrow iron cages.

A few seconds later Balthazar heard a female voice calling his name. He turned around to see the young woman crossing the street and walking towards him and Memed. It was Marika.

Balthazar smiled. 'I thought you were going home, Marika.'

'I am, honestly.' She gestured up the road. 'I came out to do some shopping. But then I thought I saw you. I live on this street. Number 78, if you ever want to come and visit. I mean for a tea, or something. I don't know many people here.'

She turned to Memed, looked him up and down, taking in his olive complexion, dark eyes and black hair. She smiled as she asked, 'Are you one of us?'

Memed returned her smile, shook his head and was about to answer when a dark-blue Mercedes saloon skidded around the corner.

Balthazar and Memed scrabbled for their weapons, but both men had pulled up the zips of their leather jackets and their pistols were inside.

The car stopped a couple of yards in front of them.

Balthazar and Memed lost just a couple of seconds as they fumbled with their jackets but that was all the men inside the Mercedes needed.

The front doors flew open. Two men dressed in black wearing black balaclavas jumped out. Nobody noticed Marika dart into the darkness.

The two gunmen held Glock 34s in a two-handed grip, legs apart, the weapons pointing at Balthazar and Memed, who were directly in their line of fire. One of the gunmen was tall and rangy, the other shorter and wiry. A third man sat in the driver's seat.

These were trained professionals, Balthazar instantly understood.

Balthazar looked at the men, then at the car. The blue Mercedes looked familiar. The left-hand headlight was smeared with dirt, the right-hand one shiny and pristine.

The taller gunman stood in front of Balthazar and Memed; the other stood to their side.

'On your knees and hands up,' the taller gunman shouted, pointing his weapon at Balthazar.

He and Memed looked at each other.

The Mercedes driver, Balthazar saw, was now reversing down Nemet Alley. He would turn around, he guessed, then reverse back down to be in position for a rapid getaway.

Balthazar took his hand out of his jacket, raised his palms to his shoulders and glanced to his right with his eyes. Memed nodded, a tiny, almost imperceptible movement.

Balthazar instantly pivoted sideways on the ball of his left foot, stepping out of the line of fire.

He lunged at the pistol with his right hand, fired a punch at the side of the gunman's head with his left.

Balthazar's fingers flew around the barrel of the Glock. The gunman struggled to free his weapon but Balthazar kept his elbow and right arm locked so he could not take control. His left fist connected with the gunman's head, but he moved sideways at the last moment and Balthazar only delivered a glancing blow.

Still, it was enough to disorientate him.

Balthazar drew his left arm back again and slapped the gunman on the back of his head with an open palm as hard as he could, his right arm still solid as he gripped the barrel of the Glock, the two men locked in a danse macabre as they struggled for control of the weapon. This time the blow connected, the hard bone of the man's skull smashing into his hand.

The gunman reeled, dizzy and disorientated.

Balthazar pivoted again, turning on his hip, his left hand shooting forward and gripping the gunman's wrist.

Now he had the gunman in a two-handed grip, one hand on his wrist and the other still grasping the weapon. Balthazar quickly turned back in, slamming his right knee sideways into the gunman's groin as he raised their arms even higher. At the same time he twisted the barrel of the gun sideways as hard and fast as he could. The gunman grunted in pain and half fell forward. This time he let go of the weapon.

Balthazar gripped the barrel of the gun in his right hand, holding it like a hammer, pivoted again, twisted his wrist and slammed the base of the stock into the gunman's solar plexus, the full force of his body behind the blow. The gunman groaned and fell forward, wheezing as he tried to catch his breath.

Balthazar now had control of the weapon. But disarming and disabling an armed assailant demands enormous concentration, courage and determination. There was no chance to check how Memed was doing.

Balthazar stepped back, the Glock 34 in his hand, and looked around.

The second gunman was standing with one leg on Memed's prone body, pointing his gun at his back. The Bosnian was unconscious and blood was seeping from the side of his head.

'Nice work, Detective,' said the tall gunman. 'Really, very impressive. But as you can see your friend is not nearly as efficient. So now we have a Mexican standoff. You can shoot me, I can shoot Memed. But we are not in the shooting business, at least not tonight.'

'Then what kind of business are we in?' asked Balthazar. He felt the anger surge through him as he kept hold of the Glock. His body was pumping adrenalin, sending his senses into sharp focus. He could hear distant traffic, smell exhaust and cigarette smoke on the freezing night air. And where was Marika?

The wiry gunman righted himself, still panting, his face pale but tight with fury, clenched his right fist and stepped towards Balthazar.

The taller man shook his head. 'Not now.' The wiry gunman stopped, staring at Balthazar, hatred blazing in his eyes.

The taller gunman continued speaking. 'Let's call it the guided discussion business, Detective. Someone wants to talk to you.'

'Then why don't they call? I'm sure they can find my number.'

'They can do that. But they believe that you will need a bit of persuasion to have this discussion. That's why we are here.'

'Who?' demanded Balthazar. 'Who sent you?'

'Come with us, and you will find out. You listen and then you can go home. I give you my word.'

'So what happens next?' asked Balthazar, still training the Glock 34 on the taller gunman. The other man, he saw, had quickly walked over to the Mercedes, which had reversed down the alley and was now parked nearby with its front facing towards Nemet Street.

The tall gunman said, 'Next is you are going to lower that gun and hand it back to my colleague, as well as your weapon and your mobile phone.'

'And what if I don't?'

'Then I will shoot your friend in the back. At the same time you will shoot me. Then my friend will shoot you. And everything will get very complicated.'

Balthazar glanced sideways. The wiry gunman was back in his two-handed stance, pointing a Glock at Balthazar again, with a look on his face that said he would be only too happy to use it. He must have picked up another weapon from the car.

The taller gunman continued talking. 'So you see, you will be dead, I will be dead and your friend here probably will be too, or at least crippled for life.' He paused. 'All because you refused to come for a little chat.'

He stepped forward. 'Look, I don't want to shoot you, Detective. Or your friend. I don't want to shoot anyone. It draws so much attention. It causes enormous hassle, especially if a cop is involved. But I will if I have to. So what do you say? Just come for a chat, then you can go home later. Eva *neni* will feed you some of her famous *turos palacsintas*. How is she, by the way? She must get lonely at night, an elderly lady living on her own. You're very important to her.'

'Is that the best you can do, threatening an old lady?'

The tall gunman shrugged. 'Who is threatening anybody? It's just an observation.' His tone changed, became harder. 'Now, Detective, much as I am enjoying our conversation, we really need to get a move on. Hand over both weapons to my colleague – yours and ours – and your phone. Give him the one in your hand, and he will remove the other pistol and your phone.'

Balthazar did not believe the gunman for a moment. Whoever had sent these men wanted to know what Balthazar knew. The likelihood of him simply taking a taxi home later was more than remote. For the moment, though, he had little choice. But he could take as much control as possible.

The tall gunman gestured at his partner. He walked over to Balthazar, who handed him back his pistol.

The wiry gunman stood at Balthazar's side, so close he could smell his odour of stale sweat and cigarettes. Balthazar braced himself for what was surely coming, after he had humiliated him in front of his boss. The man's fist slammed into Balthazar's side, under his ribcage, into his kidney. Bolts of pain shot through his back. Nausea rose in his throat and the street began to spin. He forced himself not to cry out but for a moment he thought he might collapse.

The gunman stepped back, raised his fist for another punch. The second gunman shouted, 'Stop. We need him able to speak.'

The tall gunman looked at Balthazar, his weapon still trained on him. 'All you need to do is follow orders, Detective. Then you will save yourself a whole lot of pain. Now don't move, especially not suddenly, tell us where your phone is and put your hands out and forward.'

'Inside my jacket. Left-hand side,' said Balthazar, trying to stop his legs from shaking.

The wiry gunman reached inside Balthazar's jacket and took out his iPhone, then reached for his shoulder holster and removed his Glock.

'Hands out,' said the wiry gunman. 'Unless you want one in the other kidney.'

Balthazar did as he asked. The gunman placed Balthazar's

phone and pistol inside one pocket of his jacket and removed a roll of duct tape from another.

Balthazar smiled inside when he saw what the gunman planned to use to restrain him. Duct tape, he had read recently in an international police report, was now the most popular method of restraint in an abduction. But it wasn't nearly as secure as most kidnappers believed.

Balthazar knew what was coming next – he would be put inside the car and taken to whoever wanted to speak to him. There seemed little doubt that the same people kidnapping him were connected to the death of Geza Kovacs, and the shooting on Klauzal Square. There seemed little means of avoiding getting into the vehicle. But as long as he wasn't put into the boot, he still had options. Unfortunately that probably meant taking another punch.

The sound of a mobile telephone ringing echoed across the street. The taller gunman reached inside his jacket and took out his phone with his left hand. He looked at the screen and took the call, his gun still trained on Balthazar.

The wiry gunman looked at Balthazar, his face twisted in contempt.

'I hope they are paying you well,' said Balthazar.

'Shut it, dirty Gypsy. How the fuck did you ever get to be a cop anyway?'

'They were short-staffed. Once this is all over I'll arrest you, you can be sure of that. You'll get ten years for kidnapping a cop. At least. Your employers won't care. What are they paying you for this evening's fun? Half a million forints? A million? They'll dump you like a sack of shit.'

Balthazar glanced at the taller gunman, who was still speaking on his mobile phone. He was absorbed in the conversation and not listening.

Balthazar glanced at Memed. He was still lying the floor, but seemed to be coming round. 'Actually, you'll get much more than ten years. You left your DNA all over the flat across the square where you killed Geza Kovacs.'

The gunman looked at him. 'What the fuck are you talking about? I didn't kill anyone. Who's Geza Kovacs?'

'Someone working for the same people as you. Someone with a large hole in his chest, another in his head and his brains all over the wall. Maybe your friends planted it. But you'll be going down for murder as well.'

Balthazar had no idea whether any of this was true, but it was certainly angering the gunman. He looked across at the taller gunman, who was finishing his conversation. Balthazar held out his hands. The wiry gunman wound the duct tape around his lower wrists. 'Geza had lots of friends,' Balthazar said. 'Plenty of them are in prison. I'm sure they will be pleased to meet you. You can be their *kocsog*.'

The wiry gunman said nothing. He tore the end of the duct tape and closed the binding. Once it was fastened he stepped sideways and slammed his fist into Balthazar's stomach. Balthazar stumbled forward, pain and nausea exploding inside him. For a moment he could taste the *cevapcici* and palinka again, the greasy meat and alcohol sliding back up his throat. He took deep, panting breaths, somehow managed not to vomit.

The Mercedes moved nearer and the car boot popped open. The second gunman finished his call. 'Get in,' he said to Balthazar.

'Your boss won't have a much of a conversation if you put me in there.'

'Why not?'

'You saw what just happened. Your friend here has punched

me in the kidney and the stomach. I'll puke. There's no air in there. And I will be tied up lying on my side, so when I puke I will then choke on my own vomit. So your boss won't be able to have any kind of conversation with me, guided or not.'

'And if you go in the back of the car?'

Balthazar glanced at Memed. His eyes were open and he nodded subtly. Memed was alive and just needed to get to Goran's nearby restaurant. He could leave him. Balthazar said, 'I'll manage. Just keep the window open.'

The second gunman gestured at his colleague. 'You first, get in. He'll sit between us.'

THIRTY-FOUR

Nemet Street, 8.40 p.m.

Marika watched through a hole in the construction site fence, her heart thumping and her eyes wide, as the blue Mercedes sped down the road and turned left on Rakoczi Square.

She peeked around the edge of the barrier, double-checked that the men and the car had all gone, then rushed across to the middle of the alley to where Memed was trying to sit up, blood streaming from the side of his head. He had turned pale and was shivering.

Marika knelt by his side and scrabbled for her mobile phone in the pocket of her coat, almost dropped it in her nervousness. 'Sit down, stay where you are. I'll call an ambulance.'

Memed shook his head. 'No, no ambulance. No hospital. Just help me get back to the restaurant.'

'But you are hurt. You need help.' She pulled out a packet of tissues. 'I always wanted to be a nurse,' she said as she started wiping blood from the side of his head. 'I enrolled at nursing college, you know, but I had to leave after a few months. I had to look after my family. I'm still in the helping business, it's just a different sort...' she said, gabbling after what she had just witnessed.

Memed tried to stand, but his legs gave way and he crumpled back to the ground.

Marika put her hand on his shoulder, pressed down gently for a moment. 'Just a wait a minute. They've gone now and they won't come back. I've seen enough fights. Either you will be able to get up in a little while, or not. If you can, we'll go back to the restaurant. If not, I'm definitely calling an ambulance. Deal?'

'Deal.' He sat up again and managed to crab-walk across the road onto the pavement and sit with his back to the wall. Marika handed him some more tissues.

'Give me a minute,' said Memed, wiping the side of his head. 'I'll be OK.'

A moment later a large blue Maserati coupe cruised slowly down Nemet Street. It passed the entrance to Nemet Alley, went another ten yards or so, then suddenly reversed to the corner and turned into the alley.

An overweight Gypsy man levered himself out of the driver's seat and walked across to where they were sitting. He had slicked-back black hair and coffee-coloured skin, and wore a shiny black tracksuit over a white T-shirt and expensive trainers.

'What the fuck happened?' he asked Marika.

She looked at him with relief. 'Vik. Thank God you're here. They've taken Tazi.'

Tito Grill, 8.50 p.m.

Goran looked up as a loud hooting sounded again and again.

He watched through the window as a blue Maserati slammed to a halt at speed, parking illegally on the corner of Nemet Street, stopping just millimetres from the car in front.

For a moment he feared the restaurant was being targeted until he realised the vehicle was Gaspar's car. Gaspar wasn't a very careful driver but even by his standards this was truly terrible parking. And the hooting continued.

Goran understood. He stubbed out his cigarette, stood up and signalled to Biljana that she needed to clear the restaurant.

A couple of seconds later he was already at the door as Fat Vik and Gaspar strode in, each holding up Memed between them, Marika walking behind them, still explaining what she had seen.

The other customers turned to look at the sight of the two large Gypsy men bringing in another man who could not stand very well, holding up a couple of tissues to a bloody wound on the side of his face in a vain attempt to staunch the blood. Only three tables were occupied.

Biljana quickly moved between the groups of diners, asking them to leave, as she apologised and explained that their dinner and drinks were on the house. They all knew enough not to ask questions, quickly gathered their coats and left.

Goran ushered Fat Vik, Goran, Memed and Marika through the dining area into a small back room that served as office-cum-lounge. An old-fashioned monitor and keyboard stood on top of a wooden desk in the far corner, with a large grey cash box on the edge of the desk. Nearby stood a metal filing cabinet.

A blue sofa, its sagging cushions covered in a brown nylon blanket, took up most of the facing wall. Fat Vik and Gaspar carefully lowered Memed onto the sofa, then covered him with a blanket. He was still pale and he was trembling, his brown eyes wide open. Marika sat on the edge of the sofa and straightened out the blanket, reassuring Memed that he would be OK.

'What happened?' asked Goran.

Gaspar started ranting and raving that Balthazar had been kidnapped, every other word an oath, promise of violence and bloody vengeance on the *kocsogok*, the *lofaszok*, the horse pricks, who were responsible and *kurva anyatok*, fuck their mothers.

The sweat shone on his bald head and the veins in his neck looked like steel cables. His fury was about to overtake him and he started wheezing as he spoke, suddenly reduced to gesticulating.

Fat Vik laid his hand on Gaspar's arm. 'Take it easy, boss. We need you with us – not in hospital. Let Marika explain to Goran; she was there.'

Goran nodded, gestured at Gaspar to sit down at the desk and for Marika to speak. She gave a quick, incisive summary of what she had seen through the hole in the fence.

Goran was about to answer when Biljana walked inside, carrying two more chairs. She handed one to Fat Vik and one to Marika, who took it and sat by the edge of the sofa.

Biljana said, 'We're clear now. Everyone else has left. Go back to the restaurant, I will look after him and call the doctor.' She smiled at Marika. 'Don't worry, the doctor will be here soon. Memed will be fine.' She looked down at Memed. 'Won't you, *draga*?'

Memed smiled wanly, his hand clamped to the side of his face, where the bleeding was slowing. 'Once my head stops hurting.' He turned to Marika, took her hand in his. 'Thanks. You were very brave.'

Marika looked at her hand in his with surprise, but left it there. 'I wasn't. I hid. But get better.'

Biljana laughed. 'See, I told you he will be fine. He still has an eye for a pretty girl. Now get out of here and let me get on with things.'

Marika gave Memed's hand a long squeeze, then walked back into the restaurant with the three men. Goran guided them back to the table where he had just eaten with Balthazar and they sat down.

Goran glanced at Gaspar, who still looked like he could explode at any moment. A sheen of sweat still coated his shaved head. He wore his trademark black silk shirt, with several buttons open to display a thick, solid-gold rope chain and three heavy rings on either hand, each displaying a ruby or emerald.

Gaspar was even more overweight than Fat Vik and his heavy jowls hung over the collar of his shirt. In Gypsy culture being obese was seen not as a source of shame, but pride. It showed a person able to afford to eat their fill, and much more, which was rarely the case in the history of Roma people.

Gaspar could be very generous but was also notorious for his temper, especially lately as rival gangs encroached on his territory. He poured each of them a glass of water from the jug on the table. The three men and Marika looked at each other for several moments, each processing what had just happened.

Marika took a sip and asked, 'Will Memed be OK?'

Goran nodded. 'I think so. But he'll have a sore head for a couple of days.' He shot her a knowing look. 'You can drop by if you like, and see how he is.'

Marika smiled. 'I'd like that. Meanwhile…' She reached inside her coat, took out her iPhone and placed it on the table. 'I filmed it. All of it.'

Gaspar stared at her. 'You what? How?'

'With my camera. I hid behind the fence. There are lots of holes in it. I just held the phone up behind one.' For a moment she looked worried. 'Did I do something wrong?'

Gaspar shook his head. 'No, not at all. Smart girl, well done.'

Goran stood up, walked behind the bar, and returned with a laptop and a cable. He looked at Marika then at the iPhone. She nodded.

He plugged the iPhone into his laptop, dragged the video file from her handset onto the computer's desktop. All four of them watched. The video was shaky, occasionally blurred, but it showed the sequence of events: the blue Mercedes stopping in front of Balthazar and Memed, the two men trying to take control of the guns, Memed being clubbed to the ground, Balthazar doubling over in pain as the gun butt slammed into his stomach, being forced down onto his knees, getting plasticuffed and hustled into the Mercedes.

Marika looked down at the table for a moment. 'If I was really brave I would have gone out to help or screamed or something.' Her eyes were moist and she was trembling. She swallowed and wiped her eyes with a napkin. 'It's horrible. Who were they? Why did they do this?'

'We don't know yet,' said Goran, although remembering his conversation with Balthazar he had a quite good idea of the answer to her question.

He scrolled back through the file until the Mercedes slammed to a halt on Nemet Street. The gunmen jumped out and kept moving around in front of the rear of the vehicle. Goran pressed play again – Hungarian number plates had three letters and three numbers. He could not see all six letters and numbers but the first two were KZ and there was a number 7 as well.

Fat Vik watched as Goran started and stopped the file. 'They will be false plates. There are hundreds of blue Mercedes in Budapest.'

Goran nodded. 'I know. But that might not matter. Excuse me for a minute. I need to make a quick call.' He walked out of the dining room, back towards the office. A couple of minutes later he was back and sat down again. 'We'll find him. Don't worry.'

'How?' asked Gaspar. 'How will we find him?' He poured himself a shot of Goran's slivovitz and knocked it back in one, then lit a cigarette from a gold lighter with a diamond embedded on the side. He took a deep drag then started coughing.

Fat Vik passed Gaspar a glass of water. He drank most of it in one go, took another drag on the cigarette, then stubbed it out in the ashtray in front of him, which was already half full.

Goran rested his arm on Gaspar's. 'I don't know yet, but we will.' He paused and looked at Gaspar and Fat Vik. 'Do you want to eat?'

'Eat? How can I eat when my brother has just been kidnapped by gunmen?' he answered, his voice rising.

Goran said, 'Because we need to be calm, and to think. We won't find him any faster if we sit here shouting at each other.'

Fat Vik nodded. 'He's right, boss. We are all worried sick and angry but we need to be smart here.'

Fat Vik was the only person outside the Kovacs family who could disagree with Gaspar in public. That was because he counted as family. He had grown up with Balthazar, Gaspar and their siblings, in a tiny one-room flat next door to them. His mother was a prostitute and a drug addict. She did not know who her son's father was and Fat Vik had never tried to find out. At the age of six he had discovered his mother passed out from an overdose and run next door to the Kovacs family to call for help.

Fat Vik's childhood had been spent in and out of children's homes while his mother occasionally managed to go clean and find work as a supermarket cashier. One day he came home and found her pimp had beaten her unconscious. Vik found him laughing and drinking in a nearby bar. Soon afterwards the pimp was dead; Vik was arrested for manslaughter and sent to prison for five years. He had worked for Gaspar ever since.

Gaspar nodded. 'OK. You're right. It's hard to think properly on an empty stomach.' He looked around the room for a moment, a different kind of anxiety flitting across his face. He had never eaten at Goran's place and only patronised a couple of restaurants where the owners always prepared the same dish for him: a large, rare steak topped with goose liver. 'Give the menu to Vik. He'll choose for me. He knows restaurants better than me.'

Goran instantly understood. 'There's no menu, Gaspar. *Cevapcici* or *pljeskavica*. Chips, *ajvar*, salad.'

Gaspar looked relieved. 'OK, *cevapcici*, ten.'

Goran looked at Fat Vik, who asked for the same and then at Marika. She looked down at the table, momentarily embarrassed. 'I'm sorry. I don't know what that is.'

'Like mini-sausages, you'll love them,' said Goran, kindly. 'If you don't, we'll make you something else and these two will eat them.'

At that moment an elderly man walked out and into the main dining area. Dr Gyorgy Lorand was stooped with thick grey hair and old-fashioned square glasses. His white coat was smeared with blood. 'Your friend is very lucky. He has severe bruising to his cheekbone but somehow it's not fractured. He tells me he turned away at the moment of impact. Impressive timing. I've stitched up the cut, so it should stop bleeding. But he does have a mild concussion. If you have his best interests at heart, he should be in hospital under observation,' he said pointedly, looking at Goran.

'What does Memed say?' asked Goran.

'No hospital.'

'Can you look after him, Doctor?'

He nodded. 'I suppose so. I've patched up much worse. Someone needs to check on him every hour. If he worsens, becomes unconscious, vomits or stops making sense, that could mean a brain injury, so no more arguments. Hospital. Agreed? I will be back tomorrow. But you must call an ambulance if he deteriorates. I have your word on that?'

'Agreed,' said Goran. He reached inside his trousers for his wallet.

The doctor shook his head wearily. 'Not now. We'll settle up later.' He gave Goran a pointed look. 'Check on him every hour. Call me if you need me.'

The three of them watched the doctor leave. Marika looked at Fat Vik questioningly, then at Gaspar. 'Do I have to go back out tonight?'

Gaspar shook his head, his jowls wobbling. 'No, no, not tonight. Take a couple of days off.'

He reached inside his tracksuit trouser pocket and pulled out a Louis Vuitton wallet with a thick wad of 10,000 and 20,000-forint notes inside. He peeled off several, and handed them to Marika. 'Here's 100,000. Go home once you have eaten and buy yourself something nice. Send some to your parents. I'll call you in a day or two.'

Marika looked at the money, her eyes wide with amazement.

Gaspar turned to Goran, his voice apologetic. 'Sorry, *brat*. I lost it a bit earlier. But how are we going to find him? And then we have to rescue him.'

Goran said, 'Don't worry. I have a plan.'

The door opened. The three men and Marika turned to see who was coming in.

Goran said, 'And here they are.'

THIRTY-FIVE

Grand Boulevard, 8.50 p.m.

'It's jammed solid from here, boss,' said the Mercedes driver, glancing at the Waze map on his mobile. The screen showed a thick red line from the Grand Boulevard to Nyugati Station and beyond. 'I'm going to make a sharp left at Wesselenyi, cut across the tramlines, cut through the seventh district, then zip along the embankment to the Arpad Bridge, then cross the river there.'

The tall gunman grunted a yes. 'Just get us there as quickly as you can.'

Balthazar silently absorbed this information. Wherever they were headed, they were already making slow progress, inching along the Grand Boulevard in heavy traffic. The car turned onto Wesselenyi Street and moved slowly into District VII.

Doubtless their ultimate destination was a fancy villa in the Buda hills, where most of the city's rich elite – legitimate or otherwise – lived. But this was potentially good news if they were going through his neighbourhood. Now that Memed was out of the picture Balthazar had no intentions of going anywhere for a 'guided discussion'.

He knew every inch of his own part of town: the narrow alleyways that cut between the streets, the hidden courtyards and desolate open spaces waiting to be redeveloped. It would be much easier to lose them there, amid the crowded bars and ruin pubs than in the sparsely populated far suburbs.

Wesselenyi Street was one of the district's main arteries, but this part was a narrow, one-way thoroughfare that ended at the Great Synagogue where it met Dohany Street. Cars were parked nose to tail on the left-hand side and at ninety degrees to the pavement on the right.

He needed some space for his plan to work – and a decent speed. The Mercedes drove past the artisan bakeries, hipster bars, bicycle repair shops and cafés, slowing to cross Klauzal Street. Balthazar shut his eyes for a moment, tried to ignore the pain in his side and his front. His flat was just a minute or two's drive away, but was far out of reach.

The gunmen had strapped him in with a seatbelt – which suited him perfectly. Neither of them had used theirs.

After Klauzal Street the road widened and the Mercedes speeded up as it headed towards Dohany Street. He glanced at the speedometer – the road was clear and the car was touching forty kilometres an hour – then glanced again at the headrest. It was an old-fashioned restraint, with the pad mounted on two thin metal poles.

He looked outside. The pavements were deserted.

Now.

He leaned back into the car seat and braced himself. The two men on either side sensed his movement and looked to see what he was doing.

Balthazar quickly pulled both legs up to his chest, then kicked forward as hard and fast as he could, lifting his hips and slamming the balls of his feet into the back of the headrest.

It snapped clean off, smashing into the back of the driver's head.

The driver instantly lost control of the car, which began to spin. He lurched forward, then backwards, grabbing at the steering wheel as the car skidded across the road. The gunmen on either side of Balthazar flailed wildly trying to hold onto something to stabilise themselves.

Balthazar leaned back again and shot his legs forward once more.

This time he made solid contact with the back of the driver's head. He flew forward, slamming his forehead into the steering wheel, knocking himself out.

The front airbag exploded with a loud bang.

The car spun around, hitting a bollard, then careered in the opposite direction. The G-force pushed Balthazar first into the tall gunman, then the wiry one.

The Mercedes smashed sideways into a parked white Dacia SUV, bounced off, shattering the passenger windows on his right side, showering Balthazar and the others with broken glass. The Mercedes finally stopped moving and the Dacia's alarm started howling.

Balthazar felt sick and dizzy from the impacts. Unlike the driver and the two gunmen, he had known what was coming and had braced himself. But knowledge was still not adequate protection against the G-forces that had slammed him back and forth and shaken his brain as the Mercedes impacted.

He blinked for a moment, trying to focus. He gasped as a sharp pain shot down one side of his back, as though someone had stuck a needle into the muscle and was gouging it back and forth. Something was pulled, even torn, but he ignored the pain and forced himself to move.

Both of the gunmen were half dazed, trying to understand what was happening. They had been thrown forward against the front seats with the first impact, then sideways against the car windows as the car spun. The car had no rear airbags, but Balthazar's seat belt had locked and somehow the gunmen's bodies had also cushioned him from the impacts.

He lifted his right foot and ignored the knife of pain cutting through his back.

He slammed his heel edge down as hard as he could onto the arch of the tall gunman's left foot, through his leather boot.

The gunman gasped in agony, letting rip a stream of abuse. While he was swearing, Balthazar delivered the same strike to the other gunman's right foot with his left leg. He was wearing training shoes and Balthazar felt the bones of his foot move as his heel impacted.

Balthazar threw his arms forward, rubbed the duct tape around his wrists back and forth against the jagged glass in the door frame where the window had shattered, felt it tear, then sat back and drove his arms back on either side of his ribcage. The duct tape tore slightly but his hands remained bound.

The tall gunman tried to punch him in the head but, jammed against the door frame on one side and Balthazar on the other, he could not get proper leverage for his fist.

Balthazar ignored the glancing blow. He quickly extended his arms forward again, slammed his elbows back again in the car seat. This time the duct tape tore with a loud ripping sound.

His arms free now, Balthazar undid his seat belt. He turned leftwards on his hip to make space then smashed his right elbow into the side of the tall gunman's face, then moved rightwards and slammed his left elbow into the other gunman's cheek. Had he been standing, the blows would likely have fractured their cheekbones and knocked them out. Jammed between the two men he could not deliver the proper force, but still both lurched back from the blow, grunting in pain.

Balthazar then bent his fingers in half, locking the tips against the top of his palm. He swung around from side to side, twisting his hip sideways for more reach, his hands flying across his body, smashing his right palm into the wiry gunman's face and his left into the tall gunman's nose, a human flailing machine, delivering bone-crunching blows one after another. The two men lolled forward, both semi-conscious, blood pouring from their broken noses.

All this had taken place in less than a minute.

Balthazar leaned across the tall gunman and took his weapon, then did the same with the wiry gunman. He stripped the magazines from both guns, threw them out of the car window and retrieved his pistol and his mobile.

Balthazar leaned across the tall gunman, opened the car door, then climbed out.

He staggered for a moment, suddenly overcome by a wave of dizziness and nausea, his head drooping, but he knew he had to get away.

He looked up to see two policemen both pointing their guns at him in the firing position.

'Police officer,' Balthazar shouted. 'I am a police officer. Do not shoot.'

'Put the gun down,' shouted the older policemen. '*Now.*'

'I am doing that,' said Balthazar, slowly lowering his Glock to the floor.

By now a small crowd of onlookers had gathered. A teenage girl with bright-purple hair started filming, and others soon followed.

One of the policemen gestured for Balthazar to follow him

to their nearby vehicle. The other picked up his Glock and walked behind Balthazar and the other cop. Balthazar looked at the two men as he headed to their car.

He knew most of the beat cops in District VII and VIII but these two were unfamiliar. His sixth sense suddenly kicked in – there was something not quite right here. Or maybe he was just strung out from being bounced around in the car crash, fighting the two men inside and then walking away?

Balthazar turned to the policeman next to him. He was young, in his early twenties, pale and skinny, but with several days' growth of stubble, Balthazar saw, which was against regulations. 'Which station are you from?' Balthazar asked.

'Eight. Your old stomping ground. We're heading back there now, for a debrief. Then we'll get you home,' he replied, his eyes darting right and left.

'Great. Call Tomi *bacsi* and tell him to get some of his strong coffee on,' said Balthazar.

For a second doubt flashed across the young-looking cop's face.

'Tomi *bacsi*, the custody sergeant,' said Balthazar, his adrenalin starting to flow again. He was so focused on the conversation that he did not notice the second cop take out a can of spray and move towards him.

'Of course, yeah, Tomi *bacsi*,' the young cop said, moving to stand behind him. 'I'm gonna call him from the car.'

Just as Balthazar turned to run, the second cop held out his spray in front of Balthazar's face, making sure to turn his own face to the side. A squirt of white mist hit Balthazar's mouth, nose and chin.

Balthazar raised his hands, tried to wave away the spray, braced himself for what would happen next: he would not be able to breathe properly, his eyes and nose would burn, his muscles would turn floppy and he would quickly be gasping for air.

For a second he was puzzled. Why wasn't he coughing and retching?

The street began to spin and the world turned dark.

THIRTY-SIX

Remetehegyi Way, 9.30 p.m.

Eniko sat hunched over her laptop, her stomach tight with anxiety, staring at the video that filled up the homepage of newsline.hu.

She had watched it three times by now and a flashing panel proclaimed that more footage would be uploaded soon. HERO POLICE OFFICER ABDUCTED BY FAKE COPS? DRAMA TONIGHT ON WESSELENYI STREET! blared the headline, next to a large photograph of Balthazar.

A short and shaky film, it showed the blue Mercedes skewed across the road, with its windows smashed and the driver slumped against the airbag while Balthazar staggered out of the car. He then encountered the two men in police uniforms. One stood in front of him, the other behind. The sound was unclear, overloaded with voices as if whoever was holding the camera was shouting with excitement at her friends to come and see what was happening.

One of the policemen sprayed something directly into Balthazar's face. He waved his hands, trying to bat away the mist, to no effect. The other officer, behind him, caught Balthazar as he crumpled, then dragged him to the waiting police car. The doors closed and the vehicle sped away down Wesselenyi Street. Spliced onto the end of the footage was an interview with a teenage girl with purple hair, who gave an excited account of what she had seen.

Eniko exhaled hard, sat back and closed her eyes for a moment, everything that had happened in the last couple of days rushing through her mind: Reka's video, the deepfake strategy, Reka's plan to release the truth about her family's dark wartime history and now this, Balthazar staggering from a car crash, dazed and bloodied, before being gassed and abducted.

Meanwhile, the shooting on Dob Street was giving Reka's opponents a strong attack line on the daytime and evening chat shows, accusing the prime minister and her government of losing control of the streets, letting the capital descend into lawlessness. One channel, funded by a right-wing oligarch who made no secret of his desire to depose Reka, had somehow got hold of some CCTV footage that showed the gunman on the motorcycle opening fire and was showing it continually.

Eniko opened her eyes, took a drink from her glass of water. If all that wasn't enough, it now turned out Elad wasn't missing at all, but was here, working on some kind of article or statement about Nationwide with Zsuzsa in the garden house. This was quite incredible news. Reka had promised her that this was the last secret she had been keeping from her, but how could Eniko believe that? What else was buried from Reka's dark past – or her present – that would be suddenly dumped on her?

The real question, one that Eniko was increasingly asking herself, was how much longer did she want to keep on doing this? Working for Reka had been – still was – an incredibly interesting experience, one that brought her closer to the fire, as the Hungarian saying went, than anyone else, apart from Reka herself and Akos Feher.

But over the last few months she had realised that she was still a reporter at heart. She wanted to break the news, not manage it. And there was something else she could admit to herself, if nobody else.

She missed Balthazar. She was starting to think, actually admit to herself, that she had made a terrible mistake in dumping him. Instead of moving in with him, as he had suggested, she had run away to London and worked for *Newsweek*. Looking at the video footage of him getting abducted not only made her angry, but also sick with worry.

Eniko glanced at Reka, who was standing on the other side of the room, by the large windows that opened onto the terrace, talking to Akos Feher, nodding vociferously.

Why was the prime minister so obsessed with Nationwide? It seemed a strange, even deeply unwise strategy to go to war with one of the country's largest companies a few days before an important diplomatic visit and a general election soon after that.

Especially as Nationwide was the Bardossy family business – essentially owned and run by her uncle. Of course, that was somehow tied into the whole story. Eniko knew that Reka and Karoly Bardossy could not stand each other. Their mutual antipathy was an open secret among Budapest's business and political elites. There was something deeply personal there, but what?

For now, that would have to wait. Eniko's immediate concern was Balthazar. She pressed play and watched the video clip again until the moment he stepped out of the car. She pressed pause and froze the frame. Something about Balthazar's hands. She leaned forward, focusing hard on what she saw. Yes, that was it. There were shreds of tape around his wrists. Police officers did not use duct tape – or knockout sprays.

He had been abducted twice, once in the first Mercedes that had crashed – presumably he had caused that collision – and then again.

This level of backup, to have a second car ready in case the first failed, was highly organised. Who was behind this? Somehow she knew that this was connected to Nationwide and Elad Harrari. There was too much going on in the city in the last twenty-four hours for this to be any kind of coincidence.

Eniko looked at Reka once more. She had stopped talking on her phone and walked over to Eniko with Akos. They sat on the sofa, one on either side of her.

'You look very stressed,' said Reka.

'You both need to see this,' said Eniko, pointing at her laptop screen. She gave them both a few seconds to read and absorb the headline and the photograph then pressed play.

Reka and Akos both watched the clip. Reka sat back, silent for a few moments as she processed what she had seen. Just when she thought everything – and everyone – was in place, this happened.

Eniko said, 'They aren't real cops, are they?'

She played the video segment once, this time freezing it at the point where Balthazar was waving his hands after being sprayed. Eniko pointed at the shreds of tape on his wrists. 'That's duct tape.'

At that moment Reka's mobile rang. She glanced down at the number. 'I'm sorry, Eniko, I need to take this. And he might have some answers for us.'

Reka pressed the accept button, lifted the handset to her

ear. 'Yes, Sanyi, I'm watching it now.' She mouthed 'Sandor Takacs' at Eniko, then carried on speaking. 'I don't know anything more than you do. Are they real cops?'

Reka waited for the answer. 'No, I didn't think so either. Who sent them? I am not sure. But I have a pretty good idea.'

Reka ended the call, and walked over to the picture window. She stood there for a minute or so, lost in thought. Eniko and Akos looked at each other quizzically, but said nothing.

Reka made another call. It was answered almost immediately. 'Antal, I need you to bring someone else here,' she said. 'Now, please.'

THIRTY-SEVEN

Tito Grill, 10.30 p.m.

The Council of War was composed of a veteran officer of the state security service descended from Transylvanian aristocrats, a highly skilled computer hacker who was its newest employee, the city's most powerful pimp, his consigliere, and a Serbian restaurant owner with a shadowy past.

Several of them had met before, even worked together. Last autumn Anastasia had also been held captive in the basement torture chamber of the former police villa in the Buda hills, in a neighbouring room to Balthazar. It was Gaspar and Fat Vik who had led the charge into the building, rescuing both of them, with the help of Attila Ungar after he changed sides.

Now they were gathered at a corner table inside the restaurant while Biljana and Marika ferried over a continual supply of drinks – but no alcohol, that was universally agreed, at least until they got Balthazar back – and food.

All of them had also watched the footage of Balthazar's abduction on newsline.hu, but Vivi was now hacking in and out of the city's municipal CCTV network, sitting at the corner table, with the others standing around her, trying to follow the car's progress through the city.

The footage showed the fake police car cutting through

downtown and roaring down the tramlines on the Margaret Bridge onto the Buda side, then turning right. The cameras showed the vehicle's course as it sped along the embankment, then coverage ended.

Vivi looked up at the group. 'That's it. They were headed towards Obuda.'

Gaspar, Fat Vik, Goran and Anastasia sat back down at the table. Gaspar reached for one of the toothpicks in a small plastic box.

Gaspar said, 'Can you stop the video and catch the car number plate?'

Vivi nodded. 'I already did. We also have some numbers and letters from Marika's phone footage. It's the same vehicle.'

'Check it,' said Anastasia. 'You've got direct access to the database now.'

Vivi's fingers flew over her keyboard as she entered the letters and numbers into the national database. The screen showed: *No such registration*. Vivi said, 'Fake plates.'

Gaspar looked at Anastasia. 'OK, so we know for sure what car he was in. Now what?' he asked, playing with the toothpick as he spoke. 'Is he in Obuda?'

Anastasia shrugged. 'Maybe. But he could be anywhere. There are hardly any cameras up there. There are cameras on the motorways, but he could be en route out of the city on a back route.'

Gaspar asked, 'So now what?'

Before Anastasia could answer Marika walked over with a tray of coffees, a jug of water, a plate of biscuits and a bowl full of *ropis*, salty sticks, and stood by the table for a moment. Anastasia watched as Marika looked at Gaspar several times, and the space in front of him, but then placed the plate in the centre of the table.

Marika smiled at everyone and brushed her hair back from her eyes. 'Let us know if you want anything more. The cook's gone home. But I can help, I can make chips or sandwiches. Biljana says to tell that she can cook those thingies, *cevap*… whatevers.'

'*Cevapcicis*, *dragam*,' said Goran, giving her a rare smile.

Marika turned a faint shade of pink. 'Thanks.' She looked at Vivi's screen, showing the Obuda embankment. 'Is that where he is? Will you find him?'

Fat Vik rested his arm on hers. 'Of course we will. Don't worry. How's Memed?'

'Asleep.' Marika looked at her watch. 'I've got to wake him up now to check on him.' She turned and went back to the bar.

'Sweet girl, very helpful,' said Anastasia to Gaspar, looking him in the eye.

Gaspar said nothing, started fiddling with more toothpicks.

'Brave, resourceful, thinks on her feet,' Anastasia continued.

Gaspar still did not reply. A toothpick snapped in half.

Anastasia said nothing more, letting the silence grow and the tension rise.

Gaspar blinked first. 'She keeps almost everything she earns!' he declared, his voice almost indignant.

Vivi said, 'Very generous of you.'

Gaspar looked down for a moment, then around the room as though seeking help. Fat Vik looked bashful, but said nothing. Gaspar glanced at Goran, who shrugged, amused now.

'She'd make a good nurse. Or a waitress,' said Anastasia, arching her eyebrows. 'She'd need some financial support through college. But it would be a lovely gesture. Humanitarian.'

Gaspar sat back, and sighed. '*Ertem*, *ertem*, I get it. My first college scholarship. But first, let's find my brother and get him home. How are we going to do that?'

At that moment Vivi jumped in her chair. '*Azta,* that's it,' she exclaimed loudly.

Anastasia, Gaspar, Goran and Fat Vik all turned to look at her.

'What's what?' asked Gaspar.

Vivi turned the laptop around with a flourish and pressed play on a video file. It showed a police car driving up a track through woodland to a security cabin where the road narrowed, and further passage was blocked by a barrier, which then lifted.

The police car then continued down a short, narrow tarmacked road to the house, which was surrounded by a high wall. A panel slid sideways across the wall to let the car in. The car drove inside, and the panel moved back into place. It was clear there were four people inside the car, a driver and three in the back seat, although their faces were not properly visible. 'Number 302 Mariahegyi Way. Police car with the same number plate. That has to be them,' said Vivi.

Fat Vik frowned for a moment, looked at Gaspar. 'That address sounds familiar, boss.' He peered at the computer screen. 'Looks familiar, too. Don't we know that place?'

Gaspar snapped the toothpick. 'We do. A VIP punter. Spends a lot. Diamond-rated on our customer rankings.'

'Karoly Bardossy? The boss of Nationwide,' said Anastasia. 'I checked his address earlier.'

'That's the one. We know who he is,' said Gaspar. 'We know all about him, don't we, Vik?'

Fat Vik smiled. 'Not all about him, but quite a lot. More

than most people. A real old goat. Quite impressive for his age, although the Viagra helps. Likes his nose candy as well.'

Gaspar said, 'That must be it. That's where they've taken Tazi. Play it again, please.'

Vivi did as he asked. Goran took a napkin from the small container on the table, unfolded it and started drawing.

Gaspar glanced at him for a moment, then turned back to the video. He looked at Anastasia. 'Yup, it's definitely Karoly Bardossy's place.' Gaspar turned to Fat Vik. 'Remember, we went there together. Very fancy gaff, like a palace inside.'

Anastasia asked, 'What were you doing there?'

Gaspar said, 'Negotiating. He had some special requests. They were expensive. He likes lots of girls. Three, four, all at once. Imagine. One is enough work.'

Fat Vik said, 'Like I said, a real old goat. He used to come to us until his wife died. Then he stayed at home. We sent them over in a limousine. So now we know where he is, what are we going to do about it?'

Anastasia smiled, took a cup of coffee and drank half in one go. 'OK. The obvious way forward is to tell the police and raid the place. We'd need helicopters and an armed SWAT team. I've already spoken to Sandor Takacs. We could get that in place tonight. But there are several potential problems with that plan.'

'Which are?' asked Goran.

Anastasia said, 'Firstly, we don't know for sure that Balthazar is there. We don't have any footage of Balthazar that clearly shows his face, only the police car on the track and going into the house. Even if he is there now they might take him somewhere else. It would cause a massive scandal if we launched an armed raid on the home of the country's most powerful businessmen and got it wrong. We've only got one shot, and I'm not sure we can even use that.'

'Why not?' asked Goran.

'Because it's pretty clear that Karoly Bardossy has people on the inside of the police and we don't know who they are. That was a genuine police car they used to take Balthazar on Wesselenyi Street. The plates might be fake, but it was a real vehicle. Whoever the fake cops were, they also had real uniforms. As soon the SWAT team starts planning, or they get the helicopter ready, someone could tell Karoly Bardossy and he can move Balthazar. It's very remote up there. There are a lot of woodlands and there is no CCTV coverage.'

Goran had been watching the footage and listening to the conversation as he continued scribbling on the napkin. Now he leaned forward, moved the plate of snacks aside, and put the piece of paper in the centre of the table.

'Here is plan,' he said, showing a complicated illustration of arrows, targets and pathways. 'I can call some guys. Very reliable. Two teams. Team A, two snipers in woods, shoot at security guys in cabin. Either they hide in cabin or they run out. If they hide, no problem. If they run out, Team A takes them down. Don't worry, no need to kill them. Small-calibre bullet. Only leg or shoulder. Guys in house will rush out to see what is happening, come down to cabin. Team A deals with them as well. Meanwhile Team B goes into house, finds Balthazar, takes him out.'

He quickly slapped his hands against each other several times, rotating his palms from side to side. 'Small teams. Quick in and out. Easy.'

Anastasia half smiled. 'Nice idea, but that's not going to work, Goran. We can't turn Obuda into a warzone. No guys you know. No snipers.'

Goran looked disappointed. 'But they are good guys. I trust them. I can promise. I know one sniper who could do this. Very good shot.'

'I know him too, and yes, he is very good indeed.' She gave him a look, shook her head. 'But not this time.'

Goran shrugged, picked the napkin off the table and crumpled it into a ball. He grabbed a *ropi* stick and ate it in one go. 'Your choice. Then how do we rescue Balthazar?'

Anastasia said, 'Firstly we gather as much information as possible. Then we analyse it. Then we decide on our course of action.'

Gaspar looked at Fat Vik, shook his head, exhaled. 'You *gadjes*. Gather. Analyse. Decide. So slow. Be a bit Gypsy. We get results much faster.'

Anastasia said, 'You have a better idea?'

'I do,' said Gaspar. 'Much better.'

THIRTY-EIGHT

Mariahegyi Way, Obuda, 10.45 p.m.

'We can do this the easy way or the hard way, Detective,' said Karoly Bardossy, a glass of whisky in his hand. 'This is the easy way.'

Balthazar asked, 'And the hard way?'

'There is a cellar downstairs. You really don't want to go there.'

Balthazar took in the scene around him, rapidly trying to work out his options. The two men were sitting on black leather armchairs in the lounge of the villa, a coffee table between them. A jug of water and glasses stood in the centre of the table, next to a crystal decanter of single-malt whisky.

Karoly had a large white A4 envelope in front of him. He wore a black Ralph Lauren polo shirt, cream linen trousers and soft brown-leather deck shoes. His face glowed with the semi-permatan of the very rich, his skin pink with health, his blue eyes clear. He looked relaxed, confident, a man in control of and at ease in his surroundings.

Balthazar could sense him assessing what he saw: a dishevelled Gypsy in scruffy jeans, scuffed boots, a sweatshirt and a leather jacket. Blood was seeping from a cut on his forehead. Just a few minutes ago Balthazar had still been semi-conscious and the knockout spray was still fogging his brain. Balthazar understood the power dynamics of an exchange between two people: the placing of the furniture, the body language, the expressions of dominance. Such exchanges usually took place in police interview rooms where Balthazar was in control. Karoly Bardossy's apparent insouciance was all designed to show he was in control. That had to be disrupted.

'Do you know how long you will get for abducting a police officer?' said Balthazar. 'Ten years, at least. You can be sure of that. And then there is all the other stuff. Bribery, using police vehicles, uniforms.'

Karoly shrugged, took a sip of his whisky. 'I have no idea what you are talking about. I didn't abduct you. You were brought here semi-conscious by some unknown people. I gave you first aid, cleaned you up. A doctor will come and check you over and then you will be free to leave.'

'If you didn't abduct me, then why was I brought here? Let me go now.'

Karoly smiled, revealing a mouth full of expensive dentistry and unnaturally white teeth. 'Let's not waste any more of each other's time, Detective. You will soon be free to leave. Once you have given me the information I require.'

Balthazar sat back for a moment and evaluated his captor once more. He was slim and fit-looking, but it was the trimness of a wealthy man who spent much time swimming or golfing. He could probably be overpowered quite easily.

But then what? The other man in the room, standing against the wall at the back of the salon, was a very different prospect. He was at least six feet tall, with close-cropped steel-grey hair. He was well muscled, looked very alert and had a military bearing. Balthazar had seen him before, he realised.

This was the bodyguard who had stood by Karoly with the large umbrella at the Librarian's funeral. And he was armed with a pistol in a side holster on his belt.

'Which is what information, exactly?' asked Balthazar.

'We are about to get to that.' Karoly paused. 'You're probably thinking that you could overpower me easily, then somehow escape. But you've also seen Porter behind you. He's a crack shot with that pistol. Ex-British army. You won't get very far. So that's why I think we can safely keep this civilised.'

'Like you kept it civilised with Geza Kovacs?'

Karoly kept his face impassive. 'I have no idea what you are talking about. Who is Geza Kovacs?'

'Someone who was working for you, coordinating the gun attack on Klauzal Square, but who messed up, allowed himself to be filmed on CCTV and to be recognised by me. Someone you had killed. That's murder, at least twenty years inside.'

Karoly shrugged. 'I'm sorry, Detective, I really don't know what you are talking about. I've never heard of this Geza Kovacs.' He turned to his bodyguard. 'Have you, Porter?'

'No, boss. Name means nothing.'

Balthazar said nothing. For a powerful businessman Karoly Bardossy was a bad liar, or maybe the pressure was getting to him. His voice tightened, his posture was stiff and defensive and he glanced leftwards before he answered. Porter was much better, but then if he had killed Geza Kovacs he had much more to lose.

Balthazar looked around the room. The lounge was larger than his whole apartment, with massive glass doors that opened onto the terrace. In one corner was the largest flat-screen television he had ever seen, in another a drinks bar of chrome and black leather. There were several paintings on the wall – one of which looked like a Picasso, another two by French impressionists, he guessed. The floor was a parquet of black polished hardwood, much of it covered with expensive-looking Persian rugs. But amid all the luxury something was missing, he realised. Balthazar had read about Karoly Bardossy after his meeting at the state security offices with Vivi and Anastasia. He was a widower, with one son. But there were no family pictures at all: none of Karoly's wife nor of his son.

In front of Balthazar on the table was a jug of water and some glasses. He looked at the water. His throat felt like it had been vacuumed and dry-cleaned and his head like there was an iron bar moving around inside.

Each time he moved in the chair, a dagger of pain shot up the right side of his back, although he was careful not to wince or let it show. He must have torn a muscle in the crash. No bones were broken and he had somehow managed to escape a concussion. But he had been thrown around in a high-impact collision, then drugged with something very powerful.

His limbs still felt heavy, his reactions slow. He still felt sick from the blows to his stomach and his kidney. For now, at least, he was in no condition to fight. He needed to use his wits, not his fists. And the first stage was to get Karoly Bardossy talking. The more he talked, the more information he would reveal and the more openings he would provide for Balthazar to use as leverage.

Balthazar gestured at the water. 'I'm thirsty.'

Karoly nodded. 'Drink. That's what it's there for.'

'I don't trust that. Bring me a new bottle and have someone open it in front of me.'

Karoly laughed. 'Whatever you say, Detective.' He looked at the man standing against the wall. 'Porter, you heard the man.'

Porter nodded, walked over to the bar and returned with two large bottles of spring water, one with a pink label, one with a blue. He turned to Balthazar in a parody of a waiter, his grey eyes boring into Balthazar, his distaste apparent. 'Still or sparkling? *Sir*.'

'Still.' Balthazar looked at him. 'Porter. You're British, Mr Porter? You sound British. I've spent time in London. Is that a London accent? Sounds like it, Mr Porter. South London?'

Porter did not answer, his irritation visible as he showed Balthazar the top of the bottle. The seal was unbroken. Balthazar nodded. 'Could you pour it for me, please? I'm still a bit unsteady. I don't want to drop the bottle.'

Porter grunted something in reply. Balthazar moved the glass closer to where he was sitting so that Porter needed to lean nearer to him to pour the water. Balthazar glanced at the pistol on the side of his hip. Engraved along the grip of the gun he could see the edge of a logo and the letters *BER*...

As Porter moved closer, Balthazar whispered. 'Twenty years.'

Porter did not acknowledge what Balthazar had said, but his hand trembled slightly as he poured the water.

Karoly picked up the current that flowed between the two men. 'What did you say, Detective?'

Balthazar smiled, and took a long draught of the water. 'I said thank you.' He sat back. 'Is that an original Picasso?'

'Yes. From his Blue Period. The others are a Manet and a Monet. I still get them muddled up. So easy to do that.'

'Very. How long have you owned them?'

Karoly smiled. 'They have been in the Bardossy family for a long time. We helped out some friends during the war. They were very grateful.'

'I'm sure they were. How did your family help them?' asked Balthazar.

Something flickered in Bardossy's eyes. He blinked, reached for the whisky glass.

Balthazar thought quickly. A Picasso, a Manet and a Monet. The document – Vivi's decryption was right. The paintings were real. They were here, in front of him. So who, or what, was Ber...?

There were always moments, Balthazar had learned during his career as a detective when pieces suddenly fit together and a picture emerged from the confusion of jumbled names, dates and confused witness accounts. For a second he was back on Liberty Square, reading one of the brief biographies pinned to the thin rope in front of the mawkish statue. *Tragically, they trusted the wrong person*. The hair rose on the back of his neck. Miklos and Rahel Berger. *Cigany boszorkanysag*, Gypsy witchcraft. It had never let him down yet. Ber... was Berger – Miklos and Rahel.

Karoly looked back up now, a thin smile frozen on his face, aware that he had let something slip. 'We helped them, that's all that matters. This is not a history seminar, Detective.'

'But it is, Mr Bardossy. Everything in Hungary is a history seminar. History is walking around everywhere. It's asking what you did when they came for your neighbours and how you got those nice silver candlesticks.' He paused. 'Or those lovely paintings by the artists whose names sound almost the same. We Hungarians have a lot of unfinished business.'

Karoly laughed. 'We Hungarians.'

The subtext was clear. Balthazar was a Gypsy, not a Hungarian. He yawned before he spoke, drank half a glass of water. 'Really, Mr Bardossy, an intelligent man like you. Is that the best you can do? How about the Bergers, Miklos and Rahel? I am sure they thought they were Hungarians as well.'

Karoly stiffened for a moment. He emptied his whisky glass, his anger rising. 'I have no idea what you are talking about, Detective. I told you, my family helped another family. I don't remember their names.'

Balthazar pressed harder. 'Miklos and Rahel also thought they were Hungarians, until the gendarmes came for them and put them on the train to Auschwitz. And the Bardossys got three nice new paintings to add to their collection. From people they thought they could trust. There was a lot of trusting in 1944, but much more betrayal. Do you ever think about that, when you look at your Picasso? Or the Monet, the Manet?'

'The gendarmes did not come for them. It was the SS,' said Karoly angrily. He closed his eyes for a moment, knowing that he had given too much away.

Balthazar smiled inside. His instinct was correct. 'Ah, so now we are getting somewhere. If you have never heard of Miklos and Rahel Berger, how do you know who arrested them? What's the real story here, Mr Bardossy? Elad Harrari asked a lot of questions about what happened in 1944 and now he is missing. I tried to find him and you had me abducted. What have you got to hide?'

Bardossy shrugged. 'Nothing. What does it matter now? It was a long time ago. Who cares?'

'You do. Otherwise why am I here?'

Karoly's face flushed red. 'You're here because you ask too many fucking questions. Like that Israeli, asking for access to our company archives. Why would I let him poke around in our historical records?'

'Because you have nothing to hide. Because you want the truth to come out, finally. Because you want to clear the historical record.'

Karoly laughed. 'Spare me.' He looked at Balthazar. 'Your sister, Flora, she's is in the art business isn't she? I heard she sold some pictures to my dear niece for her new office in parliament. Flora has that lovely little gallery in District VIII. On Brody Sandor Street, number 23, I believe.'

Balthazar sat upright. 'Is that a threat, Mr Bardossy?'

Karoly smiled, shook his head. 'Not at all. Just an observation. I like to keep up with the news in the art world. I hear she's going to start staying open till ten or eleven at night. Very good idea; there are so many tourists in Budapest now with money to spend. Still, Brody Sandor Street, not the best part of town for a young woman on her own at night, even in the fancy end, what do they call it now, the Palace Quarter?' The smiled turned into a smirk. 'Palaces. In District VIII, who knew?'

Balthazar breathed through his nose for several seconds, controlling his rising anger. The insults about District VIII, the slurs against its Gypsy inhabitants, were nothing new. But this was clearly a threat aimed at Flora, and could not go unanswered.

'Shall I explain something to you, Mr Bardossy?' Balthazar asked, his voice cold and measured. Porter moved away from the wall and started to walk towards Balthazar.

Karoly held up his hand. 'It's OK, Porter. Detective Kovacs wants to tell me something.' He looked at Balthazar, his eyes amused, his face flushed with alcohol. 'Go ahead, Detective. I'm listening.'

Balthazar spoke slowly and carefully, his eyes locked onto Karoly's. 'It's another story from the Second World War, Mr Bardossy.'

Bardossy stifled a yawn. 'Get on with it.'

'You know for us Gypsies, family comes before everything. We may squabble and feud among ourselves, but against the outside world, we are always united. When the Nazis came for us, here in '44, in the neighbouring countries much earlier, the families refused to be divided when they arrived at the camps. Mothers and fathers, they would not let the Germans separate them from their children. They fought, they screamed, they cursed, even on the ramp where Mengele did his selections. Sometimes the mothers attacked the Nazis by hand, scratching at their faces, gouging at their eyes. So the Nazis let them live together, in a special family camp. There was even a Gypsy uprising in Auschwitz. Who knew? Did you know?'

Karoly shook his head. 'No, I did not hear about that.'

'That was in May 1944. They attacked the SS with stones and sticks. For a while the Nazis left them alone. Then in August, they gassed everyone, almost three thousand people.' He paused. 'Including some of my relatives.'

Karoly said, 'We all lost people in the war.'

'Some families more than others, Mr Bardossy. But you are wondering why I am telling you all of this. This is why.' Balthazar paused. 'If something happens to Flora, or her gallery, the same will be visited on you and your home – but multiplied many times. This lovely house will go up in flames. You might be in it when it does. I'm the only cop in my family. The rest of my relatives don't worry about laws. They run District VIII. They have an army to call on. Our family, and all the other families. There are hundreds of us. We have codes and we live by them. Family first, before everything. In the camp at Auschwitz in 1944, or on Brody Sandor Street now. And we believe in vengeance. We're very good at it; we've been practising for centuries. You – and your business – won't know what hit you. Oh, it might take a few weeks, or months. Even a year or two. But you will never be able to sleep soundly again, or step outside without looking over your shoulder. One day we will come for you and we will find you.' Balthazar turned to look at Porter, ignoring the bolt of pain that shot up his back. 'Even with a legion of Porters. He won't be able to save you. Or himself.'

Balthazar paused. 'Now tell me why I am here.'

Karoly sit very still for several seconds, swallowed, then asked, 'Where is the Israeli?'

'I don't know.'

'Aren't you looking for him?'

'Yes. But I didn't find him yet. Why do you care?'

Karoly blinked slowly, seemed to gather his strength. 'This is how it's going to work, Detective. You are going to call your friend Anastasia. She is going to send over the memory stick that you found with your neighbour, dear Eva *neni*.' He paused. 'Yes, that memory stick. The one you took to Falk Miksa Street where whatshername, Bibi, Vivi, whatever, decrypted it. Once I have that, you are free to leave.'

Balthazar rapidly processed what he had heard. Bardossy had someone on the inside at Falk Miksa. In fact it would be surprising if he did not. Nobody could run a business empire in Hungary the size of his without a powerful network of contacts across every sector of the establishment, including the security service. 'I don't know what you are talking about,' Balthazar said.

'I think you do,' said Karoly. 'And in case you need a reminder, here it is.' He picked up the A4 envelope, opened it and handed several photographs to Balthazar. He leafed through them. Each shot was of Eva *neni*, walking in and out of the apartment building on Dob Street, chatting with her friends in the park on Klauzal Square, shopping in the market hall nearby.

Karoly sneered, 'Your Gypsy army will go to war for you or your sister, Flora. Or for Alex.'

Balthazar jerked upright at the mention of his son's name. Karoly held his hands up. 'Don't worry. I don't threaten kids. Especially such well-connected ones. I don't want the Americans on my back. But I don't think District VIII will rise up over an elderly Jewish lady, even if she is your neighbour. Look outside, it's winter. It's a nice clear night tonight, but we have weeks of snow and ice ahead. One slip, an accidental nudge from a passer-by in a hurry. What a shame to survive the Holocaust, then perish on a slippery pavement.'

This time Balthazar let the red mist descend. He knew he had one chance to take both men down. He needed Karoly out of reach and Porter well within reach. This was it and his fury drove him.

'You fucker. You piece of shit,' he snarled, as he slid towards Karoly. 'Threatening an old lady.'

Karoly jumped out of his chair and stepped away, his alarm turning to fear.

At the same time, Porter leapt forward towards Balthazar, his fists raised. Sensing Porter behind him, Balthazar clenched his right fist, whirled around and aimed a side hammer punch at Porter's groin.

His plan was that Porter would fall forward in pain. Balthazar would then rain more blows down on the back of his head and neck without having to waste time trying to stand up, slam his face into the table, then grab the whisky decanter and break it over his head. Once Porter had collapsed he could take his gun, knock Karoly out or shoot him in the leg and escape.

It was a decent plan and might have worked, had Balthazar not taken several hard punches, been hurled around in a car crash, wrenched a muscle in his back, staggered out of the car and been gassed with a knockout spray.

The side of his fist connected with Porter's groin, but his fury and adrenalin weren't enough and his arm moved too slowly.

Porter stepped sideways at the moment of impact. Balthazar felt him wince but he absorbed part of the blow in his thigh. He ignored the pain and moved back in.

A second later his right arm was around Balthazar's neck in a chokehold against his carotid artery, his left arm locking it in place. It was a deadly technique that cut off the blood supply to the brain. Unconsciousness would follow in a few seconds.

Balthazar grabbed Porter's wrist with his right hand, trying to break the stranglehold while his left flailed at Porter's eyes.

Porter ignored the blows, tightened his grip.

Balthazar reached forward for the glass in front of him on the table. He grabbed the glass and swung it at Porter's face, but his strength was fading by the second.

Porter released his left hand and blocked the glass with no difficulty, then locked it back in place.

Porter's arms felt like two steel bars. Daggers of pain shot down Balthazar's neck and back. His breathing turned ragged and shallow.

The room turned murky. Balthazar felt his limbs go weak.

The glass slipped from his hand.

Karoly said, 'OK, Porter. Stop now. He's not a threat any more.'

Porter tensed his arm muscles once more, increasing the pressure for a fraction of a second, then released Balthazar. He fell forward on the chair, coughing and wheezing, the room dark and spinning.

Karoly sat back down, smiled at Porter. 'Thank you, Porter. Very nice work. Our friend was getting a bit emotional, it seems. Now then, Detective. Needs must. Get me that memory stick.'

Balthazar slowly sat back, panting and coughing. After several seconds the room stabilised. He tried to speak but at first the words would not come. He swallowed, tried again. 'Everything on it is digitised. They will have copies.'

Karoly shrugged. 'Doesn't matter. We are living in the post-truth era. I just need to know what's there. Then I can learn from my niece's example. Nationwide has a substantial communications department, as you can imagine – with plenty of tame journalists. We will launch a pre-emptive strike, like Reka did, explain how we are being targeted with a deepfake, show how easy it is to fabricate documents, take each one apart line by line. Nobody will believe anything once we are finished. We are good at rewriting history here, always have been. Now we have a new toolkit, it's even easier.'

He smiled, poured himself some water, drank half the glass. 'I should be grateful to my niece. At the start of the week almost nobody knew what a deepfake was. Now the whole country does. Of course, the irony is that her video wasn't fake at all. It was completely genuine. But now nobody believes that. In fact people are sympathetic to her. Last time I looked her numbers were creeping back up. I've already talked to my communications people, explained there is a massive smear campaign coming, against me, against the firm, a tissue of lies and fabrications all reaching back to the war. Another deepfake. We're all ready to go.'

Karoly leaned forward. 'Now get me the memory stick. Once it's here, you can go home.'

THIRTY-NINE

Remetehegyi Way, 10.45 p.m.

Antal Kondor opened the door of the silver Audi and helped Eva *neni* out of the vehicle. She thanked him, stood still for a moment as she took in her surroundings: the row of regularly spaced villas, the carefully tended gardens, the police guard outside Reka's house.

She breathed in deeply, trying to control her emotions, keep her voice steady. 'I haven't been to Obuda for years. Decades, in fact. Better air than downtown, that's for sure.' She squinted, looked harder at Reka's house. 'Apart from the police, it looks exactly the same.'

Antal asked, 'You've been here before?'

'You could say that. A long time ago. A very long time ago, young man. In another life,' she said, still staring at the house. She looked up at Antal. 'So, are we going inside,' she asked brightly, 'or shall we stand here a bit longer getting cold?'

Reka had called Eva *neni* personally and told her that Elad was safe and wanted to see her, that she also had some information for her and she would send a car and driver to get her. There had been no question in Eva *neni*'s mind that she would accept the invitation, especially when Reka told her the address. Antal gestured for her to walk ahead, signalled to the policeman standing nearby to open the gate, and led through the front garden, inside the house to the lounge.

Eniko and Akos stood up as Eva *neni* walked into the lounge. She greeted Eniko, who she already knew, and Akos introduced himself. A few seconds later Reka appeared from a side room. She walked over to Eva *neni*, introduced herself and thanked her for coming, especially at such a late hour.

'You're welcome. Well, Prime Minister,' said Eva *neni*, looking her up and down, 'you're even prettier in person than you look on television.'

Reka smiled. 'Thank you. Please call me Reka.'

Eva *neni* nodded. 'OK. And I am Eva *neni*.' She looked around the room again. 'You said he was here. I can't see him. Where is he?'

'Come with me. I'll take you to Elad,' said Reka, as she led Eva *neni* through the garden towards the cottage.

'And Balthazar?' asked Eva *neni*.

'I won't lie to you. We are not sure. It looks like he has been kidnapped. But we will find him.' There was no need to tell Eva *neni* about the internet footage of Balthazar's abduction, Reka judged. 'We have a good idea where he might be.'

Eva *neni* stood still, her face creased with anxiety. 'Then go and get him, please.' She shook her head. 'It's all my fault. I should never have involved him.'

Reka took her hand. It felt small and cold. 'It's not your fault, Eva *neni*. You have done nothing wrong. Everything will be fine in the end.'

'I've heard that before, several times.' Eva *neni* gave her a half smile. 'It never was.'

'It will be this time. But for now, please come with me.'

Eva followed her outside and stood still for a moment. She had dressed up, Reka saw. She was wearing a dark-blue wool coat that had once been expensive, had brushed and set her hair. Beneath the bluster the elderly lady was nervous, Reka saw. She was far from her home and comfort zone, and travelling back in time.

The two women walked over to the small house. Zsuzsa and Elad were inside in the small kitchen, sitting at the table, working. The surface was covered in handwritten sheets of paper, books and piles of printouts. They looked up as the door opened.

Elad jumped up and ran over to Eva *neni*, hugging her. Zsuzsa smiled and quickly left, together with Reka.

Eva *neni* and Elad sat down at the table. Eva *neni* wagged her finger at him, mock sternly. 'Naughty boy. I was so worried about you. Two days you have been missing. I've had your parents on the phone every day. You should have called. Or sent a message or something. A few more hours and they would have called the embassy, the police, everyone. Then Reka called me.'

Elad looked bashful. 'I know. But they told me I couldn't. It might have put you in danger. I'm really sorry.'

'I forgive you. Don't do it again. So what have you found out?'

'A lot. About your parents. About this house. It's very sad. Are you sure you want to hear it?'

Eva *neni* nodded. 'They've been dead a long time.' She looked around the small room. 'I want you to tell the story. It's your story too.'

Elad stood up, looked for two pieces of paper and picked them up. 'I know. Come, Auntie, let's go through to the others.'

They gathered in the lounge. Eva *neni* sat next to Elad on the sofa, Zsuzsa next to him. Eniko and Reka sat on the armchairs, while Akos grabbed a chair from the kitchen.

Reka started speaking. 'You are probably wondering what all this is about, why this is happening now, why a historian and a journalist are working in the garden house... all sorts of questions. My family, as you know, is one of the richest in Hungary. It was rich before the war, managed to expand its wealth after 1945 and keep its riches during communism. Karoly Bardossy, my uncle, is now one of the most powerful businessmen in the country. I wondered for a long time what the real origins of our wealth were and what happened during the war. I had my suspicions, of course. I'd heard things over the years, remarks, strange references. I'd also found some documents that were very disturbing. I could not commission a Hungarian historian to investigate this. I needed an outside voice. Around this time I had a call from Erno Hartmann at the Jewish Museum, who wanted to show me the museum. I went there and I explained what I wanted to do. Erno was sympathetic, keen to help. I told him I needed someone who could dig deep, wasn't afraid of what they might find, and that I could pay all the necessary costs.'

Reka nodded at Elad. 'Erno had heard of you, knew about your work at Hebrew University, and that you understood Hungarian. He contacted you, offered you a stipend, expenses, space in his office.'

Elad started with surprise. 'You brought me over? You set this up? Hartmann never told me.'

'Yes, I did. And why should he? He promised to keep things confidential and he did.'

Elad sat very still for a moment. 'So it was you feeding me the documents. You are the source.'

Reka nodded. 'Yes. It was me. I gave you the first document. I wanted to see what you did with it, if you would use it to dig deeper or go public as soon as you got it.' Reka smiled. 'You passed the test. You kept quiet, carried on working. So I sent you the next document. Then I realised that you were in danger, so I brought you here. Not just from Uncle Karoly. There's a rogue guy at your embassy, Shlomo. He was very unhappy about your work. He was about to warn you off, in very strong terms. The last thing he wanted was a big Holocaust revelation before Alon Farkas's visit and the trade deal with Nationwide. Especially anything to do with Nationwide.'

Elad's eyes widened. 'Shlomo? I met him a couple of times. He was always so friendly, so interested in what I was doing. He asked a lot of questions.'

Reka smiled and nodded. 'Now you know why. The more you found out, the more worried he got. Then he got in touch with some people in Serbia, and we got very alarmed. That's when I brought you here. Now, over to you, Elad. Talk us through the documents.'

Elad looked down at the first sheet of paper. 'This is a copy of the first document you sent me. It's a legal agreement between Tamas Bardossy, Reka's late grandfather, and someone called Miklos Berger. Who was Miklos Berger? Well, he was the son of a family of Budapest Jewish industrialists. The family firm was called Berger Holdings. Miklos was the chairman of the board and the CEO. His father, Samuel, who founded the company, had been sick for a while and died a few weeks before the Nazis invaded. His mother had died in childbirth. Miklos was the only child. He knew that the Nazis would probably invade Hungary and take the business, so he arranged with a trusted business partner, Tamas Bardossy, a way to safeguard the family holdings, which were extensive. The Bergers owned a steel mill on Csepel Island, a bicycle manufacturing plant and several other companies.'

Elad looked around the room. He had everyone's attention. He caught Eva *neni*'s eye. She nodded and smiled at him encouragingly. Elad drank some water then carried on talking. 'So now to the details of the first document. It is dated 20 March 1944 – a day after the Germans invaded. There are two parts. In the first Miklos signed over the company to Tamas Bardossy in exchange for 50,000 Swiss francs. Both men had bank accounts in Zurich, so the transfer was simple to arrange. The agreement was confidential, of course, but could be produced if and when the Nazis tried to appropriate Berger Holdings. The key point was that this document showed there was no longer any Jewish ownership of the company. There is another paragraph about three paintings, a Picasso, a Manet and a Monet, which the Bergers also transferred to Tamas Bardossy for temporary safekeeping. And a house, a beautiful villa in the Buda hills.'

Elad paused. 'In Obuda, to be precise.'

Elad looked at Reka. She closed her eyes for a moment, swallowed, then met his gaze. She nodded, a quick, tight movement.

Everyone at the table sat very still. The only sound was the faint hum of the fridge and the soft tick of an electric clock in the kitchen.

Elad said, 'This villa. The Bergers lived here.'

Nobody spoke.

Eva *neni* wiped her eyes, then asked, 'And the second document?'

Elad picked up the second piece of paper. 'This one was also notarised by the lawyer, signed by both men, witnessed by their wives, Maria Bardossy and Rahel Berger. It says that the sales agreement wasn't genuine and was invalid. It was merely a device to cloak the ownership of Berger Holdings until the end of the war, at which point Miklos Berger, or any surviving family member, would return the 50,000 Swiss Francs to Tamas Bardossy. Bardossy would then give back the factories, the house, the paintings, the house and everything else to the Berger family.'

'But that's not what happened, is it?' asked Eniko.

Elad shook his head. 'No, it's not. Tamas Bardossy did not even pay the 50,000 francs.'

Reka said, 'But the Bardossys still got everything the Bergers owned.'

Eniko asked, 'Did the Nazis try to take over Berger Holdings?'

Elad nodded. 'Absolutely. A squad of SS officers turned up at the office to arrest Miklos Berger the day after the invasion. But they found Tamas Bardossy sitting in Miklos's office. He produced the 'Sales Agreement' – Elad made quote marks in the air – 'that showed the Bergers' firm had been sold to the Bardossy family and had no Jewish ownership. The SS officer, one Karl Buchner, left.'

'Why didn't the Germans take it all anyway?' asked Eniko. 'Why did they care about a legal agreement?'

'It's a good question,' said Elad. 'In the first few months of the occupation, at least until October 1944 when the Arrow Cross took over, the Germans wanted to keep a kind of fiction that Hungary retained some sovereignty. They needed Hungary as an ally. Admiral Horthy stayed in place, there was a Hungarian government. Berger Holdings had already been converted to military use – it was making casings for mines and shells. It was more important for the Germans to show that there was still some rule of law and Hungary was a partner, rather than a fully occupied country like Poland. Hungary was a very useful ally at a time when it was growing clear the Nazis were losing the war.'

Eniko asked, 'What happened to Miklos and Rahel?'

'They went into hiding but they were found the next day,' said Elad. His hand reached for Eva *neni*'s. 'They were sent to Auschwitz. They didn't come back.'

Zsuzsa said, 'This is the Miklos and Rahel Berger whose story is at the memorial on Liberty Square, isn't it?'

Elad nodded. 'It is.'

Zsuzsa asked, 'Did you put it there?'

Elad said, 'Yes.'

Eniko asked, 'Did Miklos and Rahel have any children?'

Eva *neni* blinked away the tears and clasped Elad's hand tightly. 'Yes,' she said. 'They had a daughter.' She paused. 'Her name was Eva.'

The atmosphere, already tense and emotional, turned electric.

'Her name still is Eva.' She swallowed hard for a moment, took a drink of water before she spoke. 'My name is Eva Hegyi now. But I was born Eva Berger. I grew up in this house, played in the garden. The day before the Germans arrived, before my parents went into hiding, I went to live with my aunt, Orsi. We knew that the Nazis had a VIP wanted list and my parents and I were on it, so they thought it was safer for me to move to Pest. We were in the heart of the ghetto. Orsi got me false papers. We survived, somehow, but Orsi didn't want me to have a Jewish-sounding name after the war, so she changed it. That is my real name. Eva Berger. Berger in German, Hegyi in Hungarian, they both mean "of the hill".'

Elad said, 'Berger, Hegyi, and in Hebrew, Harrari.'

Eva *neni* stared out of the window for a moment. 'Now I'm back on the hill.' She turned to Reka, wiped her eyes again. 'And now I know what happened, how we lost everything. Thank you for bringing me here, Reka. For bringing me back home. I wanted to come for such a long time. But I couldn't have done this on my own.'

Reka swallowed, also wiped her eyes. 'I'm so sorry this has taken so long. I had a researcher check the records for Eva Berger but we could not find anything after the war. Those were chaotic times. I thought perhaps you had died in the ghetto or emigrated. Then I read recently about how many Jewish families changed their names, Hungarianised them, after the war, and I wondered if you did. This time the researcher found your records. So then I needed to find a historian to dig out the whole story. Now I have something for you, Eva *neni*. I've been waiting a long time to give it to you.'

Reka walked over to a cupboard in the kitchen and took out a small metal box. The blue paint was faded and rusty but she had cleaned it, even oiled the hinge so it opened easily.

She handed it to Eva *neni*. 'This is yours. Everything inside once belonged to your parents. I found it many years ago, half buried in the garden. I used to play with it when I was a kid. I left it there for years, then after my parents died I brought it into the house.'

Eva *neni* stared at the metal box for a long moment. 'This is from my parents? From seventy years ago?'

Reka said, 'Yes. Would you like us to leave, Eva *neni*? We all understand that this is a very emotional moment for you.'

Eva *neni* shook her head, touched the box with a sense of wonder, her hand resting on the metal. 'No, please stay.' She looked around the room. 'You are all part of the story now. Thank you for being with me. I just wish Balthazar was here as well.'

'We all do,' said Eniko.

The table fell silent as Eva *neni* opened the box, her face suddenly childlike and full of wonder. She took out the white silk garment with the blue trim, held it to her face and inhaled. 'My father's tallis. His prayer shawl,' she said, carefully folding the garment and placing it on the table.

Next came the smaller box with all the rings. She took them out one by one, looked on the inside of the gold bands, swallowed. For a moment she could not speak. 'I remember these. My parents' wedding rings, with the date of their wedding: 10 August 1933. And my mum's ring and my father's.'

Eva *neni* looked at Reka, her face full of amazement, joy and sadness all at once. 'I don't know what to say. I never thought I would see these again.' She placed the rings next to the tallis, then took out the exercise book. She opened it, took in the heavy, blocky script. 'It's in Hebrew. I can't read Hebrew.'

She handed the book to Elad. He opened it to the first page, quickly read it, flipped through the other pages. 'It's a kind of diary. Thoughts and impressions. Miklos wrote it. I'll translate it for you.'

She reached for the book again, and Elad handed it back. She leafed through the pages. 'He wrote this? By hand? I don't have anything in his writing.'

Eva *neni* reached inside the box again, almost overwhelmed. Resting at the bottom was a small photograph of a young girl with curly blond hair in a dress with a row of buttons down the middle.

She took out the photograph, her eyes wide. 'Oh. That's me.'

Eva *neni* turned the picture over then read the inscription out loud: 'Darling Evike, we have to go away for a little while, but we love you always and forever. A million kisses, Mummy and Daddy.'

She sat very still for a moment and put the photograph down. Then the tears flowed, around the table.

FORTY

Mariahegyi Way, 11.40 p.m.

Kristof Solyom's finger hovered over the screen of his mobile phone. The number 112 was on display, which would put him through to the police. He was still hesitating because once he made the call, he would certainly lose his job.

Kristof had sat in the security cabin on the path to the Bardossy villa for ten hours a day for three months. He was immensely bored most of the time. But the work paid three times the salary of his previous position as a nightclub bouncer and there were no drunks or druggies to deal with. Porter, his boss, had made it clear that all he needed to do was open the barrier across the road when necessary, keep his eyes open for any potential intruders and keep his mouth shut.

Usually, that wasn't a problem. The regular deliveries were food from a gourmet grocery chain, small packages from a motorcyclist that Kristof knew was a runner for Budapest's high-end coke dealer and girls from an upmarket brothel on the other side of Buda. He was fine with that; whoever the boss wanted to screw, whatever he put up his nose was his business.

But he wasn't so fine with what he had seen tonight. The police car looked like a real police car, the men inside wearing police uniforms looked genuine, but what were they doing here?

Kristof had followed protocol when the cop car pulled up. He had stepped outside to see what was going on. There were three cops inside the car, one driving in the front and two in the back with someone between them.

The prisoner – and he must have been a prisoner – looked completely out of it, his head lolling forward and blood seeping from a cut on his head. He looked familiar, Kristof realised. He was pretty sure it was that Gypsy cop, the famous one who took down the terrorist last year and stopped that plot to gas everyone on Kossuth Square. What the fuck was he doing here? He looked really bad. And why wasn't he in the car when it drove back out?

The more he thought about it, the more he realised there was something wrong here, very wrong, and whatever the boss was paying it was not enough to go down for this. Kristof was just about to press the call button when a new set of headlights appeared on the CCTV screen showing the feed from the path up to the cabin.

A few seconds later the lights were shining into the cabin, on full beam. Now what? He stood up and stepped outside, held his right hand over his face to shield his eyes from the light and squinted into the night.

There was a large blue Maserati coupe about ten metres away. Kristof recognised that car, he realised. He liked cars, was saving up for one, had a good memory for people and their vehicles. There were not a lot of Maseratis in Budapest. This one looked familiar, just like the Maserati that belonged to the fat brothel owner that came to the house sometimes.

But what the hell was he doing here? No girls were expected tonight. Something really wasn't right.

Kristof waved his hand up and down, palm out, still squinting. The headlights dipped. A woman got out and started walking towards him. She was attractive enough, slim, long hair. Looked sophisticated, though, not the usual tarty type. What was this about? Maybe the boss was going upmarket, or wanted someone to talk to afterwards as well.

Kristof walked forward, wished her a good evening. She reciprocated, showed him an open wallet with some kind of ID inside.

He looked closer, closed his eyes for a moment. *Fuck*. State security. He really should have called the police.

'Your ID, please,' said Anastasia.

Kristof scrabbled for his wallet in his back pocket. Somewhere in the distance an owl hooted. He showed his ID card to her. She took his wallet, looked down at his ID card. 'Do you have a weapon on you or in the cabin? Anything I should know about?'

Kristof shook his head. 'No. Nothing.'

'Anyone else here? Are you changing shifts, waiting for a replacement?'

'No. Just me. I'm here till six in the morning.'

'Good. You are going to help us, Mr Solyom, aren't you? You saw the car that passed through here earlier. So no nonsense, no ridiculous stories. Then you might escape a prison sentence for aiding and abetting the abduction, torture and detention of a serving police officer.'

Kristof felt sick with fear. He really was in deep shit. He nodded as enthusiastically as he could. 'Sure. Whatever you need.'

Fat Vik and Gaspar got out of the car and walked towards Kristof. His eyes opened wider. They looked familiar. He was right. It was the Gypsy pimp and his sidekick. What the fuck was going on here?

Gaspar walked up to Kristof, stood a few inches from him. He could smell cigarettes, stale sweat, alcohol. Gaspar prodded Kristof in the chest, his stubby finger smashing into his ribs. 'Where is he?'

Kristof said, 'Inside.'

Gaspar jabbed his chest again, his finger like iron. 'Who else is in there?'

'The boss, and Porter, his bodyguard. He's British, ex-military. He's armed.'

Anastasia took Gaspar's hand. 'Enough. He's helping us.' She looked at Kristof. 'So there's only you, and you control the main entrance to the house from here? There're no more security people inside?'

'That's right. The boss doesn't like company. There's a short road from here to the wall around the house and one entrance, and this is the only road in.'

'Good. Open the door, call Porter and tell him we are coming.'

'What if the boss says no, doesn't want to let you in?'

Gaspar smiled, his gold teeth glinting in the harsh light. He held an envelope in his right hand, and slapped it back and forth against his left palm. 'Tell him we have some really nice souvenirs of his time in the VIP suite. The one with the purple carpet and the mirror on the ceiling. He'll definitely want to see them.'

A couple of minutes later Gaspar, Fat Vik and Anastasia were standing in the entrance lobby of the house. It was a wide, open-plan area, surrounded by glass walls, with a marble staircase at the back. A modernist sculpture, a twisted construction of black metal, stood on a plinth by the wall. The space was without a speck of dust, smelled of furniture polish and had all the warmth of a designer show home.

Porter stood in front of them, his arms crossed against his chest, his pistol in his holster. 'It's almost midnight. I have no idea what you are talking about. There is nobody here. You are trespassing. What do you want? Mr Bardossy has not requested any company tonight.'

He looked at Anastasia, asked, 'I know these two, but who the fuck are you, anyway?'

Anastasia flashed her ID for a moment before she spoke. 'State security. Place your weapon on the floor and slide it over to me.'

Porter's hand hovered over his Beretta. He looked at Anastasia for a moment as if deciding what to do.

In that second she reached for her Makarov and it was in her hand, pointing at him. 'I told you, Mr Porter. Place your weapon on the floor and slide it over to me.'

This time he obeyed. Anastasia kept her eye on him and her Makarov trained on his chest as she knelt down and picked up Porter's gun.

She handed it to Fat Vik. 'Hold this but take the magazine out.'

Anastasia said, 'We know all about you, Mr Porter. George Porter. Born 7 March 1976 in Manchester. Father unknown, mother a nurse. Enrolled in Salford University to study engineering, dropped out after two years after a fight in a nightclub which left a teenage boy in a wheelchair. Police failed to secure a conviction. Joined the army. Served in Northern Ireland in an undercover unit, in Sierra Leone, Bosnia and Kosovo. Reached the rank of captain, won several inter-service pistol shooting competitions. Expert marksman. Left the army, again under mysterious circumstances. Allegations of sexual assault, case never proven.'

Porter shrugged. 'So what? None of that means you can barge into a private home and make wild accusations about people being kidnapped.'

Anastasia said, 'You are a murder suspect, Mr Porter. We believe you killed Geza Kovacs. They were small-calibre bullets, the type fired by a Beretta. And as soon as we match the bullets to your weapon, you will be arrested.'

Porter turned pale, started to bluster.

Gaspar stepped forward, an envelope in his hand. 'Let's stop fucking about, here, George. Give this to your boss. Then bring my brother out.'

Porter said nothing, his eyes blazing with fury.

A few seconds later Karoly Bardossy appeared at the top of the stairs and slowly started making his way down. 'Visitors, at this time of night. How exciting. What is all this about?' he asked.

'Business,' said Gaspar. He walked forward, envelope in hand.

Porter stepped in front of him. Gaspar laughed.

Karoly raised his hand, looking at the envelope. 'It's OK, Porter.'

Karoly looked at Gaspar, smirking. 'Did we have an appointment, Mr Kovacs? I don't recall ordering anything from you tonight. You'll forgive me if I don't invite you inside. I wasn't expecting company.' He looked at the envelope. 'Is that for me?'

Gaspar nodded. 'Yup. Take a look.'

Karoly opened the envelope and leafed through the photographs. The smirk vanished. He turned red with fury, ripped the photographs to shreds and scattered them on the floor.

Gaspar shrugged. 'They are just prints. We have the originals, high-resolution, nicely digitised. There is much more, all ready to go. Some really nice video clips as well. And don't bother saying the pictures are fake. All the girls are ready to talk – at length and in detail about your favourite activities. You deny it all you like but everything will be all over the internet. That's a lot of coke, as well. Your communications people won't know what's hit them. Mud sticks. Your board will ask you to resign by the end of the day.'

Karoly said, 'What the fuck do you want? What is this about?'

Gaspar stepped forward, jabbed him in the chest several times with his finger. 'Bring my brother out. Now.'

FORTY-ONE

Dob Street, Saturday, 1.10 a.m.

Balthazar sat on his bed, his back against the wall, as the doctor held up various combinations of fingers, each time asking him to count.

'How many now?' she asked, showing her left index finger and three fingers on her right hand.

'Four,' said Balthazar. Exhaustion was hitting him in waves, but he knew he had to stay awake for as long as she was here. The doctor wore a white coat and stethoscope around her neck. She looked, even sounded, familiar. Where had he seen her before?

'Correct,' said the doctor. 'And now?' she asked, holding all ten fingers up.

Balthazar gave the right answer. She nodded, leaned forward and peered closely at Balthazar's eyes, before taking his blood pressure. She had already checked his breathing with the stethoscope and dressed the cut on his forehead.

'Hmmm,' she said, when she saw the blood pressure results. 'One fifty-nine over ninety. That's high, but should go down over the next hour or so.'

The doctor's name was Dora Szegedi. She was a stern, plump lady in her mid-forties with dyed red hair, blue eyes and a gold Star of David around her neck. Dr Szegedi, who usually worked as a paediatrician, had recently joined the roster of doctors kept on twenty-four-hour call by the state security service.

Once Balthazar was out of Bardossy's villa and inside Gaspar's Maserati, Anastasia had placed a blue light on the roof. Fat Vik drove at speed and they had raced through Obuda, back across Margaret Bridge, down the Grand Boulevard and to his flat on Dob Street. Fat Vik and Gaspar had helped Balthazar up the stairs into his flat. Anastasia called Dr Szegedi from the car on the way back to Dob Street. She lived nearby and had arrived a couple of minutes after the four of them. The doctor had listened to the events of the evening and immediately taken some blood samples, which were sent to a laboratory for rapid analysis. Fat Vik had gone home, but Anastasia had insisted on staying.

Dr Szegedi turned to Anastasia. 'He doesn't seem to be suffering from a concussion, and there are no signs of skull fracture or bleeding on the brain.'

'That's a relief. Thank you, Doctor,' said Anastasia.

Dr Szegedi turned back to look at Balthazar, her head to one side. 'We've met before, haven't we?'

Balthazar thought for a moment before he replied. She was right, but when? Then it came to him. It was last September. He had been investigating the death of a Syrian refugee at Keleti Station at the height of the refugee crisis when he had been surrounded by a group of men and beaten unconscious. Dr Szegedi had been working with MigSzol, the volunteers helping the migrants who were sleeping out at the station.

'Yes, at Keleti Station last autumn. You were helping out with the refugees. Then you helped me when I got knocked out.'

She fixed with him with a sharp, assessing glance. 'I did. And here we are again, patching you up. Now take your T-shirt off and lie down, please.'

Balthazar looked at Anastasia as if to say, *Is this really necessary?*

Anastasia said, 'You heard the doctor.'

His bedroom was sparsely furnished – a blue Ikea wardrobe and chest of drawers, a salvaged bedside table from a throwing-out day, with a cheap bedside lamp. The walls were a faded shade of white and there was a damp patch in the shape of Austria on the ceiling. A large double window looked out onto Klauzal Square, half covered by an ancient roller shutter.

Balthazar did as she asked, then lay back while she poked and prodded his upper body, wincing as her fingers probed his stomach and right side where he had been punched. He turned over as she checked his back and shoulders.

Dr Szegedi stepped back. 'You can sit up again. You are a lucky man, Detective Kovacs, if lucky is the word. You have substantial bruising to come, a wrenched muscle in your back but no broken ribs. There is no blood in your urine and you do not seem to have any internal injuries. I would prefer if you would check into a hospital for observation.' She paused. 'I assume you don't want to do that.'

He sat up and put his T-shirt back on. 'Thank you, Doctor. But I would really rather stay at home and rest if possible.'

A knock sounded on the bedroom door and Balthazar said, 'Come in.'

Gaspar opened the door and stepped inside with an envelope in his hand. 'This just arrived from the hospital,' he said as he handed it to Dr Szegedi.

She thanked him and opened the envelope, extracted a

sheet of paper, quickly read its contents and turned back to Balthazar. 'More good news. Your blood tests show some irregular results from the spray but nothing to worry about. They will stabilise naturally as you excrete the toxins. Sleep, Detective, that's what you need. And some proper home-cooked food. May I give you some further advice?'

Balthazar nodded, half smiling. He could guess what was coming. 'We have met twice now, Detective Kovacs. Once when you were knocked unconscious and again when you have again subjected your body to notable trauma. You are now at least sitting upright and talking. But you are in your mid-thirties. You are slower and need more time to heal than you think. You can't keep doing this to yourself.'

Balthazar glanced around the room. Anastasia was watching them both, affection and concern written on her face. Gaspar was nodding at the doctor's words, his jowls wobbling.

Balthazar asked, 'And the advice, Doctor?'

She gathered her equipment and began to pack away. 'Get a desk job, Detective.'

The doctor turned to Gaspar and Anastasia. 'If he won't go to hospital, then someone needs to stay with him tonight. If he vomits, or his condition worsens, or if he passes blood, you must call an ambulance.'

Gaspar and Anastasia looked at each other and nodded. They thanked the doctor and Gaspar walked her out to the front door of the flat.

He spent a couple of minutes in the kitchen, smiling as he looked at the photographs on Balthazar's pinboard of the two brothers as children, then walked out into the lounge. There he picked up the large framed photograph of Virag and stared at it for some time, his stubby fingers resting on her face. The doctor was right about the desk job. He had already lost a sister – and he could not lose his brother.

Gaspar put the photograph down, walked across to one of the armchairs, picked it up and carried it through to Balthazar's bedroom. His brother was fast asleep on his side. Anastasia sat on the end of the bed, watching him. Gaspar put the armchair down by the side of the bed and moved to sit in it.

Anastasia said, 'It's fine, Gaspar. I can stay with him.'

Loud voices echoed from the street for a few seconds, shouting in English, then faded as the partygoers moved past. Balthazar murmured for a moment, then fell silent.

Gaspar asked, 'Are you sure? There's nowhere to sleep properly. That chair is thirty years old. It's not very comfortable.'

'Really, I will be fine. Don't worry.'

Gaspar thought for a moment. The doctor had said someone needed to stay with him. And he was responsible for his brother. He looked at Anastasia again, understanding slowly dawning.

She smiled. 'I'll call you if anything happens. I promise.'

Gaspar nodded. Being a good brother also meant knowing when to get out of the way. He stepped forward, kissed her on the cheek. 'Thanks, Colonel. And for everything tonight.'

He walked over to Balthazar, bent over him to stroke his hair, whispered, 'Bro, try not to mess this one up.'

He switched the main light off, turning to look before he left. Anastasia was sitting in the chair by Balthazar's bed, watching him as his chest slowly rose and fell. The sound of his breathing echoed in the small space, softly lit by the pale glow of the streetlights on Klauzal Square.

FORTY-TWO

Obuda, Sunday, 9 a.m.

Reka and Karoly Bardossy stood facing each other on either side of a barbecue pit in the Obuda park. Charred pieces of wood and a half-burned log lay on the ground between them. In spring and summer teenagers gathered here for makeshift barbecues but now the fragments were covered in a thin layer of ice.

The prime minister and her uncle had agreed to meet here, on neutral territory, in the middle of a green space roughly equidistant from each of their houses. Two semicircular benches framed the barbecue pit, but nobody was sitting.

Antal Kondor stood a few feet from Reka; George Porter watched over Karoly Bardossy, although the bodyguard was now unarmed. It was a crisp, sunny winter morning, with white streaks of clouds in a clear blue sky. The air smelled fresh, of woodlands and earth. The sound of distant traffic murmured in the background.

Reka looked up for a moment, feeling the bright sun on her skin, then at Karoly. 'There's two ways this can go, Uncle.'

He snapped back, his voice taut with anger. 'What are we doing here, Reka? What the hell is this about? You don't talk to me for years, ignore all my communications, snub me at the funeral, then suddenly you summon me and I have to stand in a park with your goon watching me.'

Reka said, 'As I said, two ways.'

'Which are?'

'Public or private.'

'I don't understand what you are talking about. Why am I even here?'

Reka sighed. 'Uncle, Uncle. Can't you ever stop? It's over. It's finished. The story will be published tomorrow.'

'What story?'

'How we made our money. Where it came from. What we did to get it.'

Karoly sneered, his eyes narrowing. 'It came from running a successful business empire. From navigating a path through wars, dictatorships and terror. From looking after our interests. Like everyone else did.'

He glared at her. 'How do you think you paid for that fine Italian cashmere coat, those shoes? That fancy furniture in your house? The paintings? On your prime minister's salary? You've been spoiled all your life, Reka. You're just like everyone else. You grabbed whatever you could and enjoyed it as long as you could.'

She nodded in agreement. 'I did. It's true. But not any more. The article is written. I've read it. It's very good, very detailed. It tells how our family was friends with the Bergers, how in 1944 your father, my grandfather, promised to look after them and return their holdings to anyone who survived. And how we broke our word to them.'

He shrugged. 'Who cares? That was decades ago. Ancient history. There are hundreds, thousands of stories like that, Jews who made the wrong choice, trusted the wrong people. It was a war. Everyone looked out for themselves.'

'Not everyone, Uncle. Some people saved their Jewish friends and neighbours, looked after their homes. But we did not. We even had a legal agreement with the Bergers. And then we stole everything.'

Karoly's voice softened. 'Reka, it was wrong what happened, I know. It's a sad story, but an old one. Look, even the Israeli prime minister is coming on Monday. They want to do business with Hungary, with our firm. They've moved on. Why can't you? There's nobody to return anything to, even if we wanted to. The Bergers are all dead now.'

'No, Uncle, they are not all dead. Eva, Miklos and Rahel's daughter, survived. She's still alive. You know that. Tamas, your father, commissioned an investigation after the war. They found her, living on Dob Street. She'd changed her name to Hegyi. She lived with Orsi, Rahel's sister. I found the report in the Librarian's archive.'

Karoly laughed. 'So what? And what should Tamas have done? Handed control of a massive economic empire to a ten-year-old girl? Absurd.'

'Maybe not. But we could have helped. Even when the communists took power, we were still rich and influential. Orsi lived out her life in poverty. I found some letters from her to Tamas, explaining her story, that she was looking after Miklos and Rahel's child, asking for help. She never received a single reply. You saw those letters.'

Karoly shrugged. 'I did. The woman said they changed their name. They were chaotic times. Who knew if the story was real? Everyone was hustling for something. If we did help them, it would never end. We would be admitting guilt. They could have hired lawyers, come after us. Why are you digging this up now? What do you care?'

She stepped forward, her voice rising. 'Because I lived in

their house. I ate in their kitchen. I slept in Eva's bedroom. I played in their garden. I walked on their grave.' She stared at Karoly, the anger rising inside her. 'And nobody told me the truth. But now I know it. The whole story. There's a lot more as well in the article, about Nationwide now, the tax tricks, the river of money flowing into your private bank account. I told you, Uncle, it's over.'

Reka closed her eyes for a moment, brought herself under control. She reached into her handbag, took out a photocopy of a typewritten sheet of paper and handed it to Karoly.

He read it once, then again, slowly. 'What is this? An old piece of paper in German? Anyone could write this and claim it was genuine.'

'That paper is a record of a telephone call to the headquarters of the Gestapo, at 8.32 a.m. on 20 March 1944. It was a very short conversation. The caller gave the address where Miklos and Rahel Berger were hiding. In the cellar of a house on Gellert Hill.'

Karoly shrugged. 'And? What is this to do with me? I was two years old then.'

'Only one other person knew where the Bergers were hiding. Tamas Bardossy. Your father. My grandfather.'

He looked down at the paper, his hand trembling slightly. 'Hearsay. Conjecture. You can't prove anything.'

Reka handed Karoly another piece of paper. He glanced down at it, crumpled it up and threw it into a nearby bush.

She glanced at Antal, who bent down, picked up the paper, straightened it out and handed it to her. Reka said, 'I don't need to read it out to you. You've seen what it says. The Gestapo traced the call. The number was tapped. It was a male voice, speaking from the private line in Tamas's office.'

Karoly blustered. 'It could have been anyone. Lots of people had access to his office.'

'No they didn't. He was a very secretive man, as you know. He didn't even let his secretary in there. He was the only one who could use that number.'

'So what if it was him? The Bergers would have died anyway. The Nazis were after them. They were on the VIP wanted list.'

'Maybe they would have. Maybe not. Half the Jews of Budapest survived. The Bergers had money, contacts, friends; they might have made it. Especially if we had helped them.'

'But we didn't. Nor did most people. They were lining up to denounce their neighbours all over the country, then empty out their homes once they were gone.'

Reka stepped closer. 'Not everyone. Some people helped. They hid people, like we could have hidden the Bergers. But we didn't. So now our family's debt will finally be paid. You are going to resign all your positions at Nationwide, Uncle. You are going to donate your money, your house, your land, your property to a new charitable foundation.'

Bardossy guffawed. 'This is a joke, yes?'

'No. It is not.'

'Ridiculous. Step down, give everything away? Because of something that happened seventy years ago. Why should I? I have no intention of doing that. Where did you get this from, anyway?'

Reka stared at her uncle. His bluster was fading, his blue eyes darting from side to side. 'Admit it, Uncle. It's a relief. All these years you have been carrying the family guilt. Now you can cast it aside. You've had a copy of both of these papers for many years. You got them from the same place that I did. From the Librarian.'

She stepped closer. 'That's how he kept you and Nationwide under control. That's how you built the firm, not because you are such a smart businessman, but because you were his lackey. He gamed you, like he gamed everyone, and you followed his orders. He lusted for power, you hungered for money. You both got what you wanted. Then he died and you knew that I was poking around, trying to find out what really happened. That's why you bought 555.hu, to use it to release the video of me on Castle Hill, to bring me down. That's why you were planning to kidnap the Israeli historian. That's why you funded your ridiculous new parties, the Workers' whatever and the far-right hoodlums. But it didn't work. You are not much use without the Librarian, are you?'

Karoly stared at Reka with fury. 'Why are you doing this? Why don't you just leave things be? Everything was fine until you started asking all these questions.'

'Because it festers. It's like a slow poison. And we have to drain it.'

'I told you. I was two years old in 1944.'

She stepped closer, so close she could smell the coffee on his breath. 'Yes, but you were born long before 17 February 1991. You were forty-nine years old.'

Karoly became quite still. 'What's that got to do with anything?'

'You know what day that is?'

'Yes. A very sad day. The day Hunor died. Your father, my beloved brother. A tragic accident.'

'*Beloved*. How can you even say that word? It wasn't an accident. And now I know why.'

Karoly frowned. 'I don't understand.'

'I think you do, Uncle. You understand very well. My father knew about all of this. It all came out after the change of system in 1990. The dark secrets from the war, what we did to the Bergers, how we betrayed them, sat on their wealth and assets, built our economic empire on their ashes.'

She swallowed for a moment, looked down. 'Dad wanted to release the information. Make a clean start. A new company for a new regime, Reka, that's what he told me. Let it all out, then start again with a clean slate. That's why you arranged that accident for him. A specialist team came in from Moscow. My father was a superb skier, but he never went off-piste and he never drank while he was on the slopes. I found the papers in the Librarian's records. It's all recorded. Your request, the dates, the result. How you killed your brother. My father.' Her face crumpled for a moment. 'How could you do that? Your own brother. I was just a child.'

Karoly's face twisted in guilt and anger. 'My brother was a fool. He would have wrecked everything, just because he had a fit of conscience,' he said, almost shouting now. 'I told him, leave it for now, we'll deal with it later. Let's focus on the business, history can wait. But no, no, he would not listen. After all these years, he discovered his conscience. He told me that he had found the Bergers' daughter, that she was alive. That we could compensate her.'

'He found her? He found Eva?'

'Yes. He found her as well. He was going to tell you. But I knew once we paid her, it would never end. The reporters would be all over us. The Jewish organisations, the Americans. We would have lost the house, the company, everything.'

'So you admit it? You, Karoly Bardossy, arranged the murder of my father, your brother Hunor, because he wanted to reveal the truth about how Tamas Bardossy, your father, denounced Miklos and Rahel Berger in 1944 to the Gestapo so he could steal their assets and wealth?'

'Yes. It's true. I did that,' said Karoly, his voice dull.

Reka glanced at Antal, moved her head slightly to the side. He stepped closer to Karoly. Reka said, 'I can't hear you, Uncle.'

Karoly looked skywards, as though help might come from the heavens, his face twisted in anguish. 'Yes, yes,' he said, his voice shrill. 'I did all that. I had my brother killed because he wanted to tell the world how we set the Gestapo onto our family's Jewish friends so we could steal everything they had. In March 1944.' He stood back, panting, his breath white plumes in the air. 'That's it, Reka. My confession. After all these years. Happy now? Did I say enough? You got what you wanted?'

'Yes.' Reka wiped her eyes. 'You will resign all your positions in the company by the end of the day. You will give up the house. You will turn over all your assets. You will never work again. If you do that, I will arrange a pension for you of 300,000 forints a month.'

'Three hundred thousand forints a month? That's not even a thousand euros. How can I manage on that?' he asked, his voice incredulous.

'It's three times what Eva Hegyi gets. You'll get by.'

'No,' said Karoly. 'I won't do it.'

Reka looked at Antal. He stepped forward, took out a small digital recorder, pressed play.

Karoly's voice sounded, small and tinny, but clear: *Yes, yes. I did all that. I had my brother killed because he wanted to tell the world how we set the Gestapo onto our family's Jewish friends so we could steal everything they had. In March 1944.*

FORTY-THREE

Klauzal Square, 3 p.m.

The baker's round, jolly face stared out from a large black-and-white photograph as he weaved plaits of dough for the Sabbath challah bread. Next to him was a portrait of a woman in her thirties, her long hair pinned up as she modelled a black evening gown in an old-fashioned studio, and next to her one of Samu *bacsi* in his repair shop, bent over a desk covered with knobs, bolts and bits of wire, smiling at the camera as he fixed an ancient radio.

Eva *neni* clutched Balthazar's arm in delight as she looked at the pictures, one by one. 'And there is Rothman's, the best cake shop we ever had,' she said excitedly, pointing at a photograph of a 1970s patisserie on the other side of the square, now a falafel restaurant. 'Look at these, Tazi, I'm so pleased to see them, all the places I grew up with.'

There were six white exhibition stands, arranged in a corner of the square. Smaller lettering on each announced that the exhibition on District VII's Jewish heritage was supported by the government and the local municipality.

Balthazar read the caption on the photograph of the lady in the dress. *Rosa Hartmann, modelling one of her designs, 1974.*

He turned to Eva *neni*. 'Is she...?'

'His wife. She died just a couple of years ago. She was very elegant.'

It was a tasteful, stylish exhibition, he thought. Both locals and passers-by were stopping to look at the photographs and to read the captions. The old District VII might have mostly vanished, but at least here it was preserved.

Eva *neni* said, 'Now come, let's sit down.'

They walked over to a nearby bench. The sun was still shining but the brief warmth of the day was fading as dusk approached. 'I have something for you, Tazi,' said Eva *neni*, reaching into her pocket. 'A present.'

Balthazar smiled. 'There's no need for presents, Eva *neni*. Having you in my life is a gift every day.'

She laughed, hit his arm lightly. 'Save that stuff for your girlfriends. I almost believe you.'

'You should. It's true.'

She looked at Balthazar, her deep affection for him written on her face. 'Now stop with your nonsense.'

Balthazar looked across to the playground, where Alex was clambering on a climbing frame. Balthazar smiled as he watched his son. His carefree joy at being with his dad was was a pleasure to behold. Sarah had also seen the footage on newsline.hu of Balthazar being abducted on Wesselenyi Street – as had Alex, of course. For once Sarah did not argue or play power games: she had brought Alex over on Sunday morning and even agreed to let him stay overnight. Balthazar felt wrung out, exhausted, but also strangely relaxed. Elad was safe. So was Eva *neni*. Alex was with him, playing happily.

Eva *neni* was also watching Alex, smiling with approval. 'That's a fine young man you have there. You must be very proud of him. It can't be easy for him, bouncing back and forth between his mum and his dad.'

She glanced at Balthazar, shook her head, took a tissue from her bag, and dabbed the plaster over the cut on Balthazar's forehead. He looked at her questioningly. 'Is it bleeding again?'

Eva *neni* showed him the paper, dotted with red. 'A bit. How much longer are you going to do this, Tazi?'

'Do what?' he replied, although he understood the question perfectly. It was the same one he had been asking himself.

'Guns, shooting, fighting, getting kidnapped, gassed, beaten up. They knocked you out last year at Keleti. Now look at you. All bashed around again.'

'That's what the doctor said. She told me to get a desk job.'

'She's right and you should listen. Don't be such an *okos tojas*.' The phrase translated as 'clever egg' but meant a know-all who did not listen to others. Eva *neni* looked at him, her voice softening. 'Tazi, it's not your fault what your father and brother do. You didn't take that path. You did something else. If you have something to prove, that a Gypsy is as good as any other Hungarian, you have done. You have a son, Tazi. He needs his dad – and in one piece. You can stop now. You've done enough.'

He gave her a wry smile, wincing as he tried to sit comfortably. First the doctor and now Eva *neni*. Perhaps she was right. She usually was. Maybe it really was that simple. 'Have I?'

Eva *neni* nodded. 'Yes. And you can focus on something much more important,' she said, nodding towards Alex, then rummaging in her bag. 'Now, end of lecture. I told you I had a present. Open your right hand and close your eyes.'

Balthazar did as she asked. He felt a cold, metallic weight on his palm. He opened his eyes to see a heavy gold ring with a large black stone mounted in the middle. 'It's beautiful,

Eva *neni*. But you don't need to give me presents. I hope you haven't spent a lot of money on this.'

'I know I don't need to, Tazi, but I want to. And I didn't spend anything. This was my father's. I want you to have it. You know I have one daughter, Klara, and she's in London, and she has two daughters. There are no more men in my line of the family.' She grasped Balthazar's hand in hers and curled his fingers over the ring, her eyes glistening now. 'That's it, Tazi. No more arguing.'

'Your father's? But how?' he asked, his voice surprised.

Eva *neni* had never told him much about her parents, only that they had died in the Holocaust, and he had never pressed her. Eva *neni* looked over at Alex, who was now sitting down on the edge of the sandpit, playing with his iPhone. 'I'll tell you in a minute. And one day, hopefully not for many years, you will pass it on to Alex.'

She let go of his hand. 'Now try it for size.'

Balthazar slipped the ring onto his middle finger. It fit perfectly. He held his hand up and looked at the black stone from different angles. It was a beautiful piece of jewellery, finely crafted, masculine, but not ostentatious. The ring felt completely natural on his finger.

'Thank you. It's an honour. I'm very touched.' He glanced at her enquiringly. 'This is all tied up with what happened on Friday, at Reka's house, isn't it?'

Eva nodded. She spoke for some time, told Balthazar the story of her family, of the Bergers and the Bardossys, of the house, the paintings, the box in the garden, how she lost her parents, somehow managed to survive the ghetto. She wiped her eyes as she spoke, then smiled at him. 'So now you know.'

Balthazar sat back for a moment, looked at Miklos's ring

once more. 'So all this time, you knew that the Bardossys had your house and everything else? Didn't you want to get it back?'

'Of course. Or something, some acknowledgement at least. But under communism it was impossible, Tazi. The state took ownership. There was no compensation. Nobody wanted to draw attention to themselves, show that they were part of the old capitalist elite. That would just bring trouble. And after the change of system, the Bardossys were still really influential and important. What do you think would happen if an elderly widow in a little flat in Dob Street without much money or any political connections took on one of the most important dynasties in the country?'

'Nothing. A warning off if she persisted.'

'Exactly.'

'So what has changed now?'

'Once Reka became prime minister, I went to see Erno Hartmann at the museum on Dohany Street. He's an old friend. We went to school together. I saw Reka on television, making all the usual promises. But she looked different to the others, and she is a woman. I thought maybe she meant it, about honesty, transparency, modernising Hungary. Why not try? I had nothing to lose. I told Erno the story, of how my real name was Berger and my family lost everything to the Bardossys. He was amazed, he did not know anything about it. I didn't know the details, of course, about what happened in 1944, or about the two documents that Reka had, the ones that I just told you about. But she had visited the Jewish Museum, increased their grant, spoken publicly about the Holocaust. She went to Dohany Street synagogue once, lit a candle at the Holocaust memorial. I asked Erno, why not approach her? If she really believes all that stuff about coming to terms with the past, she could start with her own family.'

'And did he?'

'Yes, and Reka agreed to help. It turned out she had the same idea herself. Then Erno brought over Elad, my cousin, and you know the rest of the story.'

Balthazar turned to look at Eva, suddenly overcome by a wave of affection and admiration. 'You did this? You started the whole thing?'

Eva *neni* looked bashful and somewhat surprised. 'Yes. I did. It was me. I didn't expect all this to happen, though. That's why I felt so guilty about Elad when he went missing.'

He took her hand and held it gently. 'Don't. You have nothing to feel guilty about. Nothing at all.'

Balthazar looked around the square. It was a peaceful weekend scene. The sound of children playing nearby carried on the air, the smell of cooking drifted from a nearby window. Two English tourists sat on a nearby bench, looking hungover.

Yet it had happened here, in the middle of the city, the capital of the country that he called home. Which Eva *neni*, her parents, and all the other Jews and Gypsies had also called home, until it turned on them.

Eva could sense him thinking. 'Every day that I am here, that I am alive, is a kind of victory.' For a moment she had a faraway look in her eyes. 'That winter, Tazi. You cannot imagine. It was indescribable. The cold, the hunger, how it gnawed at you. People dying all around. The Arrow Cross rampaging. Hiding from them, hearing the screams and cries, the sound of the shooting.' She pointed across the square. 'Just over there, a few yards from where we are sitting. The bodies frozen, stacked up like logs. I try not to think about it too much.'

Balthazar took Eva *neni*'s hand in his, sat silently for a while, letting his thoughts run through his head. Eva *neni*'s memories. His aunt Zsoka with the scar on her face. His family members murdered at Auschwitz. The long days in the archives researching the Poraymus.

A pigeon landed on a bench nearby. The bird looked left and right, then was still for a moment, its tiny eye staring straight at Balthazar.

He looked down again at Miklos's ring on his finger, felt its cool weight on his skin. His decision, he realised, had already been made. The pigeon cooed for a moment, soared skywards.

Balthazar asked, 'And what about the house, the factories, all your family's holdings? What will happen to them now?'

'We are going to talk about what to do next. Erno will help me. We have some ideas already. A charitable foundation, some kind of school or college. But don't worry, Tazi, I'm not moving anywhere. I'll still be here to nag you. Now show me that ring again.'

Balthazar held out his hand. Eva *neni* looked at her heirloom on his finger and squeezed his knee for a moment. 'He would be very happy. It found the right home. Now, there is a condition, of course.'

Balthazar laughed, sat back on the bench. 'I thought there might be.'

'You take that nice Anastasia, the classy one, out for dinner. Somewhere nice. You go on a date.'

For a moment Balthazar was back in his bedroom, late on Saturday morning. He had woken up at eleven o'clock to see Anastasia sitting in the armchair from the lounge, bleary-eyed but still awake. She had waited while he showered and brushed his teeth. Dr Szegedi had come back to check him over again, a much briefer visit this time, pronounced him fit to be on his own. Only then had Anastasia left. Balthazar had spent the day resting, avoiding the internet, which was full of clips of him being kidnapped on Wesselenyi Street, and eating large meals of soup and *csirke paprikas* that his mother, Marta, had brought over.

'She sat with me all night, when I came back on Friday.'

Eva squeezed his knee. 'So you see. She likes you.'

'Maybe she felt responsible. But what if she says no?'

'You'll live. But trust me. She won't.'

They both looked at Alex, who had put his iPhone away and was now chatting with a young girl with long blond hair and pink jeans, who looked about his age. She was laughing, smiling, touching his arm. 'Ask Alex. He can show you how it works,' said Eva *neni*. 'That's Katika, our neighbour's daughter. He has good taste. And speaking of accompanying ladies, even not so young ones, I have a request of you.'

She reached inside her coat pocket and took a stiff card, and handed it to Balthazar.

It was an invitation, he saw, with an embossed illustration of the parliament building, lined with gilt. He read the details. 'Very fancy. It's the reception for the Israeli prime minister tomorrow evening. But it's addressed to you.'

Eva took the card back. 'I can take a guest, I have to give them the name today so they can run the security checks.' She looked him up and down. 'I think you'll pass. Now excuse me for a moment, I need to call Klara.'

Balthazar stood up, walked over to the playground. Alex ran across to greet him. 'Katika saw you on the internet. Everyone did, Dad. She thinks it's really cool.'

Balthazar looked at his son, his skinny frame, his long black hair, his mother's green eyes, his coffee-coloured skin.

His beautiful boy. He put his arm around Alex and hugged him tightly. 'And what do you think, *fiam*?'

Alex looked up at his father, touched the cut on his forehead. 'I think it's time for a new job, Dad. And a proper girlfriend. One who sticks around.'

'You may be right. Come, let's go and say hallo to Eva *neni*.'

The wind turned colder as they walked back across the square and Eva *neni* stood up. 'Klara's coming next week, with the children. I told her we have big news. Good news. But I would only explain in person.'

She smiled at Balthazar and Alex, ruffled his hair. '*Gyertek, fiuk*, come on, boys. *Palacsinta* time.'

FORTY-FOUR

KAROLY BARDOSSY FOUND DEAD IN JACUZZI

NEWS FOLLOWS REVELATIONS OF FAMILY'S WARTIME PAST

By Zsuzsa Barcsy

Special to newsline.hu

Karoly Bardossy, one of Hungary's richest and most powerful businessmen, has been found dead in his jacuzzi at his luxury villa in Obuda. Police sources said there were no initial indications of foul play, but a full investigation would follow.

Bardossy, 73, was the chairman and CEO of Nationwide Ltd., and the uncle of Prime Minister Reka Bardossy. Eniko Szalay, her spokeswoman, said: 'The prime minister is shocked and saddened by this terrible news. The death of her uncle is a great loss for Hungary's business community and the country as a whole.'

Bardossy's death comes the same day as the results of an extensive historical investigation into the origins of Nationwide Ltd. is released. The probe, by Israeli historian Elad Harrari (see accompanying story) reveals how Tamas Bardossy, the father of Karoly, took over the extensive holdings and properties of the Berger family in 1944 after the Nazis invaded. Tamas Bardossy signed an agreement with Miklos Berger, the head of the family and owner of the Bergers' industrial empire, to protect the Bergers' assets and properties and pass them on to any surviving members, once the war was over.

Soon after the agreement was signed Miklos and his wife Rahel went into hiding. But they were quickly discovered by the Gestapo, and deported to Auschwitz where they were killed. The Bergers' factories, industrial plants and other assets were all absorbed into the Bardossy family holdings. The Berger family home in Obuda is now the residence of Reka Bardossy, the same house where she grew up.

Only now, more than seventy years later, can the full story of the terrible betrayal be told.

Reka read through to the end of Zsuzsa's story, clicked on the link for Elad's investigation and read that. It was all there: the two documents were reproduced, the sales agreement between her grandfather and Miklos Berger, the second agreement nullifying it. Newsline.hu had done a thorough job: there was a video interview with Elad about his work, another with Erno Hartmann about the significance of the findings – 'extremely important, shedding valuable new light on the fate of the wealth of Hungarian Jewry' – and Zsuzsa's article was thorough and detailed. One of the video reporters had even shot a stand-up report outside the house, telling the story of how it used to be the family home of Miklos and Rahel Berger. Zsuzsa had also written an accompanying article exposing the company's tax structure and vast payments to its directors.

The business correspondent had written an analysis on the likely impact of the death of Karoly Bardossy and the wartime revelations on the firm. The former would drive the share price down for a while, he opined. The latter would cause some sound and fury for a few days, but would fade away by the end of the week. The share price would soon recover.

Reka was pleased to see that there was no mention of Eva *neni* for now, as agreed. That part of the story, that she was the daughter of Miklos and Rahel Berger and so was the heir to their empire, would come out as well. But not yet – and only when they had a media minder for her in place. Another, smaller, story reported the arrest of George Porter, Karoly Bardossy's former bodyguard, for the murder of Geza Kovacs.

Reka switched on the large flat-screen television on the other side of the room. The story was already getting picked up by the international press. 'The secret history of the Hungarian prime minister's family wealth is revealed,' announced the BBC, while CNN proclaimed, 'Hungarian oligarch dies as wartime family betrayal is revealed'. The BBC was also interviewing the Budapest correspondent for the *Economist*, a British journalist in his early fifties. 'History here is a live thing, not the dead past. It still shapes everything,' he explained.

Yes it does, thought Reka. But sometimes we can shape it too. She turned the volume down, sat back and looked around the lounge, taking in the decor, the furniture, the paintings. Was it still her house? Would she stay here? How strange to think that it wasn't her decision any more. If Eva *neni* let her, she would. If she wanted the house back, she would hand it over.

But before that, two last tasks.

There were two faded sheets of paper on the coffee table next to her phone, a handwritten note, and by them a steel mixing bowl, a lighter and the digital recorder that Antal Kondor had used in the park.

Reka spread the papers out, smoothed them down. Her uncle was dead; so was the Librarian. Nobody else knew these documents existed. She had not mentioned them to Zsuzsa or Elad. There were no scans, or photographs, or digital records.

She looked down at the yellowing sheets, German-language records of a telephone call and a telephone tap from March 1944, read them through once more. The handwritten note said, *You deserve to see these. Use them as you wish. J.T.*

She slowly tore all three into small pieces, dropped them into the steel bowl, clicked the lighter on and set them on fire. The dry, brittle paper burned quickly, turned to ashes.

Reka picked up the digital recorder, played the recording of Karoly Bardossy in the park, listened to his shrill confession once more.

Her index finger hovered over the delete button.

She pressed it.

FORTY-FIVE

Offices of newsline.hu, three weeks later

Zsuzsa Barcsy turned to the camera and said, 'Our guest today is Balthazar Kovacs. Until recently he was the country's best-known policeman. But he has now left the police force. He has been appointed director of the new Roma Historical and Cultural Foundation, which has just been set up by the government – and we are the first news organisation to interview him.'

She turned to Balthazar. 'Thank you for joining us today, Balthazar. That's quite a career change, from being a detective on the Budapest murder squad to running a historical foundation. What will the new foundation do?'

Balthazar outlined the plans for a new cultural centre for writers, musicians and artists, which would also incorporate a museum of Gypsy culture and a memorial to the Poraymus. 'We are especially pleased that Erno Hartmann, the former director of the Jewish Museum on Dohany Street, has agreed to sit on our board as an adviser,' he added.

Zsuzsa and Balthazar were sitting in newsline.hu's new studio. The news organisation was based in the former premises of 555.hu. The sprawling flat was no longer a ramshackle, hipster hang-out. It had been transformed after a substantial donation from a mystery donor. The parquet floor was slick and polished, the windows had been replaced, the walls replastered and painted. The studio had sound insulation, state-of-the-art recording and lighting equipment, a sound engineer and a producer. A photographic backdrop of Budapest at night covered one wall.

Zsuzsa and Balthazar sat in two armchairs, facing each other, talking through the issues facing Hungary's Roma. The interview went on for ten minutes or so as Balthazar outlined how the foundation would also set up a Roma research department to produce policy papers for the government. 'There is a lot of work to do, both within the Roma community and wider society. But we need to start somewhere and now is the time.'

'It sounds great – and long overdue,' said Zsuzsa. She glanced at her notes. 'And work is going ahead on the Virag Kovacs Music School, in memory of your late sister?'

Balthazar nodded. 'Yes, we hope it will open later this year. The government is being very supportive and we are very pleased about that.'

Zsuzsa smiled. 'You seem to be turning into a de facto spokesman for Hungary's Roma community. Would you consider a career in politics yourself?'

Balthazar shook his head emphatically. 'No. I've never even thought of that. And we have far too much to do at the foundation.'

A voice sounded in Zsuzsa's earpiece as the producer told her to bring the conversation to a close. 'One last question, Balthazar: why do we need a museum of Gypsy culture and the Poraymus, the Gypsy Holocaust?'

Balthazar said, 'There's a long answer and a short one to that question.'

'For now, the short one, please. But we look forward to welcoming you back soon.'

'Because it's time to tell our stories.'

'Thank you.' Zsuzsa turned back to the camera. 'And in a few moments, our next guest is Ilona Mizrachi, the former Israeli cultural attaché, recently promoted to ambassador. Ilona will be telling us in detail about the new trade and cultural agreements that were signed, after Israeli prime minister Alon Farkas's visit.'

Balthazar stepped out of the studio and into the main editorial office. Newsline.hu also had a new editor-in-chief, who was now walking towards Balthazar.

'Thanks, Tazi, that was a great interview,' said Eniko Szalay. 'It's going to be a fantastic museum. You will do a great job.'

'I hope so,' said Balthazar. He looked at Eniko. She wore a pink T-shirt and dark jeans, looked relaxed and in control. 'You seem very at home here.'

She smiled. 'That's because I am. I'm a journalist. It's good to be back. I've seen the other side and it's not for me. Reka was very gracious, though.'

Eniko stepped closer, touched his arm. 'Buy you a drink? Now? Later? I'm free this evening. There's a very cool new bar round the corner.'

For a moment, a part of Balthazar wanted to say yes, yes to a drink, yes to the dinner that would come a couple of days later and yes to everything else that would soon follow. But that was another life, an old one. Instead he smiled, shook his head. 'I'm can't, Eni, I'm busy tonight.'

He looked across the editorial floor to the reception area where she was waiting for him. 'I'm sorry, I have to go, someone's waiting for me.'

Eniko followed his line of sight, where Anastasia was sitting. Balthazar saw hurt, perhaps something like regret, flash across her eyes.

'Keep in touch, Mr Museum Director,' Eniko said, her voice businesslike now. 'We'll have you in for that follow-up interview soon.'

Balthazar and Anastasia took the stairs. Halfway down, he pulled her towards him and kissed her. Her arms slid around his neck. 'Nice chat with your ex?' she asked, half amused but with a hint of steel underneath.

'Not as nice as this one,' he said, kissing her again.

She pushed him away, laughing. 'How old are you? Sixteen?'

'Something like that.'

They walked down the rest of the staircase and stepped outside onto Blaha Lujza Square. Balthazar stood still for a moment, taking in the scene.

The busy afternoon traffic flowed down Rakoczi Way towards the Elisabeth Bridge as crowds of commuters descended into the metro station. A number-four tram trundled past, en route to Oktogon, Margaret Bridge and Buda. It was hard to believe that just a few months ago Rakoczi Way and nearby Keleti Station had been the epicentre of the international migrant crisis. For a moment Balthazar thought of Mahmoud Hejazi, the terrorist known as the Gardener, being shot dead from under his feet, the human wave of refugees trudging through here towards the Austrian border, of Simon Nazir, the Syrian from Aleppo who had sought refuge here with his wife but who had been murdered.

Anastasia looked at Balthazar, could sense the memories flowing through him. She squeezed his hand. 'OK?' she asked.

'Fine. They never found the gunman who killed the Gardener. I still wonder about that,' said Balthazar, although by now he had a pretty good idea who the sniper was.

She narrowed her eyes, put her finger to his lips. 'Case closed, Tazi. You're not a detective any more. And we have much more interesting things to talk about.' She pulled him away from Blaha Lujza Square, towards Rakoczi Square and District VIII, her hand holding his. 'Come, it's dinner time.'

'Great. Where are we going?' He laughed for a moment. 'Not the Tito Grill.'

'Even better. We're going to Jozsef Street. Your mum and dad are waiting.'

ACKNOWLEDGEMENTS

A novel has many roots. Those of *Dohany Street* reach back to 1991, when I first moved to Budapest to work as a foreign correspondent. I was instantly entranced by the city and the vivacious, welcoming Hungarian friends that I made. But Budapest, I soon realised, was haunted. It is a city rich in culture, literature, music, beautiful architecture – and ghosts. At night, when the backstreets turn still and dark, it's easy to imagine a Russian commissar or a Gestapo officer strutting down the road, the click of boot-heels on the pavement and a midnight knock on the door echoing through the silence. All that happened in living memory. Klauzal Square was a open-air mass grave in the winter of 1944–45, where frozen bodies were stacked like logs. The pavements of Budapest – and many other European cities – are peppered with *Solpersteine*, stumbling stones, small brass plaques commemorating Jewish people killed in the Holocaust. Gypsy inmates at Auschwitz fought back against the camp guards with home-made weapons in May 1944. *Dohany Street* is the third volume of a trilogy of noir crime thrillers featuring Balthazar Kovacs. A novelist's primary aim must always be to write an enthralling story, but I hope these books will also make readers, whether locals or visitors, pause for a moment, think about and perhaps even explore Budapest's hidden histories.

My thanks as always go first to my agents, Georgina Capel and Simon Shaps, the most steadfast of advocates for Balthazar and his adventures. Thanks also to Rachel Conway and Irene Baldoni for all their help and support. I have been blessed with a fine team at Head of Zeus, and I am especially grateful to my editor, Clare Gordon, for her insightful feedback and encouragement, to Louis Greenberg for his incisive copy-editing, to production supremo Christian Duck for making everything happen on time and to cover designer Ben Prior for his eye-catching artwork. Thanks also to Anthony and Nicolas Cheetham for their faith in and enthusiasm for Balthazar, and to Claire Kennedy for securing multiple translation deals. A generous grant from the Society of Authors was also much appreciated.

Many others have helped along the way. Clive Rumbold and Monika Payne, my two early readers, generously corrected spellings, pointed out repetitions and shared many useful ideas and suggestions. For fight scenes practice and Krav Maga choreography I am grateful to Gideon Hajioff, Shaun McGinley, Michele Hajioff, Melissa and everyone at the Dynamic Self Defence Academy in Hendon. Balthazar's gun defence is not perfect – every technique alters on contact with reality – but it would, I hope, work. I have never driven through a two-car roadblock but the instructions provided in the highly informative *100 Deadly Skills*, by former Navy Seal Clint Emerson, would doubtless do the job. Some years ago Peter Jenkins of ISS training (intelsecurity.co.uk) kindly let me join a course on surveillance. His book *The Theory of Covert Surveillance* is a very useful guide to this subtle art. My thanks go also to my editors at the *Financial Times*, Alec Russell, Frederick Studemann and Laura Battle, and at *The Critic* to former editors Michael Mosbacher and Bob

Lowe, and to Graham Stewart and Olivia Hartley. I hope that my thriller and television reviews at these publications have sharpened my own story-telling skills. Justin Leighton, Roger Boyes and Vesna Kojic were, as always, encouraging friends. Special thanks to Geoffrey and Sally Charin for their generous hospitality over the years, and to Michael L. Miller for showing me around Dob Street, inside and out.

In Budapest, Laszlo Reti, the acclaimed Hungarian crime writer, generously shared his knowledge and experience of police procedures and operations, as did several other former police insiders. Iain Lindsay, the former British ambassador to Hungary, kindly co-hosted the launch of the Hungarian edition of *District VIII*, the first volume of the trilogy, at the Budapest Book Festival. Thanks also to Tony Lang and the team at the wonderful Bestsellers bookshop for all their support over the years.

In cyberspace Graham Bartlett's online workshops at the Professional Writing Academy (profwritingacademy.com) on forensics, surveillance and covert policing were engaging and highly informative. As well as my own personal experiences in Budapest and Hungary I also drew on several internet resources. Centropa.org is an in-depth and often very moving digital archive, chronicling Jewish life in central and eastern Europe. Jewish Heritage Europe (jewish-heritage-europe.eu) is a rich resource for news about Jewish monuments and heritage sites. The Holocaust Memorial Day Trust (hmd.org.uk) has extensive information on the Nazi persecution of the Gypsies, including a poignant account of the life and death of Johann 'Rukeli' Trollmann, a Gypsy boxer murdered in a concentration camp. The European Roma Rights Centre (errc.org) is a comprehensive website with detailed information and reports on the current situation of Roma people across the region. The Open Society Foundations website (opensocietyfoundations.org) is also a useful and informative resource.

Over the years I have had many informative and moving conversations with my parents-in-law, Robert and Zsuzsa Ligeti, who both lived through the Holocaust in Budapest. I am grateful for their insight, memories and generosity in sharing their personal stories. Thanks most of all to my wife, Katalin, and my children, Daniel and Hannah. Their love, support and patience made creative things happen. A million thanks and as many kisses – I couldn't have written this book without you. *Dohany Street* is dedicated to the memory of my mother, Brenda LeBor. She and my late father, Maurice, were frequent visitors to Budapest while I lived there. I can still see them stepping out at the Dunapark café, on Pozsonyi Way in District XIII, as the music starts. Somewhere they are dancing.

ABOUT THE AUTHOR

ADAM LEBOR is the thriller critic of the *Financial Times* and a veteran former foreign correspondent who lived in Budapest for many years. He is the author of seven novels and eight non-fiction books, including *Hitler's Secret Bankers*, which was shortlisted for the Orwell Prize. He is an editorial trainer and writing coach for numerous publications and organisations and also writes for the *Critic* and *The Times*. He lives in London with his family.

www.adamlebor.com @adamlebor